20 Million Leagues Over the Sea

Book One of *The Nemo Paradox*

K. T. Hunter

Book One of *The Nemo Paradox*

20 Million Leagues Over the Sea is a work of fiction. Names, characters, businesses, places, events and incidents are either the products of the author's imagination or used in a fictitious manner. Any resemblance to actual persons, living or dead, or actual events is purely coincidental.

Wells, H. G. *War of the Worlds*. London: Heinemann, 1898.

Verne, Jules. *Twenty Thousand Leagues Under the Sea*. Paris: Hetzel, 1870.

Verne, Jules. *The Mysterious Island*. Paris: Hetzel, 1874.

Tennyson, Alfred. "The Lady of Shalott". 1832.

Cover Design by The Cover Collection at www.thecovercollection.com

Twin Cedars Enterprises

twincedarsenterprises@gmail.com

Printed in the United States of America

First Printing, 2015

ISBN: 098886357X
ISBN-13: 978-0-9888635-7-6

DEDICATION

For my beloved husband. Thank you for supporting my dream.

GEMMA

"Have no fear, Miss Llewellyn," the captain said. "I've done this before."

He touched a heavily gloved finger to the corner of his sharp green eyes, as if to tip an imaginary hat. He lowered it quickly to allow the white-coated technician to continue strapping him into the seat next to her.

Gemma Llewellyn had schooled her posture as much as she could to conceal her nervousness, but there was so much of it that she supposed her face was as pale as the technician's suit. That was fine. After all, a total lack of fear would draw too much attention. She hoped she seemed just nervous enough without tipping over into real hysteria.

"The Terran Industrial Alliance has seen to it that we are as well-trained as possible for space travel," he continued. "In fact, most of the crewmembers have experienced at least a half-dozen launches via the rail-gun system by this point. We've launched continuously for several years without a major incident--"

"Bloody hell, I suppose the crash into Mount Cook last spring was only a *minor* incident, then," growled a voice in the row behind them. "I suppose one must be at least a midshipman before having one's grey matter smeared across a mountainside is considered a major incident, eh?"

Gemma quirked an eyebrow at that. She had not heard a whisper about such a crash, from either the newspapers or the creeping vines of gossip that wound their way through halls of learning.

"There is a lady present, Doctor Pugh!"

The captain tried to turn in his padded seat to emphasize his point, but he was too tightly strapped in to do much more than wriggle. His tall, lean frame was well ensconced in the padded chair. Gemma thought he looked quite young to be a captain; he appeared to be not much older than her own four-and-twenty years. With his angular cheekbones, short chestnut hair, and pencil-thin mustache, he could blend in with any group of young

1

university fellows.

"Lady, my arse, Christophe," the voice replied with a snort. "A lady would be home tending to her knitting, not strutting about in a pressure suit. Sophie the Steamfitter, indeed!" He snorted again and fell silent.

Gemma looked down as her own attendant snugged up her straps. She pretended to focus on that young lady's tightly snooded hair. Mrs. Brightman had taught her that it was usually best to allow men their quibbling and not bother to argue against such statements. It was a waste of one's breath. The suit was a bit odd, but she supposed it would be just as awkward on anyone that had not already spent a great deal of time in orbit. She wondered what the Rational Dress Society would make of it.

"They ought to save that rot for the bloody tentacle-heads," her attendant whispered as she pulled back and offered Gemma a sympathetic look. "The charging coils for the rails should be close to full power now, Miss. They just loaded your trunk in the boot, too, so that ought to make this easier. Been up to the station twice meself. It's not so bad. Don't worry, love. You'll be on your way shortly."

She gestured for Gemma to lean forward, and another worker maneuvered the copper-clad helmet over her head. When they were done, Gemma nodded at the young woman as much as the helmet would allow. It wasn't the rail-gun that worried her.

"Kindly restrict your remarks to the weather, Pugh," the man next to her said. His voice took on a muffled quality as his own helmet locked into place. "And that's Captain Moreau to you."

Gemma felt a slight coolness from the sudden rush of air blowing into the helmet. She flashed the attendant an understanding smile. The woman's exasperated face would be the last she would see on Earth until their return... in over two years, if things went as planned. Gemma had thought that they would be surrounded by reporters shouting questions, especially since this was the last tender to the ship; but it was just the three of them and a few technicians. It was strange to have so little attention paid to an event that the entire world had anticipated for more than two decades. But it wasn't the mission's visibility that worried her, either.

As preparations continued around her, Gemma pondered Dr. Pugh. Since she had been a (quite literally) last-minute addition to this venture, this was her first encounter with members of the crew. She had spent the last few days just getting to the launch site in the middle of the Pacific Ocean; it had been a long journey by airship and steamer from Britain. Striking workers at some of the ports had caused more than one diversion. Gemma had wondered how Nellie Bly would have managed if she had met the same obstacles on her famous trek around the globe before the days of the Airship Network.

Then it had been two days of very intense orientation on the Launch

Coil and the ship itself. This would not have been possible before the Invasion, Mrs. Brightman had told her, as they had based the ship's design on plans found in the Martian cylinders and adapted the design to accommodate humans.

Except for the three of them, the crew and the Scientific Cohort were already on board. Since the TIA had built the ship in orbit -- it would not fly within an atmosphere -- very few people had seen more of it than drawings and schematics. The newspapers (also owned by the TIA) were rife with headlines that proclaimed the imminent and permanent defeat of the Invaders.

Dr. Pugh, whom she had never met, was the lead scientist for the expedition. She had only seen one photograph of him in the newspapers, standing next to his mentor, the celebrated naturalist Professor Aronnax, when he was much younger. She had no idea what he looked like now, and it would be several hours before she could look him in the face.

So, here was her superior, and he was insulting her even before their formal introduction. Mrs. Brightman would *not* approve. Behind the veil of the helmet, Gemma allowed her face to melt from the ladylike mask that it normally wore into a scowl. In about five hours, she would have to speak to him, ready or not. She wasn't looking forward to it.

One thing at a time, Mrs. Brightman had said.

Instead of worrying over the eventual confrontation ahead, she focused on the slight reflection of her own face in the back of the faceplate -- wide brown eyes framed with long lashes above cheeks dusted with freckles on a heart-shaped face.

The speaker in her helmet clicked on, and Captain Moreau's voice continued as if there had been no interruption. The tinny scratching of the transmission could not conceal his enthusiasm. He sounded as if he were back in London rather than right next to her.

"Just remember your emergency procedures, Miss Llewellyn. Most likely, they will not be necessary, but I do find that having something to focus upon does make things easier. Do not worry! I will ensure your safety."

Dr. Pugh's voice clicked in on the speaker next to her other ear. "Pretentious little prick," he said. "Endangering the lives of people who have no business flying about in space. Get him to tell you about the shakedown cruise to the moon someday. I'm not sure why we need a geologist on this trip, anyway."

Dr. Pugh had finally mentioned the worrisome bit: the first TIA voyage to the moon. One heard many rumors about that maiden voyage, but who knew which bits were true?

"But they insisted," he went on. "Oh, right, we've got to learn what we can while we're there, they said. Can't waste an opportunity to advance our knowledge of natural philosophy, they said. Poppycock! This is a ship of *war*, not a tea party! They are sending scientists to Mars to find better ways to kill Martians, not to convene symposia on the substrata of the Tharsis Bulge--"

The captain's voice pushed Dr. Pugh's to the background. "Never mind Dr. Pugh. He's married to his work. He's been a leading light in natural philosophy since before the Invasion. Many people born in that generation are pretty set in their ways. Not like us, Miss. No, we that came of age after the Invasion have a fresher view of the universe. I, for one, am glad that we have some ladies aboard."

They went on in that vein as the technicians checked their harnesses one last time and then backed away. The top of the capsule lowered down upon them, and she felt a thump as it locked into place. Panels flickered to life and banished the temporary darkness. There were no portholes, so she could not see the great plantation of Tesla Chargers -- an odd hybrid of electrical coils and flywheel storage -- that surrounded the launch site. She had seen them from the airship as she had arrived here. They had been charging even then, preparing for a crew launch, and they had been a startling sight. She could imagine the tongues of lightning licking the sides of the towers, ready to hurl her away from the sheltering lap of Earth. The orientation instructor had told her that the launch system used so much power that it required its own generators; otherwise, each launch would have drained the surrounding towns of the very power that they had received in return for hosting the facility in the first place.

Even through her helmet, she could hear the whoosh of cabin pressurization. She had reviewed all of these procedures the day before, in a simulation engine, but this felt far rougher. However, it was hard to think on the wonder of it all with two people having two different one-sided conversations with her at the same time. Mrs. Brightman's school had taught Gemma a great many things, but it had not prepared her for this.

"Perhaps you might lob some quartz at them," Pugh groused. "Just give us a chance to coat it with some influenza first. Now wouldn't that be a useful weapon?"

"Pugh means well," the captain said into her other ear. "Etiquette simply isn't his strong suit."

"What are you supposed to do for the forty days it'll take to get there?" the scientist continued. "They don't even have Martian rock samples for you to study yet. We're the first--"

Mercifully, a third voice joined the chorus: "Good afternoon, lady and gents, your attention please. This is your launch director. Welcome to the last tender to the TIAS *Thunder Child's Fury* on this, the 23rd of August, nineteen hundred and twenty-four. The capsule is now sealed, pressured, and ready for flight. The weather is optimal. Estimated travel time to

Shackleton Station is six hours from launch. For the moment, sit back, relax, and continue breathing in the oxygen so we can get all that nitrogen out of your systems."

"Yes, young lady, you'll want to do that," Dr. Pugh said. "I've had a touch of the bends before. Definitely something you want to avoid."

The launch director broke in again. "We are sealing the outer door of the tube. Commencing vacuum shake test in thirty seconds, mark."

At least they are getting the worst part over at the start, Gemma thought. A hard jolt rattled her teeth, harder than it had during the brief training. The wrenching and rolling was harder and more bone jarring than she remembered, but it did not last long.

"Air returning to the chamber. Prepare for lift, ten seconds," the launch director said.

Gemma heard a loud whistle and then felt a far gentler movement as the capsule moved into one of the lifts. She fought the helpless feeling that flooded her as she was tilted onto her back. The lift was turning the capsule towards the sky.

"Right," the launch director said. "Look sharp, now. Shuttle launch in five..."

"Oh, dear," sputtered Pugh.

"Four."

"What now?" demanded the captain.

"Three."

"That sixth cup of tea just kicked in."

"Two."

"Well, you'll just have to--"

"One. Take it away!"

She felt a tremendous push from behind and fought down the wild panic that tried to escape as it became more difficult to breathe. After another single hard shudder, the captain's voice broke in on her reverie. He spoke with little effort, as if the extra force of gravity on him meant nothing more than a feather pressing upon his sternum.

"Congratulations, Miss Llewellyn, you are the first female scientist to cross the sound barrier! And here's the switch to the climbing cable. It is the pinnacle of human ingenuity, is it not?"

The announcer broke in again: "Turning you over to Cable Control, now. Good luck! *Terra vigila!*"

"I mean," Dr. Pugh continued as if he'd not just been interrupted by a launch, "just because we picked up the toys that some aliens left behind, do we have to change everything?"

Gemma was sure she could tolerate another five hours of this -- she could tolerate just about anything for a short amount of time -- but she was not sure about two whole years. The only response she could give Pugh now would have been impertinent, and any response to the captain would have been flirtation. She was not ready for that.

Sweat trickled down her spine while they were climbing, climbing, climbing. The rails on which they traveled were a true marvel. They rose above the waves only during a launch. An electric current snapped it to attention when it was in use. When it was electrified, it was the largest structure ever made by humans. Otherwise, it slumbered on the water like a gargantuan iron dragon until it was shocked into life again. Its collapsibility made it easier to maintain and more resistant to the massive seasonal storms that rolled through this region of the world. Since this was the last shuttle for the Mars Mission, Gemma wondered how long it would sleep before the next launch. If they were successful, perhaps they would use it again to go to Venus. If not -- oh, that did not bear thinking on. She focused her thoughts on the inside of the shuttle, instead.

After a long stretch of cable climbing, the launch director broke in again. "Prepare for cable release... there! You are now in free fall." And with that, any downward pull that Gemma felt disappeared. The light breakfast that still lingered in her stomach threatened to emerge, but she managed to keep it down.

For the next hour, she endured the two men arguing their respective positions. The captain excused the scientist, and the scientist delivered an exhaustive lecture on the dangers of space; he informed her about how it wasn't a safe place for anyone, let alone a lady of any quality. He went on about how the world needed more women that could breed the numbers lost during the Invasion and fewer that could sweat pipes. That is, when he wasn't complaining about his bladder.

"We're so far behind in sheer numbers, I wonder if we'll ever catch up," he mused.

She wondered if he had done his own bit for King and country, then, and if he had delivered the same lecture whilst in the act.

She had endured much, much worse on previous expeditions. At the same time, while physics was the pilot on this part of her journey, she did have control over one thing. She pressed a button on the arm of her padded seat. It was large enough to accommodate her thickly gloved finger.

"Gentlemen," Gemma said, "your advice is duly noted and appreciated. However, I do believe it is time for this lady to get some beauty rest."

With that, she pressed another button, the one that silenced all transmissions except those from the launch commander. She breathed happily into the blessed silence that followed.

Moreau. The name tickled a memory at the back of her mind, but she couldn't quite place it. That bothered her; in her line of work, memory was her most valuable tool. He didn't seem French, and he certainly didn't sound like he had been anywhere near Paris.

She dozed for a while, unsure if they had ever stopped their one-sided debates. All of a sudden, she fell forward with a jerk. The shuttle had stopped floating freely. She felt a slight wobble and a distinct forward pull.

"Ah," said the captain. Somehow, he had found an override. "That would be the landing tether. They are towing us into the station bay. Almost there, now."

A few moments later, the cabin lights extinguished, and the hatch opened. A waiting crew unstrapped them and assisted them out of the small capsule. Gemma was so stiff that it was almost impossible to walk down the short ramp to the main deck without assistance. She turned to look back at Dr. Pugh, but all she could see was a very tall white jumpsuit and a helmet that was stubborn in its refusal to unclamp from its collar. The technician ushered her forward into a dressing room and left her to the ministrations of another lady waiting there.

She was very relieved to exit the awkward suit. It was a bit of a struggle even with assistance. They finally managed it after much hopping and grasping and pulling and not a little cursing on Gemma's part. Mrs. Brightman would not have approved of the cursing, but she was many miles away on the planet below and could not hear. After uttering every swear word she knew (and making up a few in the process), she was free of it. In the small cubicle where she changed, she found a washbasin and soap. The water was not as warm as she would have liked, but a wash after so many hours of sweat was refreshing. The young lady presented her with a long charcoal-gray skirt and brown button-up blouse. She had to demonstrate how the skirt worked; apparently, in space even dressing required extensive training. Flaps and buttons allowed one to be wearing a skirt or wide-legged pants, depending on what one needed at that moment.

"There are times," the technician said, with her own "skirt" buttoned into pants, "where the trousers will be more modest than the skirt. Trust me."

The blouse itself was a double-breasted jacket in a drab workaday brown material that was warm and heavy but not stiff. Copper buttons marched in a double line down its front. From its mandarin collar down to the hem just below her waist, its design had function in mind, not fashion. Buttons on the upper arm allowed the wearer to shorten the sleeves or attach sleeve protectors as needed. She had seen both techniques in laboratories in the past. A small badge sewn onto the left arm shouted that she was a member of the SCIENTIFIC COHORT.

A curious patch sat upon the right arm. In the shape of a shield, it bore a picture of a tiny steamship churning its way towards the Red Planet. The white poles of the globe shone in the harsh light of the station. Across the top of the patch was the name of her new home: *Thunder Child's Fury*. The bottom simply declared the ubiquitous war cry of *Terra Vigila!*

She brushed the patch with her left hand and adjusted the top of the blouse. She tucked her locket in and buttoned up. She left her braid alone, as they did not have time for re-dressing her great mound of hair just now.

Gemma released a resigned sigh. She did not mind the unfashionable plainness of the outfit, not really. She didn't even mind the lack of a corset or a bustle. This outfit had the stamp of the Rational Dress Society all over it. In fact, the RDS had been attempting to change the prevailing wardrobe recommended by the TIA's Ministry of Culture for years. Perhaps the RDS had finally had their way somewhere in the universe. Still, she would feel more comfortable once she was back in her own clothes. Two years in this dress would be intolerable. She was adaptable, but not that adaptable.

She found Dr. Pugh and the captain waiting for her outside of the changing rooms. This time they were debating the relative merits and dangers of the rising Socialist movement. She looked up at Pugh, who was of a size with the captain; they both towered over her. They, too, had swapped the bulky jumpsuits for similar double-breasted jackets with matching trousers. But where Moreau was a bright blue jay, Dr. Pugh was a dull turkey. Dr. Pugh's coat was the same boring brown as her own, but the captain's uniform was a midnight blue with shining silver buttons and white trim lining the high collar.

"We meet again, Miss Llewellyn," the Captain said. "I hope the clothing isn't too plain for your liking. I'm afraid we're mostly business up here in the sky. May I present Dr. Elias Pugh? Dr. Pugh, Miss Gemma Llewellyn, our new geologist."

Dr. Pugh nodded and grunted at her by way of greeting. His sparse gray hair was long enough to gather into a ponytail; such tiny flashes of rebellion were a sort of style amongst his deliberately unstylish brotherhood. His eyes were bloodshot and weary. He turned his gaze to Moreau without a word to her.

"Why are we wasting time standing here? Shouldn't we go ahead and board?"

"I'm afraid that we must delay our embarkation for a bit," the captain replied. "I've been informed that they are conducting tests on the Oberths at the moment. It is not safe to cross the gangway right now. We have a little time to spare." He smiled at Gemma. "Would you like to see the ship from the outside?"

Watch him, Mrs. Brightman had ordered. *Whatever else you do, watch him. Keep his attention.*

"Yes, I would," Gemma replied.

"I've seen it before," muttered Dr. Pugh. "But I would like to see our geologist's reaction to the view."

Captain Moreau led them down a long hallway. The walls, doors, and floors were blindingly bright. Gemma was amazed at how very clean everything was. It was far removed from the grime and mud of ancient London. The air was laden with the smell of metal, India rubber, and another chemical odour that she could not identify. The ambiance wasn't exactly fresh from the country, but it had no soot to choke upon, either.

She took time along the way to examine Dr. Pugh in more detail. He was certainly much older than in the photograph she had seen. While Moreau practically glided down the hallway, Pugh loped like a limp giraffe, poking his head ahead of him as the rest of him rushed to catch up. His hands were knobby and covered with the scars one got from years of exploring the uses of a scalpel. His lab shirt stank of formaldehyde. She was used to scientific aromas, so she did not wrinkle her nose as much as others might have. He glanced her way on occasion, but he said nothing.

Moreau was full of energy as he chatted about the station. Pugh lowered his eyelids and silently mimicked the younger man's speech when he wasn't looking. Moreau waved off the older man's sullenness as if he were humouring his slightly senile grandfather.

They entered a room on the station's outer rim. Light shone up from the baseboards along the walls. The dull thuds of their footsteps echoed as they approached the far side of the chamber. Gemma could barely see the others' faces in the semi-darkness.

"Miss Llewellyn," the captain said, "may I present to you, the apex of human achievement, the TIAS *Thunder Child's Fury.*"

Moreau pulled a lever on the adjacent wall. The deck plates hummed as a section of the wall rolled back and revealed the dark space beyond.

Gemma gasped. The ship was even larger than she had imagined. The schematics had not prepared her for this; they were just drawings and figures on paper. This beast was alive and floating below her like some magnificent creature of the sea. Enormous nozzles stretched out from either end of the ship, extending its length. It resembled a gargantuan crab ready to crawl sideways across the sky.

"Why do we have nozzles on both ends?" she asked. "I understand why they would be aft, but--"

"But why forward? For braking. We have to slow down at some point, so we can get into Mars' orbit. We'll start using those on Braking Day, partway through the trip. We figured that would be simpler than turning the ship around mid-sail."

She blinked at him.

"It's just like a sailing vessel, where one cannot just stop the ship like one stops a motor car. We're spilling wind from the sails, except we're doing it with the direction of thrust." The captain continued his story as she stared out the viewport. "She's a real beaut, isn't she? Victory Class. She's the first."

"The only," muttered Pugh.

A sea of rivets dotted its skin in straight lines of steel barnacles, broken every so often by intersecting circles of smaller nozzles. According to the schematics she had seen, these were the maneuvering thrusters, used to nudge the ship into new directions. The top of the ship was longer than the Gatwick Racetrack. The airships that she had flown in were enormous, but this behemoth dwarfed even them. It was a metallic monster suspended against waves of stars. It felt odd to see it just hanging in space, with neither ground nor water to support it. Just seeing it made her forget for a moment why they were here in this high and lonely place.

There was a slight glow to her left. She supposed that was the engine test that the captain had mentioned.

"Apex of human achievement?" Dr. Pugh snorted. "Hardly. Apex of thievery, more like. We made it the old-fashioned way. We stole it."

"We made use of the spoils of war!" Captain Moreau replied. "They invaded us. It was ours by rights."

"Bah. Theft!"

"Reverse Engineering!"

"How is it that we are not falling back to Earth?" Gemma interrupted.

Dr. Pugh snorted at the question and mumbled something about the current state of women in the natural philosophies.

The captain's voice swelled with pride as he answered. "Believe it or not, Miss Llewellyn, we are falling! We are moving fast enough sideways at the same time that we end up staying in place. It feels like we are standing still, but we are moving at an incredible rate of speed. We feel the pull of Earth beneath us as she seeks to pull us back into her embrace. That keeps the station from drifting away. The movement keeps us in place and prevents our falling. It is a perfect balance." He gave her a long searching look, and then he turned his gaze to the ship below them. "We are in orbit, my lady. Even when we are standing completely still, we are moving faster than humans have ever moved before. We are so high in the sky that we should be floating inside the station. Do you know how it is that you can stand on the floor?"

"More purloined technology," Dr. Pugh growled. "We know how to build it, but we don't understand the physics that makes it work."

The captain waved him off. "Gravity plates. They are on the ship, too."

"Thank the good Lord for that," Dr. Pugh replied. "If the ladies' skirts went flying up during tea, the Cultural Officer would be quite put out."

"The wireless transistors in our suit helmets were all ours," the captain countered. "We managed to shrink those down all on our own." He smiled down at Gemma. "So, what do you think?"

"She is... unbelievable," Gemma stammered. Her voice was a hair above a whisper as she watched the glow of the test fade away. "Astounding. I believe she's larger than the *Titanic*!"

"Ah, that lady's been plying the seas for twelve years, now," Dr. Pugh said. "This one could hold several of those old girls. She's over five hundred meters long, but most of that is for the Oberths. Do you know how she got her name, young lady?"

Everyone knew the ship's history by now, especially those orphaned by the Great Invasion. It had changed the lives of everyone on Earth. Some things are so horrible that, once glimpsed, they cannot be unseen. The Invasion had been that horrible.

It had changed *everything*.

The Launch Coil, Shackleton Station, and the ship had all been born out of one horrible, all-consuming need: vengeance.

In 1901, the last year of the long reign of Queen Victoria, they fell from the sky. The astronomers observing the flashes of gas on their nearest planetary neighbor had no idea what fire was about to rain down upon the Earth. Tentacled monsters in hollow cylinders had plummeted down onto all the continents. The creatures, all brain and no heart, had wrecked the countryside around London, destroying Woking, Leatherhead, and a hundred other villages. Other nations, from the European Continent to Africa to the Americas, had reported similar devastation across their territories.

The Invaders had left widows, orphans, and suddenly childless parents in their wake. They had smashed homes with their tripods and burnt entire forests with their heat rays. They had captured mothers, grandfathers, and little babies and drained them to the last drop of their blood.

The steamship *Thunder Child* had been one of the first vessels to fight back against the aliens. Her crew had sacrificed themselves as they destroyed one of the Martian machines that threatened a nearby vessel.

After a month of wanton destruction across the globe, the aliens perished where they stood, struck down by common pestilence. Many had called their deliverance the Wrath of God.

Gemma wasn't sure what to call it.

The Invasion had put a cork in a powder keg of Earth's own making. Tempers had flared across Europe for years before the aliens had landed. The Hague Convention of 1899 had attempted to restrain the storm many had sensed was approaching. The appearance of the Martians not long afterwards had calmed the winds, but only for a little while as the nations recovered and rebuilt. Crowned heads realized that new technologies not bound by the Convention had fallen into their laps. A hastily convened Second Hague Convention, the Invasion Conference, was called in 1902 by peace proponents around the world, including prominent industrialists and philanthropists that had managed to weather the Invasion. Scientists and "peaceniks" had called for research into the alien technology for the benefit of all; war hawks had demanded the ability to defend their people against future Invasions, from within or without. The new Treaty had forged a compromise when it founded the Terran Industrial Alliance.

Greater than a conglomerate, but not quite a superstate, the TIA had won from the Convention unprecedented rights and powers to act on a global scale. This included everything up to and including the right to declare war upon the Martians on behalf of the Treaty signatories.

The new organization had confiscated all the Martian technology it could salvage in order to research it and re-engineer it for human use. They allowed bits of it to trickle out at a time, ostensibly preserving the bulk of it for when the world could use such treasures amongst themselves in a peaceful fashion, like good little children.

Even as the TIA pushed the state of industry ahead with the Martian treasures, they fought to keep people's minds on the world that they had lost. The Ministry of Culture, a branch of the TIA that had a consulate in every capital, had frozen certain customs and sensibilities in place and time, but with the force of commerce (and the Convention's blessing) rather than that of law.

Fashion, which would normally ebb and flow with the times, was at a standstill. Hats, parasols and other accoutrements that might have died out over the years on their own became *costume de rigeur*. TIA member corporations owned every facet of public life, from the House of Worth down to the last Jacquard loom, every publishing house and newspaper, and most laboratories that studied everything from biology to astronomy. They decided what was worn and what was seen. Newer fashions (lower waistlines, higher hemlines) attempted to surface from time to time, but most of those efforts were either home-brewed or disappeared from the market quickly as their designers were quietly bought out.

In the meantime, the machines had been torn apart, examined to the last millimeter, and rebuilt to carry humans to the Red Planet. The resulting ship had been named the *Thunder Child's Fury* in memory of those who had first fought the Invaders. The official war cry of *Terra Vigila!* -- Earth, Awaken! -- marched across her hull.

A passenger on the ship rescued by the *Thunder Child* had survived to record all that he had witnessed in a journal known simply as the *Invasion Chronicle*. It had, as the Invasion Conference had decreed, become part of every schoolchild's education in every nation and every language.

That included the very private education of Gemma Llewellyn. Petunia Brightman had found her in the ashes of the Woking massacre, next to her parents' bodies. Gemma, just an infant at the time, had no memory of them. No other family members had appeared to claim her. The schoolmistress, in her kindness, had taken her in along with many other Invasion Orphans. She had given them a home, an education, and a purpose. Brightman's institution was more than just a school or an orphanage; it was home.

Gemma trembled as she turned the story over and over inside her mind. History stretched out before her in this metal monster; here was her chance to avenge her world, her unknown parents, and the loss of so many lives. She was aware that the two men were staring at her, awaiting an answer, but she kept her thoughts locked in her heart. She simply stared at the ship, trying to drink it all in.

Captain Moreau broke the long silence. "We carry part of the original *Thunder Child* with us, you know. They recovered some of the wreckage from the bottom of the Thames some time ago. They melted down the hull and used that in constructing the bits that were not part of the original Martian cylinders. Her bell is our ship's bell, cleaned, gleamed, and ready for war. We carry the heart of our predecessor with us."

They turned at the sound of footsteps behind them. A crewman appeared in the entryway to the observation deck.

"Pardon the interruption, Captain," he said with a salute. "The Oberth tests are complete, and it is safe to use the gangway now. You may board at your leisure."

The captain saluted back. "Thank you, Ensign. Dr. Pugh, Miss Llewellyn, would you please follow me?"

He led them down the corridor and took the lift to a lower deck. The upper deck had been nearly empty, but this one was aflutter with activity. Crewmen had lined up on the station side of the door during the tests; now they pushed wagons filled with provisions through the cavernous boarding area, which bristled with the blue uniforms of the crew.

The crewman that had come to fetch the captain preceded them through the door.

"Captain on deck!" he called out.

Everyone froze in a tableau of salutes.

"As you were," the captain said with a return salute. Even as the mass of people began moving again, the small party was able to navigate freely as the crew made way. Moreau was a good head taller than most of the men around him, so it was easy to follow him in the crowd, which funneled down to a single line of people and carts on the gangway.

The caravan passed through a pair of thick doors and entered a small windowless tunnel. Its floor did not feel entirely stable, and the walls looked as if they could collapse like an accordion at any moment. In an odd way, Gemma felt slightly lighter as she walked through it, almost as if she were wading through water. She felt heavier as they reached the other side.

"Ah, they still haven't fixed the manufactured gravity here," Dr. Pugh grumbled. "And we're still entering through the cargo bay. They really were in a hurry to make the launch window, weren't they?"

The other side was even busier than the station. Rows of crates and boxes marched on either side of her down the long sides of the cargo bay.

"I am sorry, Miss Llewellyn," the captain said. Some of the shine left his eyes as they looked around. "They didn't have time to complete the formal entryways. We had a substantial refit after the shakedown cruise, and some things had to wait in order for us to make the launch window, as the good Dr. Pugh stated. However, later versions of the Victory Class should have a formal reception area."

She nodded. Secretly, she was grateful for this peek behind the scenes, for this chance to see the inner workings of the *Fury*. Absent were the overwhelming aromas of tar, sea salt, and mildew that had been her constant companions since London, though the tang of hot, sweaty men was universal. A pungent undertone of barnyard crept beneath the scents of oil, rubber, and that strange fragrance that had followed her across the tunnel, lost somewhere between a seared chunk of beef and hot metal. Crates of every conceivable size lined the walls as far as she could see, and the buzz of barked orders to move this or shove that out of the way was a welcome cacophony after the stale quiet of the station.

I must be tired, she thought. *I hear hens clucking in the distance.*

"Ah, Captain!" a man's voice. "Jolly good to see you again."

They turned to see a man that might have stepped off the painted cover of *Vanity Fair*. His uniform insignia was so shiny that he practically blinded Gemma. She could smell the pomade in his hair -- Murray's Superior -- from five feet away. A pince-nez perched on his nose, and a thick handlebar moustache with the sharpest curls she had ever seen on a man concealed his thin lips.

He bowed to them. "Arthur Gordon Wallace, at your service. I am the official representative of the Terran Industrial Alliance's Ministry of Culture for this voyage. So pleased to see you again, Captain, Dr. Pugh. And who is this lovely young lady?"

As the captain introduced her, Dr. Pugh wandered away to talk to another man in laboratory brown.

"You had a pleasant trip, I trust?" asked Mr. Wallace. "We take great steps to ensure the civility of the ground and station crews."

Gemma sighed internally. As if politeness were the most vital aspect of hurtling through the sky at greater than the speed of sound. "Yes, quite. Thank you, Mr. Wallace."

"Excellent, Miss. I hope to see you again at tea tomorrow. We must remain civil, even when we are twenty million leagues from home. If you will excuse me, I must have a word in private with Captain Moreau."

She nodded and stepped away from them. Unsure of where she should go next, Gemma examined the crew bustling about her.

"Oi!" Yet another voice came at her out of the fog of noise. "Didn't I see you dancing in Luxembourg City a while ago?"

Gemma turned to see a wild-eyed crewman gawking at her. The leer on his face took her aback. She managed to squeak, "I beg your pardon?"

"I did! I did see you!" He clapped and shuffled about on the deck. His hunter green uniform -- which made him stand out from the other crewmen -- fluttered as he danced about. He shook his head in disbelief. "I swear there was a girl on stage at the Cirque du Lune not long ago... she did that Oriental dancing with lots of feathers and little else. Lovely gams, she had! You're wearing a lot more now, to be sure, but come on now, be a lamb and do a shimmy for us."

He reached for her hips. She could not tolerate such behavior, especially as a precedent for a journey such as this. Mrs. Brightman had given her specific instructions for this kind of situation. Her hand stiffened in preparation to sting his cheek with a hard slap when Dr. Pugh appeared over the young man's shoulder.

"Shoo, shoo! Off with you, cretin!" The much taller naturalist pulled at the young man's ear, making him grimace. "A scientist wouldn't be caught dead in a burlesque show, you know that! Now go make yourself useful and swab the Oberth Deck or something." He pushed the sailor down the hall and shouted after him. "Or it's out the airlock with you!"

Pugh watched the young man's retreating elbows. "Pfffft. *Booleans.*" He shook his head. "Good Lord, the people they let into space! You would think they would have had some sort of screening for this venture." He turned toward Gemma, folded his arms, and scowled down at her, as if he were just then realizing to whom he was speaking. "And what credentials do *you* bring to the table, *Miss* Llewellyn?" Dr. Pugh asked. "From whence does your dazzling fountain of geological knowledge flow? And who will get you when you return? Oxford? Trinity?"

It certainly wasn't pleasant; this drilling in front of a good portion of the crew that she would be living with for the next couple of years was profoundly inappropriate. She could not allow this to continue. With a sharp breath, Gemma drew herself up to her full height of five feet, one and one-half inches. She lifted her own narrowed eyes to look Dr. Pugh directly in the face.

"Brightman's Ladies' College," she announced.

He froze for a moment, and the sneer fell from his lips. "Brightman," he said. His mouth twisted to the left, then to the right. He swallowed, and his already narrow eyes closed even tighter, as if examining her through a microscope. It was a long moment before he spoke again. "As in, Mrs. *Petunia* Brightman?"

"Yes."

"The one that trains computers?"

"And scientists, Dr. Pugh. The very same."

"Ah. I see."

Pugh narrowed his eyes and grunted. His sudden silence was quite disconcerting. His eyes flickered from side to side as he confirmed that no one was within earshot.

"First science briefing is tomorrow," he said, with his voice hoarse and low, "two hours post-launch, in the aft laboratory conference room on the Research Deck. Maps are by the lifts. Don't be late, child, as I'm rather an exacting taskmaster. In the meantime, I will be checking in on the rest of the team. Look lively and stay sharp. Follow my lead, young Gemma, and you may just make it back to Mrs. Brightman's second-best parlor alive." He looked to her right and narrowed his eyes.

"You there!" he shouted and pointed to someone in the distance. "Be careful with that, lad! We want to give the tentacle-heads the flu, not ourselves! Oh, for Heaven's sake."

He lumbered away at what for him must have been a high rate of speed and muttered to himself. Gemma shook inside. He knew Mrs. Brightman? That was certainly unexpected. Now the question was, how much did he know? Captain Moreau's sudden appearance in the space the scientist had evacuated pushed those thoughts away.

"Pray don't fret about him," he said. "His bark is as sharp as his bite is toothless. Too many hours staring into the innards of aliens, I suppose." The young commander tugged at the hem of his jacket. "He may be the director of the Cohort, but *I* am still the captain. I won't allow him to be too rough with you."

He extended his hand to his right and gestured for someone to join them. "May I introduce you to another of our ladies? Frau Elsa Knopf, our head of housekeeping and an indispensable member of my crew. Her husband, Herr Knopf, is our resident gardener. They are the first married couple in space! Frau Knopf, may I present Miss Gemma Llewellyn, the geologist for the Cohort."

The lady inclined her head with an economy of movement. "Fraulein."

Frau Knopf was clad in a white no-nonsense chemise with thin blue stripes and straight sleeves with a distinct lack of puffs. Her sole adornment was an ebony cameo bearing a child's silhouette. Various tools -- scissors, magnifiers, and keys -- dangled from a chatelaine on her belt.

Moreau broke the silence. "Right, well and good, you've been properly introduced." He turned to Gemma. "For now, I must leave you to the gentle ministrations of Frau Knopf. She will show you to your stateroom. Allow me to bid you *Adieu*."

He touched his brow in a gesture of farewell and walked away with another officer in tow.

The matron pinned her with a stare of granite.

"Follow me, Fraulein," Frau Knopf said.

The noise of the cargo bay faded behind them as they passed through one of an infinite number of doors in the wall. They entered a lift, and it was an eternity before the doors opened to release them. Gemma's companion said little as they walked except to point out the deck maps beside the lift doors. The tools on her chatelaine clanked and tinkled with every step. As they wandered through an endless maze, they passed by what Frau Knopf called Men's Country. She got a glimpse of several barracks-style chambers, and she could hear the occupants' chatter echoing amongst the bare surfaces. What little she could see was grey, grey, and still more grey. Silver, chrome, and aluminum sparkled everywhere she looked. There was an occasional hint of India rubber amongst the metal. She saw no portholes, and she wasn't sure how deep they were inside the ship. Normally she had a good sense of direction, but right then she felt completely turned around. She had never been in such a place before. Even the steel-and-concrete monsters built on the ruins of Leatherhead and Woking were nothing compared to this severe and gleaming world. She felt dizzy.

They passed through a door guarded by a young crewman that acknowledged Frau Knopf as she approached. He started to grin at Gemma, but he quickly returned to attention when Frau Knopf pinned him with a glare.

When Frau Knopf closed the door, they crossed the border from a land of metal to one of wood and wainscoting. The harsh ceiling light of the previous corridor gave way to the soft glow of wall sconces and frosted hurricane lamps. Wine-coloured carpet deep enough to swim in muffled their footsteps, and roses of every known shade of pink fairly dripped from the soft ivory and gold wallpaper. It was as if someone had squeezed the ink from *Godey's Ladies Book* and sprayed the juice onto the walls.

"We are now in Ladies' Country," the matron said without breaking her stride. "The men are not allowed here without express invitation from me, unless there is a clear and present danger to the ladies, with the possible exception of the captain." She fingered some of the keys on her chatelaine. "By the same token, you are not to venture into their area unless I direct you to. Today, we took the fastest route, but from now on you must take a different path if you must visit the cargo bay. I doubt you will ever need to. Is that clear?"

"Perfectly," Gemma replied.

The matron continued in that vein as they turned left yet again, passing several wooden doors along the way, each marked with a number in the 600's. It felt to Gemma as if they were winding their way deeper into the ship. It was so quiet here -- except for the odd skittering sound behind the walls every now and then -- that if she didn't know better she would have thought they were alone on the ship. Did these blasted corridors ever end?

"The ladies' lavatory is here, just down the hall from your stateroom.

The sailors call it the 'head'. It is communal. Do not leave a mess. Do not exceed your daily ration of water. We only have so much, and we will not replenish it for two years. Even with the recycling, we must make it last."

Frau Knopf's accent reminded her of an adventure in Munich with a chemist earlier that year. That time she had uncovered some fraudulent experiments that purportedly studied radium but turned out to be another waste of TIA science funds. Strangely enough, her findings had seemed quite welcome back at the College. Trying to hide her smile at the memory, she only nodded like the demure young lady she was supposed to be.

"You will make your own bed, every morning, and you will make it tight," the matron continued. "No one will be waiting on you hand and foot on this ship, Fraulein. I may be the Head of Housekeeping, and you may be a scientist, but this does not make me your maid. I run a tight ship! I make sure that things get done! And I will be inspecting your room from time to time."

Gemma merely dropped her eyes and nodded assent. After Mrs. Landry's strict housekeeping back at the school, Frau Knopf would not be a problem. She suspected that dirt would run screaming from the mere mention of this lady's name.

"Here we are," the lady said as they stopped in front of a door marked *615*. She pointed to the latch that grew out of the door in the place normally occupied by a knob. "Secure the door, coming and going, always the doors," she ordered. "Also, there is a map of the rest of the ship as well as a schedule on your dressing table. Tea will not be served today, but I will bring you a small tray for your supper. Tea will be served at four o'clock tomorrow in my parlour on this deck. Please see the schedule for acceptable dress. Also, the ship's ladies meet for a knitting circle on Saturdays in my parlour after tea. Remember, promptness is a virtue."

Frau Knopf shut and latched the door before Gemma could reply. Gemma was alone at last for the first time in days. She looked about the room and saw that her steamer trunk, one she had aptly named "Old Dependable", had arrived ahead of her and in better shape than she had.

She ran her fingers lovingly over its antique lock, and then she retrieved her necklace from beneath the shelter of her blouse. She snapped the locket open and gazed at the image of the imposing matron that had sent her on this journey. In the photograph's sepia tones, it was difficult to discern the colour of the hair in that severe chignon, with not a strand out of place. Her roommate at Brightman's, Philippa, had whispered to her that it had once been as blond as Gemma's, but now grey ruled those formerly flaxen fields. Mrs. Brightman's disciplined and no-nonsense manner was captured perfectly in the tiny metal frame of the locket, packaged to follow her students no matter their posting. Commanding eyes that observed all and revealed nothing peered down an age-sharpened nose at the unknown photographer. One hand pressed into the arm of the straight-backed chair that held her. The other hand gripped a walking stick, and its ivory head of Medusa was barely visible beneath her fingers. Gemma could fill that bit in for herself; she had memorized its slithering locks over many years of being nudged back into line with it. She drew strength from her teacher's determined expression before she closed the charm.

Slipping the toggle at the end of the necklace's chain into the trunk's lock, she heard a satisfying click as the tumblers turned. She inhaled the smell of aged leather with a smile. In a life where her living space was as changeable as the weather, this trunk encompassed her only feeling of continuity, of home. As she opened it, she also allowed the compartment of her mind that contained her true self to open, as she only allowed when she was alone with the ancient trunk. The mask of the wide-eyed young scientist fell away, and her face relaxed into something more authentic. She took a deep breath as her own true thoughts unfolded like a fan that had been held closed for too long.

She examined her quarters as she unpacked. The chamber was small, but serviceable. A low bookshelf doubled as a headboard and nightstand for the bed. Everything had its twin, mirrored on either side of the room, down to the pink and gold roses on the porcelain washbasins at the foot of each bed. A pair of sturdy wardrobes occupied the space where one would normally see a window. A small desk stood between the foot of the bed and the wardrobe. It was the perfect spot for her copy of Lyell's *Principles of Geology.*

Where the walls in the men's quarters were flat grey, hers wore bright white, pink, and French country blue toile wallpaper. Ladies in Marie Antoinette gowns festooned with coral and azure ribbons danced among sprays of roses and Greek columns. A coordinating blue and white wedding-ring quilt covered the bed, and a folded white down duvet nestled by the footboard. The scene was a slice out of any of a hundred boarding houses in Guildford. It was difficult to believe that she was on a ship in the sky and not back in her room at Brightman's.

Since she was the fifth single woman aboard, and the other two pairs were already sharing quarters -- assuming that Frau Knopf shared quarters with Herr Knopf -- she had a double stateroom all to herself. It would make certain tasks all the easier. As she fingered the spine of Lyell's text, she wondered if Mrs. Brightman had had a hand in that, as well.

She pulled out a few more books, including a frayed copy of *Jane Eyre;* perhaps now she would have some time to read it. Dear Philippa had read it years before, during an illness that had brought her home from her long-term assignment at the Admiralty Computing Service. It had kept her confined for some months and had made her too weak to smile with those dimples that Gemma loved so well. Philippa had insisted that she read it, but that chance never came. Though she had never fully recovered her strength, she eventually departed for one last mission at the ACS. She had never returned.

When the teachers had emptied the girl's armoire, Gemma had nicked the book in a singular act of rebellion and hidden it in the depths of Old Dependable. In the haste of the past few days, it was the one personal item -- besides the locket, a gift from Brightman herself -- that she had refused to leave behind.

She took another deep breath and leaned her back against the door. The fact that Dr. Pugh recognized the name of her school gnawed at her. She hoped that was all he had recognized. If her true nature were discovered, there would be nowhere to hide. But there was no knock on the door just yet, so she had a little time to settle in. She reminded herself that for the next couple of years, this room was going to be home. Yes, it was small, but for her that was not an issue.

"Besides," she said to the room, "compared to my dressing room at the Cirque, it's downright palatial."

CHRISTOPHE

Turning away from the departing Frau Knopf and Miss Llewellyn, Christophe strode towards the lifts that would sweep him to the bridge. His companion jogged to catch up with his much longer stride. They traded salutes as they waited on the car. The lift door closed behind them before they spoke.

"Good to see you again, Miguel, old sport," Christophe said. "How goes the provisioning?"

"Christophe," the man replied with just a hint of Madrid peeking through his accent. "All supplies are in orbit. Seventy-five percent of them are already on board. We had to stop for the Oberth tests, but I am confident that we will have the rest loaded by this evening. Now that you and Dr. Pugh are here, all crew are present and accounted for. Who is the young lady? I did not see her on the manifest. Is she--"

"A last-minute addition to the Cohort. Miss Gemma Llewellyn, geologist."

"A scientist, eh? I am sure that Elias has plenty to say about that. Miss or Missus?"

"Miss," replied Christophe.

"Oh, no. I'm sure that Maggie will have plenty to say about *that*."

"Only if they meet, Commander Cervantes."

Miguel shook his head. "I stay out of such things, remember? How did she take your 'apex of human achievement' speech?"

"I think she liked it. Why?"

"Because I know where you'd rather be." Cervantes shook his head in mock disgust. "Ah, I am glad I am married to the ship."

"Only until you get your own command. I still think the mission should have waited until we had at least two ships ready to go. Then you would be a captain, too."

"Ha! And you would be Commodore Moreau. You are supposed to be the hero here, remember? Between you and Sophie the Steamfitter, there is no room for me on the cartes-de-visite. I could not see anyone trading my face like that."

"Perhaps when this mission is over, then, you might be Admiral," Christophe replied with a wink. "Your examinations did get higher marks than mine, after all."

"Well, not all of us are gifted with a redundant memory, *amigo*. I had to beat you somewhere."

"If I had my way, you'd get your own CDV's and be promoted right away. But I would hate to lose the best first mate in the fleet."

"I am the only first mate in the fleet," Cervantes snorted.

"Don't let Old Artur hear you say that. He's got plans for you, my friend!"

"Speaking of Admiral Thorvaldson, I noticed he didn't ride up with you to see us off. Was he even at the Launch Coil? Is everything all right?"

"I received a wireless from him yesterday. Urgent business kept him in Luxembourg City, or else he would have been here. He sends his regards, though, and wished us luck."

"It must have been some business to keep him away from the most important launch in history. Perhaps there is news on the construction of the next ship? Maybe they are finally getting started on it?"

As they exited the lift, Christophe said, "I don't know. But if we were a *real* navy, we'd wait and send a fleet, not just a single ship."

"We *are* a real navy. Just a private one. Unlike a government, the TIA has a profit margin to maintain. Which explains why they are sending us with one dropship instead of two. How we are supposed to collect the spoils of war with that dinghy? There's enough room left over in the cargo bay to have brought your little canoe with us."

"If only I could," Christophe said as they approached the bridge entrance. "But I still look forward to the day I salute you."

GEMMA

Gemma jerked awake. Some unseen alarm jangled her nerves. She pulled the cord on the headboard's lamp and looked about for the source of the clamour. A bosun's whistle screamed through the small speaker in the corner of the ceiling. She was lost in a haze of confusion. Brightman Girls normally woke up precisely when they meant to, without reliance on clocks or alarms. However, she had been in so many time zones in the past seven days that her body wasn't sure what hour it was.

She snapped her attention back to the matter at hand. Rapid focus was an ingrained habit, and one that was vital to survival in her occupation. She reminded herself that this was not Guildford. She was on a ship, many miles above Guildford. The thought made her a little dizzy. She checked the small stateroom clock; it was six A.M., ship's time. That made it five in Guildford, also, she supposed, since the ship was on Luxembourg City time. Naturally, it would be at the same o'clock as the TIA headquarters.

She made a trip to the head. She found it quite bizarre; why in the world did they need speaking tubes and storage closets in the loo? She peeked into the storage cabinet and found jugs of water and packets marked "Cold Rations". There were also boxes of Lister's Towels, which made her sigh with relief (she could only fit so many in Old Dependable) until she did a quick calculation in her head. Even with only a handful of women on board, there weren't nearly enough in the closet for their expected journey. She hoped Frau Knopf had more down in the cargo bay. There were other boxes on other shelves, but she would have to save that prying for later.

She dressed in one of the several sets of dreary blouses and skirts that awaited her in the wardrobe. It was easy to dress without aid, as the uniform apparently did not allow for a corset. She breathed a secret sigh of relief.

Score one for the Rational Dress Society, she thought.

23

She checked the schedule that Frau Knopf had left for her. Breakfast was already in progress. After that, they would be preparing for the launch. She made up her bed and tidied up a little, in case Frau Knopf decided to pop in. Mrs. Landry had taught her well; the housekeeper had always bounced a shilling on the bed to check Gemma's work. She straightened the wrinkled top of the unoccupied bed as well, though she did not remember disturbing it during her unpacking.

She set off down the empty corridor, which was quiet except for the scratching sounds behind the walls that she had heard the day before. Wooden ships squeaked and creaked, and even steamships had their groaning; perhaps the *Fury* had her own version of complaining. Gemma's stomach grumbled along with the sounds and reminded her that she had eaten little from Frau Knopf's tray the night before. Dr. Pugh's response to the name of her particular school had upset her digestion quite a bit. She could not afford Discovery so early in her journey.

In this particular case, she could not afford Discovery at all. There was nowhere to run.

After taking a few wrong turns, she found the mess hall with her nose. Thankfully, it was on the same deck as her stateroom, outside the fortress of Ladies' Country. She selected a tray and queued up with the crewmen. Being the only female there, she received many admiring looks. She ignored them as she poured her tea. The odour of fried sausages and potatoes, mixed in with that of shoe polish and McCoy's English Pomade, was overpowering; and her stomach growled again as she carried her tray to the seating area. The long tables had benches on either side, and she was uncomfortable with the thought of sitting amongst her admirers or climbing over a bench in her long skirt.

She was the object of many stares and more than a few whistles as she walked the line of tables. Some of the men -- she assumed they were non-commissioned officers -- barked at the others to stop gawking at the skirt. The room was a cornucopia of nationalities and accents, and men of many colours donned the same blue uniform. Amongst various flavours of English, she detected notes of Paris, hints of Venice, flecks of Berlin, with a seasoning of Peking, Seoul, and Bombay, along with others that she did not recognize.

There were few grey heads in the hall. Most of the sailors appeared to be her age, or just a little older. She silently wondered how many of them were Orphans. How many of them had eaten misery in the years since the Invasion, those poor souls that had not the good fortune to enjoy the shelter beneath Mrs. Brightman's wings? How many of them were here for revenge instead of adventure?

She continued down the line to the end, which was sparsely populated. She detected a feminine note in the noise of the crowd. One person in a hunter green jacket -- a blade of summer grass in a field of navy blue -- turned around, saw Gemma, and waved at her with a bright smile. Gemma realized with a bit of a shock that this was no man, no matter how short the hair. The young lady gestured for Gemma to sit next to her.

"Come sit here, love," she said. "Name's Caroline McLure. You must be Gemma!" She leaned over with a conspiratorial wink. "Frau Knopf told me we had a new member for our little knitting circle." She pointed at the man across the table from her, who was also wearing hunter green. "And this one won't bite, neither. Look, Nigel, it's our Miss Llewellyn!"

Gemma returned the girl's greetings and nodded at her companion. Caroline was about Gemma's age, perhaps a little younger. Her nut-brown hair was so short that it stunned Gemma. It fell straight from the crown, cropped short at the nape of her neck. In fact, from behind, she looked like a young boy. Gemma had had no choice in her own hairstyle; the job at hand determined her appearance, not her own desires. Still, she could not dream of wearing her own hair so short.

Except for the different colour, the young lady wore the same uniform blouse as the men, with only slight allowances here and there in the shirt for her more feminine shape. Normally, Gemma would not be able to do her own job without her lace and corsets. She glanced down at her own drab outfit and remembered the relief she had felt not an hour ago at the lack of those encumbrances.

The gentleman across the table appeared to be slightly older than Caroline. His horn-rimmed glasses and wedding ring gleamed in the overhead lights. His face was clean-shaven, lacking the TIA-encouraged muttonchops and handlebar moustache sported by many members of the crew. A book rested on the table next to his empty plate. The page bore diagrams as mysterious as hieroglyphs.

The young man stood up and bowed. "Chief Warrant Officer Nigel Davies, at your service, madam. Welcome to the *Fury*. Yeoman McLure has been looking forward to meeting you."

She inclined her head as she studied him. He sat down and returned to his book as Gemma picked up her fork.

"So, you're one o' them eggheads in the Cohort," Caroline said, pointing to the badge on Gemma's arm. "What branch, love? Astronomy? Chemistry? You into that Black Smoke inquiry?"

Gemma sliced the sausage and pricked it with the end of her fork.

"Geology," Gemma replied.

She placed the bite of meat into her mouth and hoped the young lady would leave it at that.

"You muck about with rocks?" Caroline asked. She picked up a sausage link from her own plate and popped it into her mouth. She asked while she chewed, "What the hell do you want to go all the way to Mars to look at rocks for?" She shoveled some fried potatoes into her mouth and winked at Gemma. "Don't we have plenty of 'em back home? Thought we were going to kill Martians, not study boulders."

Mr. Davies looked up from his book. "Manners, Caroline," he said in a low tone. "Remember your manners. Not everyone here is from Cheapside."

"I hear Glasgow's pebbles are lovely this time of year," Caroline giggled through bites of potato.

Gemma began to regret that she had not brought her copy of Hartley's *Ladies Book of Etiquette*, a text that bordered on the sacred for Brightman Girls. Caroline certainly needed a chapter or two of its instruction.

"And what is your department, Mr. Davies?" Gemma asked.

He removed his spectacles and placed them on the table. Pointing to the badge on his shoulder, one with a brass gear on its shield, he replied, "Informatics."

"We're Booleans," Caroline chimed in a she licked the grease from her fingers.

"Booleans?" Gemma asked. "Dr. Pugh mentioned that word yesterday. What are Booleans?"

"Oh, surely even in the ivory tower of science you've heard of Booleans," Caroline said.

"It's just a bit of jargon, Miss Llewellyn," Mr. Davies said. "It's what the crew calls us. We write code for the Engine."

"You work on the Oberth engines? It's launch day. Shouldn't you be on that deck already?"

Caroline guffawed. "Aw, no, not *those* bloody monsters. The analytical engine, love. We call it the A.E. Totally different."

"Napkin, Caroline," Mr. Davies said just as Caroline was about to wipe her fingers on her jacket. He pushed a cloth in his companion's direction. "Remember what Frau Knopf said regarding grease on the uniforms. Besides, you never know when Mr. Wallace may be lurking about. Miss Llewellyn, you may have heard them called difference engines in other circles. We run the data you scientists cook up through the gears, sum it all up, and then let the wireless blokes send it back home. It's one of the more expensive jobs, more gears than they used in all the new ACS Engines put together by far. It is based on the designs of one Charles Babbage. Oh, and of course on George Boole's principles of logic. They'd been working on that since long before the Martians came along. The Invasion just gave us the incentive to build them. It's too bad Mr. Babbage didn't live long enough to see his creations come to life."

"Did they die in the Invasion, then?"

"Did who die?" asked Caroline.

"Messers Babbage and Boole."

"Naw, 'em blokes was pushin' up daisies long before the tentacle-heads took a notion to pay us a visit," Caroline said. "But the TIA was keen on usin' Babbage's schematics. Guess the chaps wanted something that was human built on the ship."

Gemma frowned. "It sounds like most of the credit belongs to Mr. Babbage instead of Mr. Boole, then."

"Well, there's Lady Lovelace, too," Caroline said. "She was what's-his-name's daughter."

"Lord Byron," her companion said. "The poet."

"Yeah, that's him! She worked with Babbage. Knew all kinds of mathematics. Translated an article someone wrote on his engine and added more of her own ideas that we're still using! I think of her as the first true Boolean. But it's all in the name. Lovelace ain't bad, but who wants to be called a Babbage? I mean, honestly?"

Mr. Davies nodded. "True enough. I can only imagine the ribbing we would take. Well, the additional ribbing, at any rate." He turned to Gemma. "Rumour has it that you took the last tender with the captain himself. So, what is your opinion of our fearless leader?"

"He seems very--"

"He's just like Lancelot, isn't he?" Caroline asked.

Mr. Davies returned to his book with a sigh at that. Caroline continued chatting, and Gemma was more than happy to let her. In the meantime, nodding at appropriate moments, Gemma examined the rest of the mess hall. Posters and bills covered most of the back wall in a wash of colour. One read "Lights of Blue, Go to the Loo! Lights of Red, Keep Your Head!" Gemma wasn't sure she wanted to know what that was about. An illustration of Sophie the Steamfitter grinned down at them with a curve of seduction in her lips. She informed the reader that "The TIA wants YOU to help combat the Martian Threat!" The icon leaned against a smokestack in her standard outfit: black corset, miniscule skirt, and garters that held up long silk stockings.

Gemma wrinkled her nose. The corset barely contained the woman's generous bosom as it pulled her waist into an impossibly tiny circumference (even by Brightman standards). One muscular leg bent to rest her foot flat against the smokestack behind her. A bowler perched on her head at a rakish angle; her hair was nearly as short as Caroline's. One of her eyes was frozen in a permanent wink. Sophie brandished the welding torch like a pistol with its barrel pointed overhead and a tiny flame poking out the end. A rather scandalous and silly outfit, Gemma thought, for such a powerful tool. Which, she supposed, was the point.

She had worn less, herself, in the Cirque du Lune. It had been under a bit of duress -- she preferred to leave the best of her bits to the imagination -- but she had accomplished her task and gotten the attention of a certain professor of chemistry, who had preferred dancers to computers. It was unfortunate that she had been called away from that particular venture. She had been in her dressing room when she had received her summons to report back to Brightman. She had even had the correct dose of sleeping powder for the job measured out into her favourite hollow ring. She blinked when she realized that she didn't remember where she'd left it once she'd changed into her traveling clothes.

Too late to worry about that now, she thought.

That mission was done; there was no sense in fretting over spilt absinthe, as Mrs. Brightman would have said.

Gemma stared at Sophie again. Some of the sailors stopped to kiss Sophie on their way out, and the poster was slightly wrinkled from their attentions. Someone had posted a newspaper clipping declaring the winner of a horse race from the week before. Other bills simply cried "*Terra Vigila*" and "The TIA - Defender of the Earth" to the passersby. Gemma also noticed what was missing. She wore the only brown uniform in the entire room.

"Mr. Davies, where are the other members of the Cohort? Surely they eat as well."

"Oh, they tend to breakfast in their conference room on the Research Deck. One of the cabin boys carries pastries down there so they don't have to come by the galley."

"They don't frat with us much," Caroline said. "Nice of you to come here to eat, though. Say, where are you going to be during the launch? You busy?"

"Our first meeting is scheduled for after the launch," Gemma replied.

"You don't have any rocks to look at yet, then?"

"Um, no. Not yet. When is the launch, exactly?"

"It's just under a couple of hours from now. Oh, you can watch it with us!" Caroline offered. She looked at Mr. Davies and bounced in her seat. "Oh, Nigel, can she come with us? Please? It'd be wicked fun to watch it with a scientist. I can show her the A.E.! Informatics is just off the bridge, with a window that'll let us watch it all up close. You'll be in the front row!"

Mr. Davies pulled out his pocket watch, checked the time, and replaced it. "You are certainly welcome, Miss Llewellyn. Caroline is right; you won't have a better view of history in the making. I suggest we leave now, though, as we need to get the rest of Informatics settled first."

"I would be delighted to join you," Gemma replied.

Mrs. Brightman had charged her with watching the captain. They were correct; this would be an enormous opportunity. How kind of them to save her the trouble of contriving a way to access the bridge.

Caroline led the way to the tray return. Gemma realized with horror that the young lady was wearing true trousers, not the convertible skirt that

Gemma wore. She had seen women in trousers before. But they were always wide-legged, and their blouses always covered their backsides to avoid giving the local Ministry of Culture consulate a complete conniption. Could Caroline really prefer to look like a man?

The yeoman must have noticed that her legs were the object of study. She pulled at the fabric on her thigh.

"Oh, these. Just want to blend in with the mates, love. You'll find out over time that they just make the job easier. If they think of me as just another bloke, they don't get distracted. Learned the hard way."

"Crumbs, Caroline," Mr. Davies said as he pointed to some wayward bits of toast on her uniform.

Caroline chatted all the way down the corridor and all the way up in the lift. Two decks later, they walked down another long wide corridor, passing a window on the left that opened onto a chamber filled with men in hunter green busy with teletype keys. Mr. Davies pointed to it as they passed.

"Wireless Operations," he said. "You'll want to visit with them later."

A few yards away was a door guarded by two crewmen, who greeted Davies with a sharp salute. He returned it and waited for them to open the door. A second door loomed just inside that one, but they did not enter it. The new corridor curved away to either side, and they took the right passageway. It stopped at a blank wall, with two doors on the right just before the end. He opened the second door, labeled "Informatics", and gestured them through.

The Informatics chamber certainly wasn't the grand spectacle that Gemma had expected. It was small, about twice the size of her stateroom. The ceiling felt low and close. Someone had polished the wooden floors to a warm, fine sheen. A shelf ran along the wall adjacent to the right of the door and continued to the opposite side of the room. A row of modified Remington Electric typewriters stood at attention on the shelf. One was typing along by itself on a long banner of paper, as if a ghost were composing a novel. Boxes of beige cards surrounded other such machines, and two of the Booleans were using them to punch holes into the cards. A young man in the corner of the room was in the process of packing a set of these cards into a drawer. He too, wore hunter green, like the rest of the men in the room. He picked it up, inserted it into a slot in yet another wall of the chamber, and pulled down a lever.

He turned to them and smiled; but his smile quickly melted into a red-faced grimace when he laid eyes on Gemma. She had to bite her tongue at the sight. Here was her accoster of yesterday.

Caroline noticed the exchange. "Oh, I take it you've met Mr. Humboldt already?"

"Just in passing," Gemma replied. She narrowed her eyes at him and took distinct pleasure in his squirming.

"Just yesterday," he stammered. He managed a small bow. "Yeoman Roger Humboldt, at your service, Miss." He gazed for a moment into the space beyond her shoulder, as if confirming that Dr. Pugh was not there to shove him out the airlock.

"Pleased to meet you," she said with the smooth monotone that she reserved for such situations, with just the right undertone of ice to it.

He turned away, checked the hopper's progress, and lingered there as Mr. Davies introduced her to the other Booleans. The wall that held the young man's attention was the true marvel here. The hopper itself was one of two drawers in the wall, and next to them was a wide window. Beyond it was a large rack of frames. Each frame contained a double stack of turning wheels. A box on the far right held more cards, but the machine was the one punching holes this time. Gemma walked up to the glass to study it more closely.

"Ah, that is the Engine itself," Mr. Davies said. "At least, that is part of it. We feed the data into it from this location. This set of wheels performs some of the simpler calculations. Some of the more complex mechanisms are on the deck below us."

"We use these punch cards here," Caroline said, "to talk to it. That top drawer holds the instructions. We can use those over and over to run different sets of numbers. We can put the numbers, them what varies, on cards in the other one."

"I don't know how the gubbins works, exactly," said Mr. Humboldt. He pointed to the moving wheels behind the glass. "The care of the mechanical parts falls to another lot down below. We can talk to 'em via the pipephone or send a note to 'em through the pneumatics." He pointed to a set of tubes that emerged out of the far wall and terminated in a cluster of clear boxes. Hollow cylinders lingered around on the table below them. "We can send notes to several places around the ship through them. The Cohort can also send their own punched cards for us to run through the A.E. Saves a bit of shoe leather. It's off now, 'til we launch, but it's right handy." He indicated the pipephone handset on the wall. "Pipephone takes less power, though. Your voice makes the energy for it as you talk, so use them when you can."

A loud grinding noise interrupted him. Mr. Humboldt used a knob to slide open the pane of glass. He reached into one of the frames and pulled out the crushed corpse of an insect.

"Bugger!" he spat as he tossed it into the rubbish bin. "More of those blasted beetles have escaped from the Gardens again. It's like they're in the bloody walls! Now I'll have to start the job all over again."

"Watch out when you debug like that, Humboldt," Caroline said with a snort, "or you'll get your peckham rye stuck in the machinery again."

"Bugs in me algorithm. What a bother," he mumbled. "Well, I need to halt for launch, anyway. Mr. Davies, may I beg a word with you?"

As the two men conferred in the corner, Caroline tugged at Gemma's elbow. "Speaking of which, have you seen the Gardens yet, Gemma?"

"No, actually, I haven't had an opportunity to see much of the ship at all."

"Oh, you have to see 'em! Lovely bit'o'green in the middle of the sky. The taters you ate this morning came from there! And it's got lemons and limes growing, too, so we don't get scurvy way up here."

"Truly?" Gemma asked with genuine surprise. "My institute had me convinced that it would be hardtack and water for the entire trip."

"I'd be glad to take you on a tour, Miss," Mr. Humboldt said with a grin as he and Mister Davies wandered back over to them. The icy effects of her introduction had worn off quickly.

"Not without a chaperone," Mr. Davies countered. The room erupted into laughter as he glanced at the clock on the wall.

"Quiet, you lot," he said. "Getting close to time, now." He slid open the window to the bridge. Gemma was able to observe the nerve centre of the ship for the first time.

The bridge was about twice the size of the cozy Informatics chamber. Behind a raised chair stood Captain Moreau, his hands clasped behind his back. He turned his head slowly as he observed the rest of the deck and nodded his head from time to time. She could see the same reassuring (yet naughty) smile that he had given her yesterday just before their own launch. He looked more like a lad of ten lording it over a shiny new toy train than a ship's captain, despite his great stature.

He was handsome, at least by current social standards. Tall and lean, his long face shone with hope. His wide, warm smile infected the nervous crew. His spine was straight and his gait was steady as he moved about the bridge. He was almost too handsome, as if someone had carved him out of flesh, as Pygmalion had once carved a woman out of ivory. He was so impossibly good-looking that it was hard to believe that he was real and not some heroic character in a penny dreadful, a bespoke hero. Gemma allowed herself an inner smirk; handsome men always put her in a cynical mood.

A ring of workstations surrounded the command dais. At the front of the ring was a viewport similar to the station's observation deck. It looked out upon a dark pool of twinkling stars. It felt odd, seeing a night sky this time of morning. It seemed that in space, the difference between day and night took on a completely new definition.

Behind her, she could hear the Booleans shuffle cards and paper about. Out of the corner of her eye, she saw Mr. Davies pushing a notebook into Caroline's hands.

"We talked about this," he said. "Please keep your personal research in your stateroom, Yeoman."

"What," Mr. Humboldt chuckled, "did she see it again?"

"Roger, this is serious research!" Caroline replied. "The Psychical Society--"

"Shut it, you two," Davies said. "We've got work to do."

They lapsed into a barrage of technical jargon, and Gemma tuned them out as she continued to study the bridge. On the opposite side from Informatics was a matching window, and she recognized the man standing there as one of the wireless operators. Apparently, the room was long enough on that side of the ship to have windows onto both the main corridor and the bridge. She supposed that was so that they could have direct access to the bridge but also serve those who did not need the bridge.

To the left of that window sat Mr. Wallace, who was stroking his enormous mustache and glancing at his reflection in the glass panel next to him every few seconds. The officer on the other side of it added notations in a red grease pencil. He struggled to keep a straight face every time Mr. Wallace preened himself. The poor man was losing his fight.

"This is a real treat. Historic, this is," Mr. Humboldt said. "In fact, keep hold of your gear, lads. It's now all part of history! I bet people are trading our CDVs even now! Why, even me French letters will be in a museum!"

"Still in the box, like as not," another Boolean muttered.

"What sort of fuel are we using?" Gemma asked.

She was thankful that in her guise as a scientist that her questions would be part of her role instead of something suspicious. A natural philosopher was supposed to be curious.

Mr. Davies replied, "It might be better if Dr. Pugh covered that. I believe your Cohort will have a tour later today? It takes a while to explain it all."

Mr. Humboldt broke in. "Well, we have a technological wonder here, Miss L. It's sort of a multi-fuel kind of engine. Anything that has a melting point, see, can be made into what we call propellant. Although mostly we use argon gas, and lots of it, 'cause it's easy to get. What we do is heat up the gas to a really, really high temperature, hot as hell, and it gets all the electrons in the gas all excited, see. They get so happy they push themselves out the ship's backside, and Bob's your uncle. We start out a little on the slow side, but we speed up as we go, right? It's getting to where we're moving along at a pretty good clip. There's this old cove, Newton, you see, and he calculated that once you get something moving along it stays moving along until something interrupts it. So we'll just keep moving along until we get to the other place, and we'll have to be braking about halfway there or we'll pass it right up. And can you guess what we use to get it so hot? I guarantee there's no amount of coal going to get you that hot anytime soon. We use the same thing we use to send our messages to the folks back home -- radio waves!"

"Radio waves?" Gemma asked. She had seen many strange things during her forays for Mrs. Brightman, but she had never heard of using radio waves in such a manner.

"Radio waves is just part of the spectrum, you see, all 'lectromagnetics. You can use it for a lot more than sending a telly to your mum back home, let me tell you. You being a scientist, I'd figure you might know about 'lectromagnetics, though."

"She's the ship's geologist," Mr. Davies said.

"Rocks," Caroline added. "She studies rocks, Mr. Humboldt."

"Oh, well, I guess you don't have much call to study 'lectromagnety when you're gawping at rocks all day."

The bosun's whistle interrupted them.

"Attention, all hands! Make preparations for departure."

Gemma could hear the echo from the speaker as the actual man spoke into the tube just a few yards away. Mr. Davies pushed down a slider on the wall, and the speaker went silent.

"That would be Commander Cervantes, our first mate. We can hear him well enough in person," he said.

"Mr. Cervantes," the captain said, "poll the stations, if you please."

Olive-skinned and raven-haired, Mr. Cervantes rolled the names of the various stations on the bridge off his tongue in a Spanish accent that went straight to Gemma's toes.

"Dock Control, prepare to cut station mooring cables and umbilicals."

"Prepare to cut moorings and umbilicals, aye, sir."

"Life Support, switch to internal power only."

"Life support on internals, aye, sir."

"Oberth Control, confirm that the main engines are on standby and ready to commence primary plasma heating."

"Confirm engine standby, aye, sir." The officer standing by one of the round telegraphs moved its lever and watched the pointer on the neighboring telegraph move in response a moment later. "Oberths are on standby, sir."

"Thruster control," Mr. Cervantes said. "Stand by for push away from station, Mr. Goldberg."

"Thruster control, standing by, aye."

"Mr. Rathbone, confirm wireless contact with Shackleton Station and TIA headquarters."

A few moments later, the man in the Wireless window replied. "Confirmed, sir. Flare Watch reports no signs of solar activity."

Gemma noted that everyone stopped and took a deep breath at that announcement. Cervantes paused to cross himself, and then he snapped to attention in front of the captain.

"Captain Moreau, all bridge stations report ready for departure."

"Excellent, Mr. Cervantes. Mr. Rathbone, please open a voice channel from the bridge to the Station."

"Channel open, captain."

He strode over to a large microphone attached to one of the side stations. "Shackleton Station, this is Captain Moreau." Gemma detected an edge of nervous pride in his voice. "*Thunder Child's Fury* requesting permission to depart."

"Permission granted, Captain Moreau, and godspeed," came the reply through the bridge speaker. "*Terra Vigila!*"

"Mr. Cervantes, we have clearance to depart. Complete your procedures."

"Dock Control, secure the cargo bay doors," the first mate said. "Complete the retraction of all cables and gangways."

Gemma watched the responding officers at their corner stations. She anticipated feeling some rumble, even a small vibration, as these chores were completed, but she could detect nothing.

"Mr. Allston," the captain said to the officer at the bridge telegraph, "Have Chief Nesbitt commence the plasma heating sequence."

"Commence primary heating sequence, aye, sir," Mr. Allston replied. He pulled the lever on the telegraph to "CPH" and watched the responding telegraph move to a symbol that she did not recognize. "Estimated time to optimal temperature, two minutes, Captain."

"Mr. Goldberg, commence push away from the station." The captain turned to the officer at the navigation station, who was a broad-shouldered man with deep brown skin. "Mr. Pritchard, once we have cleared the station, navigate us to the launch point."

Mr. Pritchard responded, "Navigate to the launch point, aye, sir."

The crew called back the orders in a surprisingly calm fashion, as if they had rehearsed it a hundred times. She found Mr. Pritchard's cadence of speech odd. Perhaps he was an American? She knew that there would be some of them among the crew. The Martians had hit North America hard, and many of their larger cities had been devastated by Black Smoke.

She finally felt a slight movement as the ship nudged itself away from the station. She felt hollowness in the pit of her stomach. They were committed, now; this was the point of no return, and they were leaving the only world that they had ever known. She gripped the rail in front of her until her knuckles turned white and threatened to burst through her skin. Whispers of the disastrous lunar voyage curled around in her brain, and the hollow feeling in her gut ached.

The bosun's whistle echoed throughout the ship. Everyone snapped to attention. The captain's voice flowed through the speakers throughout the ship.

"This is Captain Moreau. As the entire world listens for word of our departure, I would like to share my thoughts with you. Many of us were just infants when our namesake struck the first blow against the Invading Martians, but we still carry within us the heart of that brave steamship. Many people are alive today because of the courage of her crew. Others gave their lives during the construction and maiden voyage of our own vessel. We carry that legacy forward to realms unknown. We are the first of our race to break the bonds of our mother world. We do so through human innovation and inspiration. We carry the fight back to the Red Planet to protect our loved ones back home. We do not know what awaits us there, but we are prepared to bring them low enough that they will never trouble us again. We will be free of the Martian Threat for all time. Because we as a people have the ability to turn tragedy into something greater, humanity will someday see her children in every corner of the sky. Every one of you, down to the last cabin boy and galley assistant, will have their names written in the great volume of History. Earth is awakening to claim her destiny. As we set sail, let us give meaning to the lives lived before us and give a new world to those who come after us. We walk among the stars, among the legends, where no other human has walked, in the name of all those who perished, in the name of the Terran Industrial Alliance, in the name of our Kings and Countries, and in the name of all Humanity."

Caroline whispered into Gemma's ear. "Told you he was like Lancelot, pretty speech and all."

"Bet he was up all night, writing that," Humboldt said with a cackle. Davies elbowed him in the ribs until he stifled his giggles, but his grin remained.

Captain Moreau took another deep breath and turned to the officer standing at the bridge telegraph. "Mr. Allston, what is the status of the engines?"

The officer gazed down at the pointer on the telegraph. "Captain, the engines are in departure status and are standing by to fire on your command."

"They heard his speech down in Luxembourg City," Mr. Davies explained. "We can broadcast voice as well as telegraphy. You can be sure, they've recorded it so it can be heard 'round the world. After it's been edited, of course."

In this quiet room with only a few people watching, it was hard to believe that an entire world waited breathlessly to hear this man, and that his speech would be read by schoolchildren for years to come, perhaps in a sequel to the *Invasion Chronicle*.

"Mr. Pritchard, notify me the moment we are in launch position."

"Aye, sir."

An excited tension sparked around the bridge. Everyone watched the captain, Mr. Pritchard, and each other, as the seconds stretched out like taffy. Everyone but the captain jumped when Mr. Pritchard spoke again.

"Captain, we are in launch position."

"Let us depart, then! Mr. Allston, give the word to Chief Nesbitt to engage main propulsion. All ahead full." He looked at the navigator. "Take us out, Mr. Pritchard."

Mr. Allston moved the brass telegraph lever to "All Ahead Full". The ship shuddered a bit, and the captain gave the order to check the dampeners. The shuddering stopped.

"Are you certain we have engaged the Oberths?" Gemma asked.

"Oh, most assuredly," replied Mr. Davies. "I was on the lunar shakedown voyage, Miss Llewellyn. Believe me, the dampeners have improved much since then."

"You were on that voyage?" she gasped. "Is it true that half the crew--"

"Yes, I was," he said as he lowered his voice to a whisper. He patted the chair next to him. She sat in it, and he leaned in closer so that the others could not hear. "So were Caroline and Humboldt, but none of the rest of this lot. They replaced the ones we lost. I was fortunate enough to be in a sheltered area of the ship when the flare enveloped us. So were the Captain and Mr. Pritchard. We had no warning at all. We lost many colleagues... friends... that day."

"It must be so difficult to go on another voyage after that," Gemma said.

Sympathy did not come easily to her. She could not afford to become emotionally involved in any job. It was more emulation than genuine concern. She reckoned that in the next few months she would have lots of practice. But there was something compelling about his earnestness. "It would take a great deal of fortitude to venture out again, I think."

"I owe it to them," he replied. "I owe it to them to complete what they started and make sure that they are not forgotten." He looked down at his wedding ring. "My wife is carrying our firstborn. I have to make sure they are safe. I want to ensure that my child does not live in fear that these monsters will come and take his mother away at any moment." He glanced at the rest of the Booleans, who were watching the captain through the window. "I will tell you more later. Such talk makes the rookies uneasy."

Gemma's chest tightened as he spoke. This was one of her few tender spots: encountering a fellow Orphan. He was not much older than she was, but he was most likely old enough to remember his parents.

All the Brightman Girls were Invasion Orphans. It was forbidden to discuss that fact amongst themselves, for Mrs. Brightman was their mistress and mother now. Even whispers in the dark were discouraged by the night monitors. When she was older and shared a room with just Philippa, that lesson had remained with them. Brightman had tolerated the stories of spirits and monsters (Philippa had told Gemma a deliciously wicked tall tale about a mad vivisectionist that had attempted to turn animals into people, though she could not remember his name). Her teacher had always assured her students that they were safe from such things inside the School. However, discussions of their might-have-beens were deemed fruitless and therefore forbidden. Gemma was startled to hear the Boolean speak of such a thing so openly. He said no more, and she let him be.

"Status, Mr. Cervantes?" the captain asked.

The first mate gazed at the row of brass-rimmed controls and the black needles dancing over pools of white.

"All systems running normally, sir."

"Very well, then. Let go and haul!"

There were no bumps or shakes. The chamber remained steady. Everyone in Informatics let out their breath at last and smiled at each other. Some shook hands.

"That's it?" asked Gemma.

"Yes, that's that," Mr. Davies replied. "We're on our way. It's debugging and solar flare drills until Braking Day."

"Braking Day?" Gemma asked.

"We're slowly accelerating our way towards the Red Planet. Midway through, we decelerate. As Mr. Humboldt so aptly put it, we have to start braking at the right time or we'll pass it right up. Precise timing is a must."

"It'll be a bit of a holiday, actually," said Mr. Humboldt. "We've got to get that bit right. I don't think we brought enough tea to make it to Jupiter."

The Booleans that were not on duty shuffled out. Gemma heard them moving behind her as she continued studying the bridge. At one point, the captain turned in her direction. He winked at her with the smallest of movements, then turned his attention to the bridge once more. She had watched him, as she had been ordered, but so far she had only seen a popinjay in a military jacket. She still was not sure why she was here or what exactly she was supposed to watch for; usually her missions were more specific. But she was here all the same, and she would do her job. Still, it was a little embarrassing to her that she had captured his attention with almost no effort on her part.

Caroline made her way over to stand next to Gemma and Mr. Davies as the chamber emptied.

"Do you think we'll make it past the moon this time, Nigel?" she whispered through a frown. She bit her lower lip like a lost child.

"Hush, Caroline," he replied in the same soft tone. He patted the yeoman's shoulder. "It will be all right. We've done this before. And we're better, this time."

And with that, Gemma Llewellyn, Invasion Orphan, departed for War.

CHRISTOPHE

"Now that we're underway, what's on tap for the rest of the day?"

As he asked the question, Christophe swung his lanky limbs onto the conference table and crossed his ankles. Miguel sighed, as he always did when they were alone. He sat up a little straighter in the adjacent chair and jogged the stack of papers in front of him.

"This afternoon, we have a meeting with Gun Control to discuss the final heat ray tests." He looked up from the schedule. "I'd like to be involved in those, if possible. I spent a lot of time with them on the maiden voyage, if you recall. I'd like to see that through."

"I have no objections. What else?"

"Let me see. Ah, the launch tea party is scheduled for the first dog watch--"

Christophe groaned. "Another official tea? So we can all see Wallace's shining face again?"

"Yes, and you will see plenty of him on this voyage, so I suggest you get used to it. But before that, the Cohort will tour the Oberth Deck."

"Really?" Christophe withdrew his legs from the table and sat up. "All of them?"

He sighed again. "Yes, all of them. And tomorrow we resume the classes for the midshipmen. I suggest--"

"Miguel, old sport, my old *amigo*, I think it is time to add something to the schedule."

"What?" It was Miguel's turn to groan. "Now? We just left the station. At least let the crew settle in first. You know how nervous they are about flares."

"All the more reason to go ahead and get a drill over with. You never know when one will pop up. I want to be sure that we're ready. Especially on the Oberth Deck. We have to keep our scientists safe."

38

"Christophe," Miguel said as he winced and pinched the bridge of his nose, "do I have to remind you of the trouble you had in Gibraltar last year? With the governor's daughter?"

"Miss Llewellyn looks nothing like the governor's daughter."

"The barmaid in Saint Vincent? The minister's daughter in Tortola? As your first mate, it is my duty to tell you when you act like this." As Christophe flashed a satisfied grin back at him, he continued, "I know why you named me after the creator of the Man of La Mancha. I just don't know whether I'm Don Quixote or Sancho. Some days it is both, I think."

Christophe leapt from his chair and headed for the door. "Set it up. I will pipephone you from the Oberth Deck when I'm ready to go."

Cervantes cupped his hand across his forehead. "And this is why you'll never make Admiral."

GEMMA

"Would you like to see the orrery?" Nigel asked.

Gemma was startled out of her reverie by the sudden question. She had lingered with the Booleans after the captain and his first mate had left the bridge. After the initial excitement of the launch, everyone had quickly settled down. Humboldt had turned the pneumatic tube system back on, and Caroline and the others had resumed their posts at the keypunch machines.

"I would," she replied.

She had seen such things before, and she wondered how in the world a miniature of the solar system could be so important as to need its own Boolean. At the same time, it would be good to cultivate allies on the ship. It was going to be a long voyage, and an even longer one without them.

"However," she continued, "that may need to wait for later. I have a Cohort meeting to attend, and I need to send a message back to my academy to inform them that we have set sail."

"I can show you how. Follow me, please." He turned to address the room. "Yeoman McLure, you're in charge for the moment. Contact me if you need me, or if Humboldt gets out of hand. Don't worry, Roger," he said, looking at Humboldt. "You'll get that algorithm right. I have every bit of faith in you."

He led Gemma out of the Informatics chamber and back into the corridor. After the door closed, he gently touched her elbow and then withdrew it.

"Pray, don't fret for Caroline's sake," he said. He walked slowly and spoke softly. "She will be fine. She has survived much worse than a case of the nerves. The hair bob isn't even new. She's worn it that way since we were children together at the old Wickham Textile Factory. That's where we were apprenticed, you know. The Jacquard looms there were a good

40

proving ground for Engine development, once the Neo-Luddite riots stopped. 'Twas loads better than life on the factory floor, let me tell you."

Gemma shuddered as they passed through the guarded door. Mrs. Brightman constantly reminded her Girls of the Factory Orphans: the lost fingers and limbs, the filth and starvation, and the acres upon acres of tiny graves. So many little ones had died during the brief anti-technology insurrection of 1912, just one hundred years after Ned Ludd had led a similar rebellion against machines. Many more had died just keeping the looms in operation until the machines had taken over completely, and many were homeless adults now that the textile factories were fully automated. Just how many Invasion Orphans had those monsters devoured over the years? How many times had she thanked her mistress for saving her from such horrors?

She looked up as they arrived at the wireless window.

"Here we are," Mr. Davies said. A stack of glass slates sat to one side, each with a grease pencil attached to it by a string. They resembled the glass panels that she had seen on the bridge. "Just write the recipient's name here at the top, your name, and your message below it. Then put it with the others over here. They'll send it when they review the stack, and the Admiralty will route it to the proper person. Don't worry, the A.E. keeps a record of everything we send and receive, so you can always ask us to pull it up later via punch card if you need to review it. You can also send messages up from the labs via the pneumatics." He glanced at the clock on the wall. "I must be off. See you at tea, Miss Llewellyn."

He bowed to her and strode off in the direction of the lift. Gemma picked up one of the blank slates. She appreciated his help; here at last was someone who strove for efficiency as much as she did. He would be a worthy ally.

As she wrote out her message, her eyes flickered over the box containing the stack of waiting panels. She read over the message on top in a flash, out of habit. It was nonsensical; at least, it was to the untrained eye.

There were more abbreviations in it than actual words, but that was a common enough practice. She reread the message and allowed one eyebrow to arch slightly. Ah! She wasn't the only one of her kind aboard! It did not surprise her all that much. Mrs. Brightman was certainly not alone in her particular field of endeavour. She felt a prickle in her scalp at the possibility and wondered if she had worked for the mystery sender in the past. That would prove an awkward reunion. She searched for the name of the sender or the recipient, but both were smudged and nearly unreadable. One of the operators chose that moment to collect the stack, and she lost her chance.

To cover her disappointment, she finished scribbling out her own message: "Departed Safely. Clear Sailing." Or, as someone reading it would see, "DPRT SAFE STOP CLR SLNG STOP". The "clear" keyword was an indicator that the message meant exactly what it said; nothing was hidden or encoded.

"I'll take that for you, Miss," said a man on the other side of the window. Gemma looked up into the eyes of a tall, gaunt man. His smile was gentle, and there was a twinkle in his hazel eyes. He studied her over horn-rimmed spectacles and touched his fingers to his banker's visor.

"Warrant Officer Edmund Rathbone, at your service," he said. He pointed to the badge on his arm. "Signal Corps. Don't worry, I'm new on this voyage, too. I'll be happy to send that message for you, love."

She responded, using her perfectly schooled smile. By his accent, he was definitely of Guildford stock, but she did not recognize his face.

"Would you prefer to pick up your messages here, or would you like for me to send them down the tube?" He pointed to the pneumatic tube behind him with his thumb.

"Here, please," she replied. "I could use the exercise." Even though any of her messages would be in code and therefore unreadable by most, she preferred to have them handled by as few people as possible. If he sent them by the tube, someone else might open the cylinder before she did.

She thanked him and then left to find the laboratory deck. On her way, she mulled over the enigmatic message. It was protocol to be aware of any other Brightman sorts in the vicinity.

Especially if that "other" was a Watcher.

Every Brightman Girl on a mission had a Watcher. That was also protocol. Everyone had someone that reported on their movements, requested aid if needed, or took steps to make sure that the job was completed. She had heard second-hand that sometimes those steps were less than civil. The Watchers were silent and unseen, especially where the Girls were concerned.

Gemma had rarely worried about her Watchers. She prided herself on her ability to complete a job smoothly and cleanly without intervention. She often made it a game to guess her Watcher's identity, but the missions were so short that she often had a limited time to puzzle it out.

The message she had seen had been in code. Was it from her Watcher? They were by nature unobtrusive. It would be unusual for them to leave something so obviously encoded just lying about. Of course, they may have wanted to remind her of their unseen presence; they did that sometimes. It was true that she had not given her potential Watcher much thought until now. There had been such a rush to get her to the launch point, and then the nerve-wracking process of the rail-gun launch, that this was the first time she'd had a moment to consider a Watcher. A shiver danced down her spine.

She stuffed the question into her mental steamer trunk. Now she had to prepare for her first meeting with the entire Scientific Cohort. She hoped that she had met none of them under other circumstances... one that had found particular items missing from his workbench, learnt that some of his reference tables were badly skewed, or discovered his chalkboard equations altered right after she had disappeared from his life.

She arrived at the lift. A silver-haired Asian man, who was also wearing the brown jacket and badge of the Cohort, waited there. An emerging smile carved even deeper wrinkles in his face as she approached.

"Ah, you must be Miss... Miss..."

She recognized the accent from her time in Shanghai. She nodded and smiled gently in return. He struggled once more to say her name.

"Please, call me Gemma," she replied.

"Ah, Miss Gemma, then." He bowed slightly in her direction. Another smile, this one of relief, broke across his face. "I am Professor Hui Yutai, lead physicist. Dr. Pugh told us to help you if we saw you. Have you been to the Research Deck yet? No? I will show you the way."

When the lift doors opened, he gestured for her to precede him into the car. "I am sorry I did not get to meet you yesterday when you arrived," he continued, "but I was playing with a pet project of mine and lost track of time. If you wish, later, I will show it to you. I am sure you will be busy with your own experiments, though."

Experiments, Gemma thought. *Oh, bother.*

The lift swept them away to another deck; and when they exited, she followed Hui to the right.

"The conference room for the meeting is that way," he said, pointing towards the corridor to their left. "But the laboratories are this way. Oh! And the loo is across the hall from them. Very important to know."

They entered a chamber bound in metal, wood, and glass. The scientists had stuffed every inch to the gills with all manner of contraptions for dissection and examination. The lab reminded her of so many others that she had seen (and nicked from) before, but never had she seen one this large. She did recognize a few of the tools: scalpels, microscopes, and racks of tubes filled with a rainbow of fluids. From the wall between a lab bench and a keypunch machine there emerged another pneumatic tube. A cylinder awaited retrieval in its receptacle. She saw more of the glass panels like the ones on the bridge; the rectangles bore grease-penciled equations, sketches, and words that she could not pronounce despite all her lab experience. One was covered in a tangle of C's and G's, A's and T's in impossible combinations that formed a cipher text that she could not break.

And books! So very many books! Textbooks, bound journals, handwritten notebooks, and volumes of mathematical tables smothered the lab. They towered in stacks on the shelves, lurked on the corners of tables, loitered about the floor, and generally occupied any flat surface available (real or imagined). It was a treasure-trove of secrets, low-hanging fruit ripe for the taking. They had not yet been defined as part of her job. The books could wait.

She scrutinized the men in the lab, already hard at work, as if they had been on the ship for weeks, toiling away at their glass panels. Some of them were European, but others appeared to be from India and Arabia. And naturally, she was the only female amongst them.

He guided her farther into the laboratory. "Here is the space set aside for you, Miss Gemma. I am afraid they haven't brought your equipment in from the cargo bay just yet."

Here was the only empty spot in the entire room; it was as bare as the others were full to bursting. While the other glass panels bore smudged equations and fingerprints, her own pane gleamed in the bright overhead lights. She hoped that her feeling of panic did not show on her face.

Hui continued, "Do you remember where in the cargo bay they stored your equipment? Perhaps I could put in a request for you to have it moved here."

Gemma froze as she stared at the vacant shelves. They yawned before her in a bookless abyss. Mrs. Brightman had mentioned nothing about equipment in her hurried briefing. Perhaps she had thought that the Cohort would provide it all. Even though she had been excited by the prospect of the job, Gemma was used to being the assistant or the computer, not the actual scientist. Her situation was getting more precarious by the moment, and she wasn't past the moon yet. She had to say *something*, perhaps even the truth.

"I am not sure. They sent me to replace someone else who could not make the trip, at the very last moment. I do not know where their equipment might be. Perhaps there has been some mistake?"

Hui closed his eyes for a moment and shook his head. "Oh, my, what a tragedy! Perhaps you should have visited the laboratory before we launched, so you might have requested that they send it up. But perhaps it would have made us miss the launch window. Very well. Can you tell me what experiments you had planned? Perhaps someone can loan you something?"

He was quite chatty, and she found it expedient to act as puzzled as he was; it was not difficult. The word "Experiments" was already on her emergency list of Things to Ponder; experiments would be even more difficult to fake with nonexistent paraphernalia. Her next message back to the School would be a strongly worded one.

"Perhaps you brought some samples in your personal luggage?" Hui continued. "Minerals for your non-Mars research? Some strike plates? Perhaps some gems?" He rubbed his hands together with an excited gleam in his eyes.

"No, I am sorry."

"Oh, well," he sighed as he hunched his shoulders. "I thought perhaps they might have provided you some lunar rocks to study, at the very least. Check with Dr. Pugh. Perhaps he has a few from the last voyage." He paused and clasped his hands together, lost in thought. He shrugged. "You are already here, at any rate. Perhaps we can find something for you to do."

She cringed and was no longer afraid to do so. There wasn't as much as a slide rule at her station. She had known going into this that it would be difficult enough to convince the Cohort of her abilities; looking worse than unprepared would make it nearly impossible. She had to think, and think quickly, or she was going to be in an awkward position for a very long time.

"I have heard that we will have a tour of the Oberth Engines today," Hui said, startling her out of the dark tunnel she was thinking her way down. "Dr. Pugh saw them on the last trip, but the rest of us are new here, just like you. Isn't it exciting? I have heard that they use radio waves! Radio waves! How did they ever conceive of such a thing? I cannot wait to see it!"

She breathed a quiet sigh of relief at the change of topic. Perhaps that would give her some time to think about how she was going to handle her growing List. This wasn't the first time Gemma had had to improvise, but this job was going to push her skills to the limit.

A towering stack of books walked over to them on spindly legs. "I noticed you have some storage space to spare," the stack said in an accent that had grown up somewhere near Bangalore. "Mind if I borrow a bit?"

The stack rested itself on her workbench and revealed the man behind it. His face was nearly as brown as his lab blouse, and his black hair, frosted at the temples, floated untamed about his head like a quiet storm cloud of curls. The wrinkles of his lab blouse stored the crumbs of breakfast, and his now book-free hands were stained with ink and pencil grease.

"I could not help but overhear. So, I expect you won't need your space anytime soon. Any chance I might use your shelves? And your board?" He pointed to her gleaming glass panel. "The grease pencils are not nearly as nice as chalk, I will admit, but I could use the space."

"Ah, Dr. Bidarhalli," Hui answered before she could even take a breath to respond. "Please meet the much anticipated Miss Gemma, our geologist. Miss Gemma, this is Dr. Santosh Bidarhalli, our mathematician from Hyderabad, India's City of Pearls." Shedding his fatherly smile for a moment, he shook a finger at the other scientist. "Santosh, you remember what Pugh told us yesterday. Chalk gets in the air recycling and chokes everybody." He turned to Gemma. "Pugh told me that they learned the hard way during the lunar voyage."

A familiar voice interrupted them. "Just about time, lads," Dr. Pugh said, his lanky frame filling the doorway. "Come on to the conference room. Hui, do make sure that Llewellyn doesn't get lost on the way, if you please."

For once, she was grateful for his intrusion. It gave her some time to think. She followed Hui, Bidarhalli, and the rest back down the hall and past the lift. Feeling like a lost chick in a flock of clucking brown hens, she considered her situation. Perhaps she could barter her empty space for some time with the others' books and Bunsen burners. The curious side of her mind reveled in the thought of observing their work. She hated leaving a mission before knowing the final results of her target's experiments. They would expect her to take notes; even the most socially awkward scientist would notice if she didn't scribble something every so often. She would need pens and notebooks as well. The two members she had just met seemed amenable to such a trade. With her training as a computer, she would be right at home with the mathematician's materials.

Hui pulled out a chair for her, and she sat down carefully, with her hands folded in her lap and ankles crossed beneath her long skirt. She looked about the conference room as it began to fill with the other members of the Cohort.

There were no "*Terra Vigila*" posters here. Sophie didn't do any welding in this room, Gemma supposed. In fact, the only sign on the wall that she recognized was the "Lights of Blue, Go to the Loo!" one from the mess hall. Otherwise, maps of their destination covered the walls like the tattered remnants of tapestries. Some were marked with the possible locations of seas, canals, and cities that some had glimpsed through earth-bound telescopes.

A guide to the Moon was there as well, with features that she had never seen in the newspaper articles covering the maiden voyage. On the main table sat a globe of Mars, a red-gold sphere that shone in the bright light beaming down from the ceiling panels. Books, papers, rulers, and drafting tools were scattered about the globe's base, and some were employed as weights to hold down still more maps. Bound volumes of numerical tables computed by the Admiralty Computing Service lurked beside copies of Darwin and Lyell. Gemma noted that the latter was the same edition as the one in her cabin.

A geology book amongst these fellows? Perhaps her Watcher was in this very room. *If so,* she thought, *his disguise is superb. Most of them could not infiltrate a post office.*

With much squeaking and fidgeting, they finished seating themselves. They were a room of dull brown hens, and it took a moment for the clucking to subside. A couple of them glared at her, as if she were an unexpected fly swimming in an Erlenmeyer flask of carefully distilled water. Hui and a fatherly man on her other side flashed her paternal smiles while Bidarhalli and the rest found some other scientific object to occupy their attention.

"Right," Pugh said, hunching over the head of the table. "You lot know each other, but we have a new member that I need to introduce." She could almost feel the effort he was making to avoid rolling his eyes. "Miss

Gemma Llewellyn, Ship's Geologist. Miss Llewellyn, may I present the rest of the Cohort."

He gestured to the smiling man sitting to her right. He wore a clerical collar beneath his browns.

"This is Father Abramo Alfieri, our astronomer. He's on loan to us from the Vatican Observatory." Pugh's left eye twitched. "He is also the ship's chaplain. Should we need one."

Father Alfieri stood up and bowed to Gemma as he said, "I say Mass on Sunday mornings and hear confession on Wednesday evenings after tea. Of course, I am available for spiritual counsel whenever the need arises. I have a small chapel just off the mess hall for everyone's convenience."

This time the other scientists *did* roll their eyes. They grunted in response, but they did not interrupt him. Alfieri was a small man; he was one of the few people that Gemma had met so far with whom she could literally see eye to eye. Silver hair framed his broad smiling face. His deep-set eyes twinkled above a neatly trimmed beard.

Pugh cleared his throat and continued pointing out the other men at the table.

"Professor Yuri Stanislav of St. Petersburg, Germ Sciences. And next to him, Declan Shaw, of Trinity College. They are the G-bomb experts. That's 'germ bomb' to the uninitiated."

The two men nodded at her without speaking. Shaw shot her a look that she had encountered more than once in her travels, a derisive sneer that said he already knew about her empty workspace and that he had expected nothing more than that. The other hostile glower in the room clung to the face of the man next to him.

"Alvar Berndsen, lately of Copenhagen, is my fellow biologist. He also assists the ship's surgeon from time to time. And here is our linguist and cryptanalyst, hailing from the Ottoman Empire, Abdul-Halim ibn Saeed ibn... ibn... oh heavens, I can't remember the rest. We just call him Abbie."

"Which he doesn't particularly like," Hui whispered in her ear.

The man in question stroked his luxurious beard with a studied and silent frown. Not an angry frown, as she had seen many times before, but one of deep rumination that refused to reveal its secrets.

"Abbie deciphers and translates the information we retrieved from the Martian cylinders. I suppose you are already acquainted with our resident physicist and mathematician," Pugh continued, pointing to the Hui and Bidarhalli in turn.

Gemma didn't recognize any of these fellows from any of her previous jobs; she was thankful for that.

"Now that that's over with, let's crack on. Most of you are quite familiar with the plan, but I will review for our latecomers." He managed to say this without staring at her this time. "Our first order of business as the Cohort is to improve our knowledge of the Red Planet itself. As we get a better view of it with our telescopes, we will see what is where and revise our maps. We're not certain of their accuracy by any means. There has been some argument back home over whether the canals marked on the maps truly exist or if they are mere artifacts of our telescopes. But these," he pointed out red circles on one of the maps, "are our best guesses as to the locations of the main population centres. We have reckoned that these are the best targets for our attack run. Shaw, where are we on the payload development?"

Father Alfieri fidgeted in his seat and interrupted before Shaw had a chance to reply. "So, the suggestion that we might parley with them has been put aside?"

Pugh sighed. "Once again, Father, we don't think they'd be very keen," Pugh replied. "I know the Church has a vested interest in increasing its flock, but from what we can tell, the Martians evolved for War, not theological debate."

"So the plan for genocide is still in place," the priest said. "I had hoped... but there is time yet. What do we intend to do, if a victory is achieved, then? Or not achieved?"

It was an interesting way to ask the question: "*What happens if we lose?*" Those unsaid words hung in the air between the two men like the foul odour of sulphurous eggs.

With a sharp glance at the priest, Shaw answered, "With the payload we've devised, victory is a foregone conclusion. We're not using simple explosives, Father. We're going to introduce the rest of the population to the little buggers that their friends met on Earth. We've even improved a few of them to speed up the process."

"Diseased weapons?" Gemma asked, surprised that the question actually escaped her lips.

"Of course. It's the best way to preserve the existing infrastructure," Stanislav said. "For the second part of the Mission."

"Yes, yes," Pugh said with a sneer. "The much vaunted Secondary Mission. Which we all know to be the Primary. Naturally, we have to have something left to steal."

A blue-coated sailor leaned into the room. "We're ready for you down below, Dr. Pugh."

Dr. Pugh seemed relieved by the interruption. They filed out of the room and followed the young man to the lift, which took a couple of trips to ferry them all to the Oberth Deck. Gemma stayed beside Dr. Pugh during the trip down.

"We did have some ideas of our own once, you know," Dr. Pugh said to her. "Before the Invasion, that is. There was some flirtation with chemical rockets. Some people have always had dreams of going to the stars, and they felt that rocketry was the key."

"Rocketry?" Gemma asked. She had heard the term bandied about during one of her previous jobs, but she had gleaned very little in the way of useful information.

"I'll leave it to our good physicist to explain," Pugh replied as they exited the lift and passed the sign for the Oberth Deck.

"Have you ridden a bicycle before, Miss Gemma?" Hui asked.

She shook her head. "No, but I have seen them in London."

"Well," he continued, "when I ride one, it looks like I am pushing the pedals to move the wheels. What I am really doing is pushing against the ground, the Earth itself, to move forward. That thing I push against is called the *working mass*, to use the precise phrase. I can use the brakes to slow down or stop. And of course, there is friction on the road to slow me down as well."

The group turned a corner in the corridor and waited before a heavy door as their guide turned a large valve wheel to open it.

"In space," Hui said, "a ship has no ground, no gravity, to push against to move. So it has to bring its own working mass, yes? In rocketry, that working mass is the fuel. It is funneled out of the rear of the ship, which pushes it in the opposite direction. And there is no friction to slow it down." The door swung open as he talked, and they followed the guide through. "Simple enough, at least in theory--"

Hui gasped, and so did Gemma as she followed his eyes up, up, and up. This chamber seemed to have no ceiling! They stepped deeper into the chill of the cavern before them.

It was a veritable jungle of brass and steel, abloom with valve wheels and gauges of every size. Pipes climbed the walls like strangler vines and ran in every direction. The few spaces not claimed by pipes were plastered with warning signs that shouted all the dreadful consequences of a fuel leak or a solar flare, along with directions to the closest head. Gemma wondered about this obsession with toilets among the crew, thinking it might be a sign of some deficiency. Did one make water more often in space? So far, that had not been her experience.

A cylindrical tank dominated the vast chamber. Pipes of all sizes extended from it, running both fore and aft. Row upon row of barrels marched beside it. Each barrel had its own large gauge, like a cyclopean eye staring out over its fellows. The black tank itself had its own great bank of indicators in the shadows beneath it. A cluster of men monitored these instruments as they consulted clipboards and muttered amongst themselves.

"In practice, it wasn't so simple," Dr. Pugh said, picking up Hui's train of thought. Gemma thought she detected a note of boredom in his voice. It took her a moment to remember that he had seen all this before, and to him it was just another cold section of the ship.

"The problem was heat," Dr. Pugh said. "Look at it this way. You have to provide so much kinetic energy to reach a certain velocity, and you have to get to a certain velocity to go a certain distance in a reasonable amount of time. To get that velocity, you have to burn very hot indeed, and that sort of temperature tends to melt the very nozzle that uses it for propulsion! What a dreadful pickle! So we had to figure out some method of producing the thrust without actually melting the ship in the process! We fought with it and fought with it and there seemed no way round it ... until the Invasion. Once the little buggers had been harvested by the grim reaper, we peeked into their cylinders and found a solution."

He walked towards the tank. Most of the other scientists had wandered off and were running up and down the aisles of barrels by this point, so he was talking to Gemma alone. "They had plans for other ships, ones much greater than cylinders. Enormous ships that could move thousands of such creatures vast distances across the stars. They injected energy into a propellant gas," he said as he pointed up at the tank with a long bony finger, "without touching it. Using a technology that we were already familiar with. Radio waves."

They stopped at the last row of barrels just before the tank itself, very near to the men monitoring the instruments.

"The main fuel is argon gas, which is stored in this monstrosity. We can divert it to the aft nozzles, as we are now, for forward thrust. Later on, to slow down, we can divert it to the forward nozzles. For Braking Day." He pointed to each set of pipes in turn. "We convert the gas into a plasma working mass by heating it to an incredibly high temperature using radio waves. At the same time, we have to have electric power to produce those radio waves. We have a different fuel for that, a variation of helium, helium-3, also known as--"

"Tralphium!"

The word escaped Gemma's lips like a restless hound bounding over a fence for a run out. It was the one word (besides argon) that she had understood in his entire speech. She could see the word scrawled across her mind's eye in chalk letters. It had been the topic of her previous target's research. While he had refused all possible computers and assistants, he had loved to show off his cleverness to his new dancing-girl mistress. She had studied it whenever she had the chance between the glasses of champagne he pushed on her, and she had memorized every word and symbol. Most of it had not made any sort of sense at the time, but she still carried a clear image of it in her head.

The substance was much in demand on Earth, and Mrs. Brightman had been keen to discover the TIA's secret source of this very rare element. Naturally, the scientist had not written *that* particular fact on his board. Gemma had been on the verge of uncovering said fact when she had been pulled away for this mission. The connection startled her. Was Brightman still pursuing the tralphium, then? What did that have to do with watching the captain?

She discovered that the Cohort had regrouped at her yelp, and they were all gawking at her. She straightened her blouse and lifted her chin, for now they were discussing a topic to which she could contribute.

"Tralphium," she began, "an isotope of helium in which the nucleus has lost one of its neutrons; since it only has three particles in its nucleus, we call it Helium-3. It is not radioactive, and it can burn cleanly when used as a fuel. Much, much cleaner than coal. It can be fused with itself inside a magnetic containment field, resulting in loose protons that can be used to produce current directly. The problem is that the substance is very rare on Earth. Helium itself is lighter than air, so free helium on the surface just escapes from the atmosphere."

"Well-spoken," said a member of the group at the monitoring station. "Couldn't have said it any better myself."

They all turned to face the man, only to find that it was Captain Moreau, his tall form emerging from the shadows beneath the tank.

"Indeed," Dr. Pugh replied with hooded eyes. He fixed Gemma with his stare, but she simply stared right back and refused to wriggle beneath those pinning pupils.

"Actually," the captain continued, "the tralphium is not our fuel, as such. We use it to generate the electric power that then heats the argon, which is the actual fuel. We distribute the remainder of that power throughout the ship. This chamber is the only place we use gas. The rest of the ship gets pure electricity! Too volatile, otherwise!" He grinned at Gemma, who was still too stunned by his sudden appearance to respond. "Honestly, we could use any gas. Very clever, these Martians. They could use almost anything they picked up along the way as fuel, so they didn't have to load up for the entire journey at once if they didn't feel like it. At least in the larger ship designs, since the cylinders were purely ballistic. We haven't quite figured the collection bit out yet, though, so we still have to lug this tank of argon with us. Thankfully it's cheap to obtain and easy to find, unlike the tralphium. It was good enough a design to even get old Hermann Oberth himself to give up his infatuation with chemical rocketry."

Gemma pondered the next logical question. Would anyone else need the answer so badly? Should she just radio the information she had to Brightman anyway, considering that tralphium had been the object of her previous assignment? Surely they would not have consigned her to two years in this great void and her possible (even likely) demise to steal a secret within the first couple of days?

"And where did we find the tralphium we are using now?" The Russian saved her the trouble of asking.

"Ah, yes, the million shilling question," the Captain replied. "Any of you that were cleared for this trip are cleared to have some word about it, even though I can't give you the *exact* location. But I can tell you this much: we didn't stay a month on the Moon just to hop around like bunnies."

The MOON? Oh, crickets, Gemma thought. *Mrs. Brightman will have the Girls working triple time!*

At that moment, the dim yellowish lights in the chamber winked off, replaced by an icy blue glow. A clanging alarm echoed in the darkness. A voice chanted over the speaking tube and warned them about a flare alert. Gemma jumped at the blast of sound, as did most of the Cohort.

Dr. Pugh looked at the Captain and asked, "The head?"

"Over there," he said as he pointed towards the wall that they had followed into the chamber. He touched Gemma's elbow and guided her that way. "They weren't expecting many ladies down here. I'm afraid there's only the one closet, so you'll have to lodge with us," he said as they hurried across the floor. "Just don't tell Mr. Wallace."

The rest of the men scrambled into the room ahead of them, and the trio were the last to squeeze in. The Cohort and the monitoring group were jammed in so tightly cheek-to-jowl that it was difficult to secure the door. Gemma found herself wedged sideways between the captain and Pugh. It seemed that Moreau's long arms had nowhere else to go except around her shoulders; this had the effect of pressing her cheek firmly into his chest. Navy blue wool and a tiny view of the door filled her vision. Occasional voices crackled over the speaker mounted on the wall as various departments reported to anyone listening that they were safe.

"Flares? Already?" someone in the back demanded, his voice fraught with anxiety. "Alfieri, aren't we at solar minimum? I thought you didn't see any sunspots during your last observation!"

"Oh, pipe down, Abbie," growled Dr. Pugh from behind her. "Bidarhalli, mind my elbow!" He whispered, and Christophe mouthed the words in imitation as he spoke, "I wonder if Napoleon had to deal with this insanity when he took all those savants to Egypt!"

The priest's smooth voice answered. "Yes, yes, the sun should be quite calm now. Perhaps, being so early in the voyage, this is merely a drill? Perhaps the captain would enlighten us?"

The captain merely cleared his throat and said, "So, we meet again, Dr. Pugh." He sounded as if he were some hero in a penny dreadful greeting his arch-nemesis in a dank corner of London.

"Fancy seeing you here, Chris -- Captain." Even though she couldn't see his face, she could hear a hint of a smile in the old man's voice.

"Well," Alfieri said, to no one in particular, "with the new protocols, we should be well-shielded here for several hours, if necessary."

A general groan at the thought of imitating a tin of sardines for that length of time hatched among them. She could feel the press of the young man's body in places where she shouldn't be feeling it, but he didn't seem to be shy about the situation at all. Pulling away from him would only nestle her closer to Pugh, whose own shrinking reticence matched her own. She growled inwardly. Moreau was far too jolly about the situation for it to be anything than what he had planned. Silently, she hoped her mission included a swift kick in the nether regions for this cad. At the very least, she hoped her orders didn't rule it out.

The Irishman and the Russian were fussing at each other about poking, and Pugh kept telling them to shut it. Every time the captain spoke, she caught a noseful of spearmint, as if he had spent the morning gargling with Doctor Norton's Men-T-Fresh Tonic. Its strength made her eyes water, but it did tend to mask the understink of fear and sweat in the teeming chamber. It was getting hot, and there was little fresh air blowing in through a vent in the corner above them. She felt a little faint. She wished she had a fan with her, and she grunted.

He must have felt her rumble, as she sensed a subsequent chuckle in the man. "Have no fear, Miss Llewellyn. I've done this before."

It was Pugh's turn to grunt. "Unfortunately, he has," he said. At that moment, Shaw and Stanislav squawked again, and he grumbled. "Good Lord! I'd almost rather be stuck in the broom closet with a gaggle of Martians! At least they have the virtue of silence."

"We normally don't have so many crewmembers in this part of the Oberth deck at once," the captain said with a hearty laugh that vibrated through her rib cage. "Perhaps we'll rethink the closet size on the next refit. Or include one for the ladies down here."

"*If* we have a refit." Pugh fidgeted behind her as he spoke. "In case Mr. Wallace asks, Llewellyn, I don't normally include the head in the Oberth tour."

Gemma finally found her voice. "Why are we in here, of all places?"

"Flares, child," Alfieri responded. "Every once in a while the solar disk reaches out with steaming tendrils and sends powerful energies hurtling through the skies. We are usually protected by Earth's atmosphere and magnetic fields--"

Shaw interrupted, "Well, except for that time in '59! Remember the big one that Carrington saw, and all those telegraph fires--"

"Yes, yes, but that was rather an extreme one," replied the astronomer, "with aurorae you could read by! But on Earth, we are protected from such things. Mostly. In space, we surrender those protections. Like our fuel, we have to bring it along with us. We humans need extra shelter during those times."

"Well, that makes sense enough," she replied, "but why not just shield the entire ship?"

"That is exactly what the Martians did," the captain replied. "But they used simple cylinders. I don't know much about Martian economics, but I'm certain that the cost of lining those buckets is much less dear than lining a ship like ours."

"Please note that the *Fury* is a far cry from a simple cylinder," said Pugh. "Being lobbed about like tinned beef might be good enough for them, but to me that manner of travel is just plain silly."

"And in the TIA, we don't do silly," the captain muttered under his breath, so low that only Gemma could hear. She could feel the vibrations of his words. "We copied their means of space travel--"

"*Stole*, you mean," Pugh interjected.

"I prefer *improved upon*," Moreau shot back. "But you must admit that we did invent the state-of-the-art water closet."

"Hrumph," Pugh retorted. "If the Martians had actually had bladders, we'd have stolen their privies, too!"

"It's just as well," cried someone in the back. "Can you imagine trying to take a wee with equipment designed for a bundle of limbs when you've only got the two!"

"Lady present!" barked the captain.

Commentary in the back of the room ceased.

Gemma craned her neck up to look at the young man's face; she knew when she was being distracted. She had gotten the idea that solar flares were nothing to trifle with; how long would this one last, and how long would they be trapped?

"It makes a sort of sense," he explained, beaming a smile down at her, "as people usually keep themselves within easy distance of the head, and we have them on every deck. We all know where they are, even when we can't find anything else. Why bother creating two rooms when one would do? Although I admit I did not expect to be chock-a-block with a clutch of scientists at the time."

There was some pain behind that smile, though, that would be difficult for anyone less trained than Gemma to detect. She had just glimpsed a hard-won pearl of wisdom.

Cervantes' voice hissed from the speaking tube. "Captain Moreau, this is the bridge. All departments have reported in. All crew accounted for; they all reached the shelters within two minutes. Is the Cohort with you on the Oberth Deck?"

Gemma could feel, rather than hear, the young captain's inner sigh of relief at that report. He leaned his face against the wall to reach the speaking tube just inside the door.

"Aye, Mr. Cervantes, they are all here with me. We'll work on the timing, but pass on my compliments to the crew for their rapid response. Secure from panic stations."

Moreau managed to work his arm into a position to open the door. They popped out of it like hot chestnuts. Gemma hopped out of the way of the spilling Cohort. She sucked in the cold air of the vast chamber and now felt grateful for it. It had been frighteningly large before, but the wide-open space was now welcome. The difference was not lost on her; it was a matter of frame of reference, she supposed.

"Good drill, everyone, good drill," Moreau said. He pointed to one of the men from the Engineering group. "Good job, Chief Nesbitt. Expect more of those in the future. Want to keep everyone safe."

The blue bulbs were now dark, and the normal yellow-white ones were bright once more. Gemma had not noticed the extra bulbs before the drill, but now she saw other bulbs in the ceiling. Red and green bulbs flanked the blue ones. She wondered if the red one meant *fire*. She hoped that if so, she would never see it lit. She had no idea what the green one might mean. She made a mental note to ask Pugh about the other lights later.

Pugh led them over to the tank and the rows of barrels and continued his lecture as if nothing at all had happened. Gemma followed suit and pulled at her jacket to straighten it. It was a convenient way to avoid the gaze of the captain, who lagged behind their little group.

"As we were saying before we were so rudely interrupted," Pugh said as he stared daggers at the captain, "the argon in this tank is the fuel that provides the ship's working mass. In order to create thrust, we inject the gas into a chamber and superheat it to create plasma, which we eject out the nozzles at the extreme end of the ship. Now, to heat that plasma, we use radio waves, which in turn--"

"Dr. Pugh," Bidarhalli interrupted. "Please, can you explain how radio waves can do such a thing?"

"With a prodigious great antenna," chirped the captain.

"Of course, we have to have electric power in order to generate said waves," Dr. Pugh continued.

"And run the rest of the ship, as well," the captain said. "We don't just run the engines with that electricity. We feed that power to motors and charge the batteries, in these flywheels over here," he said, pointing to the rows of shining barrels. "We keep these fellows charged up and then power the rest of the ship off of them. If power production should be interrupted, we can run life support off the batteries for quite some time."

"How long, Captain?" asked Shaw.

"Long enough to get the main power back online and spin up the flywheels again. There are more of them beyond that wall there." He pointed at the bulkhead through which the tank passed, like a spirit disappearing into a wall. "The rest of the Oberth Engine is there."

Including the tralphium and the radio antenna, Gemma thought. She could feel some finality about the way the scientist and the captain were moving. *We've seen what they wanted us to see. The tour ends here, I'll wager.*

"And since we had the honour of participating in a flare drill," Pugh growled with a meaningful jerk of his chin towards the captain, "we have run out of the time allotted for the tour. We will postpone the rest of it 'til later."

This last caused an eruption groans from the Cohort, but the sudden turn of events was not lost on Gemma.

"We have yet to determine the effects of using technology that we ourselves did not create," Pugh said, motioning his flock back towards the door. "Who knows what gaps there are in our knowledge? What else might we need to survive the ravages of space? We discovered some of those gaps on the lunar voyage, and our sailors paid the price. What price will we pay this time?"

Gemma glanced back at the instrument panel underneath the tank as he spoke. The professor was correct; this ship was far more than a simple cylinder. It would have sent old Ned Ludd's lads into conniptions. And yet all the instruments seemed designed for humans with two hands, not for rotund beasts with tentacles. Even if the *Fury*'s mechanisms were not part of her mission, she still wanted to know: who had designed *them*?

Dr. Pugh's remark about the Martians having the virtue of silence came back to her. She hoped that he had not brought any pickled specimens of the beasts with him. That would truly be beyond the pale.

CHRISTOPHE

She is lovely, lovely indeed, Christophe thought. He strode down the corridor to his stateroom. His long strides covered the distance in short order.

Captaincy had its privileges, but it had its downside, too; it was often a lonely position. Command of a space ship was doubly so. He was thankful for Cervantes. They had been together for so long that Miguel often anticipated Christophe's commands before he thought of them himself. But there were some empty places that even his foster brother could not fill.

The Cultural Officer was outside the normal chain of command, but the thought of confiding in Wallace made him cringe. The man meant well, but he was a walking bundle of rules and etiquette. Christophe liked Nigel Davies, and his assistant Yeoman McLure was attractive in her own fashion; but fraternizing with the Booleans was against protocol. The Knopfs had been family friends for many years, but they had kept to themselves since the loss of their son during the maiden voyage. Sometimes he felt that the mourning cameo that the good Frau wore was more than just a token of remembrance. He felt a jab in his ribs every time he saw it.

But Miss Llewellyn... she was new. The Cohort was outside the chain of command, so the fraternization rules did not apply. Here, perhaps, was a female with whom he could connect. He was happy enough when he was on-duty, which was most of the time; but in his rare down time, he was lonely for the company of the fairer sex, especially one that was so ship-shape and in Bristol fashion. It relieved him to know that he had an entire case of Men-T-Fresh Tonic in his storage locker.

Overall, he was satisfied with his crew. Hard workers, all, not a snobbish bone in their bodies, not even the officers. He remembered Mr. Wallace's look of horror when he learned that there would be no Lords at his outer-space teas, and that memory made him smile. He bore no malice towards the Cultural Officer, who was only trying to do his job. It wasn't easy keeping a boatload of sailors from degenerating into savages with ladies on board. It was a responsibility that the two of them shared, though Christophe did enjoy tweaking him with a bit of harmless impropriety from time to time.

Miss Llewellyn! Now there is a lady! He had met many women in his time, from the maids at Tesla's estate in New Zealand to the girls he had encountered whilst he had plied the seas of the South Pacific. They had been warm and happy girls who had been sad to see him go. He could never stay in one place for long. He had been training to lead a crew to another world. He had always been moving from port to port, never staying anywhere long enough to form lasting friendships outside of his crew and Pugh's colleagues.

He had known no other goal. Mars had danced in front of him since his nursery days. He had spent his youth traversing the globe in order to learn how to leave it. He had worked his way up through the ranks on every manner of vessel -- with Miguel as his shadow -- from tall ships to tramp steamers to dirigibles, earning his command. Many of his former crewmates served under him now.

The TIA had done more than teach him how to command. They had shown him the devastation of the Invasion. They had tried to build in him the same anger and hatred that they had, so that he would be the perfect commander for a mission of revenge.

Instead of fury, though, he felt -- well, he wasn't sure if there was any word at all for what he felt. On many days, he was a bouillabaisse of sentiments, though he tried to conceal it. His crew needed a strong, solid captain, and that's all he allowed them to see. These villains had trampled the world with their tripods, and he should hate them with all the burning fire he could muster, like all the posters and bills told him to; and yet, and yet, if not for them, Dr. Pugh would not have met Maggie. And then he, Christophe Moreau, simply would not exist.

He dragged his hand across the top of a book, the one that always sat on his desk: the journal of his mentor's mentor, Professor Aronnax. The cover was soiled and rippled from decades of salt air and dirty fingerprints. Dog-eared and wrinkled pages clung together in a binding that was near-broken in a few spots. He was surprised that the words had not fallen out. The book had traveled farther than most people. Pugh had trained Christophe to take it with him, everywhere he went, and to read from it every day, like some sort of nautical devotional. He already knew it, word for word, but there was still something invigorating about seeing the words in Aronnax's own hand. Christophe had even read parts of it aloud to Maggie from time to time. She always enjoyed his tales of the wide ocean. He had whiled away many hours with her, recounting the sunsets reflected in the world's many horizons. She had shivered when he had spoken about the terrifying squalls that he had sailed through, and she had applauded the tales of the beautiful girls waiting for him on the other side of those tempests. She loved it when he read to her, especially the stories of Mark Twain. Even though he had them memorized, he had still hauled them up from the *Kiwi Clipper*. They were as much friends to him as the brass spyglass nestled amongst them. It was as useless here as the old pirate shirt hanging in his closet, but he needed that little drop of seafaring life close by.

He was certain that the women on Mars would not wear crowns of exotic flowers nor smell of coconut milk. The crew would be packed together in the *Fury* for quite some time, though, so in a sense he would not be "moving on" anytime soon. So perhaps he could talk to this Lady, hear her stories, examine the minute details of her dresses and her manners, or take a turn with her in the Garden. He could already picture her face among the cherry blossoms there, with petals falling all around her like pink snow.

He sighed the sigh of poets and rolled into his hammock -- hanging where his bed should have been -- for a brief rest before his next duty shift.

The wall above his desk was a veritable scrapbook of his numerous adventures. Plastered with daguerrotypes, tickets, and CDVs, it was a task to see the bulkhead beneath them. Tiny magnets that he had smuggled out of Dr. Pugh's office held them in place. He looked up at one picture of himself and the good scientist on one of their voyages and mock-saluted it. They were surrounded by portraits of Commander Maury, Lord Nelson, and Robert FitzRoy on the deck of the *Beagle* with Darwin. Sophie the Steamfitter peeked out at him from her hiding place between two pages of Maury's *Sailing Directions* in the row of books just below them.

An image of Tesla, another titan of his childhood, marked the *Fury's* entry in the latest edition of *Jane's Fighting Ships*. According to Pugh, the inventor had struggled before the Invasion and had just wanted a chance for his devices to be used, a chance to be proven right. Somehow, the tripods had not been able to get within several miles of Tesla's Wardenclyffe Tower on Long Island in America; the TIA had been eager to find out how he had managed such a feat. They had set him up with new facilities in New Zealand not long after that and given him his chance at glory. His new Tower in the mountains had beamed power all over the small island nation, including Dr. Pugh's laboratory. On his wall, Christophe had a tintype of the exterior of the Tower, a latter-day castle keep of scaffolding and wire.

Like Pugh, Tesla had been both fascinated and repelled by the information that they had found in the alien cylinders. Christophe had seen the inside of one of the vessels. There were no banks of instruments or controls of any sort. It was as if they had crammed themselves into tins and waited for their ballistic missiles to smash into something. The plans they had found inside the cylinders were much more complex.

Tesla, Pugh, and a host of other men had convened at that Tower many times during Christophe's youth. Often they were joined by another man, Hermann Oberth, who had assisted Tesla in the final designs of the main engine and the maneuvering thrusters for the *Fury*.

As Christophe had grown up, he had been included more and more in their conversations, though it had taken him ages to comprehend even a handful of their words. From what he could gather, Tesla had managed the design of the plasma radio antenna, but Oberth had resigned his first love of chemical rocketry to help them solve the problem of generating the needed power. Tesla had been eager to work on that problem as well, but the TIA ministers had grown anxious about their timeline. Just before the lunar voyage, they'd drawn lots to determine the namesake of the engine itself -- would it be the young upstart Oberth, or the elderly wizard Tesla?

Tesla had not been very happy about the outcome, but the TIA had just increased the funding on his death ray experiments with Hui to soften the blow.

Using his foot, Christophe pushed away from the wall, making the hammock sway a little, since there were no ocean swells to do it for him. He was thankful and relieved that the drill had gone well. Maggie's idea had worked, after all. She would be pleased. Oberth had been a bit miffed about her contributions at first, as he did not consider her a proper scientist, but thankfully cooler heads had prevailed. The head might not be the most dignified of places to shelter, but over the years, he had found that dignity and good sense did not always mix well. Besides, there was the possibility of needing to shelter from a flare for hours at a time; one might need to take a wee during that time, so they would have needed toilets in the shelters at any rate. The combination of the two was a sheer stroke of genius on Maggie's part, in his opinion.

He couldn't tell if the close quarters had embarrassed the young lady or not. As beautiful as she was, Miss Llewellyn's face was an inscrutable mask. Other girls he had known would have been giggly and wriggly and talked too loud and far too much, but she had remained steady. He was eager to tell Maggie about her. But Maggie was busy now; it would have to wait.

He wiggled his toes inside his shoes and sighed. He missed strolling barefoot across the teak deck of the *Kiwi*, along with the endless wind and the smell of salt on the air. He longed for the hot sun on his face and could feel himself growing paler already as his tan faded beneath the artificial lights. He had resigned himself to the irony that he might be leaving those wonders behind forever in his voyage to ensure that they would endure. But he also knew that good company could outweigh many miseries.

Yes, Gemma Llewellyn is a damned fine lady, he thought to himself as he rocked his hammock again. He wondered what she thought of him.

GEMMA

What a wanker! Gemma thought.

The more she thought about the captain's tentacles wound around her in the water closet, the angrier she became. It wasn't the most ladylike of thoughts, but she was alone in the corridor after blowing her way past the rest of the Cohort and taking the lift back to the laboratory alone. There was no one to see or care. Mrs. Brightman was many miles away, out of the grabby grasp of that man, so her opinion really did not count. She marched down the corridor in a haze of fury. Only long years of training kept her from muttering her thoughts aloud.

Certainly, he was handsome; there was no doubt about that. She had met handsome men aplenty. Not all natural philosophers resembled Methuselah's elder brother. Mrs. Brightman had carefully, carefully taught her over the years to resist the charms of her targets, to the point where most of them repelled her, no matter their looks.

All men are tools to achieve an end, her headmistress had said. *Their affections are beneath you. They are not worthy of your true feelings.*

To her, Moreau was too beautiful and too warm to be real, especially now that she had seen him (and felt him and smelt him) up close. It was as if someone had drawn Sir Lancelot onto one of Mr. Humboldt's punch cards and shoved it into the Analytical Engine, only to have a randy captain pop out on the other side. The farcical image made her feel a trifle better, and her anger simmered down to a mere boil. She squared her shoulders and marched on towards Dr. Pugh's study, suddenly feeling a little less like she was answering a summons to the headmaster's office.

Pugh had sent her ahead of him, as he needed to chat with Hui and Father Alfieri. She puzzled over his line of thinking; with his reaction to her yesterday, why would he send her to his office unescorted? She could only conclude that he didn't use it as his real office any more than Mrs.

Brightman used the College's second-best parlour as hers. She wondered where his true office was.

Dr. Pugh's chamber was quite small. The clutter within made it feel even smaller. This wasn't just the garden-variety sort of untidiness; she suspected some of the piles of paper pre-dated the lunar voyage. She scanned the room without touching anything, as was her habit when she had no particular objective in mind. Stacks of notebooks and journals were scattered all over the chamber, along with several editions of the *Invasion Chronicle*. A salad of languages and scripts, from Chinese to Arabic, marched across the loose pages that concealed what must have been his desk. She could make out the name "Moreau" at the bottom of one sheet that peeked out from underneath a book, but she dared not touch it no matter how much her fingers itched. He was The Captain; his name was liable to appear all over the ship. Her mission was yet too undefined to be caught sneaking about now, but oh! How she fought it! It would simply have to wait.

Many other scientists back on Earth would have given their left arm to be where Gemma was standing now. It once again amazed her how Mrs. Brightman had managed to arrange her appointment. Out of habit, she felt a burning urge to uncover the secrets buried in these notes; again, she had to restrain her curiosity. Discovery would not do so early in her journey, when Pugh could lurch through the door at any moment. It would not do to confirm his suspicions.

Daguerreotypes and CDVs covered the wall. A young Pugh stood next to the famous Professor Aronnax of *Nautilus* fame in one. Another image showed a slightly older Pugh and a boy that resembled a younger version of the captain.

Others were not so pleasant. Photographs recorded the systematic dissection of viscera emerging from a mass of desiccated tentacles. Artificial tints highlighted the sparse internal organs. Zoological drawings reduced the world's nightmares to simple blotches of ink and watercolour.

Every other picture she had seen -- from the *Invasion Chronicle* to the annual memorial issue of *The Daily Telegraph* -- had been mocked-up horrors of enormous beaks dripping with imitation saliva and sprouting rubbery limbs. Some enterprising soul had even turned a tidy profit off CDVs of the Martians, sold in tobacco shops alongside penny dreadfuls and the TIA-published *Adventures of Tommy the Terran & Sophie the Steamfitter*. Here, the monsters appeared labeled and diagrammed as if they were merely worms; they made the previous illustrations seem ridiculous and exaggerated.

Gemma wrinkled her nose slightly at the faint stink of formaldehyde that permeated the room. Another underlying odour intertwined with it, one that she could not identify. Her time in laboratories had exposed her to many such unknowns. She had seen -- and smelt -- far worse in person when she had worked for the Roman vivisectionist in the year prior. She tried to imagine these particular images on the wall of Mrs. Brightman's second-best parlour alongside the ever-present vases of lilacs. A girlish giggle escaped her mouth.

"What do you find so amusing, Miss Llewellyn?"

She turned to see Pugh lurking in the doorway. He had a terrible habit of sneaking up on her. Very few men had been able to creep up behind her so easily in the past, except for perhaps that one fellow in Shanghai. Gemma had made certain that he was no longer a concern.

"You arrived here rather quickly for someone so unfamiliar with the ship," he growled.

He picked up a small metal charm from the desk, from somewhere beneath a piece of paper, and shoved it into his watch pocket. He wasn't fast enough to conceal it from Gemma. She knew a mourning locket when she saw one. Even this many years after the Invasion, they were as common as watches.

"Drat that Alfieri, anyway," he muttered. "He held me up longer than I thought. I certainly don't want you in my office alone again. Ever. Is that clear?"

"Yes, Dr. Pugh."

"So, let us be direct. I am very familiar with the business of your so-called College. Did Petunia send you here for me?"

"Mrs. Brightman made no mention of you, sir." That much was true, though she swallowed hard at the mention of her mistress' given name.

He cleared his throat before continuing. "You are here for *something*, though. However, since your being here is probably not your choice, I won't have you put out the nearest airlock. At least, not unless you give me a specific reason to."

Gemma had never been this close to someone naming her true role. Her heart pounded hard in her chest, and it felt like the blows of a blacksmith's hammer on hot steel. Her worst nightmare -- besides that of the Martians returning -- had always been *Discovery*. That business with the gentleman in Shanghai had been a horrible mess. Despite her skills, she had barely escaped with her life. And now she could not elude the consequences of using those skills. She needed other means of protection besides escape.

Pugh slumped into his chair and regarded her with weary eyes. "I'm sure that if you were here for me, you wouldn't tell me. In any case, I wouldn't still be here to ask the question. But perhaps you can tell me a few other things about yourself. How much notice were you given of this particular voyage?"

"Two days. Someone else was set to go, but they were removed at the last moment."

It then struck her how odd that was. She was accustomed to doing exactly as ordered, with little notice, and without question, and with her real name. It was indeed strange that one would undertake the most perilous journey known to humankind without at least a fortnight's preparation. She frowned. She had never had the leisure to consider the strangeness of it all.

"Two days," Dr. Pugh muttered. "Hrmph. Even in our rapidly moving modern age, even with all the means at your teacher's disposal, that is not much time at all to prepare for this sort of adventure. I will assume she pressed you into service, for whatever reason. Probably to watch me, as that is what Petunia does. Watch people. And steal science. Though this is a pretty long reach, even for the Belladonna of Guildford. Do you have any idea whom you replaced?"

She shook her head. Again, this was truth; Mrs. Brightman had simply told her that she was replacing another and that she was to watch the captain, with more specific orders to follow after her departure. For her own part, she had jumped at the chance to play at being a scientist rather than just a silly lab bunny; she knew by now that that was not going to be as enjoyable as she had first hoped.

"So, can you tell me how you know so much about tralphium? I know you didn't *assist* the foremost expert. Professor Rosencrantz is not known for his fondness for female aides."

No, Gemma thought, *but his predilection for snogging can-can girls in his laboratory isn't exactly a secret, either.* There was no need for Pugh to know that bit of news or how she gotten access to Rosencrantz's chalkboard, so she kept silent.

"So I know about you. What you are. And you know I know. And we're not even past the moon yet. But it would be hypocritical of me to send you packing, considering the means by which we are actually out here. How dishonest is it to pickpocket a thief? Can you tell me that?" When she didn't answer, he kept on. "You are stuck, and so am I. Whatever are we to do with each other, young lady?"

She didn't know how to respond. All the usual reactions to Discovery were null and void here; of course she was stuck. But how could *he* be stuck? She was sure that within minutes of becoming aware of the situation, Captain Moreau would have her gulping vacuum before she could say *Terra vigila*.

"Everyone on the ship has to be worth the recycled air they breathe," Dr. Pugh said. "If you are going to pretend to be a scientist, we might as well bring you up to speed. What is the difference between monticellite and kirschsteinite, my dear geologist?"

She cleared her throat. "Both are members of the olivine group. Monticellite has calcium and magnesium mixed in with its silicate. The other has calcium and iron. Olivine is thought to be the most abundant mineral on Earth."

"Such a textbook answer. Well, good that you know a bit about minerals. We also found olivine on the lunar surface, you know. Or, I think, you *should* know. That's one of the things you might want to look for on Mars, should you actually be allowed off the ship. And how are you in Mathematics? Convert 59 kilograms to newtons. For someone on Earth, that is, not Mars. Feel free to round up."

She studied the patterns in the whitewashed ceiling as she reckoned the numbers in her head. One of her previous targets had been very keen on that particular formula; it was seared into her brain-pan.

It was the life of a Brightman Girl to serve the school's clients, sometimes as laboratory assistants and sometimes as computers. Granted, the work was usually done in someone else's laboratory for said client. They accessed carefully hoarded (and sometimes classified) data for Brightman's customers, who were hidden in their own veil of secrecy from the Girls.

A well-trained team of computers -- almost always female, as they were cheaper than their male counterparts -- could tear data apart and crunch through a set of equations much faster than one person alone. That left the scientist -- almost always male, Sophie the Steamfitter not being well known in those circles -- free to observe and lecture. It also left them free to take credit for all the work. The Girls spent more time drilling their arithmetic than they did their etiquette. Philippa had been especially adept at maths.

"Five hundred and seventy-nine."

"Very well. Can you calculate the mass of a planet using the period and orbital radius of one of its moons?"

She fell silent and pointedly examined one of the zoological sketches on the wall. The tentacle on it seemed to wave at her.

"So, you do have some ability, but not much. What more could one expect from a computer? Not that I've personally had a basis for comparison." He cleared his throat. "You can calculate a figure, and quickly, if you know the formula. We shall have to build upon that. Prepare to drink deeply from the Fountain of Knowledge, young Gemma. You are about to go back to school, a much better one. You are in the company of some of the finest minds in history. By the time we reach Mars, you shall be worthy of that company. Even if it kills you." He rifled through a stack of papers and retrieved a copy of Lyell's book. "If they don't get the heat ray up and running by then, it may just."

"I have that one already." She nearly bit her lip for letting that slip. The book was too important to her work to let someone take it away.

"Really? Perhaps Petunia was thinking ahead. So, do you subscribe to Uniformitarianism, or are you more of a Catastrophist?"

She blinked for a moment. "One should not mix ammonia with chlorine," she replied with a coquettish smile.

"Very well. Something simpler. Is the crust of Mars thought to be basaltic or granitic?"

"I can name the Kings of England," she replied. She pursed her lips. It was no use pretending, now.

"But you don't know enough to form your own opinion, I see. Well, Florence Bascom, you're not. I doubt you're worthy enough to polish her rock hammers." His eyelids flickered until they closed, then he sighed deeply and opened them again. "Well, it's a fine kettle of squid that you're in now, mademoiselle. One wonders if you have even read your copy of Lyell. Can you at least tell me what you have done in the past? Besides computing equations and typing notes and..." He broke off suddenly and narrowed his eyes with stinging disapproval. "Other duties as assigned?"

She lifted her chin. "Taking samples. Measuring and weighing."

"*Hrumph*. Rocks? Soil? Blood?"

"Whatever was required to complete the job," she replied through clenched teeth.

"I see."

He sorted through another stack of books on a corner of his desk.

"You are a fool, Miss Gemma," he continued as he set a volume aside. "But I can tell you are not a complete fool. And it is within that incompleteness that we shall work. No need to let the others know about your particular...*ahem*...situation, shall we say. So, here it is. I find myself in a completely different sort of pickle. My laboratory assistant was unable to make the trip. Couldn't shake the ague. And while that might have provided some raw material for weapons development, it would not be wise to make the rest of us ill along the way. So perhaps it's serendipitous that you're here. You can aid me in some of my own investigations. If you have a constitution of iron, that is. At least you won't have to unlearn any previous bad laboratory habits. I'm rather particular. Since you lack anything in the way of instruments, we'll tell the others that you are aiding me in return for using a few of mine. That will keep the hounds at bay for a bit. But just a bit. I've worked with Alfieri before. He has all the busybody tendencies of a priest and none of the reclusiveness of an astronomer! In the meantime -- oh, where is it--"

He excavated yet another stack of journals. "Ah, here 'tis. A rather basic chemistry text and some maps of our destination, such as they are. Spend this evening memorizing as many features of the Red Planet as possible. It won't be much, but it is a start. Honestly, as a Cohort, we don't know much now anyway. I suggest you start reading after tea, which starts in about an hour. Take these to your stateroom for the evening, but starting tomorrow, you will read in my office when you are on duty. It won't do for the others to see you reading such basic stuff. They'll ask all sorts of questions. Regular hen-party, they are. Worse than any women, let me tell you."

"I can start now, if you like," Gemma said. She chose to ignore the implied insult; really, she had worked for enough scientists that she couldn't argue with him on that point. At least it was something to do.

"Oh, no," he said, pulling his pocket watch out of his trousers. Unlike Mr. Davies' watch, it looked like it had not met a polishing rag since before the Invasion. She thought she caught a glimpse of an image on the inside of the cover, but he snapped it shut too quickly for her to see it.

"You need to go get dressed," he said. "Tea is not optional. Mr. Wallace is quite particular about that, especially for the officers and members of the Cohort. Frau Knopf's parlor, 4 o'clock. Sharp. Absolutely no laboratory coats! Gloves wouldn't hurt, if you have any with you. Hats for the ladies are optional in the parlour, however. They are only required when one is out-of-doors."

"*Out-of-doors?*"

"And they've made it a rule to not discuss science during tea. Some nonsense about Wallace being squirmy about entrails. Can you imagine? Anyway, you have a respite for now." He pointed at the stack of paper in front of her and said, "I expect you to know that map by heart by this time tomorrow. You are a scientist, now, Llewellyn," he said with a sneer. "Please try to conduct yourself as one."

She tucked the loose maps and the chemistry book under her arm and exited the office. She avoided her forlorn workspace and the eyes of the Cohort on her way back to the lift. The corridors stretched out forever, but after a few wrong turns she was back at door number 615.

She set the stack down on her desk and sighed. Questions chased each other round her mind like a pack of hounds that had caught the fox's scent. Experiments and rocks? Engines and bugs? Out-of-doors? Tea in outer space? Assist Dr. Pugh?

Oh, crickets, Gemma thought. *This mission gets curiouser and curiouser.*

She quivered in a brief moment of horror and hoped again that the good professor had not brought a pickled specimen of a Martian with him. She wasn't sure she could bear being on the same ship as such a monster, let alone the same room. She was grateful that none of the Martians had survived the Invasion.

Gemma opened the wardrobe and studied its meagre contents, which consisted of the ill-fitting lab blouses and skirts that the TIA had provided and a few items that she had unpacked from Old Dependable. In her whirlwind pass through Guildford, she had had just enough time to toss in a few frocks. They cowered on the far side of the wardrobe rod, limp and wrinkled from the journey. She only had three decent petticoats with her; she truly had packed in a hurry. They had on the ship what they had on the ship, and she was going to have to make do with her limited resources. It was not the first time she'd had to make do, but it was the first time this far from home.

The Knitting Circle of Doom might come in handy, after all. If Frau

Knopf could teach her how to knit something other than a net or a noose, that is. Gemma's skill wasn't exactly up to the standards of *Godey's Ladies' Book*. The Domestic Arts were not emphasized at the Brightman College; they were only taught when they served her mistress's needs. To Gemma, knitting needles were things one jammed into the back of someone else's skull when missions went badly. In which case, she hoped Dr. Pugh didn't visit the Knitting Circles.

She settled on a satin frock that didn't require a multitude of petticoats. It had a fitted waist, but it was not as tailored as others. The skirt was unadorned, but the lavender lent its simplicity an air of elegance. The neckline dipped low and squared off at the bosom. Her décolleté hid behind a demure lace blouse worn underneath the dress. It made her feel safe from Mr. Humboldt's leering smile. The sleeves puffed out just enough on her upper arms to be attractive without pretending vanity.

She would not need assistance with the corset. Brightman Girls often had to dress without aid, so Mrs. Brightman had issued each of them bespoke corsets that laced in the front without additional aid. She had been out of her stays for the past couple of days, which was highly unusual for her. Such binding articles of clothing were not allowed to be worn during launch, and they didn't really work well with the uniform she had been given. Men had designed them for men, after all. No wonder she had felt so off-kilter; she wasn't used to breathing so deeply! She winced. She'd had jobs before where she needed to be unlaced for a while, and it was always painful to stuff herself back into the whalebones.

Mrs. Brightman's waist training program had been vigorous. The headmistress had felt forced to lock some of the younger girls into their trainer corsets with chains so they wouldn't slip out of them overnight, and she had the only key. The pain and sleeplessness, Mrs. Brightman had once told them, was a small sacrifice for a greater cause. Learning how to breathe in tight lacing was an art, and it had taken even Gemma a while to master it. To her, it was an unavoidable evil. Some of the other Girls had enjoyed the tight lacing after a while; they could barely stand getting out of their stays long enough to bathe.

She didn't blame Mrs. Brightman for that, of course; to Gemma, it was more the styles at large. It wasn't the first time she had agreed -- secretly -- with the Rational Dress Society. In her opinion, the fashion industry needed to crawl out of the clutches of the Ministry of Culture and design fresh styles once again. She had made a great study of the photographs in Brightman's third-best parlour. Images of the teacher's days as a member of Pickering's astronomy harem at Harvard with her own teacher, Annie Cannon, graced its walls. Other pictures depicted Brightman as she had moved from observatory to laboratory, so frustrated with each institute's reluctance to appoint a female scientist to their ranks -- however qualified she might be -- that she had established her own. Gemma knew every word of that story and every fold of the dresses worn by the women in those photographs. She would have blended in with them at tea; even her newest frocks would have been fashionable the day before the Invasion.

Gemma had managed to pack her favourite reticule, the black velvet one with the glass-beaded fringe and the hidden pocket in the back. It was stylish but not flashy, perfect for someone in her occupation. She hoped it would amend her ensemble's other shortcomings.

Her stomach growled its displeasure. She had missed lunch. Her body complained about the sudden reintroduction of a corset, and again she devoutly wished that the Ministry of Culture had decided on the Empire waist of Jane Austen's day rather than the far more restrictive couture of 1901.

Finally dressed, she made her way to tea with just moments to spare. After twists, turns, and more than one backtrack, she located a metal door bearing the rather dull appellation of PARLOUR in plain letters. She stared at the latch, unsure of the protocol here. Should she go on in? Should she knock? Where was everyone else?

She heard footsteps echoing behind her and spotted an approaching cluster of Booleans. They chatted gaily amongst themselves.

"--and I'm sure the rocks are all rubies," chirped one of them. She recognized the voice as Mr. Humboldt's and cringed. He continued, his voice bouncing off the metal walls, "Why else would it be red?"

Gemma recognized the individual faces as they approached the door.

Caroline argued back. "I just don't see that. It looks all rusty to me, mate. We should really ask Miss Llewellyn!" The yeoman beamed as she recognized Gemma. "It's our geologist! She'll know!"

Gemma cringed even more and made a great effort to hide her discomfort. She composed her face and attempted to take a deep breath before answering, but the newly resumed corset cut her off. For once, Mr. Humboldt came to her rescue.

"We'll suss it all out when we get there, won't we, Miss L? Be sure to cut me in on a percentage when you get them gems graded. Come on, you lot, I'm peckish!"

He led them through the door, beyond which tea was already in full swing. They passed beneath a portiere of heavy burgundy velvet into another world. The curtain guarded the top of a frame that separated that door from warmly coloured oak-paneled walls. Their footsteps were silent, muffled by a deep navy blue carpet with pink and powder blue roses running along its border. Light glowed softly from frosted lamps. The low music of violins and flutes poured out of a gramophone horn. The room was as delicate as the corridor had been harsh, an acre of Ladies' Country in the middle of the common land. Once the door closed, it was difficult for

Gemma to imagine the giant Oberth engines several decks away hurtling them through the deep dark sky.

Mr. Davies led them to the main table to their right, and Gemma's stomach complained again as the scent of cinnamon and ginger tickled her nose. She ignored the cluster of bridge officers gathered in the middle of the room and made a beeline for the food.

An ivory crochet-lace cloth covered a long table that fairly groaned with mounds of delicacies. A tall silver samovar dominated the feast. On the front was the ship's monogram, "TCF", in an old calligraphic style, as if some monk of yore had taken a momentary break from illuminating a Bible to inscribe the curled letters. The glittering pot was steeped in a fog of oil of bergamot.

"That's our auto-electric-samovar," Mr. Davies remarked from behind her in the queue. "His Majesty King George gifted it to us when he christened the ship. It keeps the water hot, so tea is always ready for serving. The tea concentrate is in the little pot up there." He pointed to a porcelain teapot covered in blue and white roses that perched on top of the samovar. "Just pour some in your cup and add the water and stir it round. A little dab will do you, though, so be careful."

He dropped a lump of sugar into his teacup. It seemed too dainty and fragile for even his relatively small hands. She gazed about the room and bit back a laugh. All of the men were holding their teacups carefully, as their fingers barely fit through the tiny handles. Mr. Wallace circulated through the room, demonstrating how to hold their pinkies in the air whilst avoiding making slurping sounds as they drank.

Gemma replied, "There's not a lot of room for the actual tea, at Tea, is there?"

"I think it's a secret water preservation technique, giving us just a thimbleful enough to call it a Tea," he whispered with a conspiratorial wink. "*Entre nous*, Frau Knopf measures every drop of water to conserve it as we go, especially after all the gallons we swill at breakfast. Don't expect this big a spread on a daily basis. Oh, and watch the sugar. It's got to last. When it runs out, we'll only have the honey."

As Gemma started to ask about the source of the honey supply, the aforementioned Frau appeared through another door beside the table. She placed a tray in the lone empty spot on the cloth. She nodded at Gemma and scanned the table as if confirming something on her mental checklist. The tail of her long Irish lace coat wafted around the corner as she swept through the door again.

"Bosworth jumbles!" Caroline cried with delight as she examined the new tray. "I haven't had these in ages!"

The young lady popped one, then another, of the "S"-shaped sweet biscuits onto her plate. Mr. Davies gently reminded her to save some for everyone else as she reached for a third. With a blush, she moved along. Gemma retrieved one for herself. Mrs. Brightman had not believed in sweets at tea, despite Mrs. Landry's love of baking; event teas in the best parlour were usually heavy on the cheese. She picked up a jumble and sniffed it. It seemed worthy of her attention, so she rested it on her plate and continued.

It was difficult to select which treats deserved a spot on such a tiny platter: cucumber sandwiches on pumpernickel bread, currant-spotted scones and Devonshire cream, mounds of cheese, and one astonishing apple streusel cake that dominated an entire section of the table. Lurking in the shadow of the cake were plates piled high with fat rascals. Surrounding it all were small pots of strawberry preserves, lemon curd, and a rather tasty-looking rose petal jam. At least, she thought it was rose petal; Knopf had hand-labeled it, and Gemma's German was a little rusty.

She skipped the actual teacups for the moment and focused on filling her small plate, picking a couple of pastries for herself along with a dollop each of cream and lemon curd. It was nice to enjoy some of the perks of the job, for once. As she leaned over to pick one up, her corset reminded her that there wasn't much room in there for perks.

A long gilt-framed mirror graced the wall above the table. Gemma stood with Caroline just off the side of the table as they waited for Mr. Davies to finish building his plate. She used the perch to observe the room's reflection, which showed her the captain and first officer conversing with Pugh and Hui. She still saw nothing worth reporting beyond the man's patronizing smile at Hui's wild scientific gesturing as he rattled on about something he called a "button lamp". Mr. Davies, plate in hand, whispered something to Caroline and then sailed past the trio with a nod. He headed for a whist table on the other side of the room and settled into one of its chairs. Caroline stayed with her and made unladylike smacking noises as she slurped her tea and enjoyed the use of a madeleine as a cream-delivery device.

As she nibbled a biscuit, Gemma was distracted by the sight of Rathbone appearing in the mirror and heading straight for her.

"Miss," the wireless officer said as he held out a piece of paper, "a message arrived for you just before I came down. Thought you'd need it before tomorrow morning."

He handed it over to her with an expectant look on his face, as if he wanted to see her read it. She thanked him politely, set her plate down, and slipped the message into her reticule. One major Brightman Rule was *always read messages in private*. It would do no good to read it at this point, anyway. Without her copy of Lyell, it was just gibberish.

"I hope we captured it proper," he said. "Nothing but a stream of numbers."

She remembered the message she had seen that morning and wondered if he had noted its oddness as well.

"I'm sure it's fine," she replied in a smooth tone. "Thank you, Mr. Rathbone."

"My pleasure, Miss," he replied. She detected a dash of disappointment in his voice.

She turned her attention back to her plate as he walked away. The cream had an odd tang to it that she could not identify. Caroline caught her frown.

"Goat's milk," Caroline whispered through a mouthful of jumble. "We only have goat's milk on the *Fury*."

"I'm surprised we have fresh milk at all," Gemma replied.

"Cows wouldn't fit on the stable deck," she replied, matter-of-factly, as if livestock amongst the stars were a common thing. Caroline pointed at a set of shelves along one of the parlour walls. "Oh, look! They remembered the books! Brilliant!"

On the way over to the small library, bits of conversation washed by Gemma's ears. She listened for any information worth forwarding to Brightman and filed the more useful tidbits in her brain. The Booleans weren't the only ones speculating about what they might find on Mars, other than Martians. Some wondered what sort of cities such creatures would build; others were curious about the new technological wonders they would find. Many, however, shared Mr. Humboldt's wide-eyed dreams of treasure. Aside from a few nervous whispers about the moon amongst the more junior officers, all spoke of certain victory.

They halted in front of a set of bookshelves. Secured to the wall with enormous bolts, each shelf had a bar across its front. She scanned the shelves for likely reading material. She figured that her copy of *Principles of Geology* would drive her mad after the first six months; that is, if she actually bothered to read it. Various translations of the Bible sat alongside a volume of the *Upanishads*. Next to them rested Blavatsky's *Isis Unveiled*. Were there Theosophists aboard? She wondered what Father Alfieri would have to say about that.

She found some Austen and Twain alongside two different editions of *A Tale of Two Cities*. A copy of Shelley's *Frankenstein* leaned against Stoker's *Dracula*. The Thomas Hardy books made her smile; Gemma felt that this was about as *Far From the Madding Crowd* as one could get.

Between a set of Thoreau and several volumes of Shakespeare were multiple editions of the *Invasion Chronicle*. Atlases and books on astronomy were scattered across one of the low tables near the fireplace. Some of the crew had not wasted any time getting to the books. Mr. Rathbone rested on the sofa on the far side of the room, sans banker's visor, with a tiny teacup in one hand and a copy of Childers' *The Riddle of the Sands* in the other. He was pointedly ignoring Mr. Humboldt, who was jabbering away next to him over a plate piled high with Singing Hinnies. Another officer was paging through *Myths of the Ancient World*.

"Do you enjoy reading, then?" Caroline asked her between bites of cake. "Ever read these?"

She pointed at a book with the name "Burroughs" on the spine. "I like this one, especially. It's about this bloke, John Carter, that goes to Mars -- except them Martians, they calls it Barsoom, and these tentacle-heads can actually talk -- and then Carter kills 'em all with one of their own heat rays and brings all their gold back home to Earth. He settles down with a nice girl in Derbyshire, and we never have to worry about them beasties again. Hope we make it true." She peered over Gemma's shoulder at the captain, who was now leaning against the mantelpiece and deep in conversation with Cervantes. The two men had neatly avoided the teacup debate by sipping tumblers of amber liquid instead. "Wonder if Carter looked anything like him. Don't you think he looks right posh in that uniform?"

Gemma barely stopped herself from spurting her tea over her companion at that remark. As Caroline carried on, pointing out the Sophie the Steamfitter series on the bottom shelf, Father Alfieri approached them. Sporting a coal-black cassock with his priest's collar instead of laboratory brown, he gestured at the shelves.

"There are so many books out there, even after the Invasion!" he exclaimed, his eyes twinkling. "A few of them even manage to see the light of day outside the TIA publishing houses. It was difficult to choose which ones to bring on the voyage. Some are from my family's private library, you know. There are so many on my father's estate that it would take more than one lifetime to read them all."

Gemma selected the most innocent smile out of her collection and replied, "Thank you, Father. Even if I cannot read all of them on this voyage, at least I will not be bored in the meantime. It was very generous of your family to donate them."

Alfieri chuckled. "Indeed! Miss Llewellyn and Yeoman McLure, correct? I understand from Dr. Pugh that there was some tragic mishap with your scientific equipment, Miss Llewellyn," he replied. He clicked his tongue against his teeth. "I share your disappointment. It is a hazard of the scientific adventurer's occupation, wouldn't you say? For that is what we are. Adventurers. I think I may have a solution for you, at least a partial one, if you are interested."

"You have my attention," she said.

"Very good. Like you, most of my samples are millions of miles away! Stars are rather difficult to stuff into a microscope slide, wouldn't you agree? I use a telescope instead. Might I suggest you take a peep or two through it? You never know what wonders of creation you might see. Yes? Very well, then. Drop by my observatory any time. If you will excuse me, ladies."

He wandered off, leaving Gemma wondering what motivation he would have to help her. It would be a new thing for her, having a priest as an asset. It was Mrs. Brightman's opinion that it would not be that difficult to get a priest to spill secrets; they simply did not have any of scientific benefit. Gemma had never stepped foot inside a confessional, but she was sure that tralphium was a rare topic of discussion there.

Caroline tugged at her elbow and suggested that they circulate around the room. Mr. Wallace was getting a bit near their side of the parlour, so Gemma did not object. On the way, Caroline pointed out other officers that Gemma had not yet met, including the ship's surgeon, Dr. Hansard, who was worrying the mouthpiece of his unlit pipe between his teeth beneath a "No Smoking" plaque.

She allowed Caroline to prattle on as they made their way across the floor. The Boolean linked arms with her and chattered away about everything from Mr. Davies' impending child to the ship's archery league. Gemma only half-listened to her new ally; she nodded and uttered an "oh, my" or "how delightful" here and there with impeccable timing. The other half of her brain observed the movements of the captain as he left his perch at the mantel and meandered his way through the cluster of officers and midshipmen that had just approached him.

"Oh, you like the fireplace, then?" Caroline asked. "It's just for show, really. Open flames aren't allowed on the ship. Even Frau Knopf has to cook with electric power. It's too bad, though. I think fireplaces are so romantic, don't you?"

They encountered Mr. Davies in the far corner, still at the whist table. He stared into his pocket-watch with a furrowed brow. He closed it as they approached and got to his feet.

"Ladies," he greeted them. "We've put in our required appearance here. I have some business in the orrery to complete today. Would you care to have a peek at it, Miss Llewellyn? Caroline can chaperone us, if you wish."

Curiosity about the much-discussed orrery mixed with her interest over the message she had just received from Rathbone. The Boolean was correct, though. They had all three been seen by Frau Knopf and had managed to avoid Mr. Wallace so far. She took a final sip of tea and pondered his offer.

"Of course, Mr. Davies," she replied at last. "If you'll allow me a few moments in my quarters--"

"To change back into your uniform," Caroline said, completing her thought. "I know you must be miserable, back in your corset! I can give her half an hour, then go fetch her, Nigel. I'm off duty for the day, anyways, and I could use a sit-down, meself, for a few minutes. Oh, and one last jumble!"

CHRISTOPHE

Christophe could feel Cervantes' gaze boring into him as Miss Llewellyn slipped out of the parlour with the two Booleans.

"I would be careful of that one, *amigo*," said the first mate in a low whisper.

"McLure?" Christophe replied in the same quiet tone. "I'm aware of her interest, old sport, but don't worry yourself on that account. I can quote you a mile of protocols between us."

"Not her. The geologist."

"Miss Llewellyn?"

"There's more to that one than meets the eye. Nothing escapes her notice. She studies everything and everybody. Even through the mirror, if necessary."

"What, what? *You* were actually watching a girl?" He leaned in closer, smirking at his friend. "I didn't think she was your type. Not enough engines."

Miguel looked about them as he tugged Christophe over to the whist table that Chief Davies had vacated moments before.

"I am serious. I survived as long as I did in Madrid before Pugh found me because I learned how to read people. She watched you on the bridge during the launch, too, but not with the same eyes as our young Boolean. She is looking for something."

Christophe cast him a sideways glance. "You said the same thing about the girl at Admiralty Computing. Remember, the pretty dark-haired one with the dimples? But she only had eyes for Booleans."

"*Sí*, I remember. But it wasn't just me. Even Maggie agreed that girl was trouble. And Pugh had warned you to stay away from the computers! But just because we were wrong then doesn't mean you shouldn't be wary now," Miguel said, concern etched on his face. As Mr. Holomek, one of the midshipmen, approached them with a question dancing around his face, he added, "It could be nothing. But until we know more about her, it would not hurt to keep your distance."

GEMMA

Alone at last, Gemma pulled the paper out of her reticule and smoothed it out on the desk. The stack of notes and maps that Dr. Pugh had given her were on the corner, crying out for attention. She reached for her copy of Lyell and found that it was on the opposite side of the desk from where she had left it. She narrowed her eyes as she retrieved it. She calmed herself with the thought that Frau Knopf must have inspected her room already.

She rested the book next to the message. She didn't open the volume yet, as she did not yet know what page she would need. Taking up her pencil, she set about calculating just that.

The message itself was fairly short and simple: "DATA FROM 1924-23-08 2ND SMPL". After that was a series of numbers divided into triplets.

The first step was to look at the date provided and the number that followed. The fact that it was a "data sample" label was just to veil -- however thinly -- the meaning of the numbers. Normal procedure was to sum up the digits in the date, take the result, sum that up, and repeat the procedure until the number was the number of digits dictated by the number following the date. In this case, she reduced the date to two digits.

One plus nine plus two plus four plus... she worked the sum in her head, reducing it until she came up with eleven. She then opened her copy of Lyell to that page, which in itself was just a page of geology text. No one who picked up the book would notice anything unusual about it, as there *was* nothing unusual about it. Alone, it was just a book; there was no reason to hide it, so there was no reason to fear a sudden inspection of the room.

She examined the first triplet: 18 1 1. She located the 18th line on the page and then found the first word and the first letter of that particular word: "A". She wrote that letter above the first triplet in a light hand. The next triplet, 1 4 2, led her to an "R". She continued until she completed the first word: "ARTEMIS".

Artemis. Greek goddess of the hunt, twin sister of Apollo. The first word of her first received message on a job designated her code name for that mission, if she had not received one already. She had used every name from "Rose" in Shanghai to "Eve" in Prague in the past; why not add the name of a goddess to the list?

The next sets of triplets revealed the entire message: "ARTEMIS JESTER CHURCH SEAT TEST ORION OUI FRENCH CRYSTAL".

She smiled; the double encryption that Mrs. Brightman favoured was a bit of insurance. If anyone recognized the book cipher in the message and broke it, they would not understand the plaintext. It was usually gibberish, and it had the added effect of making some people believe that they had made a mistake.

All Brightman Girls memorized the Messaging Protocol at a young age. None of it was ever committed to writing. Much of her earlier training had involved prodigious rote memorization to prepare her mind for this type of exercise. To Gemma, it was just another facet of her mistress's brilliance, and yet again she was grateful that such a genius had seen fit to take her in. In the Brightman Protocol, in the first message received on a mission, the second word indicated the code name of her target: "JESTER".

Third word or even a phrase... some clue as to who the target was, in the event that the target had not been pre-determined or if the target had changed. "CHURCH" by itself might have led her to Alfieri, but "CHURCH SEAT" made her think differently. Mrs. Brightman loved to play with words and sounds in her messages. A "church seat" was a "pew". She didn't even have to say that one aloud to realize that "JESTER" was the head of the Cohort. Gemma had noticed over the years that Mrs. Brightman reserved that particular code name for the more troublesome targets. The use of it here on top of what she had gleaned from Pugh earlier told her much about their mutuality of feeling.

So, Gemma was Artemis. Pugh was Jester, which was surprising, given her previous admonition to watch the captain. She continued through the message, looking for an explanation for the change. The verb, "TEST", was a standard action word in the Brightman vocabulary; it really meant "EXAMINE" or "INVESTIGATE" the item that followed next, which was usually more direct: "ORION".

That stopped her short. "Orion" was a constellation, representing the Hunter. He was also the companion of the namesake of her code designation. If she recalled correctly, Artemis actually killed Orion -- in some stories, by accident, in others, not so much.

Was Orion a person? An experiment? That was the flaw with the double-cipher system. Not every situation was covered by pre-arranged code words, and sometimes one was left to decipher a third layer on one's own. Sometimes there were clues, though, in the rest of the message:

"FRENCH CRYSTAL". "Crystal" always meant "watch", as in "look into a crystal ball and see". As for "French", she suspected that Brightman had meant "Moreau". So "Orion" had something to do with the captain. She supposed that that was her assignment. At the very least, this was consistent with Brightman's last words to her. But her specific mission was no clearer.

She committed the plaintext to memory. Now she did have something that would not bear Discovery; she had to dispose of the decrypted message somehow. It certainly could not stay in her room; it had to remain free of any tools of her craft. She did not feel comfortable burying it in the sand of the fire bucket by her door. There was no telling what Frau Knopf would include in her threatened "inspections". Normally Gemma would burn it. On Earth, fireplaces were always within easy reach, but not here. Some of the Brightman Girls simply ate their messages. She had discovered the hard way that ink simply did not agree with her system, and she did not want to have to explain the mess in her stateroom to Frau Knopf in case it decided to come back up.

This job was going to wring every bit of innovation out of her. There might be an incinerator for refuse somewhere on the ship, but she did not know where it was and likely could not explain her presence there if she were seen. There was a possibility of ejecting it from the ship, but she did not want to deal with questions in case someone monitored the airlocks. She wanted to give them a wide berth, anyway. If she were on a steamship, she could toss the paper off the back of the boat (downwind, of course).

Nothing out here in the wild dark sky was the same. She wondered if the unknown sender of the mysterious message in the wireless window faced the same dilemma. Gemma still felt a need to work out the text of that message as well, if she could determine the cipher used. But that particular mystery could wait.

She could still taste the goat's-milk cream from the tea. She wished she had a mint -- and then she had an even better idea. If she could get her new bosom friend Caroline to take her to visit the goats, one of the cud-chewing beasts might just have an extra snack that evening. She folded the paper and tucked it into her reticule.

She would need to send a response in the morning. At the moment, though, she did not have any news for them. She did have a question, and it was one deeper than "where is my bloody gear?" She still did not remember how Moreau's name seemed so familiar to her. She would ask about his pedigree. That might also give her a clue about Orion, in case the two were related somehow.

She released a long sigh of relief. The orrery would be as good a place as any to begin her search for "Orion". After she changed back into her browns, she picked up Dr. Pugh's notes and skimmed the first page. Perhaps she could glean from them why the Red Planet was red, to have some tidbit of news for her new allies. A few minutes later, as she heard Caroline's knock on her door, she realized it was time to get to work.

"It's not to scale, of course," Mr. Davies said, "but it works for our purposes."

He stood at the side of the chamber with his hands clasped behind his back. He had discarded his hunter green for a set of oil-stained dungarees. There was a hint of pride in his stance as he stared across the waist-high rail that separated them from the behemoth mechanism beyond.

The orrery was more like a garden, except that planets grew in the place of roses; instead of blooming amongst the music of birdsong and crickets, they thrived within the beetle-like tick-tick-ticking of clockwork gears. The high domed ceiling gave the chamber the air of a small cathedral. Smaller niches bubbled off the sides of the room, like chapels around an ambulatory. In place of an altar, there was a great gleaming orb that represented the Sun. Circling about this metal giant was a series of pole-mounted globes that glided along shiny brass tracks.

"I count only four worlds here, Mr. Davies," Gemma observed. She may not be a true scientist, but she did know a few things about natural philosophy. "I believe there are more in the solar system, are there not?"

"Indeed, Miss Llewellyn. Point of order, though. When we are all off duty and just us chickens," he said, pointing to himself and to Caroline, "please feel free to call me Nigel."

"And call me Caroline," the other Boolean said with a nod.

"Fair enough," she replied, "but only if you call me Gemma. Let us reserve the 'Miss' for when Mr. Wallace graces us with his presence."

"Fair enough," Nigel replied with the slightest hint of a smile. "We only had time to add a few globes. Mostly we wished to display our destination, so we stopped with Mars. There's room to add one or two more, but it may be a later Victory Class vessel that gets to add Jupiter. Assuming they leave enough room for the proper gearage underneath."

"Gearage?"

"Yes. That's what keeps it all moving. It's just like the smaller models, where the planets orbit the sun on rotating poles. They are still connected here, but underneath the floor. The gearage takes up an entire chamber on the deck beneath us."

The planets were turning, turning, turning. The entire works had been polished to a blinding brightness. The Earth's globe was a stunning blue and green sphere with a silvery moon ambling around it. The satellite itself was mounted on its own pole and driven by its own gearage, visible above Earth's orbital track. Any observer would have to mind those gears when taking a closer peek at Earth.

Mars was decorated with various shades of red, from scarlet to cinnabar to crimson, with splotches of coffee colour here and there to indicate topographical features -- ones she had seen on Pugh's maps. She recognized this globe as the twin of the one she had seen in the conference room earlier that day, only less dusty. The icy poles were highlighted in hues of stark bright white and light blue.

Nigel looked over his mechanical wonder as if it were his firstborn. For once, she was able to listen to someone speak about technology without having to plot some way of filching it from them. She found the sensation refreshing.

"You'll notice that Mars and Earth are close together in their grooves at the moment," Nigel continued. "They are in opposition this year. That's what determined our launch window, you know. Otherwise, the trip would take much longer. You'll be able to watch them move apart over time. The Earth moves much faster than Mars, as it's closer to the Sun. The folks back home will see Mars go backwards in the sky, but that's just because Earth is passing it by."

"Do Venus and Mercury outpace us, in turn?" Gemma asked. "They are closer to the Sun than we are."

Nigel gave her an approving nod. "Good observation. Yes, indeed."

The other planets moved slowly, but they kept churning along, just the same. They rotated as they moved along in their tracks, circles within circles. She could feel the gearage below them, the sound of it just within range of her hearing, almost like a great clock ticking beneath her feet.

"Is Venus broken?" she asked. "It's moving along the track, but I don't believe it is revolving." She squinted at the sphere again, comparing its revolutions to those of the Earth's sphere. "Half a moment! It's revolving backwards, Nigel."

Caroline giggled as Nigel nodded at Gemma again. "You have keen eyes," he said. "I assure you that it is not broken. We discovered in the past year that Venus revolves in the opposite direction as Earth. We've been watching that planet rather closely. We observed several Martian cylinders heading there not long after our own Invasion. Ironic that they are the ones that improved our technology to the point where we could watch them!"

"Imagine how odd it would be," Caroline said, "with the sun rising in the West!"

Gemma frowned. She had heard of the Martian launch to Venus -- it was in the *Invasion Chronicle*, after all -- but something about it bothered her.

"If they flew to Venus, then why are we going to Mars?"

"The consensus is that it was just a small Invasion force," Nigel replied. "Our mission is to destroy the main nest, to prevent any more such forces from going out. The Venusians, if there are any, are on their own, unfortunately. We only have the one ship, so far. We're not even certain that Venus is inhabited beneath those roiling clouds. We know that Mars is."

"Besides," Caroline said, "it's more likely there'll be technology on Mars."

"One of the purposes of the orrery is to keep up morale," Nigel said. "It displays our current location." He pointed at the space between the globes of Earth and Mars. "It's difficult to see, but it is there."

There it was, a tiny model of a ship floating between the Earth and the Moon, suspended from a much smaller gearage system hidden in the dome above them.

"You can go in and get a closer look," Nigel said. "The globes move slowly enough that you can avoid them. Mind the gap in the track, though. Wouldn't want you falling in."

Gemma stepped beyond the rail barrier. She crossed the gleaming brass tracks of the orbit of Mars and its two circling moons and wandered between it and the Earth. The wire from which the ship was suspended was so thin it was nearly invisible. She had to stand on her toes to get a good look at it. Like the ship on her shoulder patch, the model was a tiny steamship.

Caroline laughed at her expression. "Cap'n has a sense of humour," she said. "It was his idea to use a model of the original *Thunder Child*. I think it's brilliant!"

"I am glad you approve, Mr. McLure," a voice called out from the door.

They all turned to see the captain standing just inside the chamber. Nigel and Caroline snapped to attention with a sharp salute. Gemma squared her shoulders and hid her hands in the folds of her skirt. The reticule hanging from her wrist bounced off her leg and reminded her of its incriminating contents. She felt a renewed sense of urgency to destroy it, but she did not feel safe exiting too quickly.

"As you were. Oh, don't mind me, Miss Llewellyn," the captain said. Moreau had planted his feet as if he were on the deck of a boat on the rolling main instead of on a ship with manufactured gravity. Perhaps he still had his sea legs.

"Pray continue your examination. I'd like to hear your observations, as a natural philosopher, of our little treasure here. What else do you notice?"

Gemma bit the inside of her lip, trying to think of something clever to say. This was all so new to her. It was time to bring her powers of observation to bear. She looked at the tiny model again and mentally traced its course.

"The ship is not aimed at Mars, Captain. It is heading for empty space."

"Ah, perhaps I can clear that mystery up for you, my lady. We cannot drive straight there, as if we were in a motor car. We are riding the currents and the winds on the sea of space, except now it is gravity and orbits with which we must contend. We are not so much driving there as sailing there, jumping from orbit to orbit rather than following a road. Like a whaler chasing its prey, we are aiming for a moving target. We're used to destinations standing still when we are on Earth. But we are not on Earth any more. We have to change our frame of reference when we think about movement out here in the wilds of space."

"I agree," Nigel said. "We are aiming for where it will be when we are in the vicinity, rather than where it is now. As you can see here, everything in the universe is always in motion."

Moreau picked up the thread again. "We're plodding along now at a paltry kilometre per second, so we'll reach the orbit of the moon on the fourth day of our journey. We won't actually pass by the moon, though, as it is waning crescent now. It will be new moon by then, and on the other side of the planet from us. We will simply cross the line of its orbit. A good milestone, nonetheless, as we will accelerate from there. Just giving the engines a good shakedown. Then we'll speed up until Braking Day and take our time decelerating to our destination. Mr. Davies, have you shown Miss Llewellyn the other feature of the orrery yet? May I?"

The captain sauntered over to a large switch on the wall just inside the chamber door. As he flipped it down, the chamber went dark, except for the sun in the middle. It painted the room in a soft warm twilight. The others moved past the railing and stood with her. The tallest figure stopped beside her and pointed to the ceiling.

"Look up," he said gently.

She gasped. In a day so full of wonders, it was difficult to imagine one more. Above the spheres that marched so serenely around the tracks of brass was a series of glowing stars. The North Star shone brightly above them. She didn't know the names of the other stars, but she did recognize the constellations they formed. The Zodiac glittered in a great circle across the ceiling. Next to Taurus the Bull was Orion, the Hunter himself. Gemma stared at it, the distinctive pattern holding his ground in front of the Bull.

"Luminescent paint," Moreau continued, keeping his voice low, as if he were whispering in a library. He pointed to a crimson star in Orion. "Betelgeuse is even the correct shade of red."

He wasn't standing as close to Gemma as he had during the Flare Drill, but he was close enough to make her uncomfortable. The two Booleans stood just beyond him. Even in the darkness, she could feel that Caroline's eyes were full of her own close-up view of the captain. The young lady hadn't made a peep since Moreau had entered the room.

The rendering of Orion reminded her of Brightman's message, and she wondered if this tableau, as beautiful as it was, concealed any of the secrets that she was to uncover. At the moment, she could not see how. If she did have free access to this room, though, then she would have plenty of time to search.

The four of them stood in silence, with only the grinding of the gears below them to break the stillness. She turned slowly, looking at each of the constellations in turn, trying to ignore the cloud of Men-T-Fresh Tonic that enveloped the man beside her.

She stepped away from the group, making a great show of studying Virgo. For now, it was better to maintain her distance, even if that did have the effect of attracting him even more, as it did some men. She stopped beside Caroline.

"It feels like night is all around us," Gemma whispered to Caroline.

"Oh, it just seems that way, Miss Llewellyn," she replied. She was still whispering, but Gemma noticed the subtle slip back into formality. "But if you think about it, it's always daytime, too."

"All the universe is in motion, all the time," Moreau said.

His sudden interjection into their private conversation made Gemma narrow her eyes in annoyance, even though she knew her expression could not be seen in the darkness. She could hear Caroline fidgeting next to her as the captain continued to speak.

"Over the course of a day on Earth, it feels like we are sitting still and the sun is moving, but really it is the planet's rotation that creates night and day. Now that you are out in space, Miss Llewellyn, you will have to think differently about the world. You are out in the great blue yonder, where the sun never sets."

He paused. There was hopefulness in his words, some expectation in them that begged for some poetic reply from her. Gemma maintained her steely silence.

"Well." Moreau broke the silence with a single clap of his hands. "I must be on my way. I thought I would check in on my way back to the bridge. I need to join the next watch since it's our first day out. If you'll pardon me, Miss Llewellyn. Mr. Davies, Mr. McLure, carry on!"

The two Booleans saluted him in the shadows. When he left, Caroline silently walked to the door and turned the lights back on. She slipped out the door without another word, leaving Gemma and Nigel blinking at each other in the harsh light.

Gemma raised her eyebrows and looked at him, but he did not seem as surprised as she was.

"Interesting," he observed.

Gemma answered him with an expectant look.

Nigel took a deep breath before he responded to her unspoken question. "You're new to the ship, so you may not have noticed. The orrery is nowhere near the shortest path from the bridge to the parlour."

"Oh," Gemma replied softly.

"I'd like to show you something else, if you have the time," he said.

When she nodded, he said, "Please, follow me."

He dimmed the lights again and led her to one of the smaller bubbles off the main chamber. He pulled a lever. The wall rolled back the same way the wall at the station had, revealing the deep black of space beyond. The stars twinkled in the far distance, much farther and colder than the ones on the ceiling. It gave her the feeling that she could just step through the window and dive into the night.

"I thought I would show you the real thing," Nigel said softly. He stared out at the darkness with a far-away look behind his spectacles. "I think of my wife every time I come here. She would love this view. She loves the stars so. Last year, the plan was for her to come with us as part of Frau Knopf's staff. But then we found out she was with child. I told her perhaps next time a ship launches, but not for War--"

"But if we were not going to War, Nigel," Gemma pointed out, "we might not be going at all. Bureaucracies love to waste money internally, but they require extraordinary circumstances and rewards to explore. They don't just toddle off to see something just because it's there. Even the original explorers searched for gold for their kings and souls for their pope. Surely you've seen this in your time in the TIA."

"I believe you are correct. If we find resources on Mars, the Railroad Barons will find a way to bring them home." He lowered his voice to a whisper and glanced towards the still-open door. "I also wanted to make a private request of you, outside of Caroline's hearing."

"Oh?"

Was she wrong about Nigel's being a gentleman? She tensed, waiting for what would come next. She was used to times like these, but she did not enjoy them.

"You probably are aware that Caroline is very fond of you. She has not had many friends of the female persuasion. We met in a factory. Do you remember me telling you about the Jacquard looms?"

Gemma nodded, and he continued. "She was so bright and clever. I couldn't bear her being stuck on the floor with the other factory girls. It was so dirty and dangerous! But the owners were not part of our new Enlightened Age. They only wanted boys for apprentices for loom card coding." He rested his hand on the window for a moment and went on. "So I turned her into a boy. On the outside, at least. I cut her hair one night to look like mine and gave her my other set of trousers. She was young enough to still resemble a boy then, if you take my meaning."

Gemma nodded. She, too, had looked rather boyish before she had blossomed.

"They didn't care that one orphan girl had run away, only to be replaced by a very capable boy. So we trained together. I taught her how to walk and talk like a boy. It helped her survive long enough that by the time it was obvious she was something else, it did not matter. She was brilliant at coding the machines. When the TIA started recruiting Booleans for the Admiralty Computing Service, they were so hungry for code that they didn't care. One of our instructors insisted she was Lady Lovelace reborn! All the same, I had to discourage other cadets from harassing her too much. But I think the costs of her boyish mannerisms are going to outweigh the benefits, should we make it back home. She's like a sister to me, Gemma. I'd like to see her happy, with a family of her own, someday." He gazed out the window again. "My wife has tried to teach her some etiquette. They are thick as thieves when we're all home. But it's going to be a while before they see each other again." He smiled at Gemma. "What I'm trying to say is this: I hope you return her fondness. She needs a lady friend while she is out here in space. I think she's a bit intimidated by Frau Knopf, and Knopf's assistants are shy of her. Would you do me a great favour and teach her -- teach her to be ladylike? She may still need to be tomboyish around the crew, but with some practice, perhaps she can be a proper lady when she gets back home?"

Ah, so he was still a gentleman. Gemma was secretly relieved at that. It was a simple enough request, and it might keep her occupied, should Pugh allow her any downtime. At the thought of the scientist, she had an idea.

"I would be happy to help in any way I can," she replied. "I do have some questions of my own, if you can answer them."

"Yes?"

"Is there some sort of relationship between the captain and Dr. Pugh? They seem so much alike that I thought they might be related."

Nigel smiled at the query. "I will admit to a certain grouchy affection between them, but as for the rest, I couldn't say. Mr. Humboldt is the true expert on ship's scuttlebutt. I'm sure he will gladly regale you with what he knows. But it will be up to you to decide if he's telling the truth, or spinning a yarn to impress an attractive young lady. I will say, though, that your thought has occurred to more than one person."

Gemma returned his smile. He seemed a worthy ally, after all. His concern for his fellow Boolean spoke well of him. Gemma wondered if he was aware of Caroline's other problem.

Gemma knew a "crush" when she saw one, but usually it was the other way round -- usually it was the man who was smitten with her. Caroline was going the right way for a broken heart with her admiration of Moreau. Even if he were attracted to the yeoman -- and Gemma was of the opinion that he preferred a different type of girl -- there were kilometres of fraternization rules between them.

The TIA could take a page or two from Brightman's handbook. She had told her Girls to expect such things to happen from time to time. She had given them the signs to watch for and the means to expunge any such sentiments from themselves before they got out of hand. They did not serve her benefactress and thus had no useful purpose. Gemma found it silly -- and rather unfair -- for the TIA to make such grand rules without teaching the skills needed to avoid breaking them. She would give her new asset a few pointers if she could do so without risking Discovery. As it was, she would need to be prepared for much weeping and gnashing of teeth from the poor girl in the near future. It was unfortunate that Gemma had left most of her handkerchiefs behind. She was going to need them before they returned.

If they returned. Gemma shrugged off the thought. Even if the worst happened, at least it was all for Mrs. Brightman's sake. She knew she could never repay her saviour for rescuing her from a fate of cropped hair and trousers.

"Thank you," Nigel said. He closed the window shield and wiped his hands on his dungarees. "I am relieved that she will have a friend. If you'll excuse me, Gemma, I need to change and check in with the Booleans on the second dog watch. It's only a two-hour watch, but I'd like to make sure things are going smoothly, it being our first day. Have a pleasant evening, Miss. Oh, and please feel free to join us for breakfast again, if you like."

He slipped out of the room, leaving Gemma alone with the churning orrery. So many things were turning here, more than just the little planets. They kept gliding along, little by little, never stopping, and it made her a little dizzy.

She distracted herself with the glowing splotches of light on the ceiling. She studied the figure of Orion, wondering if it contained what Mrs. Brightman wanted. The weight of the reticule on her wrist brought her mind back to her next task. Soon after, she left the room, off in search of hungry goats, leaving the miniature solar system revolving in the darkness beneath the Hunter in the sky.

CHRISTOPHE

After seeing the glowing orb of the orrery, Christophe missed the sun on his face even more. He kept waiting for the sea breeze that never came. The air circulating past his command chair stirred his hair a bit, but it was not the same. He unfolded his tall frame from the chair and braced his legs as he stood at the edge of the bridge, anticipating the rolling of nonexistent waves. The Atlantic currents ran in his blood. The Pacific salt was ground into his soul. He belonged on the prow of his boat, bare toes clinging to the figurehead, with the freedom of the unbounded sea.

He kept himself sane by reminding himself that he was protecting those turquoise waters. He tried to convince himself that now he had the freedom of the unbounded skies, but that freedom did not feel real. On the *Kiwi Clipper*, he had been the undisputed master of his world. There were always opportunities for adventure at the next port, for meeting other ships at sea, for imagining what was just over the horizon. Now he was chained by regulations, so many that he thought his head would burst. Out here, there was no horizon. Now there were no ports save one, and there was nothing but Death awaiting him there. His hope -- a slim hope -- was that it was the death of the Enemy and not his crew.

He scanned the glass panels that lined the lower ring of the bridge. The men examined them intently, making notations here and there of the *Fury's* position and status. Departmental reports flowed in over the speaking tubes and the pipephone from time to time.

He had gone to the moon and back with most of these men already. They had survived the flare that had killed nearly half the crew on that maiden voyage. They had also seen him choke back the panic and horror of it all so that he could lead the rest of them back home. They seemed to trust him. He also knew that once they knocked off for the day, their watch complete, they would relax in the mess hall, quaff their daily ration of lager, trade CDVs, and dream of the treasures they would find at the end of their journey.

He would not quash their dreams of glory, but he did not share them. His treasure was the sun sparkling on the waves of the Caribbean and the warm smiles of the girls waiting for him in Tahiti. His riches were in the oakum and teak of the *Kiwi Clipper*, sitting in safe harbour, awaiting the return of her master.

"Growlers ahead, sir," Cervantes said, breaking Christophe from his reverie. "Most seem to be small, but I recommend strengthening the forward navigational shields as a precaution."

Growlers were the equivalent of icebergs in the sky, and he refused to lose to a chunk of rock. Even dust could damage a ship below the waterline at this speed; and in space, everything was below the waterline. He was thankful for the shields, even if their Martian origins gave Pugh conniptions. Without them, this voyage would not make it past the first meteor shower. They could maneuver around the larger growlers, but the dust was much harder to see, much less avoid.

"I agree," Christophe replied. "Strengthen the shields, Mr. Cervantes."

At least for the moment, he was not under the watchful eye of Mr. Wallace. The cultural officer was still at tea with the officers from the first dog watch, ensuring that they did not smash the china. Everyone had a purpose, but he was puzzled as to why the TIA had wasted a precious billet on such a role. He was sure they had their reasons, however unspoken. People rarely served a single function on any ship. Even on the *Kiwi*, the cook also trimmed the sailors' hair. On this ship, Herr Knopf would shear their locks in addition to tending to the massive Gardens. If Mr. Wallace served another function on the *Fury*, the TIA had not seen fit to inform him of it.

He would do as he was ordered, he told himself over and over again. He would do what it took to protect the *Fury's* crew and live up to the valour and sacrifice of her namesake. He would protect the Earth, and her bright turquoise seas, with all his heart. But he would not enjoy it.

I am a sailor, not a warrior, he thought.

He wasn't sure that the TIA had picked the right star to steer by. He had attended some of their councils, but he had not been given a voice in them. That was unfortunate, because he did have some thoughts of his own on the matter.

There were many schools of thought in the Terran Industrial Alliance, and not all of them were beating the drum for genocide. Some had advocated a diplomacy-first solution, using the mere threat of violence to secure some kind of armistice with the Martians. Others desired a reconnaissance mission, to discover more about the Martians, albeit secretly, before making any kind of move against them. Others -- captains of industry rather than ships -- insisted that total revenge was called for and that nothing less would be tolerated by the citizens of Earth. Naturally, such an attack would need to leave their infrastructure intact. Their voices had been the loudest, and their orders had been for a full-on attack.

The crew had been inundated with mountains of Sophie the Steamfitter CDVs and heady cries of *Terra vigila*. He wondered if any of them wrestled with the orders the way he did, if any of them stayed awake at night wondering if they were doing the right thing. He didn't know if, when they finally reached the Red Planet, he would be able to give The Order.

He inspected the stations as he strolled along the rings of the bridge. He felt a bit sluggish as he approached the point opposite his command chair.

"Mr. Cervantes, does the artificial gravity feel heavier here to you?" he asked with a playful grin. "Would you please have Mr. Nesbitt give the bridge plates a look-see at his convenience?"

Cervantes replied in the affirmative, with a knowing smile of his own at the corner of his mouth. He still had a straight face, though, and that simply would not do.

"Mr. Nesbitt is inspecting the engines on the dropship at the moment, Captain," he replied. "I'll add it to his list."

"Oh, it can wait," Christophe said. "We certainly want the *Iron Wind* in Bristol fashion!"

He continued to tour the panels, nodding gravely as a captain should, as his thoughts swirled in eddies. Would the heat ray come online after the issues encountered on the lunar voyage? Would the Oberths continue to function smoothly? Would they be able to defend themselves if the Martians attacked first?

He brushed his fingers along the edge of a station. He could only feel the hum of the Oberths, but it was nothing like the thrum of the deck of the *Kiwi* when she was in the groove. Tall ships were living beings to Christophe, and the *Kiwi* was an extension of his own limbs. The *Fury* -- technological wonder that she may be -- was just an enormous mechanism. He had no bond with her; she was a stranger. She was made of metal, not teak that had once pulsed with life itself. Steel didn't even feel dead, for how can something that had never lived be dead? How could he master something that had no heart, no soul? How could he sail into battle on a ship that he didn't know, and that didn't know him?

Everything so far was routine. He would stay for the rest of the dog watch, complete his log entries, and then retire for the evening. He would have enjoyed a conversation with Miss Llewellyn, but after the events of the day it would be too awkward to cross into Ladies' Country, captain's privileges notwithstanding. Perhaps he could take a turn in the Gardens. If this ship had a heart, it lived there.

His gaze fell upon the open windows of Informatics and

Communications. He did not have to be near Maggie to speak to her, but conversing in person was so much better. He made his way to the Ready Room, which served as his office and conference room, just down the corridor from the bridge. He secured the door behind him and strolled to the far wall.

A wooden mural depicting the history of Terran ships sprawled across its surface, from a picture of Odysseus' ship sneaking past Scylla and Charybdis to Nelson's *Victory* at Trafalgar. The *Nautilus* swam beneath the original *Thunder Child* as it faced down a Martian walking machine. Christophe never tired of viewing the minute details of the *Santa Maria* or even the small tribute to his own *Kiwi Clipper*.

He traced a particular wave in the top half of the wall three times, and then he pushed in the figureheads of the *Kiwi* and the *Santa Maria* simultaneously. They were far apart; only someone with his long reach (or a well-timed companion) could hope to unlock this combination. After a soft click and grinding sound, the wooden panel receded and slid to his left to reveal a dimly lit tunnel. He entered the corridor and used a lever beside a rack of various small arms (and one very sharp sword) to close the panel behind him.

Yes, a good long talk with Maggie always cheered him up.

GEMMA

"Llewellyn, *do* try to keep up."

Dr. Pugh fussed yet again. For the past three days, he had taught her the intricacies of the chemistry used in his research. Her brain, famous in the Brightman Girl circle for its nimbleness, felt taxed to its maximum capacity.

"Of course, Dr. Pugh."

She had cultivated a vast reservoir of patience over the years, but her lessons with the elderly professor were consuming it at a vastly accelerated rate. Gemma felt every inch the ignorant schoolgirl, called on the carpet in front of an exasperated headmaster. She stood a little straighter and squinted at the glass panel again.

A sketched series of broken honeycomb cells covered it, each labeled with various chemical symbols. Some of the "cell" walls had double lines, and some had additional lines sticking out from the corners, just hanging out in the air. These extra fiddly bits and corners were the source of her mental fuzziness. Gemma had spent enough time in labs to recognize the symbols for nitrogen, oxygen, and hydrogen. It was difficult to adjust to the unlabeled corners representing carbon, and sometimes carbon and hydrogen at the same time.

Bollocks, she thought, allowing her thoughts to run to the unladylike. *Why don't they just write the C and the H where they belong? Why do they have to be so bloody sneaky about it?*

"To continue," he said, "we were discussing the Code of Life. This architectural blueprint contained in every cell determines the entirety of a cell's life: its functions, its behavior, and its potential life span. Thanks to the Martians, we know much about the Code's components: nucleic acids, sugars, phosphates, *et cetera*.

"We had an extensive knowledge of these components before the Invasion, to be sure. We were well on our way to working out the Code of

92

Life without their help. We knew about the chemical guanine back in 1844," he said, pointing to one of the honeycomb cells on the panel. "It was first extracted from bird guano, hence the name."

He paused and looked at Gemma, waiting possibly to see if her face would twist itself in disgust. When it did not, he continued.

His large-knuckled index finger tapped the others as he talked. "Adenine, 1885. Thymine and cytosine, just a year apart in the 1890s. We knew there was some kind of Code thanks to that old Swiss fellow, Miescher, back in '69. Kossel figured out in '78 that there were five primary nucleobases, including what you see here plus one other. We knew about guanine for ages, but it took a while to determine its purpose and relationship to the others. Now, Llewellyn, can you tell me from your vast laboratory experience" -- he cleared his throat here -- "how you think the Code works? How does it store instructions for its miniscule Analytical Engine?"

Gemma reached into the pocket of her skirt and fiddled with the grease pencil concealed there. She had used it to decode messages on her stateroom mirror for the past couple of days. She had wrestled with how to decode safely after her first attempt to feed her first message to the goats. Shreds and scraps of paper already lingered there, leavings from the goats' previous snacks, and what she had found on them confirmed her suspicions: there were others like her on the *Fury*. The message that she found there was rather pedestrian, what looked like a recipe, but there was no mistaking that someone wanted to hide it. She wasn't the only one who had considered the goats as a disposal method. She was glad that the mysterious other person had tried it first, so that she could avoid their mistake and potential Discovery. She doubted it had been her Watcher, if she even had one aboard. Gemma had never known Brightman to use recipes in her normal rotation of ciphers.

She had eaten the scrap of paper, after all, washing it down with plenty of Darjeeling and some leftover Bosworth jumbles nicked from the galley. Frau Knopf, at least, had been pleased about her little treat. It was the stout matron's firm opinion that Gemma was too skinny, and she was not shy in expressing said opinion to anyone within earshot.

On the panel was a column of letters to the right of the honeycombs, in sets of three: CGA, CGG, CGC, TAG. They suspiciously resembled her own decoding work.

Gemma had filched one of the grease pencils from her own glass panel the morning after the encounter with the goats. She thought she might have trouble doing it on the sly, but she was almost disappointed at how easy it had been. Bidarhalli always had his back to her station -- at least he had the few times she had visited it -- as he sweated over a set of equations on his own panel. The Russian and Shaw had their own isolated lab next door and were rarely in the communal lab. She was rather grateful for that, as they were working with some rather nasty bits of pestilence. It was the same with Alfieri, who divided his time between his telescope and the tiny chapel, each in different parts of the ship. The other biologist, Berndsen, spent a lot of time with the ship's surgeon. Hui was in a state of constant distraction with his own pet project and constant flow of messages from the New Zealand labs. The linguist spent most of his time in the Cohort conference room and in the Informatics chamber on the bridge. He made great use of the Analytical Engine and worked closely with Humboldt, of all people.

The pencil now had a permanent nest in her pocket. Frau Knopf might be curious if she found one in her stateroom, since it lacked any glass panel other than the mirror, but no one could argue with a scientist carrying one in their pocket. In fact, at the moment she found it to be quite inspirational.

"It's rather like a cipher, isn't it?" she asked. She pointed at the column. "The letters there, each one represents one of those chemicals. A combination of those chemical letters -- like CGA -- carries a meaning. Like an alphabet making up words that only the cell can understand. Are there always just three in a set?"

Pugh goggled at her and then rocked back and forth on his enormous feet, as if he weren't sure whether to be peeved or pleased. "Yes, as far as we know."

"Well then, with three-letter words, four possible letters, that makes, what, sixty-four possible combinations?"

"Mathematics is certainly not your weak point, Llewellyn," he replied, apparently choosing to be pleased, after all. "Indeed, though we don't think there are sixty-four separate meanings for those 'words', so to speak, not really. Some instructions can be represented by any of a set of such words. For example, if the cell needs to assemble the amino acid alanine, the Code could use either CGA, CGG, CGT, or CGC to represent that instruction."

She pointed at the last one in the column. "Synonyms, then. What about this one? What does TAG mean?"

"Oh, that one. Amino acids don't appear singly. They are assembled in chains. A chain is encoded in one of these sets of three, and then the blueprint tells it when to stop the chain. TAG is one of several combinations that tells the part of the cell doing the assembly to stop."

"Like the word 'STOP' in a wireless message?"

"Precisely."

"Are there any other combinations for 'STOP'?"

He grinned at her for that one. It was a fleeting ripple across his large and wrinkled face, but it was a grin nonetheless. "TAA and TGA, child. I'll expect you to recite all of them back to me tomorrow."

If he had expected her to be nervous at that, he was mistaken. Mrs. Brightman had ground memorization into her Girls' heads, and Gemma had been her prize student in that category.

"Are all the combinations accounted for?"

He turned back to the glass panel and started to add lines to the honeycombs. "Most of them, but not all. Research is continuous," he said. "I can always ask Maggie where we are on that, though."

"Maggie?" she asked. "Who is that?"

Dr. Pugh stopped writing on the board for a second. His hand hung there in midair, grease pencil at the ready, but writing nothing.

"A... fellow researcher," Pugh said. He cleared his throat.

A sweetheart, perhaps? Gemma thought to herself. She was puzzled. Pugh was not married, as far as she knew. Widowed, possibly. There should be no issue with forming an attachment with someone else. Unless he just did not like to share information about his affections with his colleagues. He *was* British, after all.

Pugh coughed into his hand before he continued drawing on the panel, his back to her. "So, I'm given to understand that you break your fasts with the Booleans?"

She decided not to press him on the matter. There was plenty of time to allow him to let more tidbits slip out. Besides, that bit of information did not seem likely to lead her to Orion. However, demonstrating that she could keep mum with his personal secrets might build some trust.

"Yes, Dr. Pugh," she replied with a deep sigh. "With Chief Davies and Yeoman McLure. Mostly we discuss the proper way to curtsy and Nigel's impending fatherhood. The baby is due soon, I hear."

He waved an acknowledgement, back still to her, as she prattled on. Then she realized that she was *prattling*, but perhaps it was because the Booleans made her feel a part of the crew. Granted, it was easier to do her job when she was not attached to the people around her -- Mrs. Brightman always said so. But she found herself appreciating their efforts, nonetheless.

She removed her hand from her pocket and smoothed her skirts. She asked, "That wouldn't constitute a breach of protocol, would it?"

"Oh, my, no!" he said, turning to look at her at last with widened eyes. "No, not a bit. I think it's splendid. In fact, I meant to encourage it. It would do you much good to have friends your own age. I am sure that, given your Peculiar Occupation, you have had little opportunity for that."

"Indeed," was her only reply, as a fleeting image of Philippa flickered across her mind.

What in the world was motivating this man to be kind to her -- in his own gruff fashion -- rather than chucking her out the airlock? There was no anger in his voice, just a wistfulness that recalled the mourning locket he had hidden.

She just hoped that in this flurry of activity -- she hadn't forgotten the looming Knitting Circle of Doom -- that she would have time to track down the elusive Orion. Few details on what exactly that was -- a plan, a formula, a tool -- were forthcoming. Opportunities to search were even fewer. Pugh did not leave her in the office alone, ever. It was so piled high with papers and journals that it would take months to paw through it all even if she were locked into the office in solitary confinement.

"So," she said with a slight swallow, asking the question that she had been dreading to ask yet still felt she must, "you haven't told the captain about me yet?"

"No. I don't plan to. If I did, it would put him in a spot to do something about it. If he had to do what the regulations say he has to do, he would be very put out. We can't allow anything to interfere with his ability to make war on the Martians, now can we? And I certainly don't wish to lose my newest protégé." He nodded at her sigh of relief. "Just watch yourself, though, young lady. I can't control what other people see or say to him. Just make sure he doesn't find out otherwise."

She nodded. Discovery was always a danger no matter the mission, and she still wasn't entirely sure she could trust this man. She was entirely at his mercy, and there was nothing else to do but trust him.

"There is something else you can do for me," he said.

He pulled two thick ledgers out of the pile and handed them to her. The one on top was ancient, tattered, and smelt of the sea.

"When you have a moment, I have a slight mystery for you to help me solve. Hui has his pet projects, and I have mine. Here are two different accounts of events revolving around a certain man of personal interest to me. One was written by my mentor, Professor Aronnax. Captain Moreau has carried it with him for many years. Now it is in your care. The other is written by a source that is not quite as familiar to the public. I want you to read them both and tell me what discrepancies you find, if any. If you find any -- and I believe you shall -- I'd like for you to help me resolve them. You've spent your life gathering and calculating data for others. Let's see if you can draw any conclusions worth a damn. It is a separate issue from the Code of Life, but it does have a little bearing on our situation. You *can* read French, I take it?"

She nodded as she clasped the books to her. Was he handing her busywork or the keys to the kingdom? She was a Brightman Girl pretending to be a geologist on a ship sailing the sky to Mars. Right now, anything was possible.

"Good. At least Petunia taught you *something* useful. You may keep them here until after the moon-crossing party. No need to lug those beasts about." He took out his pocket watch and studied the time for a moment, lingering to gaze at its interior. "In fact, let's knock off early today. It's just about time for the moon-crossing party, anyway. It will go all afternoon through the duty shift changes so everyone can go at some point," he remarked. "It seems that my initial assessment of this mission was inaccurate. This particular war seems to be an endless set of tea parties, after all."

CHRISTOPHE

"Welcome back to the *Fury*, gentlemen," Christophe said to the dozen midshipmen gathered around his conference table. "And welcome back to officer training. Mr. Cervantes and I look forward to continuing your education. We can't let your fellows back at the Academy pass you up." He tapped the tattered copy of *The Influence of Sea Power Upon History* resting in front of him. "It's been a busy few weeks since we last met, but you should have found time to read the first section of Admiral Mahan here. Yes, Mr. Dreyfus."

The third junior officer to his left spoke in a Parisian accent. "*Oui*, I mean, yes, sir, I have read it. But I must wonder, what use will it be? How can nautical maneuvers be relevant out here?"

"Captain, I must agree," added the fellow across from Dreyfus, Mr. Adebayo, who stroked the spine of his own book with elegant brown fingers. "He was required reading at the Nigerian naval academy as well. His analysis of the battle of Trafalgar is useful for warfare in the Mediterranean, but not in space."

Christophe perched on the edge of the table behind him and beamed his smile across the group. He winked at Cervantes as he remembered their own debates on this very issue over cold bottles of ale on the *Kiwi*. "Excellent question. Does anyone have an answer for Mr. Adebayo and Mr. Dreyfus?"

Silence reflected the same question in the eyes of the middies, from Desai and Holomek all the way back to Alatas and Owen at the far end of the table.

"Mahan himself tells us in the first section." Christophe closed his eyes and inhaled deeply, allowing his faculties to retrieve the proper memory. "'*The theatre of war may be larger or smaller, its difficulties more or less pronounced, the contending armies more or less great, the necessary movements more or less easy, but these are simply differences of scale, of degree, not of kind.'"*

Christophe shared a knowing look with his first mate. He brandished the book before the group. "We certainly have changed our theatre, gentlemen, but good strategy is good strategy. That is what Mahan is trying to tell us. Our tactics may have to change as our vessels and weapons change, but the wisdom of cutting off your opponent's communications before they can cut off yours still holds water, even out here. Yes, Mr. Holomek?"

"But how can we do that? We don't entirely understand how they communicate, aside from the telepathic theory. We cannot interfere with their wireless, because they do not use it. I mean, how do you stop someone from speaking with their mind?"

"Again, that falls under tactics," Christophe said. "Tactics that we will have to work out ourselves. We have to start somewhere, though, and Mahan is the best source we have. As for the rest, well, we're working on it. And perhaps one of us in this very room will write *The Influence of Space Power Upon History.*"

Cervantes added, "We are off the map, gentlemen, and we must chart our own way from here. Therein lies the danger."

"And the glory!" Christophe added. "It is the price we pay for our place in history. We are the first to study matters astronautical, to explore the celestime, as it were, rather than the maritime."

Cervantes joined in, as if on cue. "We intend to build upon, rather than replace, the existing principles of war. They may be all that will save us."

"Can they save us if the Martians meet us en route?" asked Dreyfus. "Even though we have only one ship?"

"There are advantages in any situation, if you look for them," Cervantes replied. "We may be more difficult to detect than a fleet would be. And they may not consider a single ship a threat. Their cylinders were mostly ballistic in nature and had only basic thrusters. We can out-maneuver them quite easily. Also, our weapons' payload is self-propagating, so we don't need as many bombs to have the same impact."

"Can these strategies save us if there is someone else out here besides the Martians?" Holomek asked. "Or if they have ships other than the cylinders? Built from the other plans we found with them?"

"Or if we collide with a growler? Or run out of fuel?" asked Alatas.

"Could they have worked on the moon?" Owen had a catch in his voice. "Could they have saved Karl?"

Christophe willed his face into a neutral expression before he locked eyes with the younger man, who had been Karl's closest friend on the maiden voyage. He could see the late midshipman's face clearly in Owen's eyes, as clearly as he saw the silhouette on the cameo that Frau Knopf wore around her throat every day.

"No. We weren't at war with the sun," Christophe replied in a cool and even voice, "any more than foundering tall ships were at war with the icebergs that sank them. The strategies for dealing with Nature are entirely different. In fact, sometimes the best you can do is get out of Her way. We have found that in space, without the protection of Earth's atmosphere and magnetic field, doing so is far more difficult."

Cervantes added, "It was our collective ignorance of what lies out here that took our friends from us. We could not save Karl or the rest of them then, but that experience can save us now. And so can the experiences of others. In that light, let us continue with Mahan. What can we learn from Nelson and the Battle of the Nile?"

After an hour of Christophe rattling off pages of prose and Cervantes interpreting him, the middies filed out of the room and headed for their various duty stations. Christophe collapsed into the chair at the head of the table and rubbed the bridge of his nose. As he fought the urge to take a nap before his next watch, he felt Cervantes' gaze upon him.

"Are you all right?" the first mate asked.

"Well, it is the one question on everybody's mind, isn't it? They had to ask it, sooner or later. They have a right to ask it. Whether they believe my answer or not is another story."

"I know that, *amigo*. But do you believe your answer?" He stepped over to the plaque mounted on the wall behind Adebayo's chair. The memorial plaque, the one that was too large and contained too many names, thumped against the bulkhead as Cervantes ran his index finger across the name *Karl Knopf, Midshipman*.

"What do you want me to do? Order them to forget what happened? I can't command their feelings."

"They should never forget what happened. And neither should you. It will keep them alive, every time those blue lights come on," Cervantes said as he ambled around the conference table. He stopped in front of the opposite wall and rested his hand on the mural of ships carved into it. "Yes, they do doubt. What we are doing dances on the line between courage and idiocy. But they are all volunteers, and they are still here. And so am I."

Christophe chuckled and swung his long legs onto the top of the table. "Of course you are. You're the next Mahan!" Crossing his ankles, he continued, "I wouldn't dream of venturing without you, Miguel. You keep me grounded. Though out here that is in a purely metaphorical sense, of course."

"Of course! Well, someone has to steer the ship while you give the ladies the Cook's Tour," Cervantes replied with the barest hint of a smile at the corners of his lips. "Besides, I wouldn't let you tilt at windmills without me."

"Is that what we're doing? Tilting at windmills?"

"From a certain point a view. We're voyagers in a universe that is trying its damnedest to kill us. That's why they are celebrating the moon crossing today. Why it's a crew party and not one of Wallace's. Because we have learned from this." He tapped the image of the *Fury*. "And because we have made it this far, this time."

"Blast! The party! I nearly forgot!" Christophe leapt out of the chair and pulled out his watch. "Do you think the Cohort will be there?"

"I'm certain Elias will have some of them in tow." Cervantes squinted at him with questioning eyes. "Wait, you're not planning to--"

"When does it start?"

"Ten minutes ago."

The urge to nap dissipated, and Christophe burst out of the room, barely hearing Cervantes' shouted reminder that the party was not in the parlour this time.

GEMMA

As they made their way through the ship, Gemma and Dr. Pugh passed clusters of sailors hovering in the corridors. A current of unease flowed through their chatter.

"Why are they so nervous?" Gemma whispered to Pugh. "It is just a party, isn't it? No hazing or anything?"

"They are almost to the moon, and they haven't had a glitch yet."

"A glitch?"

He chuckled. "Nautical folk have always been a superstitious lot. Those who sail the solar winds, doubly so. On the maiden voyage, everything went swimmingly until the return trip, and they are afraid if they don't have a small glitch now, at the beginning, then something much worse will happen later. It doesn't help that there are women aboard."

Gemma stopped in her tracks and looked up at him. She very nearly stomped her foot. "What on Earth -- pardon me, that sounds silly now -- why would that be a problem?"

"Oh, long-standing tradition, you know. Women were thought to be bad luck back in the days of the old wooden ships. We had to jump through several hoops to convince the crew at large to let Caroline and Frau Knopf on the lunar voyage without complaint. Perhaps they were afraid that the ladies would spend too much time mooning over the captain to get their work done."

"What rubbish," she replied with a crisp snort. She took off down the corridor again at a quick march.

Pugh's cackling laughter echoed down the corridor. "That's what I like about you, Llewellyn. You are completely unencumbered by notions of romance." His long legs soon caught him up with her, even with his usual languorous strides. "In fact, it's your one redeeming quality."

"I'll take that as a compliment, Dr. Pugh." Notions of romance were the last thing she needed.

As they crossed the orrery's threshold, Caroline greeted them at the door with a handful of red and white bunting. Nigel was polishing the brass pole that held up Venus, and he was in high spirits.

"So, it seems we shall get past the moon at last," Nigel said as he walked past her, his voice heavy with relief. He twirled his polishing rag in the air like a noisemaker. "So far, so good. The Oberths are purring along, no fights amongst the crew, and the goats have escaped their pen only once so far! It's going swimmingly. Just wish we'd have one small hitch before we cross the line. I'd be more at ease."

There were only a handful of crewmen in the chamber so far, but more could be heard coming down the hallway. They were joking and singing songs bawdy enough to indicate that Mr. Wallace was not yet in sight, and they were dressed in a mix of duty uniforms and civilian ensembles. Mr. Rathbone pulled a fiddle out of its case and tuned it, and Frau Knopf put the finishing touches on a table brimming with pastries.

The diminutive *Thunder Child's Fury* had indeed moved since her last visit. The pale ball of a moon was almost between the Earth and the sun, nearly on the other side of the planet from them. The miniscule ship, which was crawling away from Earth at a snail's pace, was just about to pass the imaginary circle traced by the slender pole holding the lunar sphere. The atmosphere held all the crackle and energy of a New Year's Eve party where everyone prayed that midnight actually arrived.

Gemma had attended many parties in her day, but they were usually working parties for her: a bit of sleeping potion in champagne here, a bit of seduction there with a strategically placed fan or teasing glimpse of ankle, or simply the proper choice of words in the proper ear. And now twice in a week she was attending a party at which she was merely a guest. She wasn't sure what to do, so she dropped into her observational mode and scanned the room, in case there was some clue about Orion there, other than the one on the ceiling.

Mr. Humboldt ambled along the brass pathway of Earth's orbit, on the other side of the sun from the rest of the group. He wore a cobbled-together ensemble consisting of a wrinkled wool waistcoat that had last seen daylight before the Martians had landed and a pair of ghastly jacquard-woven purple and green paisley pants. They had been meant as a rebellion against the Ministry of Culture's fashion guidelines, but they were so cruel to the eyes that even the Rational Dress Society would not defend them.

Humboldt stumbled a bit as he came around the track, further soiling his poorly tied ascot with his spilt drink. Gemma suspected that there was more than just tea in his cup. He staggered up to Caroline, who had finished with the bunting and returned to the circle of planets. With the hairs on the back of her neck rippling across her skin, Gemma slipped over to join their conversation.

"Scuttlebutt has it that Pugh raised him," he said in an exaggerated whisper. "Adopted him, you might say. Found him, see, in what was left of Luxembourg City after the Invasion. They got hit hard by the Black Smoke. Almost nobody left. Dr. Pugh was in the first group they allowed in after the tentacle-heads died. He either found him, or found his mother about to give birth to him. Not sure which."

"So Cap'n's an Orphan?" Caroline asked, with a bit of water gathering in one eye. There was a quiver in her voice, and she rested her fingers on her chest. "Like us?"

He hesitated before answering. His eyes darted right and left, as if looking for the subject of his conversation, who was not yet in the room.

Gemma desperately wished that Caroline had not asked Humboldt about what was obviously her favourite topic. She squinted at him in warning, but he ignored the look and kept talking, enjoying his enraptured audience.

"Well, like you and Nigel, yes. Sort of. But bloody rich, though. There was a lot of bees and honey in that city before the Invasion, if you take m'meanin', and most of the buildings was still standing when it was all over. Just the folks was dead. The gold was still there, see, and they took it all."

More crewmembers filtered into the orrery, bringing a murmur of treasure and adventure with them, as well as the low-grade anxiety about the lack of any incident so far. Their mutterings echoed among the planetary flowers in Nigel's little garden. Some of them cast ogling looks in Gemma's direction.

Mr. Rathbone played the opening bars of a tune, "Jack Star's Shanty", which had been a popular number at the Cirque du Lune. Nigel sang the shantyman's portion in a surprisingly agreeable voice while others called back the chorus.

Humboldt's gaze flickered over to his crewmates before he waddled over to the turning orb of the Earth and stabbed his finger in the general direction of Western Europe.

"Why d'you think the TIA picked it as their headquarters? Didn't have a lot of building to do, just clean up and move in. Turned from a ghost town into a bloody world capital. Where do you think the money to fund this mission comes from? The Crown contributed some, so did the Vatican Bank, sure, but most of it came from the TIA proper. It ain't got no taxin' power, and there's no tributes nor aid from the rebuildin' countries. It's all found gold and profits, see? In fact, I hear that the TIA is sending aid to *them*."

He leaned in closer and nudged Gemma's upper arm with his elbow. Ignoring her smouldering don't-touch-me stare, he blathered on. "I think they gave him a big allowance out of it. He's got his own little boat, y'see, what they call the *Kiwi Clipper*."

He leaned still closer to Gemma. She wrinkled her nose at the close proximity of his liquour-laden breath and his hair pomade. Faint flashes of the face of the Man from Shanghai flickered in the back of her mind. That man had smelled of the same pomade. She stiffened out of pure instinct.

"Must've been the same time you was learnin' how to dance, love." He grasped Gemma's wrist. She could feel white heat pricking the back her eyeballs. She couldn't stand for him to bring that up, not again, especially in front of Caroline.

"Don't touch me," Gemma growled in tones low and dangerous.

Caroline started at the sound of it, but Humboldt just chuckled and held on. He waggled his shaggy eyebrows at the young Boolean. Every word he spoke brought the ghost of Shanghai closer.

"Pretty sure I saw this little lovely down at the Cirque du Lune, or one that was her very image. I hear tell she's supposed to teach you how to be a lady."

His hand crawled up Gemma's arm, a five-limbed spider making its way toward her shoulder. The heat from his hand was burning her... the Man from Shanghai was reaching for her again...

"Maybe she can teach you to--"

Quick as a thunderbolt, Humboldt was on his back, and Gemma's heel was at his throat. The instinctive reaction pulsed through her before she was aware of it. The move was swift, as Madame Liu had taught them, one fluid motion that any witness would be hard-pressed to describe, except for the finish. One arm was trapped beneath the man, and the other was twisted and ensnared in her much smaller hand. He didn't breathe. He didn't even twitch beneath her patent-leather-shod foot. He just stared at her, with the same look of terror in his eyes as the Man from Shanghai. That was who she saw, not the quivering Humboldt, in a haze of red.

It was only the lack of brass on her heel -- this time -- that had prevented a replay of that bloody coup de grace. As it was, all she had to do was apply a little pressure with her foot--

And then she heard the silence. Suddenly she was no longer in some grimy back alley in China. Mr. Rathbone's fiddle screeched to a halt. The endless speculation about ruby-encrusted El Dorados and Cibolas died instantly. CDVs froze in the air, mid-trade. Teacups paused between saucer and lips. The only sound besides Humboldt's eventual squeal for mercy was the eternal turning of the gears below their feet and the revolving of the model planets, which ignored everything. As shocked as they all were, the globes kept on turning.

Gemma quaked with a rage that she had not felt in years. Caroline pulled at her gently and urged her to release the man. That gave Gemma the bolster that she needed in the face of Discovery. Ladies didn't ram their offenders into the floor; at worst they gave them a good sharp slap with a dose of righteous indignation, Sophie the Steamfitter notwithstanding. Certainly geologists were not known to be a violent lot. Convinced her mask had been ripped away, she slowly removed her foot from his throat.

She had just done more damage to herself than Humboldt ever could, with all his drunken rambling. Her face went numb, and she released the breath that she hadn't known that she was holding. It was entirely possible that she would be popping out of an airlock any moment now. Pugh wouldn't have to report her Peculiar Occupation to the captain now, not when half the crew had witnessed her act of savagery.

She dusted her hands and straightened her drab laboratory blouse as if it were a royal robe in her most severe we-are-not-amused posture.

"And that, my dear Caroline," she said with the same coolness one would use to explain the number of pence to a shilling, "is how one deals with obnoxious party guests, according to *Mrs. Beeton's Book of Household Management.* Tomorrow's lesson will be in self-defence with hatpins. Tea?"

Gemma marched over to the food-laden table by the door. Her posture dared the rest of them to utter a word. She could feel the faces of everyone -- including Mr. Humboldt -- gaping at her back in stunned disbelief.

"I didn't mean no harm, love," Humboldt managed to squeak in a hoarse voice.

He sounded surprised that he could speak at all. She studiously kept her back to him as she picked up a gold-trimmed plate and plunked petit fours onto it with enough force to shatter their icing. She held out another plate from the stack to Caroline, who had not left her side, with a shaking hand.

Everyone stared at her.

Everyone, that is, except Dr. Pugh, who had stationed himself beside a mound of scones at the end of the table. He merely muttered into his tea something about the lad deserving a horse-whipping.

There was a sudden cry of "Huzzah!" from the men in the room, and the sailors clapped each other on the shoulder. The tense cord of anxiety had been cut, somehow. As their cheers of joy faded once more into background murmurs, Captain Moreau burst through the door, slightly short of breath, as if he had been running all the way from the bridge.

There was a quick cry of "Captain on deck", and all the crewmembers snapped to attention.

"As you were," the captain managed to huff out. He joined Pugh by the table and said quietly, "Awfully sorry to be late. What did I miss?"

Gemma froze as the rest of the crew relaxed. She braced herself for the report, the deep-etched frown on the fresh face of the captain, the wailing of the tender-hearted Caroline, the sudden grasping of her arms, the quick-step march down the corridor to the nearest airlock. They would completely skip clapping her in irons to await her fate. Resistance would be undignified and worse than useless. And worse, she had failed her mistress, absolutely failed, due to her own lack of control. She hadn't even made it past the moon. There was nowhere to go. She wondered if landing in vacuum would hurt.

All the crewmembers turned their heads in different directions, looking anywhere except at the captain. Some of them whistled. Others studied their CDVs as if they contained the secrets of the universe, and still others examined the constellations on the ceiling. Pugh stuffed an entire Bosworth jumble into his mouth. Caroline stirred a fifth sugar cube into her tea and swore to Gemma that she never knew that being a lady could be so exciting. Mr. Humboldt, with his ascot tied to hide the darkening bruise on his neck, was utterly silent.

"Oh, nothing really, Captain," Pugh replied around a mouthful of pastry. He pointed to the tiny model of the *Fury*. It had just crossed the invisible border that they had all been anticipating for days. "Just a minor glitch, is all."

CHRISTOPHE

"Ah, I thought I would find you here," Christophe said, "especially since your usual thoughtful spot had been invaded."

Miguel looked up from the table with a smile. "I had all the party I could stand on launch day." He gestured at the coils and glass balls lined up before him in smart rows. "Thought the Leyden pistols could use some attention. And the armoury was quiet, for once."

"And I had all I could stand on the lunar voyage. But overall, it was a quieter affair then I'd expected. Like some company?" Christophe pulled up a stool opposite Cervantes and snatched a coil and an empty frame. "I am glad they found a way to reduce the voltage on these. But I wonder what old Nemo would say if he knew we had turned the power down on his design?"

Cervantes chuckled. "Who knows what he would have to say about anything? He used his electric rifles to hunt food, not Martians. His men were so loyal, he'd never dream of having to use it against one of them."

"I wouldn't dream of using it against our own, either. One of the benefits of an all-volunteer force." He picked some marble-sized balls out of a container on the side of the table and rolled them around in his hand. "Still, I wouldn't want to be on the business end of one of these again, even on the non-lethal setting. Once in training was more than enough. Quite the nasty shock."

"I have a distinct appreciation for the Leyden Effect, as well," Cervantes replied with a shiver, "but who knows what will happen out here, Christophe? We have to be ready for anything. At least it is our technology, even if Nemo didn't mean it to be used this way. That ought to make Elias happy, along with what the bombs are carrying. The payload is definitely of human manufacture."

Christophe did not reply. He simply picked up the next piece and snapped it into place. Cervantes loaded three of the steel balls into his pistol, set the safety, and slid it into its charging canister.

As he returned it to the nest of other pistols on the rack, Cervantes said, "The orders still trouble you, yes?"

"There were more protestors in Wellington before we left. They weren't striking for workers' rights or suffrage this time. They rejected the notion of, oh, what was it that one sign said? 'Unlimited warfare'? Miguel, what if Alfieri is right? What if the Martians sue for peace? What do we do?"

"The middies got you thinking, didn't they? Christophe, we have never spoken with them. How would we even know if they asked for parley?"

"Exactly, old sport. Well, Maggie might."

"We're not sure if even Maggie can understand them. Or our linguist in the Cohort. Our orders are fairly simple: eliminate the Martian threat by any means necessary and return with any war prizes. 'Any means necessary' could mean anything from the G-bombs to a strongly worded letter to their mothers, if we knew where to send it. There may be a loophole, though." He cleared his throat. "If they do manage to communicate with us clearly enough before we make orbit, and they have something to offer, I'm sure the TIA would be willing to deal. An advantage of being a private navy."

"And if they can't communicate?"

"We follow our orders. And pray."

GEMMA

At breakfast the next day, the mess hall had a different air about it. There were no wolf-whistles as Gemma stood in line to receive her bacon. There were no cat-calls as she made her way back to the table that she shared with Nigel and Caroline. There were a few respectful nods here and there from the sailors as she passed them, but they allowed her to walk by in peace. When she arrived at the table, she found Mr. Pritchard there as well. The navigator was in deep conversation with the two Booleans, and she heard intense negotiations taking place as she approached.

"I've got a Poe, a Queen Victoria, a Professor Aronnax, and a really nice one of Louis Daguerre himself," Pritchard said in a voice that rolled across the room like a lazy summer thunder. "I'll trade all of these for that Viscount Nelson."

Nigel stroked his chin in deep thought as he considered the offer, but he stood when he saw Gemma. Caroline followed suit with a smile, and Mr. Pritchard stood as well. A mountain of a man, he would have towered over the captain.

"Ma'am," he said with a nod. "Pleasure to see you this fine mornin'. Lieutenant Commander Hieronymus Pritchard, navigator. And you must be our Miss Llewellyn." As they all sat down, he slid his stack of CDVs closer to him to clear a space for her tray. "Let me make some room for you here. We're just doing a little tradin'."

She returned his greeting with more of a tremor in her voice than she liked. She had been shaky since she had left the orrery the day before, slipping out as soon as she could escape Dr. Pugh's notice. Violence should always be the last resort. It frightened her when she lost control like that.

She nibbled at a piece of the crisp, salty bacon and scanned the notices on the wall as the other three continued trading. Caroline was keen on a picture of a stage actress, and Mr. Pritchard wanted one of her Dickens cards in return.

The number of notices on the wall had grown over the last few days. Above the usual Sophie the Steamfitter propaganda was a long banner declaring the number of days left until Braking Day, which would mark the halfway point in their voyage. The newspaper had been replaced with a typewritten sheet entitled 'Wireless News'. According to its headline, France and Germany were bickering over the Alsace and Lorraine provinces again. There were more calls for labour strikes among the employees of the major steel manufacturers, which also happened to be major stakeholders in the TIA.

"Do you like the bacon, Miss Llewellyn?" Mr. Pritchard asked.

The sudden question gave her a start. She replied, "Well, yes. It's quite tasty, in fact. How big a supply did we bring with us? Enough for the whole journey?"

"Well," he said, a bit of shy pride creeping into his smooth voice, "it comes from my hometown. I was raised by Shakers down in Kentucky. What you have there is the best that Pleasant Hill hogs have to offer."

"Shakers?" she asked.

"What you might call a religious community. The members don't marry, but they do take in orphans and raise them 'til they're old enough to decide to join or leave. There were plenty of us to take in after the Invasion, let me tell you, so they were plenty busy. I left -- I wanted to get married someday -- but I still keep in touch with them. They're my family. They gave me a great education. They had one of the best schools in what was left of the country after the Martians got through with us."

"Were all the schools destroyed?" Caroline asked.

"No, we just lost a lot of people, teachers included. My guardians did a fair job with the three R's. Carpentry, too," he said as he flexed his muscular hands. "They're famous for their chairs, you know, and there was a lot of rebuilding to do. Their teaching was good enough to get me into the Academy and onto the *Fury*. Some of the Shakers came down to see me off and gave me plenty of good food for the journey, too. They are pacifists, you know, so they aren't exactly screaming *Terra vigila* right now. Sort of a blessing for me, I s'pose. I miss 'em."

His description reminded her a little bit of her own school. Mrs. Brightman, too, had taken in many orphans, but never had anyone asked to leave. Of course, she didn't recall anyone asking her if she wanted to. It had never occurred to her to do so. The thought stuck in her mind like a thorn.

"We brought lots of it," Pritchard continued in a jovial tone, "but it prob'ly won't last the entire journey. Not with hungry scientists on board." He motioned at Gemma's rapidly emptying plate with his chin.

"We do have some live meat on the stable deck, Ron," Nigel said. "But it won't be table-ready for a while. Until then, most of the swine act as disposal units for the galley scraps. They have a special dumbwaiter that takes buckets straight from the galleys down to the stable deck. A conveyer belt takes it the rest of the way, so the, um, fresh country air, as they say, doesn't seep back into the galleys. Whatever the pigs -- er -- produce from that goes to fertilize the Gardens. Frau Knopf frowns on waste of any sort, and we need to keep her happy."

Pritchard guffawed. "Oh, ain't that the truth. She got angry with this one fella, last trip out, when he complained that the bacon wasn't done to his liking. She burnt his bacon -- only his bacon, mind you -- for the rest of the trip." He said to Gemma in an exaggerated whisper, "You like your bacon. I'd stay on her good side, if I were you."

Caroline, who had been studying one of Pritchard's cards, looked up and asked, "Gemma, do you have any cards to trade? Don't want to leave you out, love."

Gemma shook her head. "Oh, no, Caroline," she replied. "My studies leave little time for much collecting. Except for rocks, of course."

Caroline laughed until she snorted. "Well, 'bout time you started, right? Most of us have 'em. Gives us something to do. Here," she said, "start with one o'mine. A hero for my hero. You did defend my honour last night, after all." She handed Gemma a card emblazoned with the sultry smirk of Sophie the Steamfitter. "I've got three of this one."

Mr. Pritchard slid one of his cards over to her. "A Robert Frost, for the pretty lady," he said. "Since you brought us good luck."

Nigel grinned at her. "How chivalrous of you, Ron! Well, I can't be left out! Would you like a Viscount Nelson, Miss Gemma?"

"Hey, that one's mine!" Pritchard chuckled. "Give her your *God Speed*. Everybody needs one of the captain."

Nigel drew a card from the deck in front of him and held it up. Caroline gasped at the sight of it. It was a reproduction of Edmund Leighton's painting *God Speed*, which had become very popular over the past few years: a medieval lady, leaning across a stone railing, tied a red kerchief token onto an armoured knight's arm, with said knight on horseback, ready to ride to war. Only this time, it was Sophie the Steamfitter on the railing, corset and short skirt in place with a bit of cheek peeping out, with Moreau's helmeted visage gazing up at her with gross affection. Gemma groaned inwardly at the tackiness of it, thankful that it was just a painting. She wasn't sure she could stomach a real-life image of such tripe.

Caroline, on the other hand, bounced in her chair. "I can't believe it! You have one, you actually have one," she squealed. "Oh, Nigel, please--"

"Now, now, Yeoman," he said gently as he offered the card to Gemma with a flourish. "I suggest you set up a trade with Miss Llewellyn here, if you want it." He leaned towards Gemma and said, "Look sharp with this one. She's a crafty trader. My wife trained her well."

"Gettin' mighty thick in here," Pritchard chuckled, waving his hand in front of him as if chasing an unpleasant odour away. "I think I'll take my leave. I need to head on up to the bridge, anyway. Heat ray tests later today, you know. Pleasure to meet you, Miss Llewellyn. Chief, ladies, I bid you good day." He gathered his cards and walked away.

Caroline showed Gemma the rest of her deck, which she seemed ready to trade in its entirety for that one tawdry card. Another one appeared at Gemma's elbow. She turned to look at the giver and saw only the retreating back of a hunter green jacket. The dog-eared card bore a blueprint of the *Fury*.

Once Pritchard was out of earshot, Nigel leaned a little closer to Gemma and said in a low voice, "Don't worry about Humboldt. As his boss, I have to do something about his behaviour of yesterday. I won't put him in the brig, as much as he deserves it, since I'd have to log his actual offense with the captain--"

"--and that would be bad luck," said Caroline.

Gemma gave the pair an odd look.

"Well," Nigel said, "let's just say that we don't examine a good omen's teeth too closely 'round here. And I think you gave him a good dose of humiliation to boot, so for the most part I think he's been put in his place."

"Roger ain't a bad chap, Gemma, not really," said Caroline, "not until he gets into his cups. Which he does a lot, so he can forget what his family did to him."

"Caroline!" Nigel snapped.

"Family?"

"She ought to know, Nigel. He ain't no Orphan, not like us. His family's rich. Old money. They got estates up in Kent, I think. Roger's always been a bit wild, I reckon, and one day they just got shot of him. Paid him to stay out of England. And he did, for a long time, 'til the Academy went looking for Boolean candidates for the mission. TIA didn't care about family backgrounds, long as we were good in maths. He signed on, but then his family cut him off entirely. A bit strange, really, since you can't get farther away than Mars."

"A true remittance man?" Gemma asked. "I thought they were just in stories. Then he is still an orphan, after a fashion, isn't he?"

Nigel answered, "He's had some rough patches, to be sure, but that doesn't excuse his actions. I'll give him some extra duties or something, though, and remind him to behave himself. I'll have him archive the wireless messages or muck out the stable deck. Maybe both."

"What you did was amazing, though," Caroline chirped before popping another forkful of eggs into her mouth. "Never seen a scientist move like that before. Your school may be as tough as the Academy. Tougher, maybe."

Gemma wondered how Caroline could be so cheerful all the time, with all the hardships she had endured, having to live her life in a hideous uniform and look like a boy. She simply could not understand it, and she was thankful yet again to her mistress for rescuing her from such things; but deep inside she began to wonder if she was correct in thinking that Caroline must be unhappy.

Over the course of breakfast, the pile of cards grew at Gemma's side as crew left for duty. By the time she was finished eating, she had acquired five Dickens, a Darwin, two Queen Victorias, two Lord Nelsons, a Baron Robert Baden-Powell, and a picture of a rather sad-looking India rubber Martian.

Noticing Gemma's grimace, Nigel explained, "Oh, that's just the Martian from the Badger 'n' Tentacle down in Hammersmith. Leave it to the British to commemorate the Invasion with a pub."

"I hear they built the bar out of the leg of a walking machine," Caroline added. "Wonder how that got that past the TIA salvagers."

Caroline then traded a picture of another pub, The Falcon, Battersea, and one of the Badger and Tentacle, for the Moreau card, much to Gemma's relief. She couldn't bear the thought of *that man* knowing that she was toting his face about in her pocket. Gemma was amazed to see a CDV of a pub; apparently, there was an entire series of them.

"Humboldt's trying to get the entire set," Caroline explained. "He's been bothering me for this one for a while."

Anything was better, in Gemma's opinion, than that horrid painting. She would have given the card to Caroline freely, just to be shot of it, if Nigel had not insisted on a trade.

The Booleans bid her a good day as they left the table. Gemma jogged the cards into a neat stack. She didn't have enough time to return them to her room before reporting to Pugh's office for the day. She'd simply have to endure his ribbing -- or his advice, she wasn't sure which was worse -- about them. At least he wouldn't see her with the Moreau card. Her new collection did make her breathe more easily, though. This little pat on the back from her shipmates was the bolster that she needed.

It was time to work on her special assignment: the reading of the two ledgers. She could face them now; she felt lighter and freer than she had in a very long time. The crew wasn't afraid of her even after her tussle with Humboldt. She was surprised at how much delight that gave her. Perhaps it was because there was no physical escape from this place. She was going to be with them longer than she'd ever been with a target before. The farther the ship crawled along its course, the less it seemed possible that there was a Watcher aboard. It had been hard enough to smuggle her in -- how much harder it would have been to get two on the ship! She had time, and time again, before they reached Mars to find Orion.

There was no Watcher.

There couldn't be.

In the lift, she considered the possibility that Brightman had meant OBERTH instead of ORION. The analytical part of her mind quickly discarded the notion. Most previous assignments had concerned small, portable oddments of science that were easy to move and study, like an equation, a photograph, or a chemical sample. Gemma found the notion of hiding the great Oberth engines in the school cellar amusing. This mission did seem to have thrown all the usual rules out the window, true, but surely Orion was a formula, a file, something that she could transmit via wireless or smuggle off the ship upon her return. Assuming she did return.

She shook off the morbid thought and spent the rest of the morning in a corner of Dr. Pugh's office, sandwiched between two columns of musty books. She knew that it was entirely possible that Orion was within arms' reach, but she did not dare rifle through those notes, not with Dr. Pugh right across the room. He drew odd twisting ladders upon the glass panel, looked down at his notes, grunted, then erased and redrew. It was hard to focus at times over the squeak-squeak of his writing, but she was able to make some headway into the material he'd given her. It was a refreshing respite from the deluge of chemistry notes bubbling in her head.

She recognized the first after a few pages. It was an account of the adventures of Pugh's mentor, Professor Aronnax, on the *Nautilus*. She had read it at Mrs. Brightman's insistence long ago. The professor and two other men had had a remarkable adventure with the legendary Captain Nemo decades ago, back in 1867. Brightman had explained how it was an important example of scientific observation, and some of the information had come in handy when she had assisted an oceanographer in Sicily for a few months. He had studied the maelstrom that had swallowed Nemo's vessel after Aronnax had escaped it. She had no idea why this account might apply to their trip to Mars; did Pugh expect to encounter a giant squid in space?

She was deep into the description of Nemo's mollusk collection when Dr. Pugh interrupted her study with a tray of cheese and biscuits for a light lunch. After fussing over the cheddar and potted Stilton, he planted her in front of the glass panels once more and launched into another lecture.

She examined the sketches, which were little more than intertwined and overlapping vertical lines. They resembled spiral staircases and were a stark contrast to the honeycombs he had drawn before. The one on the left, labeled "HUMAN", had its pair of lines connected at regular intervals with smaller horizontal straight ones. The "MARTIAN" one on the right was similar, but the connecting lines were so close together that they almost melded into a single block of colour. The overarching label was "THE CODE OF LIFE".

"You were correct the other day. It *is* like a numerical cipher, except it uses combinations of chemicals instead of numbers. The truly odd thing that we've found is that humans and Martians use the same chemicals for their Codes of Life, even though they originated on different worlds. At the same time, there are differences. Do you see them?"

Blast the Socratic method, Gemma grumbled to herself whilst doing her best to keep a semblance of placidity on her face. "The Martian one has more connecting lines," she replied after a moment's consideration. "The information is denser."

Pugh nodded. "Quite correct. We believe that they could carry out their major functions of life using the same density as human Code. So why the extra? That's the mystery we are trying to solve."

He cleared his throat after a moment of her silence. "Feel privileged, Llewellyn," he said. "This is the heart of my research. There are those who would kill to get even a glimpse of it. Nevertheless, it wouldn't matter if you were to share it back with your mistress. There are no Martians available for her to examine or to make use of, so the information would be useless to her."

Gemma asked, "If all the Martians on Earth are dead, and we already have a plan to destroy the remaining ones on Mars, why are we even bothering to study their Codes?" She pointed to the diagrams on the panel. "And how did you decipher all of that? Did the Martians carry machines with them to perform this sort of analysis? Isn't that all a bit advanced? And if they did, why would they bring that sort of machine with them when they meant to conquer?"

Dr. Pugh was silent for a moment, and she wondered what flour the gears in his head was grinding.

"Science!" he roared, jabbing a large gnarled finger into the air. "Because we must know the secrets of the Universe!"

She blinked at him, slowly, with no emotion on her face. Governments did not fund science and exploration "just because". She had a feeling that even the Martians did not attack "just because". There was always a reason behind funding, or war, no matter how strange or irrational that reason may be. She allowed her face to say all of this to him in a stony silence.

He cleared his throat, lowered his hand, and resumed his normal growly countenance.

"I should have known that that wouldn't work with you, Llewellyn," he continued. "But, you know, I had to try."

"Of course," she replied with her best commiserating smile. She gazed at the photographs on his office wall for a long moment, and Dr. Pugh's reasons -- if not the TIA's -- suddenly seemed very clear to her.

She continued in a softer tone. "It's so Captain Moreau doesn't have to give the order, isn't it?" she asked at last. "I think deep down you agree with

Alfieri. That you think this mission is genocide. Just like they have to have a reason to explore, they also have to have a reason, at times, *not* to kill. You are looking for that reason, aren't you?"

"Yes," he sighed with a resigned slump of his shoulders. "It's no use playing the cold natural philosopher with you, is it? You have no heart yourself, but you can see right through mine. It is a horrid Order, an absolute nightmare. I don't want Christophe to have to execute it. He doesn't want to do it, not really. But he will, if that is what they order him to do. I'm hoping to give them a reason to rescind those orders, or to at least amend them."

To hear that she had no heart was no insult. A heart would only get in the way of her work.

She asked, "Even if it means this journey was all for nothing?"

"Yes, even so."

Gemma felt a pang of sympathy for the man. She had found murder to be a messy business, what with dispensing of weapons and leaving false clues and so forth. The subsequent memories and nightmares were never pleasant, either. If it did not serve her mistress, and was not in immediate self-defence, she had no use for the extra baggage that came with the act. Except for that nasty piece of work in Shanghai, she had usually found a way to escape such situations, rather than kill.

For the Martians, however, she would gladly make an exception.

"I believe we have something in common with them," he said as he pointed to the panel. "I want to know exactly what that commonality is. Can we use it? That is, can we use it to make a case for not killing them *all?*" He set the pencil down into its tray. "I think your analytical abilities will be of great help in finding that reason. Christophe was raised to command, to lead, not to be a mass murderer. Not to live with this on his conscience."

Gemma inhaled sharply as she prepared to reply, but her words were lost in a sudden rumble that rolled through the deckplate beneath them like a deep, close thunder. She reached out for the desk to steady herself, looking to Dr. Pugh for some clue as to whether or not this was normal.

It decidedly was not. His eyes went wide, and his face lost all colour. He was listening, as Gemma was, to the exclamations of the other members of the Cohort down the hall. Their yelps of excitement and surprise echoed off the metal walls of the corridor.

"Good heavens!" he exclaimed.

"I take it that this was unexpected?" Gemma asked.

"Completely, completely unexpected. I hope the engines weren't affected. We're still accel--"

The pipephone bell rang, and he picked it up with an irritated acknowledgement. Gemma watched his eyes grow wide as he listened to the voice on the other end of the line.

"What's wrong, lad?" Dr. Pugh asked. His trembling hands had difficulty holding the handset. "Say again?"

Gemma could hear broken pieces of the other person's words. "Heat ray test... mate hurt... fire..."

"Fire?" Pugh exclaimed. "I'm on my way."

Pugh hung up the pipephone. He jogged towards the corridor with his long loping gait without a word to Gemma, who followed him long enough to watch him catch the lift. Bidarhalli and Hui dashed out behind her. They each grasped one of the sand-filled fire buckets that dotted the walls.

"Fire on the ship," Hui muttered, "is bad. Very bad." They carried the buckets back into the laboratory and left her alone again.

With no direction, no hint as to when he would return, she returned to the office. She stared at the panel and the journals that she had been reading. Another journal was open on the corner of the desk. It had been exposed and forgotten in his rush out the door. Not one to waste an opportunity, Gemma circled around to view it. There was no guarantee, of course, but he was likely to be gone for some time. She examined the page without touching it, hoping to read it without leaving behind any evidence that she had even noticed it. As untidy and disorganized as Pugh might seem, he would know if a single speck of dust was out of place.

She gazed down at the wrinkled page with its smudged notes and sketches. Some of them were identical to what he had just shown her on the glass panel. No secrets there.

A sentence began at the bottom of the right-hand page: "*In the course of our experiments, we found that Orion*" and nothing more.

Orion. It did exist. She paused to think about her own alias: Artemis. The two were connected in Greek mythology; Orion was the hunting companion of Artemis. In fact, in some myths, Artemis was the slayer of Orion, sometimes by accident and sometimes on purpose, depending on the particular version of the story. Knowing Brightman's complex sense of humour, Gemma wondered if Orion was a person as well. Part of her hoped that the connection was not a hint of what she was expected to do with Orion, once found, but she would carry out whatever was required of her. She owed Mrs. Brightman no less than that. All she needed to do was turn the page to move forward. She knew she could do it quickly, deftly, without moving the book... why did she find herself hesitating now, when she had been handed Orion on a silver platter?

The image of a disappointed and angry Pugh rose in her mind like mist condensing out of the very air. She found herself cringing at the prospect, but she didn't know why. She found herself struggling to move her hand at all. Her index finger froze an inch from the page and hovered there.

The simple turning of a page had never seemed such a complex matter. The reading of an open and forgotten page was trivial, innocent even -- but the turning of it felt fraught with -- what was it -- could it be guilt? Guilt for what? He was her only protection here on the *Fury*, but that was not all. Something in her ached at the thought of betraying what little trust he had shown her, leaving his work open to her in this way. She could not explain the feeling.

Everyone has a motivation, Mrs. Brightman had always said. *Everyone has a key that you have only to grasp and turn.*

Many times the key was predictable, almost pedestrian, like pleasures of the flesh. She had already concluded that the captain was firmly in this category. But such was not always the case. Some were turned by the avoidance of pain. And there were some whose keys were of a very different sort. Not warm flesh in their bed, but a willing ear, a friendly smile, or a soft word. They craved someone to impress, to make them feel powerful, genius, needed.

No one performs for free, Mrs. Brightman had instructed her. *No one. There is always a price. There is always a key.* Never had Gemma encountered someone whose key she could not turn. It was her special gift.

She had discovered Pugh's key: Christophe Moreau. He had rushed to the captain's side without hesitation at the slightest call. He had even left her alone in his office, after all his ominous warnings to the contrary. Worry and concern had been etched deeply into his face as he departed. Whatever their true relationship was, Pugh acted for Moreau's benefit. If only she had the will to turn that key, Pugh would be putty in her hands, no matter what he knew about her. Even Orion would not be safe from her.

But how could she turn the key, if she could not turn the page?

CHRISTOPHE

"Can someone please tell me how in the bloody hell we left Shackleton without testing the heat ray?" Pugh shouted into the chamber.

Christophe tried to hide the helplessness that threatened to crush him inside. He knelt on the floor at the head of Cervantes' crumpled form, surrounded by a pile of shattered metal, gears, and wires. A gritty concoction of sand and blood soiled his crisp uniform. Christophe looked back down at Miguel's burnt and melted face; he barely recognized his childhood companion.

The ship's surgeon was already there, tending to an endless list of injuries: burns, lacerations, and limbs jutting out at impossible angles. At least the man was blessedly unconscious. As it was, Christophe's hands were slick with his blood as he tried to halt the flood of crimson. There were so many tears in his flesh, though, that Christophe felt like he was plugging one of a million holes in a dike; there weren't enough hands in the room to do the job properly.

Dr. Pugh knelt next to him, pushed the empty fire bucket out of the way, and asked in a gentler voice, "What happened, son?"

Christophe pointed at the open control panel with his chin. He stammered, "We were test-firing the heat ray against some of the growlers. Miguel reported that one of the valve gears had a problem. Prevented the ray from firing. He was trying to fix it when there was an explosion. Miguel was deep in at the time and took the brunt. We managed to get the fire out before it spread. The other crewmen were able to walk themselves down to sick bay, but he..."

Christophe drifted off, sucked in a short shallow breath, and tried to rein in the wild winds of his feelings. Dr. Pugh rested a hand on his shoulder and gave it a firm squeeze. The pair looked at the surgeon.

"What do you reckon, Paul?" Pugh asked.

Christophe regarded Dr. Paul Hansard with a studied frown. He had seen that solemn look too many times on the lunar voyage; it was engraved into his brain, even without the aid of the redundant memory that Miguel always teased him about.

"Mr. Owen and the others will be fine, but Cervantes' injuries are quite severe," the doctor said. "I need to get him to the surgery. I may be able to staunch the bleeding. It's the burns that concern me, especially the ones in his lungs."

There was a shuffle at the door. Mr. Rathbone entered and took in the scene with horrified eyes. Christophe watched the man navigate around the mud of sand and blood. He shifted a loose sheaf of undelivered messages to his other hand, saluted, and said, "You sent for me, Captain?"

Dr. Pugh withdrew his hand from Christophe's shoulder. The scientist rubbed the edge of his sharp chin with the bony knuckle of his index finger. It was one of their many secret signals to each other. This one, which told him to keep his chin up, bolstered Christophe as he replied. He nodded in response to the salute, since he could not release the pressure on Cervantes' arm.

"Just a moment, if you please, Mr. Rathbone. Let's get Mr. Cervantes squared away first."

Corpsmen surged through the door behind Rathbone, who moved against the wall to allow them to bring in a stretcher. They carefully rolled the injured man onto it and lifted him from the floor. One of the corpsmen took over Christophe's pressure point, and the others that were not holding up the stretcher were pouring styptic powder on the myriad wounds. They moved him in a slow scrum towards the door.

"Hold on, Miguel," Christophe said to his friend's still form. "Hold on, old sport. The *Fury* needs you!"

To Dr. Hansard he said, "Please keep me informed. Do you think we should get Father Alfieri?"

The surgeon shuffled along with his corpsmen, careful to avoid jostling his charge. "Oh, heavens, I hope not. But you might send someone for him to come down. His presence would be a comfort to Cervantes, at any rate. I'd keep this off the speaking tubes for the moment, until we know something."

"I'll be glad to fetch him," Rathbone volunteered.

Christophe nodded at both of them, feeling unsteady as he heard the sand crunch beneath his feet. At least with Miguel around, he had some vestige of his days at sea with him. He could feel that tenuous thread slipping away. Biting his lip, he wished he could lend his friend some of his own strength.

When the surgeon's crew was gone, Christophe turned to the waiting wireless officer, who could not tear his gaze away from the blackened walls of the chamber and the bits of jagged metal embedded in them.

"We need to report this incident back to the Admiralty," Christophe said. "Please send a message to Thorvaldson that we have had an incident with the heat ray test."

Rathbone swept the scene once more with his gaze and arched a wary eyebrow. "An incident, sir?"

"Yes, a severe incident, Mr. Rathbone." His reply was rather harsher than he had intended. "Tell him that a full report will follow by the end of the day. No more than that, Rathbone. We need to assess what happened here and make sure what we say is accurate. And tell no one else, yet, of what you've seen. I need to address the crew myself on that account. Except for Father Alfieri, of course. Just tell him that Cervantes is injured and that his presence is needed in sick bay. The doctor will fill him in on the rest. Make sure no one else hears you. Dismissed, Mr. Rathbone."

"Aye Aye, Captain," Rathbone replied with another sharp salute. He turned on his heel and left the chamber.

Pugh and Christophe were alone in the filthy, smoky room, with the acrid smell of electrical fire and burnt skin lingering about them.

Christophe thought his voice would shatter into a million pieces. "What will we do without him? He's the best sailor on the ship. He always kept a cool head at the wheel. There were icicles on his nose when we rounded Cape Horn, and he didn't even blink! Even the winds of the Furious Fifties couldn't drive him from his post." He paced across the small chamber. He caught himself against an unshredded strip of console when he encountered a sandless pool of blood and nearly lost his balance.

"Blast it all, Elias!" Christophe said, pounding his fist on the console and snarling. "What absolute bollocks! If only the Martians were pirates on the Spanish Main! We wouldn't need a bloody heat ray. I could use a cutlass and a musket or a good cannon or two. A pox on space travel!"

"Time to captain up, Christophe," Pugh said, after giving him a moment to catch his breath. "Keep busy. Before you write your report for headquarters, even before you run to sick bay, make arrangements for the fire buckets to be refilled straight away, especially the sodium bicarbonate, in case the fires flare up again. I do hope we brought enough, if this is any indication of what is to come. Someone needs to be on watch in here in case it does flare up, or in case--"

"In case someone decides to come back and try again? Do you think it was sabotage, then?" Christophe asked in a low voice, futilely attempting to brush the sand off his hands and casting a furtive glance at the still-open door. "Admiral Thorvaldson was concerned that we might have agents aboard, but I had hoped he was just paranoid. Who would do such a thing? They would endanger themselves as well as the ship."

"Do you think someone may have wanted to harm Miguel in

particular?"

"How could they be sure it would be him at that very moment? Besides, the men respect him. And he liked everyone except--"

He stopped, not wanting to speak the name that came to his lips.

"Except?"

"He was concerned about Miss Llewellyn. Not about anything specific, but you know how suspicious he is sometimes. I can't believe it, though. She's no killer. I'd stake my life on it."

Alarm crossed the elderly scientist's face. He pursed his lips before he said, "I'm not sure of anything yet. I need to have someone take a closer look at the gubbins here before we start clapping people in irons. But not until the fire buckets are refilled. That fire might flare up again, and I would hate to be the one on the business end of it. At the same time, I would say that on the surface, this is no great surprise. Honestly, they never really understood the entire workings of the Martian version of the ray, no matter how many times old Abbie translated what we found. Even Maggie couldn't get it to work, if you recall. I warned them, but they wouldn't listen. I can't lay the blame on the gun crews or Cervantes. Or you, for that matter, son. There is a high price to be paid, though, for trying to wage war with stolen weapons."

"And Miguel paid it."

A surge of fury pulsed through him. He knew it was time to take charge, no matter what was happening with his first mate. His jaw clenched tightly with anger, but his thoughts were clearing.

"I feel responsible, Elias. As skipper of this ship, I agreed that we should launch now. We needed the heat ray to defend ourselves in case we met any resistance. The launch window was closing. At the next opposition, we'd be out of solar minimum, and we'd have had a much greater chance of repeating the disaster of the lunar voyage. I didn't want to lose anyone else that way." He took a deep breath and felt a veil fall between him and the gnawing anxiety over his first mate. "We need some kind of contingency plan for ship to ship fighting in case we cannot repair it. We don't want to be caught with our trousers down if Martians meet us halfway. Those G-bombs aren't guided missiles. They're useless unless we're in orbit. What does the Cohort have that we might use in its stead?"

Pugh ruminated for a moment. "I need to talk to Hui. Perhaps it's time his pet project took centre stage. I need to discuss it with Maggie, as well, then compose the right message for the boys back home, after we've dealt with the more immediate issues." Pugh chewed on his lip. "Do you think Old Nicky still has that volume of Tennyson you gave him last Christmas?"

"I gave you both one," Christophe replied, puzzled.

"Precisely, my boy," Pugh said with a mysterious smile. "Buck up. We will see this through."

"One last thing," Christophe said. "Maggie will need to know. About Cervantes, I mean. I don't know how to tell her." Despair struggled to get through his shield of captainship again. "She'll be distraught."

Pugh said in a low whisper, "She may know already. You manage things up here, Captain. I'll handle Maggie. I'll have some of the Cohort go over the scene here. We'll meet in your Ready Room as soon as possible to report our findings. We both have work to do." He loped out of the chamber. "Don't forget the fire buckets, son," he called over his shoulder. Pugh's voice faded as he moved down the corridor. "Rathbone, hold the lift for me, there's a good lad!"

Christophe stared down at his hands. He tried to curl his fingers, but they were too stiff from the mixture of sand and blood drying on them.

Captain, he thought to himself, wondering if he really deserved that title, after all.

GEMMA

Gemma could smell the chamber before she reached it. The stink of burnt flesh and the iron of spilt blood were unmistakable. She had been in enough laboratories over the past few years to know a horrific accident when she smelt it.

As they approached the entrance, the captain emerged. He was so changed that Gemma thought she was looking at a different man. The brash countenance and the sharpness of his eyes had vanished; in their place was the saddest face she had ever seen. A bloodstained scarecrow had replaced the bright blue jay that just a few days ago had told her to have no fear. Deep lines furrowed either side of the frown scraped across his face. It was as if a heavy mist had veiled the sun. She looked from his face to his hands, where he clutched a towel stiff with drying crimson. She would much rather see the rakish captain than this wretched fellow.

"Miss Llewellyn, Dr. Pugh," he said, greeting them with a curt nod. His sad eyes widened a little at the sight of Gemma. He looked at her in confusion, then at Dr. Pugh. His voice was so diminished that her heart ached in a way it hadn't since she had lost Philippa.

"Will Dr. Hui be joining you?" asked the captain.

"In a bit," Dr. Pugh replied.

"Very well. We've refilled the fire buckets, and I've confirmed that the speaking tubes are in working order. Should I stay, in case--"

"We should be fine, Captain," Pugh replied. "I know you have other duties that require your attention. I'll be by later to present our findings." The elderly scientist leaned closer to the young man and whispered the rest. Gemma's keen hearing still picked up his next words: "I've asked Knopf to send a tray up to your Ready Room. Keep up your strength, son."

Son? Gemma thought as he took his leave of them and made his way down the corridor at a funereal pace.

She noted once more how both men had the same tall, lean frame. She *was* supposed to watch the captain, after all, in addition to finding Orion. She was not convinced that they were unrelated -- either the captain and Orion, or the captain and Dr. Pugh. Humboldt's theory that Pugh had "found" an orphaned Moreau seemed less and less likely to her.

As she observed the captain's slow gait, she wasn't sure if she felt irritation or dismay, or equal parts of both. The world spoke of him as Arthur returned, or even Nemo, risen from the grave and taking the *Nautilus* to the stars. She chided herself for reading too many of Aronnax's notes. The real Nemo was more likely to kick the Oberths up a notch, slide right past Mars, and leave the teeming masses of humanity behind. In that case, they had better hope that the captain was not Nemo returned. There was small chance of that, anyway. Moreau was nothing like him... except perhaps his reaction to the current situation. Nemo may not have been a man of the people, but he had had a deep attachment to his crew.

She considered that for a moment. *Wouldn't it be ironic,* she thought, *if they had resurrected Nemo, but ended up with all the wrong bits?*

Dr. Pugh led her through the door, and she shook her head free of such flights of fancy. Even though she was not exactly a novice to grisly situations, she still grimaced at the sight. Before Dr. Pugh could address her again, her eyes swept the chamber: blackened and scarred walls, bits of metal and gears spread hither and yon, and a dried mud of more blood and sand on the floor, with a dusting of pink-stained powder over it all.

Dr. Pugh secured the door and leaned upon it, his giant praying mantis-like arms folded against his brown jacket. "Please, please tell me that you had nothing to do with this. Please tell me that this was not your mission."

She shook her head. "No. Mrs. Brightman is in the habit of appropriating technology, Dr. Pugh. Not destroying it."

"You must admit, Miss Llewellyn, that the entire idea of this mission breaks all the normal Brightman protocols."

"I assure you, this was not my doing. I did not know where this chamber was until now. And what possible motivation would I have to do so? It would put me in as much danger as the rest of you. Are you certain it was not just an accident?"

"That is what I am trying to ascertain. With Petunia, you never know. *You* might only steal science, but *she* is certainly not above sacrificing one of her Girls to avenge herself. Hell hath no fury like the scorned Belladonna of Guildford." He held a hand up to stop the obvious question that sprang to her lips. "Oh, not now, not now. I did not think it was you, but I had to ask. I've already spoken with the Gun Control lads, and they don't recall seeing you in this area at any point. They'd remember the swishing of skirts, of that I'm certain." He took a deep breath, then released it. "What a relief. I did not want to think that my brightest student--"

"What do you need, Dr. Pugh?"

"I need you to role-play for me, Gemma. I need for you to turn your Brightman Eye to a higher purpose. If it had been your mission to fool about with the heat ray, why would you do it?"

"Most likely, to gather information to send back. Notes, drawings, schematics, that sort of thing. A photograph or two of what was behind the panel, if I could manage it."

"Would you need flash powder, still?"

"Yes."

"Hmmm. Do we see any evidence of it? Perhaps someone else in your Peculiar Occupation was at work here?"

The spectre of a possible Watcher arose once more in her mind.

"We can look for flash powder," Gemma mused, "but it may be difficult to trace it in the rest of this mess. But I would also add that one would need chemicals and a private space in which to develop any film." She knelt on the cleanest spot she could find to get a closer look at a piece of shrapnel. "There is one other problem."

The panel shard bore the name "Squid's Bane"; she smiled faintly at the nod to maritime tradition. She squinted, as much to think about her next point as to see what lay in the shadows beneath a chunk of ruined panel.

"And that would be?" asked Pugh.

"How useful would the images be? We will not return to Earth for some time. We cannot transmit those images to Earth from here. We haven't advanced *that* much, unless the Booleans have figured it out and haven't told anybody. I'm certain that any images captured on this mission will have to be stored until our return. Whoever wanted those images back home would have to be very patient, indeed. Surely, they would have retrieved such information before we left, whilst the shuttles were still moving back and forth. It seems a bit late for that sort of skulduggery now."

There was something underneath the broken panel. It appeared to be a charred slip of paper. She was not quite sure if she should reach for it and disturb the evidence. It might be important; it might be nothing but doodles sketched by a bored sailor.

"Hmmmm. Well, I do have to tell you," Pugh said as he walked over to the scorched wall on the far side of the room, "that within the TIA there are various philosophies concerning this mission. One small but vocal faction did not want this mission to go forward at all. Perhaps someone wants us to fail early, and turn round, but in such a way that we can still make it home. That would explain why they sabotaged the heat ray, rather than the Oberths."

Gemma sat back on her heels and gazed at other parts of the chamber, hoping that Pugh hadn't noticed she'd seen something.

"A Peacenik? Or a Neo-Luddite? There are many such. But it does seem like a waste of resources."

Pugh chuckled and leaned forward into the wall. One long finger traced the blackened scar that raced across it. "I see that Petunia did not neglect your political education. Not everyone is obsessed with the Martians, you see. Some are more concerned about other Terrans. And not in a polite way."

Whilst his back was turned, she answered, but only to cover the noise of grasping the paper between two fingertips.

"But why not cause the malfunction back at Shackleton? Why take the chance out here, past the moon? Sabotage at this point doesn't make sense. The saboteur would be in just as much danger as the rest of us."

She sensed he was turning, so she released her paper -- it felt like a card -- and turned to study another pile of debris before he could fully view her.

"So, perhaps an accident," he said. "I certainly hope poor Miguel doesn't snuff it because a bolt was out of place. Hardly a blaze of glory. He deserves better."

The elderly scientist shuffled over to the gaping hole that had tried to eat the first mate. He bent over as much as he could to peer into it. He grunted as he did so, and Gemma took advantage of the noise to retrieve the card and drop it into the pocket of her skirt. It might be nothing. It might be everything. But she wanted to examine it before revealing what she had found.

"It's no good," his muffled voice told her. "I'll need an electric torch to see up in here. I'm not mechanically minded. We'll need for an engineer to take a look." He backed his head out, and his voice grew louder. "Perhaps one of the gun crew lads if they aren't too injured. Maybe Nesbitt or Pritchard. He's good at this sort of thing. Hui, too, might want to have a gander. I think we're damned lucky we didn't have a hull breach."

He struggled to stand back up. Gemma hopped to her feet and sprinted over to help him. He smiled in spite of his arthritic groans.

"Ah, your knees are some decades younger, I'm afraid," he said through a wince. "Don't grow old, child. Who knows what Brightman will do when it is time to put you out to pasture?" He coughed and finished straightening himself up. "Thank you, Miss. That will be all for now, I think. I want the scene to be undisturbed until Hui has seen it. Until then, find something useful to do, why don't you? I don't think I have to remind you that it's better if you keep this quiet. Let the captain make any announcements about this."

"Yes, Dr. Pugh. Should you need me--"

"I'll give you a screech down the pipephone. Highly unlikely today, I should think. Should you have any additional ideas, though, leave a note on my office door. Go have a cup of tea or something, there's a good lass."

"Dr. Pugh."

"Yes, Gemma?"

"Why do you care? I mean, why do you care to turn my abilities to a higher purpose, as you said?"

He blinked at her and did not speak for a moment. When he finally did, he asked, "What happens to you Girls when you are too old to ply your trade? When your charms fade? You won't be young forever, Gemma. You will need somewhere to go." He cleared his throat. He waved her on. "Now, go, child. I'm busy."

She turned to go, leaving him to puzzle over the scene and herself to puzzle over the enigma of Dr. Elias Pugh.

With the first free time that she had had in a while, she wasn't sure what to do with herself. She had not yet picked up her wireless messages for the day. After what she'd seen, a good brisk walk to the command deck might be refreshing.

Once there, she received a folded message from one of the junior officers through the window. The stack of waiting messages was quite tall, with the attached grease pencils dangling from the sides of the frames. She couldn't see around the window into the bridge, but she could hear the edge of panic in their voices. They might not know everything, but they had all felt the rumble of the explosion.

"I wasn't the glitch for this mission, after all," Gemma whispered aloud to no one.

It was not quite time for tea, so she headed back to the privacy of her stateroom to decode the message. She grabbed her grease pencil and her volume of Lyell and set to work.

She decoded it, letter by letter, thinking more about the situation around her than the message. She ran her fingers up and down the lines of text, counting, and wrote another letter on the mirror.

The blackened walls of the gun control room and the blood on its floor tugged at her mind. Was it sabotage? Was it an accident? The only thing she did know was that she was not the cause. She thought about Dr. Pugh and his strange -- and somewhat endearing -- need for her to assist him. She thought about the captain and the hollow look in his eyes.

When she scribed the last letter onto the glass, she stepped back and read the message there. Then she reread it, her mouth agape in growing horror.

NAUGHTY ARTEMIS. STOP PLAYING SHANGHAI. FIND ORION.

Gemma had not yet informed Brightman of the incident with Humboldt. In fact, she had not intended to, after the crew's positive reaction. What good would such a report serve? How else would she find out, being so far away?

Gemma had managed to convince herself that it would be impossible to smuggle two people aboard.

But *someone* had reported back to Brightman. Only Brightman would know about the Man from Shanghai.

Someone was Watching.

CHRISTOPHE

Christophe stared into the blank page of his log and tapped the pen against the desk. The words to describe what had happened would not shake themselves loose from his stunned mind.

Thorvaldson needed more details than Rathbone's hurried missive. But how could he distill the acrid stink of smoke, the drying crimson mud on the floor, and a man's agony into something so small as words? What alchemy transformed such heavy thoughts into invisible waves that flew back to Earth? How could he say that their only defence was now useless? That they were sorely unprepared for this battle? That this great iron beast had tried to devour yet another member of his crew? That the lunar voyage had been just an appetizer for her? That this was all a big mistake?

Grateful to be alone so no one could see his trembling hands, Christophe set it down, word after word, until the page was full.

GEMMA

There is a Watcher here.

The thought nailed her to the spot. It crawled across her skin like a mass of angry spiders. Who was it? Was he -- or she -- searching for Orion as well? Or were they to ensure that she did not abandon her mission? How long did she have before they took action against her?

The brief peace that she had found on the ship was now shattered into as many jagged pieces as the console that had shredded Cervantes. A peace she didn't know she needed was gone.

When she was able to move again, her mind set to work. She was used to playing with her Watcher's identity, as a game to alleviate some of the ennui of her more humdrum assignments. But this was not going to be a game. She examined her first clue: the message itself.

On further study, she saw something that she had not noticed earlier. Part of the message, the header, did not seem quite right. She couldn't put her finger on it, but something was not the way it should be. It wasn't wrong enough that she couldn't decrypt it, of course, but something did not fit.

Perhaps the message wasn't even authentic. That would be even worse. If it were not Brightman, or her Watcher, that had sent it, then there was someone else on board who knew what she was, someone who knew Brightman's code. The extra copy of Lyell in the Cohort Conference room strengthened that possibility.

She paced her room; she was a restless tiger in a shrinking cage. The *Fury* on any other day felt like a colossal vessel, but now it shriveled about her.

Her intestines melted into jelly as realization washed over her again. Alone with her anxiety, her nerves rattled like dry leaves in a frigid winter gale. There was no one to turn to here, no Philippa, no Mrs. Brightman, even. She found herself wishing for Pritchard's deep rolling voice or Nigel's wit or Caroline's cheerfulness to distract her. But she could not let them see her fear. She could not reveal its source. She must present a placid surface to them. She must bury the maelstrom.

Authenticating the message was the only way to move forward. But how?

Crickets, she thought. *Blast Humboldt for starting all this.*

Humboldt. She remembered something Nigel had said about him earlier, something about him working with the wireless messages and the analytical engine. Would he have a full record of the message? As much as she wanted to avoid the cretin -- the only person on the ship that was possibly more boorish than the captain -- Humboldt might be her only hope.

She retraced her steps to the command deck, except this time she headed for Informatics. She wasn't sure where Humboldt would be this time of day, but Informatics was the best place to start.

Sure enough, he was there, slaving away over a cardpunch machine. There were a few other Booleans present, but Nigel and Caroline were not among them. Perhaps their shift had ended for the day. That was fine with Gemma. This would be easier without them. The fewer people that knew about her little issue, the better.

She timed her footsteps with the regular clack of his typing so that he could not hear her approach. As she moved closer, Gemma surmised that this must be his normal station, as the wall behind it fairly groaned with the CDVs of pubs that hung upon it; The Blind Beggar, The Dove, and Dirty Dick's at the top overlaid pictures of The George and The Grapes. And, of course, there was the inevitable row of Sophie the Steamfitter cards lined up below them. She patted her skirt pocket and felt the weight of the cards she had received that morning. The Falcon and the Badger and Tentacle, absent from the wall, were in her stack. She straightened her spine and took a deep breath before tapping him on the shoulder.

Humboldt yelped and nearly fell out of his seat. He cringed at the sight of her.

"Oh, it's you."

"I apologize for the intrusion, Mr. Humboldt."

He turned back to his work and started typing again. Gemma retrieved her small stack of CDVs. Her fingers brushed the edge of the burnt one as she pulled them out of her pocket. She had nearly forgotten it in the chaos of her latest message. She left it hidden and rifled through the stack to find the two pub cards.

She dangled the Badger and Tentacle in front of Humboldt's face. His fingers froze after one last agitated CLACK, and he looked up at her with suspicion dancing in his eyes.

"I believe we started off on the wrong foot, Mr. Humboldt. I've come to make amends," she said with the sweetest voice she could summon. "I've brought a peace offering for your collection."

He tapped his fingers on the edge of the keypunch and stirred in his seat.

"Are you certain, Miss Llewellyn? M'pride is still bruised." He rubbed his hip and continued with a pout, "Not to mention m'arse."

Ah, the negotiations begin, Gemma thought. *Good.*

She waved the other pub card in front of him in the most tantalizing way possible, as if she were wafting the enticing fragrance of bacon towards him.

"I'll make you a deal, Mr. Humboldt. If you keep your hands off me, I'll keep my boots off you. Agreed?"

He gave the cards a hungry look. "What else you want?"

"A favour."

She set the CDVs down on the right side of his desk and showed him the ciphertext message.

"Mr. Davies has informed me that you are archiving the wireless messages on the keypunch machine for the analytical engine."

"Yes," he replied. He lowered his voice so that the others in the room could not hear. "Actually, I'm working on a way to archive them on the keypunch as they come in, so we don't have to do it manually, and I don't get stuck with it. Don't tell the other blokes, though. If it don't work -- well, me pride has taken enough of a beating lately, you see."

"Brilliant idea, Mr. Humboldt," she replied, and if she were honest with herself, she would think that he was very clever indeed. Perhaps he wasn't as thick as she had thought. "But for now, I just need to retrieve a copy of this message, if you can find it. Can you do that for me?"

He took the paper from her hand and studied it. "It'll be hard to find."

"But not impossible?"

"Aw, no, Miss. I can try to match this string of numbers here. Just takes longer, that's all." He squinted at her. "Will this make us square, then? I'm pulling lots of extra duty here, you see. I'm missing out on all the best card games."

She produced her most beatific smile for him. "I promise, Mr. Humboldt, that I will speak to Nigel on your behalf, if you are able to find it."

"It might take some time, though, Miss L. I've got a stack of Mr. Wallace's messages to work through." He pointed to the stack of pages to his left.

"What in the world would a Cultural Officer have to report? Did we not bring enough monogrammed handkerchiefs or something?"

"Oh, you'd be surprised at how many messages he sends. They are all encoded, o'course, everyone's is, but you don't always need to know what they said. Plenty o'juicy stuff to be found anyway, if you know where to look."

"Oh, really?"

As Mrs. Brightman would have said, *Information is where you find it.*

"Honestly!" Humboldt replied.

She deliberately widened her eyes and focused all of her attention on him. It was one of her better intelligence-gathering techniques, and it defeated torture hands-down.

"It's all in the higher-level data," he continued. He pointed at the partial header in her message. "Metadata, as we call it here in Informatics. Who he sends messages to, when he sends 'em, how often, how long they are, how the message is laid out. I can tell you who's sending messages to his wife *and* to his sweetheart and when, I can. I can tell you who's reporting on a regular basis, or who is supposed to and is constantly late."

He leaned closer and whispered, "Wallace sends *loads* of messages. Mostly at night, ship's time. To lots of different people. He thinks we're just typists, but we Booleans are more than that. We recognize patterns, see? That's how we write code. We see patterns in data and tell the A.E. what to do with 'em. Don't underestimate your Booleans, Miss Llewellyn. Even without the actual text o' the message, we know things. And sometimes we can guess the rest." He tapped the side of his nose and waggled his eyebrows at her. "Everyone's got a pattern, Miss L. Everyone. If you know a body's pattern, you can read 'em like a book. And when they break that pattern, you can tell even more."

"What do you mean?"

She decided to let this little fountain of knowledge babble for as long as he wished. His talk of patterns interested her, and his description of the engine code tickled her inner computer. Mrs. Brightman was quite fortunate that more scientists could not access these machines, at least not yet; they would remove the need for her Girls.

"Like if the cipher text pattern changes," Humboldt said. "Either the sender is talking to someone new, or his code's been broken. But so far, Wallace's hasn't changed." He pushed his chair back and spread his hands as he spoke. "Just imagine, Miss L, what would happen if everyone had one of these engines! It would change everything! Even more than the Invasion changed us. Personally, I think that's why the TIA has a monopoly on their use. You have to have a license to have one, you see, not to mention a herd of Booleans to run it. They want to control how fast the world changes, methinks."

Gemma did imagine, as he carried on. A host of analytical engines would certainly put Mrs. Brightman out of business, and quickly. But she couldn't tell the Boolean that. She merely nodded with astonishment at his cleverness.

"Another obstacle is the data storage. Them cards are a right pain in the arse, having to feed 'em in every time a body wants to run a programme. If we could access our data more quickly, I doubt if even the TIA could prevent universities and banks and governments from building their own."

He adjusted his hunter green jacket and sat up straighter in his chair. He picked up the CDVs and rested them next to one of the Sophie cards.

"I'm on the job, Miss. I like the one of the Badger and Tentacle especially. M'cousin Jules runs it, you know! Them cards in particular are rare. Even I couldn't get one before we left." He smiled at her. "But I have to let you know, it'll take a while to do what you're asking. You run on and do some science or something. I'll let you know when I find anything."

"Very well. Pax?"

"Pax."

After they shook hands on it, Gemma left the chamber in a slight daze. Humboldt was not as dim as she had reckoned.

Could he be? No, surely not, she thought. If he were her Watcher, why would he agree to help her?

She could not help but feel anxious, though she did feel better for having taken some sort of action. Had she just tipped her hand to the Watcher that she was looking for him? She got a firm grip on her thoughts and decided to believe that she had just added a new ally to her growing list. The ghost of the Man from Shanghai retreated into the shadows of her memory, as he always did when she patched up an ill-conceived kick on her part.

She looked up at the clock next to the lift. It was getting late. Her belly reminded her that between decoding her message and visiting Humboldt, she had missed both tea and dinner. Even though she was tired, she knew that her unsettled mind would not allow her to sleep. She could not bear the thought of pacing in her cabin until Pugh called for her.

She touched the slip of CDV in her pocket. The corridor was empty; only the night crew was on duty by now, and most of them were on the command deck. She paused at the lift and took out the card. Looking up at her was the upper half of a portrait of Sophie the Steamfitter.

Did it belong to one of the gun crew? Or perhaps to Cervantes himself? Or did someone else leave it behind? Perhaps it slipped out of a pocket whilst the panel was open? It was difficult to tell by the card. Sophie cards were ubiquitous on the *Fury*. Except for the burn and tear across the bottom, there was nothing unique about this one. She considered showing it to Dr. Pugh, but she didn't feel ready to do that just yet.

She took the lift to the laboratory deck. She would take advantage of ship's night and search once more for the Orion file, as her mistress demanded. She walked by the open door of the laboratory and saw

Bidarhalli's back blocking one of his panels, the one with the ridiculous equations that never changed.

They reminded her of her brief time in a Belgian laboratory. In her guise as "Claire Bisette", she had deliberately miscalculated entries in a ballistics chart. She had not lied when she had told Pugh that Brightman was not in the habit of destroying technology; but even her mistress broke habits every now and then. Not stealing the data had been a strange sensation for her, and only her gratitude to Mrs. Brightman had assuaged her smarting pride as she had typed the mistakes whilst the true numbers danced behind her eyes. It had been a delicate business, mucking the figures up just enough to skew the researcher's results but not enough to be immediately obvious. She had been overjoyed to leave that mysterious job behind her. Filching a formula was not a problem, as it also sated her own inquisitiveness, but deliberate errors went against her grain.

Bidarhalli studied a piece of paper, followed the lines of the equation with his grease pencil with an absentminded hum, and then wrote a character in the column to the right of the equations. It was so quiet that she could hear the pencil squeaking against the glass.

So, she was not the only one that had discovered the trick to safer decoding. She held her breath, prayed that the man would not hear her, and squinted at the distant panel. It was no good; the plaintext was in Hindi. Gemma knew many languages, but Hindi was not among them.

She took the lift to another deck and paced the corridor. In the quiet of ship's night, she could hear the voice of the *Fury*. A steady background drone hummed like a busy washerwoman, punctuated by skittering and scrabbling from the vents that was faint enough to hide behind the busy noises of ship's day. She wondered if she were hearing some of Humboldt's algorithmic bugs in the air ducts.

She paced for what seemed like hours, and still her mind refused to settle. Could Bidarhalli have sent that mysterious message on the first day? Or did he use encoded messages as a matter of course, like most of the Cohort? If so, why decode it when everyone else was off duty, if the plaintext was not readable to anyone but him? Could he be her Watcher?

Her heart raced like a wild horse with no rider to restrain it. She wanted nothing more than to run, but there was nowhere to go. She stood still and pulled the reins on her breathing to get it back under control. The ship seemed so cramped and close. If only she could take a turn outside ... it had been so long since she had seen the sun... other than the one in the orrery... Nigel's little garden...

She remembered the Gardens as suddenly as she had remembered Humboldt earlier. Why not? She did not know if they were locked down at night, but she had plenty of time on her hands to find out. A little time in the green might settle her mind, though she could not imagine ever sleeping again.

Soon she found herself in front of one of the Garden doors; there were four, according to the schematics, on various sides of the chamber. There was a slight hiss as the door released, and she could feel moisture stealing out of the opening.

A bill next to the door sported a flirty Sophie the Steamfitter outfitted with a speech bubble and little else, admonishing the reader to "KEEP DOOR CLOSED TO KEEP MOISTURE AND PESTS WHERE THEY BELONG". So, this must be the place from whence Humboldt's bug had escaped, only to be crushed in the gears of the A.E.

Despite her fretfulness, she did manage to smirk at the "Hats Required" sign next to the bill as she passed through the door. There were a few caps and hats on pegs, along with a gaudy straw hat for the ladies, covered in horrid faux cabbage roses and a wide mauve ribbon. A matching parasol hung next to it. Gemma left them untouched. Surely, the very proper Cultural Officer was abed at this hour, and such niceties could be set aside. Unless, as Humboldt had indicated, he was busy composing wireless messages. Instead, she released her hair from its braid. She shook it loose and let it hang free.

She stepped through the lock and inhaled the humid air, refreshingly wet after the arid corridor. After she secured the door, she was left in darkness, with only a series of what appeared to be streetlamps illuminating a brick path ahead. Apparently, the Gardens followed the ship's clock and let the trees sleep. The sudden nightfall startled her a little, after her near-continuous time under harsh lights.

She meandered along the path, breathing in the smell of earthly things, things that she didn't know she missed. Here was the perfume of roses, and there the scent of turned soil. She smelt water, running water, here in the depths of space! She thought she heard the gurgling of a current over stones in the distance. It felt luxuriant, almost sinful, to just walk and take it all in. No secret signals to watch for, no messages to pry out of hidden places, no bullets to dodge. There was no Man from Shanghai to haunt her footsteps here, as he did far too often these days. Just one foot in front of another. How long had it been since she could do that? Just walk?

She ran her hands through her loose hair, enjoying the privacy of the late-night path. The crew's night shift was much smaller than the day shift, and most of them were on the bridge or the Oberth deck. She was certain she would have as much time alone here as she wanted. She just hoped that the Watcher, whoever that happened to be, hadn't followed her.

The sound of water faded a little as she passed through an iron gate between two tall maple trees. The light of the nearby lamp glinted off the feathers of a brass eagle perched on one of the posts.

The path turned and moved farther away from the rippling of water. In its place was a new sound: raucous laughter. Someone was having a grand old time here. She sniffed in irritation, disappointed by the interruption. She turned to work her way back to the corridor when she thought she detected a familiar tone in his merriment. Curiosity got the better of her, and she continued in her original direction. Soon she caught sight of a gazebo on a small hill, and she made her way towards it. The lights grew brighter and more numerous as she closed in on it. The juniper trees that lined the path dripped with tiny flecks of illumination, like nests of fairies.

Someone was sitting on one of the benches with his back to her. A tall man in a sleeveless undershirt lounged next to his navy blue jacket, draped across the gazebo's railing. All was quiet for a moment, and then she heard the rasp of a page turning, then another far more quickly than she would have guessed. He chuckled for a moment, and then he threw his head back in a full rolling howl. The laughter was contagious, and she found herself smiling at it in spite of herself. She took a step back and turned to leave him alone, but one of his hoots pulled his head in her direction. He must have caught her out of the corner of his eye. It was the captain! Of all people!

"Oh, hullo, Miss Llewellyn," he said as he wiped a joyous tear from his cheek. He chuckled again, only slightly embarrassed, and gestured for her to come closer. "Glad to see someone else enjoying the night air."

"I beg your pardon," she replied. "I did not mean to disturb you. I thought--"

"It's quite all right, Miss. Please, join me." He pointed to the bench on the other side of the gazebo door. "I assure you, I won't bite. Company would not be amiss right now."

Her hand wandered to her cheek, and she fretted about the disheveled state of her hair, more for the sake of a mentor leagues upon leagues away than the sake of the man before her. It felt most unladylike, and she could hear Mrs. Brightman's chiding in the back of her mind. Then she noticed his bare feet, with his long toes wiggling in the freedom of the cool air. His boots and socks lay askew beside him on the bench, just underneath his jacket. She decided that her hair matched the situation perfectly and let it alone.

He held the book out to her. "Ever read any Twain?"

Here he was, the one she was supposed to observe, asking her to sit with him. It wasn't supposed to be this easy. At the same time, she knew that people showed more of their true selves in the quiet of the night. She walked up the stairs with her skirt slightly lifted to avoid tripping on the hem and sat down on the bench opposite him.

She observed him for a moment before answering. He held a hairy fruit in his other hand. A few bites were missing from it, showing green flesh flecked with tiny black seeds. As he moved, she could see the dark outline of a tattoo on his right arm. The limbs of an inky Martian flashed in and out of view as the captain turned and settled himself into a more comfortable position.

"I can't say that I have, Captain."

"Oh, please, there is no one else here. I insist that no one stand on ceremony after midnight. Especially while I'm reading Mr. Twain here. Call me Christophe."

She hesitated. *Just us chickens*, Nigel had said earlier. It wasn't just the Booleans that were tired of all the Mr. Wallaces of the world. She flashed a coy smile at him.

"Christophe, then."

"At least while we're here, in the gazebo. Outside the Gardens, I still have to be Captain, you know." He stuck his thumbs underneath the narrow straps of his undershirt, and his face melted into a frumpy expression. "Must keep up the show for the crew."

She raised an eyebrow at that. This was not the person that she had expected to find, not at all.

"Tell me, Miss Llewellyn, how is it that an educated lady such as yourself has not had time to enjoy *Following the Equator*? I find Mr. Twain's humour quite refreshing." He took a bite out of the fruit in his hand, sucking in his breath a little to keep the juice from dribbling onto his thin shirt.

She took a deep breath before answering. His eyes were so bright in the gazebo's light. The boorish captain had been left at the door; here before her was a jovial lad that she had never seen before.

"My expeditions do not usually leave time for leisure."

"How sad! I think if we all had a daily dose of him, we'd all be more relaxed. I find that we're a bit stuffy here on the *Fury*."

"Oh, my, what would Mr. Wallace say to that?" she replied with a chortle that wasn't entirely false.

It was part of her role to titter at jokes, no matter how banal they were. She had not had an honest laugh in so long that it fell onto her mind like a rain shower in a parched valley. It seemed that Mr. Twain was contagious. She could not help but notice that Christophe had a wide and generous mouth. His smile occupied half the acreage of his elastic face.

When the moment had passed, she asked, "Might I inquire after Mr. Cervantes? I haven't heard any updates. I understand that his injuries are rather severe."

He slumped his long frame forward, a little deflated, the spell of laughter shattered.

"Not good," he said, more soberly than before. "He's resting now, under sedation. Dr. Hansard didn't want me hovering over him as he worked. He couldn't -- or wouldn't -- give me a prognosis, but I'm certain that his situation is rather dire. The doctor ordered me to get some rest, but I am far too restless for sleep."

"I know the feeling," Gemma replied. "I apologize. I did not mean to bring you down."

She could see more of the tattoo now, as he hunched over in silent remembrance. Two of the Martian's tentacles intertwined above its head in the shape of a heart, and the name "Maggie" emerged into the space between.

"We were raised together, you know," he said. She returned her gaze to his face as he spoke, hoping he would continue volunteering information. "Miguel lost his family in the Invasion. Pugh caught him picking his coat pocket in Madrid. We were both just boys, then. I asked Pugh if we could keep him. I wanted a brother more than I wanted anything else. He was so raggedy and hungry, like a Spanish Oliver Twist, that even a cranky old scientist couldn't say 'no'. He didn't even remember his surname, so I gave him one."

"You named him? You named him Miguel *Cervantes*?"

"Yes! I was very fond of *Don Quixote*. And, as it turns out, he's a better sailor than I am." He paused and considered her as he took another bite of the fruit. He flicked a bit of the juice from the edge of his mouth and swallowed before speaking again. "Were you orphaned in the Invasion, Miss Llewellyn?" he asked gently. He hesitated when he saw the slight scowl on her face. "I'm sorry, perhaps that was a bit too forward." He waved the words away. "Forget I asked. Tell you what, then. Ask a question of me, to make us square."

"Just one."

"Yes?"

"What is that hairy little fruit you are eating? I have never seen its like."

"Ah," he said, looking at the object in question. "This is a kiwi, from New Zealand. Lovely country, wonderful people. And the food! Oh, such food you have never seen. I loved this particular fruit so much that Pugh suggested I name my ship after it."

He popped the last bite of the kiwi into his mouth and chewed it with a thoughtful look on his face.

"Your ship?"

"Oh, I've been on several, in my time. This being the first *space* ship, ever, they had to train me on what they had available." He ran the fingers of his now kiwi-less hand through his hair and down to his neck, which he scratched languorously. "Tall ships. Small ships. Steamers. Airships. Anything they could get their hands on. Even a submarine! But there was one little boat that was all mine. The *Kiwi Clipper*. Oh, a lovelier sea bird you've never seen, all teak and hemp and sail, with the most beautiful mermaid on the figurehead, you could see her--"

He stopped for a moment, realizing that his hands were tracing curves in the air. He dropped his hands to his knees. "Well, she was very pretty.

Cervantes served with me on most of those ships, including the *Kiwi*."

His voice drifted off. Christophe licked his lips and absently wiped his other hand on his trousers. "I think when I return to Earth, I will retire to the sea. And you, what would you like to do once this mission is over? Is there anywhere you'd like to call home?"

Gemma averted her gaze to the path leading away from the other side of the gazebo. A few trees were visible in the chandelier's light and in the sparkling cords of lights wound through the trees, but soon everything faded into the darkness of the chamber. She did not know how to answer. She had never thought about what was next. No one had ever asked her what she wanted, until now. She simply moved from job to job, mission to mission, always the errand-runner for others and never for herself, with occasional breathers in the College's dormitory in Guildford. She sat in stunned silence. She listened to the rustling of the trees and the distant croak of a frog. She heard a plop afterward, as if the frog had decided it was time for a swim.

If her face became well known after this journey, would she still have a place as one of Brightman's computers? Or would an Earth-bound scientist recognize her from a previous mission? It had not occurred to her that she might be difficult to place upon her return.

After a long moment, she uttered one of the most truthful sentences of her life: "I don't know."

"Oh, I'm sure you'll be busy with the Mars findings for years and years after our return. Lectures and papers and symposia and all that, you know. You'll be famous!" He chuckled again. "I highly recommend a lecture tour in New Zealand. The rocks near Christchurch are quite lovely, I hear."

He rambled on. The sound of his voice painted colorful pictures in her mind that distracted her from her present danger. The *Aurora Australis* hovered in her mind's eye as he described it, a curtain of eerie light casting a veil over the night sky. His hands carved the air as he told tales of the Turquoise Sea, off the coast of Italy, where the water was so clear that ships seemed to float on air. The sunlight sparkled on the waves like diamonds scattered by the hand of Neptune himself.

"And watching the full moon rise upon the water!" Christophe exclaimed. "It is so very big, so very, very big, enormous! Like nothing you've ever seen. I watched it rise every time I had a chance, knowing that someday I'd be sailing there. I -- I didn't know -- I never knew how big it really was until I got there."

He rested his hands on his knees and stared down at them. She knew he was thinking of that ill-fated maiden voyage. He finally spoke again. "And now I'm taking us to Mars."

She found that just watching and listening answered more questions than she could have asked. He took his duties seriously, but he seemed to crave kiwis and salt water more than power. His worry over Cervantes and his feeling of responsibility tempered his arrogance. That cockiness merely concealed the sailor that lingered deep in his heart, the one that liked the feel of his toes around the rough rigging of sails.

Would he hold up under the pressure? Or would he waver?

He had trained all his life for this mission, he told her. She realized, in a way, so had she. She had been taught to hate the Martians, so carefully, carefully taught. She had learned to grasp science, even if she did not have a full appreciation of it. She had been taught to observe, to analyze, and to evaluate; but she had not been allowed to conclude. All of that was coming to the fore on this journey, as Pugh sought her opinions in a way no one ever had.

They had something in common, after all.

Christophe stretched and yawned. His toes wiggled and clenched. With his arms above his head and his legs extended halfway across the gazebo, he seemed twice as tall as usual. He pulled himself back in and retrieved a wayward sock.

"Well, Miss Llewellyn, we both have duties in the morning. I appreciate your listening to my ramblings. I do believe I can follow Dr. Hansard's orders now. I think the same prescription would apply to you."

Gemma stood up, feeling lighter than she had in a while. "I believe you are correct."

She turned, shuffling her feet a little on the boards of the gazebo, unsure of which path to take.

"Oh, sorry," he said as he pulled on his jacket. He pointed to his left. "The fastest route to Ladies' Country is that way. My quarters are in that direction." He pointed to the opposite path. "Would you care for an escort?"

She smiled and shook her head. She had made some headway in gaining information on him, and she felt much better, but she didn't need to give him any improper ideas.

"I think I can find my way. Sleep well, Christophe."

Gemma turned and made her way down the stairs. She could feel his eyes on her back as she strode away.

"Good night, Miss Llewellyn," he called after her.

She turned back and watched him button his coat for a moment. Then she said, "It's Gemma. Just Gemma. And good night."

CHRISTOPHE

Christophe settled into a chair next to Cervantes' cot and shuffled · typewritten pages in his hands.

"Time for our staff meeting, Mr. Cervantes. I have to catch you up on the news so you won't be behind when you get back to work."

Cervantes, thickly bandaged and pumped full of Dr. Hansard's most powerful sedatives, lay still and sleeping as Christophe's words spilled over him.

"Mr. Pritchard is helping out whilst you are under the weather," Christophe continued. "You've taught him well! The Oberths are running smoothly, and the navigational shields are keeping the growlers out of the way. I know how you worry about that. One less thing to fret about whilst you recover.

"You would have enjoyed tea yesterday, old sport. Frau Knopf made flan with that recipe you found. Mr. Holomek was especially fond of it. Once you're up and about, we'll ask her to make it again." He flipped to the next page. "Oh, and a baby goat was born this morning on the stable deck."

He waited a moment, listening to his first mate's slow and laboured breathing, looking for any sign of movement. When he saw none, he cleared his throat and adjusted the cloth-covered privacy wall behind him.

"There is some news from back home, as well. In Paris, they're protesting at the local Ministry of Culture. Some nonsense about dress patterns. Some corset-burning going on down on Rue de Passy. What a sight that must be! The Rational Dress Society is behind that one, I'll wager."

Christophe looked up from the paper. Had Miguel stirred? He waited for a few heartbeats to see, but the injured man did not budge.

"Admiral Thorvaldson has wired more serious news. He sends his regards to you, by the way, and wishes you a speedy recovery. The next captain in the fleet needs to be in top shape!"

Christophe's forced cheerfulness tasted sour in his mouth, but he pressed on.

"The Tsar and the Kaiser have put their heads together -- they're cousins, you know -- and are registering a joint protest against the TIA. They want the Science Division to release their research on Martian technology to the general public. Apparently, they are a bit chagrined that the French got to keep what they salvaged. The Alliance is pushing back, though. They've bottled up both straits around the Sea of Marmara -- remember those beautiful beaches on Gallipoli? -- and only TIA-owned ships make it through. Shipping is piling up in the Black Sea *and* the Aegean. I don't have your head for politics. I have no idea how that one's going to end up. But that needn't concern us now. There's nothing we can do from here, anyway. So long as the crew doesn't take sides, we should be fine."

Dr. Hansard appeared at the foot of the bed with an orderly, who was bearing a tray laden with fresh bandages and a syringe.

"Begging your pardon, Captain," he said. "Time for his next treatment. We need a little space."

"Of course. Please keep me informed." Christophe unfolded himself from the chair and tucked the sheaf of papers beneath his arm. He leaned down and whispered to Cervantes, "And Maggie sends her love, as always."

GEMMA

Over the next week, Gemma saw very little of Dr. Pugh. The morning after her late conversation with Christophe, she had slept right through the morning duty alarm. She had skipped breakfast and made straight for Pugh's office, only to find the door locked.

"In a meeting, Llewellyn," he had called through the door. "I'm afraid we'll be in here for some time. You'll find your notes in your laboratory workspace. I'll call should I need you."

When she had tried to ask a question, the only answer she received was a dismissive "Good day!"

She received the same "Good day!" for the next few mornings, until she decided to wait for his call, after all.

Every night, visions of Aronnax's giant squid haunted her little patches of sleep. One night, after discovering the armoire door had been left unlatched in another of Frau Knopf's mystery inspections, she had dreamed that it danced round her room and poked its tentacles into Old Dependable. Another night it rifled through her volume of Lyell. She blamed it on the captain's tattoo.

The early morning solar flare drill a few days later did not help, either. At least this time she was in Ladies' Country, and she only had to share the space with Caroline. Frau Knopf and her assistants were already on breakfast duty in the galleys. Gemma took advantage of the quiet moment to inquire about the Lister's Towels in the storage cabinet.

"Aw, them's just for redundancy," Caroline explained. "This is what you want." She bent down and retrieved one of the smaller boxes on a low shelf. Handing it to Gemma, she said, "This is brand new! Well, the idea's been around for a while, but Frau Knopf redesigned it so it really works. I think she's applied for a patent, actually."

"What is it?"

"A cup. Takes care of your ladies' days needs with less than half the trouble of those Lister things. Reusable, even. It'll work for years if you treat it right, but we brought four for each of us girls, just in case. Less to bring, nothing to throw away. You know, it's another reason why they didn't want us on the ship. I reckon the Quartermaster thought we'd have a cargo bay full of them towels!" She snorted. "But Frau Knopf wasn't having none of that. She said it was downright silly to let something natural get in the way of us going to space." She pointed to the box. "There's a tract inside that tells you all about it."

"Impressive," Gemma said as she scanned the discreet label on the side of the box. "Perhaps we'll see them at Selfridge's someday, and Frau Knopf will join the ranks of the wealthy."

"Under the counter, most like, but yeah. But now they'll have to think of some other excuse to keep us Earthbound."

Pritchard's voice crackled over the speaking tube to check in on them, and the blue alert light above the latched door faded.

"C'mon," said Caroline, "let's take this box to your cabin and go have some chips and eggs. We have a little time before my shift begins."

Breakfast with the Booleans, and Mr. Pritchard more often than not, was a welcome respite, although the daily Wireless News did little for her appetite. The steel worker strikes continued back on Earth, and the Socialists were calling for a general strike. The Kaiser had renewed his annual demands for access to the TIA's Martian research, this time with the backing of the Tsar. Chips and eggs were served with a side of tension as the crew debated the news, although the French and German sailors had made a pact to leave the matter of Alsace and Lorraine up to their respective governments, for now.

That Saturday came and went, and the Knitting Circle of Doom was cancelled by Frau Knopf, as she was assisting in the care of Cervantes.

During the day, having no other work to do, she reviewed the journals Pugh had given her. She finished Aronnax's in due course, and she felt a delicious frisson of sympathetic terror as he described the frightful last moments of the *Nautilus* in the famous maelstrom near the coast of Norway. It was even more thrilling to read it in the original author's spidery handwriting. 1868 had not been a good year for old Nemo.

For as little as she saw Dr. Pugh, she saw Christophe enough to make up the difference. He was always late for tea, as he spent much of his off-duty time at his first mate's bedside; but when he did arrive, he sought her out. One day, he handed her his copy of *Following the Equator*. He had read the rest of it to the sleeping Cervantes and decided that she could use some light reading.

Every day, once tea was over, Christophe would find some excuse to walk in whatever direction she happened to go, which was usually the

Gardens. He kept trying to take a turn with her along those winding paths, to point out the patches of growing beans and chives. She allowed it, as it was part of her mission. In fact, Brightman's messages demanded more and more detail about the man, his attributes, and his habits. However, there was nothing more exciting to report than that he had a keen fascination with Mark Twain, hairy green fruit, his sailing vessel, and his injured first mate. There was nothing worth the electricity it would take to transmit it back, yet she encoded it anyway.

Moreau never mentioned the name that lurked upon his arm, and she dropped that particular detail from her reports. She did not know if the captain had a woman, and she did not care, except for the fact that Maggie might tie in to whatever Orion was. Gemma was a computer at heart, and she needed data to do her work. She only had tiny pieces, and not nearly enough to churn out any sort of solution. Leads were few, but she had time. She waited. She would report the name when she had something to report.

More often than not, their promenade did not get as far as the central gazebo before someone came to fetch him, usually in Dr. Pugh's name. She would finish her stroll alone along paths lined with angelica, savory, and lemon verbena. She knew of a botanist or two that would have sold their mother's eyeteeth to trade places with Herr Knopf. He waddled through every so often, loaded down with baskets of orange and lemon peels from the galleys. Their entire conversation consisted of nods and grunts as he passed by before disappearing behind a triple-locked door on the side of the Gardens, tucked away behind blackberry briars.

One day she came upon Caroline, looking forlorn amongst the cabbages. She gripped a notebook -- similar to one of Pugh's except considerably more rumpled -- to her chest and greeted Gemma with a glum expression.

"It was here. I know it!" Caroline said.

"What was here?"

Caroline stepped over some crushed cabbage heads and stopped next to Gemma. The Boolean leaned in close and whispered, "The ghost."

"Pardon?"

"Oh, haven't you heard? The *Fury* is haunted."

"You don't say," replied Gemma. She swallowed the laugh that threatened to burst forth and nearly hiccoughed from the strain. "Is that what the notebook is for?"

"Yes! Ask anybody. We've heard it creepin' through the halls at night. Sometimes I can hear people walking in the corridors, sometimes right next to me, but there ain't nothing there!" She shoved the book into Gemma's hands. "This is for the Psychical Society. I told them about the ghosts, when we were ramping up for this mission, and they asked me to take notes for 'em. They might let me publish a paper. I might even get a photograph or two, if I can use the Cohort's camera."

Gemma paged through the handwritten notes and scanned a few, more out of politeness than actual curiosity. "Camera?" she asked.

"They've got one for the telescope. It can take normal pictures, too. It doesn't need flash powder, so maybe it won't scare the ghost."

The wreck of the heat ray flared across Gemma's mind. Pugh had asked about a camera. She wondered if they had found any flash powder in the debris, or if he had remembered this little fact about the Cohort's own camera. At this rate, Caroline knew more about Gemma's department than she did.

"Whose ghost, do you think?" Gemma asked, hoping for more unexpected news.

"Some of the others thinks it's the ones what died on the lunar voyage."

"You don't agree?"

"No, no. And here's why. I heard it on the trip out, *before* the flare. Whatever it is, it's been in the ship since she launched the first time."

"Don't you mean, *on* the ship?"

"Nah. *In.*"

"And you aren't afraid of it?"

"Not as much as I am of the Martians." As she took the book back from Gemma, she added, "Oh, don't be afraid, love. It just walks round the ship. This ghost ain't hurt nothin' nor nobody, except for smashing some vegetation in the Gardens from time to time." She jerked her thumb in the direction of the ruined cabbages.

"You sure it's not just the goats from the stable deck?"

"I checked. They've not been up here since day before yesterday. And the cabbages were fine when I took my walk yesterday."

"Ever thought of going into real science? You have a keen eye for observation."

"It is real science!" she protested. Then her face fell. "It's also the only thing I could get. Being a girl and all."

Gemma nodded, as it was a tale she had heard before, another stanza of Brightman's song. She took Caroline's elbow and steered the despondent Boolean along the path towards the more relaxing air near the chamomile patch.

"Is Informatics considered a science?" Gemma asked.

"More like a trade, the way we do it. I want to do research. Find stuff out. Like you do."

"Well, then, I would be interested in reading your paper when you're finished."

* * *

It wasn't just tea and walks with Christophe. In fact, sometimes Gemma wondered if there was more than one of him, he turned up so often. He had visited the laboratory a few times while she was reading the Aronnax journal. Most officers visiting the lab finished their business quickly, but Christophe poked, prodded, and sniffed everything that the scientists would let him, along with a few things that made them squawk. He keypunched cards with restless energy, fiddled with the pneumatics settings, and flipped through every book he could get his hands on. He checked in with Hui, who was surrounded by a mountain of wireless messages and the guts of some sort of cannon. He discussed the G-bombs with Stanislav and Shaw. He even got a word or two in with the taciturn Berndsen, who rarely looked up from his microscope.

As a computer, Gemma had spent many hours churning out numbers in cramped warrens stuffed behind laboratories. In the past, she had transmitted the formulas and the steps for calculating them, the computing plans, back to the College, using whatever means might be at hand, even carrier pigeon once upon a time. Most of the time it was tedious, dull work; on one mission she had computed cube roots until spots danced before her eyes, but at least it had been useful. She felt useless now, just reading, though Pugh had tried to convince her that reading was a significant part of scientific research.

This far in, she could tell that her "pet project" had nothing to do with the elusive Orion. Now she had little hope of reading the one document she had seen in Dr. Pugh's office, though she had wired back an encrypted message indicating she had seen the name there. She even included a helpful tidbit about Frau Knopf's miraculous invention, which she had the opportunity to use in the meanwhile; it would make field work far more comfortable for the other Girls. She hoped that those breadcrumbs of news would buy her a little time. She cursed herself for not taking a closer look while she had had the chance.

The more she searched, the more she was convinced that Orion had nothing to do with the ship itself. The research that Brightman had collected over the past few years indicated that the Terran governments were interested in weapons they could use on Earth. Caroline had been in earnest when she had asked Gemma about the Black Smoke research. Philippa had been involved in the propagation calculations for that very study at the ACS. Her results, furtively whispered in the darkness of their room, had made Gemma's skin crawl.

Perhaps Orion had something to do with the heat ray? Though goodness knew there were plenty of ways to capture that data on Earth, if one knew where to look. Anna, another Brightman Girl whose skills lay in directions other than mathematics, had been embedded as a French minister's mistress for several years. She had provided enough intelligence on that nation's heat ray designs that Brightman could build one of her own, if she so desired. By the same token, the Cohort's pestilential G-bombs were hardly a secret. Their mechanisms were fairly conventional, and the diseases they carried were not exactly exotic.

Gemma reported back any breadcrumb that she could find, from details of the Oberths to the workings of the A.E. to the idiosyncrasies of the Cohort members (Bidarhalli would only use blue grease pencils, the linguist loathed strawberry jam), in case any of it led Brightman to clarify her orders. In return, she merely received instructions to spend more time with the captain.

Moreau made that part frustratingly easy. The captain's antics were the only thing distracting her from the tedium of reading and the anxiety of searching for the ill-defined Orion. He was like a very tall, very determined cat that demanded attention whenever she started working.

After her talk with Caroline, Gemma decided to visit Alfieri and his telescope (and his telescope's camera). He greeted her warmly and spent the afternoon showing her the massive device and the points of light in its viewing field.

"How is it that you are such an expert on solar flares?" she asked.

"Oh, I had the good fortune of attending some of the lectures of the British Astronomical Association. Met one of the founders there, one Elizabeth Brown. Quite the solar observer!"

"I thought women weren't in the societies." It had been a particular sore point with Mrs. Brightman.

"Well, there aren't any in the actual Royal Society, unfortunately. Quite a loss! I picked up most of my solar lore from her. She made sure ladies were part of the BAA from the beginning." He pointed the telescope to another area of the sky and motioned for her to look into the eyepiece. "There are other routes to science besides the Royal Society, if one knows where to look. And, I hope, as we progress, even that will change. Wisdom is where you find it."

She could almost hear the stars whispering to her as she peered into the eyepiece, reminding her of what had brought her to the observatory.

"Can you photograph what you see?" she asked.

"Certainly. We have a camera that mounts upon the eyepiece. I expect we'll be taking quite a few as we get closer to Mars."

"Is it easy to use?"

"Oh, anyone could use it after a few minutes' worth of instruction. I could show you how, if you like."

A few minutes later, after very little effort, said camera was mounted on the telescope. The mechanism was simple to use, and the camera was lighter than she had expected.

"Is it very portable?"

"It's designed to be. We can use it to record a variety of scientific phenomena, not just with the telescope. It's available to anyone who wishes to use it. I think your friend Yeoman McLure has even put in a request for it."

"So not just the Cohort?"

"Various departments have used it since we left. Herr Knopf borrows it from time to time to record plant growth in the Gardens. Wallace likes photos of the crew in action. That sort of thing. We have plenty of film, and the development lab is just over there." He pointed to a door on the far side of the observatory. "Just don't open the door when the *Occupied* sign is up."

"Of course," she replied, keeping her buzzing thoughts to herself. Should she remind Dr. Pugh of this, for his investigation? "Don't want to let the light in."

"Funny thing, light. Remember as you observe, we see the light of the past," Alfieri said.

"The past?"

"Yes. It takes light time to get to us. Even at the incredible speed it travels, it takes time to move across space. For example, if you look at Mars from Earth, you see the Mars of several minutes ago, not the Mars of that very instant. We see Mars in the past, even if just the very recent past."

"If we went far enough away from Earth -- and had a powerful enough telescope -- could we watch the Invasion happen? Or see the world before the Invasion?" she asked. But her real question, a question she never would have dared ask in earshot of Mrs. Brightman, a question she would not have dared think of before this voyage, was "*Could I see my parents?*"

"Yes," he replied with a sage nod, seeming to hear even the unspoken question. "We couldn't affect that past, but we could witness it. And it might affect us."

"Affect us? How?"

"Only in a reactionary sense. What if we witnessed events that heretofore we had only heard about? What if we saw a completely different version than the tale we had been told? The way we react to the past often influences our present. And our future."

"As we get closer to Mars," Gemma said, "I suppose we have less and less time between the present we bring with us and the past that we see. What happens when the two collide?"

"I suppose we'll find out together, my child."

Days blurred together. Breakfast presented her with the trading of CDVs and updates on Nigel's impending fatherhood. Then it was reading and still more reading, with no Dr. Pugh and no news of his investigation, even after she had left him a note about the camera beneath his door.

Humboldt managed to find her every day as she walked from the mess hall to the laboratory to report that he had still not found the original version of her message. He searched at every spare moment, even though his "extra duties" had ended two days after Gemma had had a word with Nigel.

In the meantime, she cringed every time Rathbone handed her a new message. She was amazed at how many ways one could say "*get on with it*". It no longer amazed her that Brightman had not sent any gear along. Of course she hadn't. It was an excuse for Pugh to find her something else to do.

She dreaded ship's night. The squid refused to leave her dreams alone. One night it curled up on the other bed in her stateroom with Christophe, who was reading the Aronnax journal to it. Yet another night, it waltzed with the Man from Shanghai.

One night her mind simply refused to rest. She slipped into the carpeted corridor outside her cabin and paced along the wall sconces; the ever-present scratching sounds in the wall seemed especially loud in the hush of ship's night. When she approached a turn, she heard a soft whisper.

Years of training pressed her against the wall. As silently as she could, she slid down into a crouch and peered around the corner. Expecting to find some male intruder, she instead saw Caroline, who was whispering into an air vent and scribbling in her notebook. Gemma retreated to her stateroom and allowed the Yeoman to do her ghostly research in peace.

She was not the only one under strain. Hui looked tousled and weary as he slaved over the cannon he was building. Nigel's nerves were stretched to the limit as the time of his wife's delivery approached, and he distracted himself with long nights in the orrery. When she saw Christophe, the shine in his eyes was still there, albeit accompanied by ever-deepening lines around his eyelids. She suspected that he was spending more nights in sick bay than he was in his own cabin.

Everyone was on edge since the heat ray incident. No one had mentioned "sabotage" officially, but it was still widely whispered in the mess hall. The theories ran the usual gamut, from the ridiculous to the sublime, of what would happen next. They grew wilder as the number on the "Days Til Braking Day" banner grew ever smaller.

Cervantes seemed to be the only one on the ship getting any real sleep.

The following Friday, thirteen days until Braking Day, she was re-reading parts of the Aronnax journal, wondering what in the world Pugh could be thinking in assigning her such a task, when she could have been assisting in his investigation.

Agitated, she flipped to the back of the journal and read the last page. She found some handwritten notes on the inside of its back flap. It contained a list of names in various scripts, a "COMPUTER ROSTER" for the Aronnax Laboratory, E. Pugh assisting, dated two years prior to the Invasion. Out of curiosity, Gemma skimmed the names on the list and stopped at a very familiar name: "PEARL ADDISON".

She brushed the tip of a finger across the name. She knew that script almost better than her own; "Pearl Addison" was one of Mrs. Brightman's favourite aliases, from her days before the Invasion. Her pulse raced. Dr. Pugh had all but admitted that he had a connection with Mrs. Brightman, and here it was, inscribed in fading ink. Mrs. Brightman rarely talked of her days before the School. Was this the "discrepancy" that Dr. Pugh had asked her to find?

She looked up, halfway anticipating that the captain would stride through the door at any moment. He had been curiously absent that day. She glanced around the lab at the other scientists. Hui measured and calibrated away in his own little world. Bidarhalli muttered to himself in his own language. She could hear the faint bickering of the Germ Sciences team in the next room.

She checked the clock above the door. It was far past the time for his usual check-in with the Cohort. She tapped the tip of her pencil against the lab desk, lost in thought, until she saw Berndsen glowering at her. She held the pencil still, and he returned to his microscope.

She flicked her eyes to the door. No captain. The change in pattern -- as Humboldt would have remarked -- was disturbing. Before she knew it, she was walking towards the corridor. She had half a mind to search for him and half a mind to call herself an idiot for doing so.

At the door, she met none other than Dr. Pugh, who looked considerably more rumpled than usual.

"Ah, Gemma, just the person I was looking for." His voice was heavy with weariness. "Come with me, please. I need you."

"Dr. Pugh, I--"

He loped away toward the lift and gestured at her over his shoulder to follow.

"No time, no time," he said. "We have to go now. We're needed. The captain needs us."

Father Alfieri met them as they entered sick bay. The place smelt as strongly of antiseptic as Gun Control had smelt of blood and smoke. It was not as large as she had anticipated. There were only ten beds, two of which were occupied by victims of more pedestrian accidents. A group of men spilled out from behind a privacy screen. She recognized the ship's surgeon, now dressed in a white version of the ship's uniform, and a few other officers. The top of Christophe's head stuck out just above the top of the screen, and she caught a few glimpses of him as he chopped at the air with his fists. His hair was tousled, and his normally starched uniform dripped wrinkles. He lobbed harsh words at the other men as her group approached.

"Dr. Hansard, I cannot possibly allow you to do this!" The desperation in his voice was even louder than his words.

The surgeon, clutching an unlabeled bottle, replied, "I don't want to do this either, Captain, but my orders for this kind of situation are quite clear. With these injuries, we cannot hope that Cervantes will see Earth again, even if we make it back. Neither will he die right away. He will linger for weeks, Captain. Weeks. And he will be in agony the entire time."

Mr. Wallace took up the thread when the doctor had finished. "The TIA has given you special dispensation in these cases, Captain. I've reviewed the protocols, and they certainly apply here. His burns are deep, so deep that his body cannot repair the damage, and neither can we. Please, in the name of mercy, Captain." He turned to see the approaching priest. "Ah, Father Alfieri." He noticed Gemma standing next to Pugh. The Cultural Officer stepped in front of the bed, shielding Cervantes from her view. "Why did you bring this young lady? She does not need to see this!"

"I requested her," interjected Dr. Pugh. "Miss Llewellyn is now my assistant, and I need her."

Behind Wallace was Frau Knopf, by the head of the bed, glowering at the rest of them. Gemma could feel Christophe's gaze on her as Dr. Pugh leaned down to speak, but the captain did not stop his passionate discourse.

"I am afraid he's quite wild now," Dr. Pugh whispered. "He has the power to end Cervantes' ordeal, but he refuses to use it. He can't see that we can't fix this. Leaving Cervantes like this will only prolong the lad's suffering."

"So soon?" Gemma hissed back. "This just happened."

"Look, we've seen injuries like this before, on the previous voyage. We kept the victims alive because we were so close to Earth that we could get them home within a few days. Frau Knopf's son was among them. We couldn't help them. They took a long time to die, child. A long time. It was horrid, horrid! We can send people into space, but we cannot heal these kinds of injuries!" The beseeching in the elderly scientist's voice was as earnest as that in Christophe's, which carried over the entire chamber. "The Admiralty created some new regulations for this very situation. We'll be out here for quite some time, remember. It's the only thing we can do for him. The only thing. I cannot bear to see him like this. I know you of all people can understand."

"Such an act belongs in the doctor's hands," Gemma replied with irritation at the hinted request. "Why do you need me?"

"Christophe has to give the order." Dr. Pugh swallowed hard. "They can't do it without his approval. But he won't give it. He won't listen to me. I thought he might listen to you."

"To me?"

"After your... conversations."

"What?" Gemma asked in shock. How could Christophe have told this man about their private moments, as innocent as they were?

"How do you know--"

Dr. Pugh shook his head and rested his hand on her narrow shoulder. "Never mind. Later. Talk some sense into him. Please, Gemma."

Dr. Pugh released her, and they rejoined the group of men at the foot of Cervantes' bed. She stood at the corner and looked at the mummy that lay upon it. Only the mouth of the first mate emerged from the swaddling bandages, and the breath that came out of it was laboured. She sensed that the only reason he wasn't screaming was the heavy sedation.

The dispute burned around her, and no one would agree with Christophe. Pugh's words about Christophe and "The Order" trailed across her memory. It dawned on her now that he might not be capable of giving such an order, when it came down to it.

Christophe turned to her as he looked for support, any support at all.

"Gemma! Tell him we cannot do this! Please!"

The others started, stunned at his familiarity with her. Pugh glared at her with a *get on with it* expression.

Gemma wrangled Christophe away from the cluster of men and into the doctor's small office. He argued with her every step of the way. She latched the door behind her as firmly as she could without slamming it. To pull punches now would be foolish. They had no time for this nonsense. The *Fury* had already lost its capable first mate. It could not afford to lose its commander to grief and mawkishness. How in the world could the TIA have put faith in such a man?

"Enough!" she exclaimed. "Christophe Moreau, you must do this."

The stunned expression on his face only strengthened her resolve, even though her words struck him like bullets.

She pressed on in his silence. "You are not here to play at being Sinbad the Sailor," she continued, using the same tone Mrs. Brightman had used with her after the Shanghai Incident. "We. Are. At. War. If you are going to be *Captain* Moreau, you are going to have to make the tough decisions."

"Even if it means that I am signing the death warrant of a man who has been my friend since childhood? My brother?" His voice grew louder with each word. The barest hint of water shone on the lower lid of his left eye and threatened to emerge.

What would she do, if it were dear Philippa on that bed with no hope of recovery? Would she make the same decision if it had been her friend's porcelain skin that had been melted, her dear one's glossy black hair that had been scorched away?

"Yes, even so," she said. She spoke slowly and evenly. "You are the commander. The lives of the crew, even mine, even your own, are in your hands, Captain! You have to make this call."

"How can you be so cold?" His voice rasped in disbelief. She could feel anger coiling up within him, an anger that surprised her after her talk with the happy young lad in the Gardens, the barefoot one that read Twain. "Gemma, I am not a machine. Are you? I thought you of all people would understand."

"Why, because I'm a woman?" she asked.

"I thought--"

"You're *not* thinking. At least not with your brain. That's the problem. Think, Captain. Remember. On your last voyage, you lost half your crew, but you survived that particular loss. You will survive this one."

"Do not presume to lecture me. I've seen death before, many times. Don't you think I have?" He blinked, hard, and sat down on the doctor's desk. "When you're at sea, Death is a member of your crew! Sometimes it's brutal. Scurvy eating away their teeth. Gales sweeping them overboard like toys. Water so cold that they freeze to death before we can pull them out. But it was Death's decision to take them, not mine. I've never had to murder a member of my own crew before. I've never had to give such an order before."

This man had been hailed as a Deliverer, a Warrior; up close, his much-vaunted iron will was no more substantial than Sophie the Steamfitter's garter belt. Gemma confronted an awful truth: that this man lacked the will to do what must be done. If he could not give The Order once they reached the Red Planet, the *Fury* would be lost. Gemma could not allow that. She had a mission to complete, even if she did not yet understand it.

"Pugh has sheltered you far too much," she declared. "You are in a savage land now, far more savage than the sea. You cannot give any quarter, for you will receive none. Death is also on the *Fury's* roster. Are you his commander, or is he yours?" She poked his chest with rapid taps, like a radio operator sending a telegram. The pokes grew harder with every word. "Get this through your thick pate: Cervantes is only the first. Get used to it."

"You're just a geologist, Miss Llewellyn." He knocked her hand away. It was hard enough to feel but gentle enough to avoid injuring her. "You play with rocks all day. What do you know of holding a life in your hands?"

The Man from Shanghai would have told him that she knew plenty. Her icy gaze bore into him. Her face was blank of sentiment.

"He is your friend, Christophe. You owe him release."

She reached for his hand and held it between her two smaller ones. It was clammy. He looked at that hand and pursed his lips. He pressed his trembling fingers into the top of her hand in silent response.

She continued, "I am not saying this won't haunt you. It will. Of that I have no doubt. But that does not relieve you of your responsibility. The only thing you can do for him now is find the cause of his demise. Like it or not, this is the job you took on when you put on that uniform."

"You question my courage?"

"No. Your judgment."

He jerked his hand away from her as if her palms were burning coals. He squeezed his eyes shut, removing her from his sight so he could avoid her words. A single hot tear escaped from his shut eyelid. It ran down his face, dripped off his jaw, and splashed onto the floor. When he opened his eyes again, they brimmed with fury.

"You heartless beast," he snarled.

He wiped the cuff of his sleeve across his cheek and marched out the door. She let him go without a word. It was his turn to act.

Gemma stood there, frozen to the spot, her heart a glacier, listening through the open door as he gave the order to Dr. Hansard. He was the courageous captain, the darling hero of the CDVs, once more; the lighthearted lad was back in the Garden where he belonged. As Christophe spoke to the surgeon, she could feel the fragile connection that they had formed over the last few days snap. Whatever it had been -- friendship, attraction, simple commiseration, she did not know -- it was gone now.

She slipped out into sick bay and leaned against the wall, forcing herself to witness that which she had advocated. She owed Cervantes that much, stranger though he was, because she would have done the same for Philippa.

At least the captain got to say goodbye. At least he had that much. With Philippa, there had been no hand to hold, no forehead to kiss, no eyes to close, no body to bury. She had simply not returned.

She remembered the day that Mrs. Brightman had told the Girls that one of their number was not coming home. Mrs. Brightman had always discouraged displays of sentiment. All Gemma had been able to do was stare out the window, into the grey misty rain, and let the sky weep for her. The wind had wailed in her stead. When she had been exhausted enough, she had simply sat back in the chair in front of the fire in Brightman's third-best parlour and stared into the flames. She had simply listened to the thunder.

Even now, she could not tolerate passionate scenes. On that dark day long ago, she had closed the door -- forever, she had thought -- on attachments to any other person. That chamber inside of her, that aspect of Gemma Llewellyn, was dead. It only felt a flicker of phantom pain every now and then, like the itching an amputee might feel in a missing arm. She knew what this action would cost the captain.

Mrs. Brightman had not allowed her to wallow in her grief then, and she could not allow Christophe to wallow in his own grief now. The rest of the ship depended on him to hold it together. She would rather have him hate her for knocking him about with the baton of reality than see him as a pitiful and pathetic creature lashing about for comfort. She could offer him neither succour nor absolution, but she could offer him the distraction of anger.

Everyone has a key that you have only to grasp and turn, Mrs. Brightman had said.

Gemma had found the captain's key, and that key was cruelty.

She leaned her head back against the wall, letting the background hum of the ship sing to her. Even the skittering and scratching in the walls had a wretched tone to them. Part of her wished she were back on Earth, where she could hear it rain, where she could just lean back and listen to the thunder. That was all she could do here, lean against the wall to witness a dying man's last rites and listen to the thunder in his captain's heart.

CHRISTOPHE

"Cervantes' death was a complete and utter waste."

Christophe's words lashed out across the table at Pugh and Wallace. He felt the loss keenly, as if someone had hacked off his right arm. Anger and frustration thrashed inside him, threatening to break free. It was a struggle to stay in his seat.

Wallace responded in a calm, composed voice. "I disagree, Captain. Our late first mate is a hero. He died in the line of duty. In the hands of the right journalist, no death is ever wasted."

"What, what?" Christophe snarled in growing disbelief. Was the geologist's coldness infecting the rest of the ship? It was bad enough that he remembered every frozen word she had uttered in perfect detail. The conversation replayed in his head, even when he tried to stop it. Did he have to hear it from everyone else?

Wallace's tone was arid and precise. He might as well have been discussing train schedules. "You've provided us with a genuine hero, Captain, and that's precisely what we need at the moment. Sophie the Steamfitter has taken our friend to her plump white bosom. People will devour that image. They will remember him with every cry of *Terra vigila.*"

"Not to mention enshrine him over the lager taps at the Badger and Tentacle," Pugh growled.

Wallace waved the response away. "Why, there are memorial CDVs on the presses as we speak."

"So soon?" asked Dr. Pugh.

"Why do you think we took photos of the crew before we launched? We only missed the geologist, and, well, no one would miss her."

Christophe had noticed the busy photographers that had swarmed the launch site for weeks, and he had noticed their absence on the day he had departed. He had assumed that all the photographs had been for historical purposes. Apparently, history had not been their only motive. He felt a chill go down his spine as he thought about the TIA, preparing to commemorate the deaths of his crew, one at a time or otherwise.

Wallace continued, "His death is unfortunate, to be sure. But even death has its uses." He leaned over the table and scratched at the grain of the wood with a short stubby finger. "A hero may keep the wolves of a world war at bay a little longer, Captain. This will suit our true mission. Just wait. You will see. Victory is relative."

Wallace droned on about history and victory. Christophe tuned him out and recalled his younger self, lying in a hammock on the deck of the *Kiwi*, staring at the stars and dreaming about sailing among them. He had imagined the parades and the parties for his crew upon their triumphant return. Now he wanted to visit that younger Christophe, shake him out of that hammock, and order him to keep his bare feet planted on that teak deck. Now he knew. He knew what space was. Cold and empty, empty except for darkness and death. His great adventurer's theme had become a funeral march.

Wallace tapped the list in front of him with his fountain pen and recalled Christophe's attention to the matters at hand.

"We need to inform his next of kin," the Cultural Officer said.

Christophe shut his eyes and stared into the darkness behind his lids, trying to do something, anything, to hold on to himself. "I am his next of kin. So is Dr. Pugh."

"No wife?"

"The *Fury* was his life entire," Christophe said with a shake of his head.

He might have been talking about himself. He opened his eyes and forced them to focus on Wallace. He had to have captain's eyes now.

"Personal effects?"

"Everything he owned is in his stateroom. He led a sailor's life. He traveled lightly."

Wallace nodded as he checked off another line on his list. "We'll need to move them so that the new first mate can take possession of his cabin. You do realize you will have to appoint an acting first mate, yes?"

Christophe nodded. He was indeed aware of that need, but he had tried to put it from his mind. It would be too final.

There was so much to do. A death was the end of the story for some, and the beginning of another chapter for others. He would have to grit his teeth in the face of this shifting wind, put his hand on the wheel, and steer once more. Gemma's harsh words of yesterday still echoed deep inside him. She had been right; deep down he knew she had been right even as she had said it. That didn't make hearing the words any less excruciating.

"I think that can wait until after the memorial service, can it not?" Dr. Pugh asked. "The crew needs some time--"

"The crew needs to keep doing its job, Dr. Pugh," Wallace said. "We need a first mate on the job now. They need their chain of command." He jotted down a few words in the margins of his paper. As he wrote, he said, "However, I think we can wait on the change of quarters until after the memorial service. Will that be acceptable, Captain?"

"Yes, Mr. Wallace. That would be acceptable." He could not, would not, give in to this sinking weakness in the pit of his stomach. There was too much to do, and he would do his friend no honours by staring into space for the rest of the journey. "I will recommend Mr. Pritchard."

"And the memorial service? Do you agree that the suggested service in the protocols--"

"Yes. I know the protocols only too well. It's much like the burials at sea. Your people thought of everything."

"Just prepared for every conceivable contingency, Captain. We can pull it together today and have it, say, tomorrow evening after the day shifts come off duty?"

Christophe nodded wearily. How could a man's life boil down to lines on a checklist?

Mr. Wallace checked his next item with a determined stroke of the pen. "Any progress on the investigation into the actual cause of the explosion?"

Dr. Pugh chimed in. "The findings are still preliminary. We haven't found any evidence of an explosive device. It appears that the mechanism itself was misaligned. Nesbitt believes one of the valve gears was loose. We haven't ruled out sabotage, but we have nothing to support it, either. Not yet."

"Very well. Let me know the instant your people have anything else to report. How is Hui coming along on the alternative weapon? Will we be able to defend the ship, should it become necessary?"

"At this point, who knows? He is putting every possible hour into it."

Christophe replied, "I'm giving them until Braking Day to have something workable. If not, we may have to consider aborting the mission."

Dr. Pugh's response was dry. "Either that, or invite the tentacle-heads over for tea. But I don't think they'll be very keen."

Mr. Wallace pinned them both with his steely gaze. "That will be up to the Admiralty. So far, I don't see a reason to abort our mission. Not our true mission." He set his pen down beside the checklist. "We have to keep the world united for as long as possible. Many of the old arguments are surfacing again, gentlemen. The Invasion and the Hague Treaty have held things in check for a while, longer than we could have hoped, but the effects are starting to fade. Without external enemies to distract us, the Treaty is just so many words on paper. War would have been a nightmare even before the Martians. We did our best to collect their technology, but it was impossible to confiscate it all. Word has it that Germany has detailed battle plans, ready to go at a moment's notice. Russia has created their own version of the Black Smoke, even though it violates the very first Hague Convention of '99! France has improved upon the walking machines and dabbled with the Heat Ray. No more metal breastplates and horsehair helmets for them. The days of Napoleonic formations are over. How much worse will war be now?"

Wallace rapped his knuckles on the table. "We have to keep their eyes on us, on this ship, for as long as possible, until we can find some other way to quell the tensions." He showed them another page inscribed with his precise penmanship. "I've written an article on Cervantes' heroic sacrifice that will be published in every newspaper around the world. We can get considerable mileage out of this incident. Considerable. And if anything else happens?" He shrugged. "Pressing on in the face of adversity? Even better." He jogged his papers into a neat stack. "I suggest we meet again later today with Father Alfieri to go over the final details of the memorial service. Any objections?"

When Mr. Wallace finally left the room, Christophe shuddered at the man's calculating demeanor. It chilled him to the bone to think that the death of the sea-hardened, sunbaked first mate, the finest man and most capable sailor he had ever known, would be just another tool to someone back on Earth. He was too shaken to even rage about it, as he had the day before. At least Gemma had had Cervantes' best interests in mind.

"True mission?" Christophe asked. "True. Mission. Elias, do you know anything about this?"

Pugh shook his head and leaned back in his chair to stretch his impossibly long legs out beneath the table. He stared up at the ceiling, as if he could find the secrets of the universe written there.

"No," he replied without looking at the captain. "But I should have guessed. Why else send only one ship, instead of waiting for the fleet to be finished?" He mumbled something harsh under his breath. "Well, there's nothing we can do about it now. We are well on our way." Then he sighed deeply and placed his hands behind his head, continuing his study of the ceiling.

"Something else has come to my attention, Elias, that may have something to do with the explosion. It may be small, but I didn't want to mention it in front of Wallace, just in case. Not yet, anyway."

"You don't trust him. Don't blame you. What's going on?"

"Frau Knopf reported to me this morning that some of the emergency cold rations are missing from the cargo bay. The count is off from last week's inspection. Not enough to be a crisis, but enough to get her notice. Not that anything escapes it. What do you reckon, Elias?"

"Can't be because Maggie was feeling a mite peckish," Elias replied, still boring holes into the ceiling with his eyes. "I see no great cause for concern.

Wouldn't hurt to poke around the cargo bay. Perhaps they just got moved."

"Or maybe we have a stowaway. Maybe one of the Shackleton lot decided to tag along. I'll have the lads in charge of the bay have a look round when they have a moment. It's a lot of ground to cover."

Pugh sat up in his chair. His voice shifted to a more fatherly tone. "How are you holding up, son?"

Christophe took a deep breath and stared down at his hands, clenched into white-knuckled fists. He flexed them, feeling where his fingernails had nipped his palms. Without looking up, he asked the question that had been haunting him since the day before.

"Yesterday, when we -- when I -- why did you ask Miss Llewellyn to be there?"

"You wouldn't listen to me. I thought you might listen to her. Lately, you seem to have become rather attached to that young lady," Pugh admitted.

Christophe straightened in his chair and grasped the edge of the table. "Attached? Who said--"

"Maggie."

Christophe snorted. "Maggie talks too much."

The scientist pegged him with a knowing look. "Maggie doesn't talk at all, son."

"You know what I mean. Anyway, there is no need to worry on that account anymore."

The air of concern that Pugh had carried with him the past few days grew heavier. "If you must blame anyone--"

"She's so... so very cold. She's not who I thought she was."

"Who did you think she was?"

"A lady."

"Oh, that she is. At least, the lady that she was taught to be." Pugh shifted his lanky frame in the chair. "She never lied to you about that, son. You only saw what you wanted to see. Cold? Perhaps. Practical? Logical? Definitely. One must have some store of logic to be a computer."

"A computer? I thought she was a geologist."

"That bit *is* a lie. But I try not to blame Llewellyn for that." Pugh took out his pocket watch and fidgeted with it. "Let me tell you something about her 'college'. They do teach science and mathematics, but to create computers, not scientists. Computers that infiltrate laboratories and take what Brightman wants."

"Why would anyone send their children to such a place?"

"No one 'sends' their children there. It's not just a school. It's an orphanage. It's a prison. The beast that runs the place is as heartless a creature as you'll ever find. She raised our Gemma, if you can call what she did *raising*. The girl has known nothing else. Gemma doesn't know how to love, Christophe. She can't know. She's never known what it's like to be loved. Petunia Brightman doesn't have a maternal bone in her body. Believe me, she would have been far better off being raised by Martians."

Christophe sputtered, "How do you know this?"

"I make it my business to know these things."

"Sounds like you know from personal experience."

"I do. Very personal." He sat up, his chair groaning in protest, and leaned over the table. "Did you ever wonder why I had no computers of my own? Why I never made use of the Admiralty Computing Services for my work? Besides the fact that I was afraid you'd try to get under their skirts?"

Christophe bit his lip at that and shrugged.

Pugh continued, "It was bloody inconvenient, doing a lot of the computation myself before we got the analytical engines, but computers are far too dangerous. Before the Invasion, my mentor made heavy use of them. One of my tasks was to oversee their work. One particularly bright computer caught Aronnax's eye, a certain Petunia Brightman. Except we knew her as Pearl Addison. We were engaged in a line of inquiry that was severely confidential."

Christophe frowned. "You rarely mention your research from that time. But you were both biologists. What could have been so confidential before the Invasion?"

"It was secret because such research was highly controversial. Still is, actually. We researched the inheritance of traits, specifically that of genius. You've heard it called 'eugenics'. That research was why I was picked for the TIA study of Martian Code, you know. Aronnax's main source of funding was the Wollstonecraft Foundation."

"One of the founding organizations of the TIA."

"Precisely. Addison -- that is, Brightman -- was fascinated by the topic. She rose in the ranks of the computers, and she soon created the computing plans that they used to plow through mounds of data. She could do more than calculate. She understood the meaning behind the numbers, and she devoured any literature on the subject she could lay her hands on. She had a keen mind, and her charms won over Aronnax, even though he was a confirmed lifelong bachelor. She seduced him, she stole his secrets from him, and then she abandoned him. She sold the information to his fiercest rival and started her purported school off the profits. Years of work, lost to a fair face." Pugh sighed at the memory. "He never really recovered from that betrayal. He lived on, for a while, but he was never the same. I think that when he did die, it was of a broken heart."

"Why would anyone do such a thing?"

"Only Brightman herself knows. She had tried to make it as a scientist in her own right years before, but she could never break out of the computer harems. She was stymied at every turn. The scientific community has not been kind to those of the fairer sex."

"But there are lady scientists, aren't there? What about Madame Curie? Or the botanist that designed our Gardens? Alice Eastwood?"

"Yes, they are out there. Eastwood did a smashing job on our Gardens, and Curie has done some wonderful work with radium. But society doesn't seem to be interested in a woman doing pure research, doing science for the sake of science. Curie had a difficult time getting funding for her radium until a journalist convinced people of her desire to treat cancer with it or some such maternal nonsense. Yet even she had more of a place than Brightman did. Somewhere along the way, Brightman decided that if she could not join them, she would beat them, and make her living by taking from those who had rejected her."

A very dark question occurred to Christophe, one that disturbed him even more than Gemma's behaviour of the day before. "Do you think that Miss Llewellyn is here to steal from us? Is that even her real name? Do you think she could be a--" He stopped, not wanting to utter the word that perched on the tip of his tongue. It was a dangerous word. He picked up a stray fountain pen on the table and rolled it through his fingers. "That's a very serious charge."

"I try to hold her in a different category than Brightman. That woman's methods certainly show in Gemma's behavior, however. Most of her previous jobs involved computing, you know."

"She's never mentioned it."

"I'm sure she has mentioned very little. I'm certain she *listens* very well, though. Part of her charms. And part of the danger, for Brightman systematically and methodically drains them of any capacity for warmth or affection. And yet somehow she fills them with eternal gratitude towards her for saving them from an orphan's life. They have no other higher power than their headmistress, no other god before her. The TIA propagandists could learn a great deal from her methods." Dr. Pugh shook his head in disgust. "Brightman may train computers, but in the process she creates machines."

Christophe tossed the fountain pen back onto the desk. "There are days when I think it would be easier to be a machine. If love did that to Aronnax, what use is it, then? What use is there in loving?"

Pugh caressed the watch with his long fingers. He popped it open and handed it to Christophe with a slow hand.

"A great deal of use, son. Don't avoid love. It's what holds us together in this savage world. Just don't let it kill you, all the same."

Christophe looked at the photograph that he had seen many times over the course of his life, the one of Pugh's late wife and child, the family that he had lost in the Invasion. He gave Pugh a puzzled frown. "There's something else you aren't telling me."

Pugh flashed him a brief glimpse of a smile. "I've had my eye on Brightman for some time. Partly because of Aronnax." He pointed to the watch. "Partly because of her."

"Your wife?"

"My daughter."

"Your daughter?"

"I don't think she died in the Invasion."

"What? But I thought--"

"More than one person turned the Invasion to their advantage, Christophe. A crisis can ferret out the best and the worst that humanity has to offer. Brightman harvested the Invasion Orphans for her own uses. The Martians left her quite a crop. But, perhaps even worse, she did not limit herself to orphans."

Christophe looked at him with growing horror as he pushed the watch back to Pugh. "Why have you never told me this?"

"What possible good would it have done you? You didn't need the distraction. I wasn't with my wife when the Invasion hit. I was in Paris, settling Aronnax's estate. By the time I was able to get back to Woking, it was too late. I found my wife but not my child. She was simply gone." He snapped the pocket watch closed. "I've been trying to locate my daughter ever since. In the intervening years, I've discovered that Brightman was in Woking at that time. Collecting. There is a strong chance that my child is among Brightman's so-called students. It's been difficult to confirm that, though. My daughter was still a babe in arms when the Invasion came, so we would not recognize each other now. Brightman has a network of people that keep her cache of students incredibly secure, so it has been a chore to access them."

"How could she have gotten away with this for so long? I mean, to hire out so many girls that leave their employer all of a sudden, so often? Surely someone would have noticed."

"Even the legitimate computers do not last long. Many march out of the laboratory and straight down the aisle. At least, that is what most people expect to happen. It's even easier when they never use the same name twice. That's what happens when you put people beneath your notice, Christophe. They become invisible. It gives them a kind of power over you, if they only realize it. And if they do realize it, as Brightman did, then it's Katy-bar-the-door." He rolled the watch between his hands. "To stick to the point, some of the Code of Life research that we've done might help me confirm my suspicions. I once hired a man to track the Girls in the field and get a sample from them, like a lock of hair, so I could find someone with enough Code in common with me. There were two likely girls left of the right age. One is reportedly deceased. Killed in Action, as it were. He tracked the other one to a laboratory in Shanghai."

Christophe's face went numb. "What happened? Did he find the girl?"

"Don't know. The local constabulary found him in an alley with a crushed windpipe. There was no sample on his person or at his hotel. They never discovered his murderer's identity, but I'm certain it was one of Brightman's lot. She took boys as well, kept in a separate facility. They do the truly nasty jobs, including keeping a watch out for the Girls. After word of that incident got out, no other investigator would go near my case."

"Surely the TIA could--"

"An international consortium of robber barons and self-aggrandizing philanthropists that thinks of itself as a sovereign nation has better things to do than look for a girl that everyone assumes perished a quarter-century ago. I had to take matters into my own hands to get access to that one last living candidate, and now she is a member of the Cohort. That bit was relatively simple, in the end. Petunia has friends in high places. Friends that are also my friends. How else would she have... no. No. I think I've said too much on that account. All I can say is, ask me no more. Not now. As far as I know, Gemma hasn't stolen anything, even when she's had ample temptation and opportunity. Of course, I have kept her 'visible' and in my notice as much as possible. Her wireless messages are in cipher, like everyone else's, but they are far too short and too infrequent to include anything vital. She hasn't yet found what Brightman wants. No crimes have been committed, as of yet, so there is nothing for you to do here. There is a possibility that she really is a scientist. Or she will be, when I am done with her." He stuffed the watch back into his pocket. "Let me deal with our Miss Llewellyn. I need to know."

"You haven't confirmed it yet?"

"I've been trying to gain her trust, first. I'm a bit nervous about finding out the truth, finding out that -- that you may have a sister, in a manner of speaking." Dr. Pugh unfolded himself from the chair and yawned. "You have things to settle here, so I will take my leave. I will let you know what I discover."

He departed, leaving the young captain alone with his thoughts. In all his life, he had never known Elias to keep anything from him; now he had just revealed something so deeply held that Christophe had never even guessed at it. What else had he kept hidden all these years?

He recoiled from the idea of what Brightman had done. Discipline aboard ship was always strict, sometimes cruel, but there was always a reason behind its severity. Life at sea was brutal, and discipline was required just to survive. He had heard that schools could be difficult, but he could not imagine any reason why life at any school would need to be harsher than life on the waves.

He could not puzzle out why someone would want to browbeat those wide brown eyes and that upturned nose dusted with freckles into some sort of unfeeling automaton. And now there was a possibility that this strange girl was part of Pugh's family, and by extension part of Christophe's family. It unnerved him to think that he had felt more than brotherly affection for her before the incident with Cervantes. A small part of him was grateful to Pugh for holding him back from further pursuit, as agonizing as the process had been.

Sister. Stranger. Definite Victim. Possible Thief. He didn't know which to hope for. He was so stunned from Miguel's sudden absence that he could not endure any more shocking revelations. He could use a long talk with Maggie, but he had no time for it.

One thing was certain, though. He had known Pugh long enough to know that if Gemma Llewellyn were indeed his daughter, this Petunia Brightman would have hell to pay. She was not the only one with friends in high places.

GEMMA

The dreaded Knitting Circle of Doom was upon her.

The picture was surreal: Gemma hurtled through space at a heretofore-inconceivable speed to rain destruction down on a faraway world full of slimy tentacled aliens, and in the meantime, she faced down the steely menace of a crochet hook.

She had dreaded it like nothing else. Gemma was equipped to discuss science with scientists, or at least to bob her head in feigned interest. She could pump numbers through an equation in the blink of an eye. Despite all of her training and accomplishments, she had no idea of what to say to the other ladies. She knew how to hold her teacup and how to be coy with men. But in a group of women who were not Brightman trained, she was lost.

It was not even much of a break from her strange research for Dr. Pugh. The second journal, written by an engineer named Cyrus Smith, seemed to have no connection to Aronnax at all, at least in the parts she had read. Smith's story began in 1865, two years before Aronnax's adventure. His escape with several other men from imprisonment during the Americans' Civil War had been a thrilling tale. She found the hurricane that they had encountered to be a bit fantastic, but no less so than Nemo's giant squid. Having nothing else to do, she had plowed on through the text, hoping to find some glimmer of Orion in it.

The knowledge that Caroline would be at the Circle had been some small comfort to Gemma, as she had grown quite fond of the girl. However, when she got to the parlour, Caroline's chair was empty.

"There are only seven of us on the ship!" Frau Knopf snarled to no one in particular. She had put away the teacups and now sipped from a tumbler of liquid that smelt of evergreens and cinnamon. "How can we have a proper circle with only five!"

The miscount caught Gemma's attention, but she chalked it up to the matron's irritation and to the general excitement over the news that Nigel's wife had gone into labour that morning.

Gemma looked past her steel nemesis and studied the women around her. These women had spent most of their time in the galley and the stables on the journey so far, and this was the first time she had seen them. As it turned out, she didn't have to worry about what to say to them; they barely spoke English. She could hear them whispering to each other in some Eastern European tongue. They consulted each other on their various pieces of handwork and cast the occasional suspicious glance at Gemma. Frau Knopf read a poem aloud to them while they worked, so Gemma did not have to converse at all. Gemma didn't know whether to feel awkward or relieved.

Frau Knopf had stated that the wool had been sheared off the *Fury*'s own herd of sheep, down on the stable deck. She had then handed Gemma the crochet hook, a hank of black thread, and a pattern for making lace written in German. She had said little else; the matron did not seem inclined to idle chatter.

As Gemma struggled to grasp the pattern, Frau Knopf read to them. To Gemma's ears, it was a lot of nonsense about a lady trapped in a tower in the days of Camelot. Frustrated, she set the booklet aside and listened for a moment.

> *There she weaves by night and day*
> *A magic web with colours gay.*
> *She has heard a whisper say,*
> *A curse is on her if she stay*
> *To look down to Camelot.*
> *She knows not what the curse may be,*
> *And so she weaveth steadily,*
> *And little other care hath she,*
> *The Lady of Shalott.*

"What rubbish," Gemma muttered under her breath.

Even as she whispered them, her words did not feel quite real. They felt hollow and rehearsed, as if from a script written by someone else. She found herself hanging on to the words in spite of herself. Besides, she did not want to give the good matron a reason to withhold her daily bacon.

> *And moving thro' a mirror clear*
> *That hangs before her all the year,*
> *Shadows of the world appear.*
> *There she sees the highway near*

Winding down to Camelot:
There the river eddy whirls,
And there the surly village-churls,
And the red cloaks of market girls,
Pass onward from Shalott.

Sometimes a troop of damsels glad,
An abbot on an ambling pad,
Sometimes a curly shepherd-lad,
Or long-hair'd page in crimson clad,
Goes by to tower'd Camelot;
And sometimes thro' the mirror blue
The knights come riding two and two:
She hath no loyal knight and true,
The Lady of Shalott.

But in her web she still delights
To weave the mirror's magic sights,
For often thro' the silent nights
A funeral, with plumes and lights
And music, went to Camelot:
Or when the moon was overhead,
Came two young lovers lately wed;
"I am half-sick of shadows," said
The Lady of Shalott.

The delicate thread hung limp in Gemma's hand as the last two lines lodged in her heart like an arrow. *I am half-sick of shadows*, Philippa had once said to her, not long before she had left on her final journey. Had this poem been in Philippa's little library, too? Was this the beauty that she had tried to share with her?

"Bah," Frau Knopf said as she put the book down. "I will finish this next time."

She said something to one of the other ladies in their language, and one of them rose in reply. She reached behind the bookshelf into some dark and hidden place, retrieved an unlabeled record, and replaced the eternal strings and flutes with it. When she lowered the needle, a new music emerged from the horn, one that Gemma had never heard on the wireless in London. A voice of pure velvet crooned to her absent lover in a tone both mournful and seductive. A muted trumpet and wailing clarinet shadowed her words and punctuated the lonesome moan of her song.

"Ah," mused Frau Knopf as she closed her eyes and bobbed her head along with the music, "I am so very glad that the Martians missed New

Orleans. There are some things even the TIA censors cannot keep silent."

"I've never heard this kind of music before," Gemma said.

"It's the blues. American blues. Helps exorcise one's own sorrows. As does this." She swirled the liquid in her tumbler and stared into it. "Mr. Pritchard smuggled the albums up with the bacon. Not illegal, mind you, but Mr. Wallace, he has no ear for it. My Karl--"

A clamour of rattling interrupted her, and they all turned to see Caroline bursting through the door. She stopped just inside and bent over, hands on her knees, trying to catch her breath. Frau Knopf rose and touched her shoulder.

"Whatever is the matter, child?" Frau Knopf demanded.

"I'm all right," Caroline gasped as she looked around the room. "It's Nigel. He just got a message. About his wife, I think. He's gone wild! He won't let me near him! Gemma, d'you think you could get some sense out of him? Father Alfieri is in a meeting with the captain and Mr. Wallace about the memorial service, and the yeoman won't let me in to see them. But Nigel respects you, he does. I think he might talk to you."

Gemma stood up and tossed the crochet hook into her chair with a mixture of urgency and relief. What was it about her that made people think such things? Who, exactly, had appointed her ship's counselor, she wondered. Still, she was not about to look a gift escape hatch in the mouth.

"Go on, Fraulein," Frau Knopf said. "Take care of our young father."

"Where is he?" Gemma asked.

"Somewhere in the Gardens. I'll show you. Please!"

On the winding path, past the roses and the cherry trees, they passed crewmembers that pointed the way to Nigel. They found him in the gazebo, in a state of near-collapse on one of its benches.

He clutched a message to his chest with one hand. His other hand hid his face from the world. His ever-present glasses sat on the bench next to him, ignored, as if the words could not be true if he could not see them.

Caroline urged Gemma to go ahead without her. She sat on one of the benches beside the path just out of sight and waited.

As Gemma approached him, she wondered what could possibly have upset the calm and unflappable Nigel. She had never heard a cross word from the man.

He didn't notice her approach until she mounted the steps. Her sudden presence startled him. He met her with stranger's eyes, eyes that were empty of the calm determination that normally inhabited them. Gemma could now understand why Caroline was so distraught.

"Nigel? Caroline asked me to come. What--"

"She's gone," he said, choking on the words. He moaned. "Oh, Gemma, she's gone." He crumpled the paper even more in his hand and pushed his fist into his scrunched-up eyes.

Gemma sat down next to him, her knee barely touching his. She brushed her fingertips against the crushed paper between his fingers.

"May I?" she asked in the gentlest voice she could summon.

He didn't reply. She reached for his fist and very slowly pulled it away from his chest. He didn't resist as she opened his hand, finger by finger, and retrieved the message, now ragged and damp. She smoothed the sheet between her fingers, careful to keep it from further damage. Years of uncovering the secrets of others left her no qualms about prying into Nigel's privacy. This was the first time she had done such a thing for someone's benefit besides Mrs. Brightman's; but there was a first time for everything.

The message was shockingly brief, appallingly stark in its plaintext clarity, considering the weight it carried:

WE REGRET TO INFORM YOU THAT MRS DAVIES DEPARTED THIS LIFE AT 3:57 AM AT ISLINGTON LYING-IN HOSPITAL STOP INFANT GIRL ALIVE AND WELL STOP PLEASE RADIO BACK WISHES FOR DISPOSITION STOP BRIGHTMAN SCHOOL REQUESTS CUSTODY UNTIL YOUR RETURN STOP

Gemma had to read it three times before the message registered. Mrs. Brightman sought custody of Nigel's child. Nigel's wife, his entire world, Caroline's dearest friend, was dead.

All this technology, all this wonder! They can send us to Mars, but they can't keep a woman from dying in childbed?

Even in her cool analytical mind, that seemed unbalanced, wrong. Something rumbled deep inside, and she felt a flood of anger sweep over her, even stronger than the anger she had felt when she had confronted the captain about Cervantes. Gemma had not felt -- or allowed herself to feel -- such a rush of emotion for so long that it made her dizzy. The cold efficiency of the word "disposition" incensed her. It was a strange sensation for her. Should she not be glad that Mrs. Brightman was gaining a new pupil, a new Girl to carry on the cause?

Nigel was shaking with silent sobs next to her. She could feel a fever of grief rolling off him, and she reached for his hand. She was no great comforter; she had no instinct for it. But Nigel had always been kind to her. He was one of the few men that had treated her as a friend and a colleague, not just a cog in a machine or a bit of fluff to flirt with. She could not allow him to bear his grief alone, yet she did not know which key to grasp to calm him down. So she simply held his hand.

"I wasn't there," he cried at last. "Oh, my Jennie, my sweet Jennie. I should've stayed." His intake of breath was ragged, as if he were breathing through shredded lungs. "She died amongst strangers, Gemma. We were all she had. Caroline and me. I won't even be there to bury her poor little body. Or take care of my daughter. Oh, my little, little child. Will I ever see her face?"

"I wish the wireless could transmit images," Gemma said softly as she squeezed his fingers. "It would help if you could at least see her picture."

"I have a photograph," he said, finally gaining some lucidity. "Of Jennie, I mean. I don't think you've seen it." He fumbled in his pocket, pulled out his watch, and popped it open. "Here she is. My Jennie."

Gemma gave him the warmest smile she could summon as he handed her the watch. She had been curious about it for a while. Men always kept important thoughts in their watches. As she opened it, she saw a watch face with no hands. Instead, there was a lock of glossy black hair, curled up behind a small pane of glass, opposite the photograph.

"I don't have anyone to take care of her," Nigel went on as she studied the wedding picture. His voice was rough and broken. "No family. Neither did Jennie. We're all orphans, you see."

He took a deep breath before continuing. "Brightman's school, your school, has offered to take her. I think -- I think that would be good, yes? They can make her like you--"

"Oh, my, yes," she said, nearly automatically. "They--"

Her next words froze in her throat.

The woman's face was not the face of a stranger.

There, staring into the camera, seated next to Nigel and draped in lace, was her beloved Philippa.

The Philippa that Mrs. Brightman had told her was dead.

She could hear Dr. Pugh asking the question: *Who knows what Brightman will do when it is time to put you out to pasture?*

Gemma was a talented computer, one of the best. It was not difficult for her to put the picture and the question together. And the sum burned her.

Her mind spun into a maelstrom. Everything Mrs. Brightman had taught her, every rule, every aphorism, every bit of discipline, tore itself loose from the walls of her mind in that moment. The lie burned her like acid from one of the lab's test tubes poured on her heart.

Philippa. The one person she had truly loved. The one whose death -- once a lie, now a horrible truth -- had seared her heart and cauterized it closed, leaving her with hatred of the Martians and gratitude to Mrs. Brightman as her only acceptable passions.

Some rescue! The other Invasion Orphans on the ship did not seem half so miserable with their lot as she had been led to believe. Trapping her finest student on a ship full of them had been a grave miscalculation.

175

Philippa had been alive. Alive, and vital. The face in the photograph looked happy, happier than Gemma had ever seen her. She choked back a sob of her own, stuffing her own grief back down deep into herself, fearing she would lose all control.

Gemma felt as if she would never be calm again.

"Gemma?" Nigel asked. "Are you all right? You look as if you've seen a ghost." He swallowed hard. "Had you met her before? Did you know--"

"No, no!" Gemma protested. She snapped the watch closed. "Nigel, your child is not an orphan! Not while you live! We're not dead. Not yet."

She suddenly felt fiercely protective of this infant, the only part of her dear friend left in the world. Here, at least, was one last service that she could perform for Philippa.

"Nigel, listen to me," she said. "Whatever comes, we must not allow Brightman to have your daughter. You have to trust me on this."

He gaped at her in bewilderment. "I don't -- I don't understand. You--"

"Trust me," she repeated. "She'd be better off raised in a factory."

He continued to gawp in stunned disbelief, as confounded as the captain had been in Hansard's office. "Why?"

"Later," she replied. "Time is of the essence, Nigel. We have to move now."

She was fully aware of how swiftly Brightman would move on this. If the hospital did not give up the child willingly, the woman would find another way to take her. She stood up, placed her finger under Nigel's chin and raised his hot red face. The message crackled in her free hand.

"Chin up, Davies. Give me some time. Send them a message. Stall them any way you can. In the meantime, I'll speak to the captain. Surely he has contacts in the TIA that can aid a crewmember on this historic mission. I'll send Caroline to go with you to the wireless. Collect your wits."

She gave his hand one last squeeze, and he managed a nod in reply. Gemma trooped down the tree-lined path towards Caroline's hiding place and told the Boolean to attend to Nigel. She left the pair far behind her as she went. Her mind was awhirl with what she was about to do. A great key turned in the guts of her mind, a key in the shape of Philippa. Once that door opened, there was no turning back.

She was marching through her own Gethsemane, for she had no doubt that Petunia Brightman would discover her hand in this. It did not matter if Brightman had a Watcher to do the job now or if she waited until their return home, she would find some way to avenge this betrayal. From the moment she requested help, Gemma would be living on borrowed time. She did not care. Brightman had already taken the best part of her, and Gemma felt that the rest of her life would just be marking time, anyway.

She had no clue how she would win this race, here, millions of leagues over the sea, but she was going to win. She had to win. Nothing else mattered now, not the Watcher, not Orion, not the captain. Nothing. It didn't matter anymore what Humboldt discovered about the message; its meaning had winked out of existence as soon as Gemma had seen that photograph. The only thing that mattered was saving Philippa's child from her own Man from Shanghai. She had the very weapons that Brightman -- her new target -- had given her. She had her wits, her cunning, and her own connections on the ship. She was going to Mars, for heaven's sake. If she could go to Mars, she could do anything.

And Mrs. Brightman?

Mrs. Brightman could go to Hell.

Gemma rolled into Informatics like a runaway freight train.

"Mr. Humboldt!" she snapped as she crossed the threshold.

Humboldt jumped up from his workstation as if a firecracker had gone off underneath his chair. "Miss L?" His words froze as he noticed the crumpled piece of paper in her hand. "Is it about the Chief? He left in such a hurry. We're all worried."

"Yes, yes," she said, lowering her voice. She cast a glance at the closed bridge window. "I need to speak to the captain immediately. It cannot wait. Can you get me onto the bridge?"

"He's in a meeting, I think, down in his Ready Room. Rumour has it that he's promoting Mr. Pritchard to first mate. I can take you there if you don't know where it is, if it's that much of a rush."

He led her out of the chamber with no hesitation. *I have to give Humboldt this*, she thought to herself, *he doesn't dawdle about when he's truly needed.*

As they rumbled past the Wireless Room, Rathbone leaned out the window and waved a sheaf of paper at her.

"Messages for you, Miss Llewellyn," he called after them. "They're marked--"

"Sod off!" she barked without turning her head or slowing her stride.

The time for ladylike behaviour had expired. All she could think of now was Philippa's child. She could feel the ghost of the Man from Shanghai dogging her footsteps now. She sped up to escape him even as she followed Humboldt to an area that she had never seen before. They passed Father Alfieri and Mr. Wallace on the way. Without stopping, she informed Father Alfieri that Chief Davies required his presence. The captain and Pugh appeared just ahead. The echo of their rapid footfalls around the sharp metal walls startled the elderly scientist.

"What's all this kerfuffle?" Pugh demanded as she and Humboldt skidded to a stop. The scientist's eyes widened as he saw her escort, as if Humboldt were the last person he expected to see with her. "Miss Llewellyn, explain yourself!"

Humboldt hung back behind her as he tried to catch his breath. Gemma thought she caught the movement of his salute to the captain out of the corner of her eye as she leaned over, one hand on her knees, too breathless too speak. Instead, she shoved the crumpled message, now a mass of damp and tattered pulp, into the scientist's face. As he scanned it, Christophe leaned over Pugh's arm and read it with him.

"Bloody hell!" exclaimed Pugh. "How would she even know about this child?"

"They must--" Gemma began, casting a glance at Christophe. Even now, she must be careful. If anyone needed to know Mrs. Davies' true identity, Nigel should know first. Besides, what she was about to say might even be true. "I suppose she keeps a watch on all the lying-in hospitals for orphans, Dr. Pugh."

Christophe pointed at the message. "But she's not orphaned yet. How can the hospital allow--"

"He knows already? You told him about the College?" Gemma was on the edge of shrieking. As confused as he was, he wasn't confused enough. Could the captain know about her, already? Had Pugh already betrayed her? She tried to ignore the klaxon that clanged in her head. "Can you do something, Dr. Pugh?" Gemma pleaded. "You know. You know we can't let this happen. You know why. And Nigel has no one else but us. The crew." As she pointed at each of the four of them with a sweep of her hand, she came close to choking on her words.

Christophe broke in. "Dr. Pugh, do you think the security office in Battersea might be able--"

"I don't think they are equipped to handle a newborn, Captain," Pugh replied. "They're not exactly a foundling hospital."

"She is not a foundling!" Gemma shouted. She shuddered and lowered her voice. She balled her hands into fists and realized she was still holding Nigel's watch. As she slipped it into her skirt pocket, an idea occurred to her. "What about this Maggie you're always going on about?" she demanded. "Can't she fetch the child?"

Christophe stared at Pugh, alarm writ large upon his face. "You told her about Maggie?"

Pugh stumbled and shook his head so hard it nearly popped off his spine. "Oh, dear. Oh, dear, dear, dear, dear."

"You told her. About Maggie."

"Not now, Captain!" Pugh let a nervous chuckle escape him. "Gemma, child, I'm afraid Maggie's not in London at the moment. Not even close."

Gemma's voice rippled in a near-laugh of frustration. "Even if she's in the bloody Antarctic, surely she's closer than we are?"

Christophe and Pugh looked at her, looked at each other with widening eyes, and then back at her, with unspoken words crackling in the silence between them.

"Isn't she?" Gemma asked.

They looked at each other again, and the tense silence stretched out like molasses.

"Well?" Gemma demanded.

"Well," Pugh said at last, "it certainly wouldn't hurt to consult with her, at the very least."

Saluting as he did so, Humboldt stepped up to join them. Gemma had almost forgotten that he was there. "Captain, begging your pardon, sir, this is downright tragic. Miss L, Miss Llewellyn, I mean, is right. We can't let the Chief's baby girl go to an orphanage! I don't know who this Maggie person is, but perhaps I might be of assistance."

Gemma was ready for relief from any quarter. "Yes?"

"The Chief's been good to me, Miss L. I'd love a chance to return the favour. You know me, I'm normally all mouth and no trousers, but I might be able to do something here."

"What can you do, Mr. Humboldt?" the captain asked.

"My cousin Jules could go get her."

"Your cousin?" Christophe crossed his arms and leaned back into the wall with one eyebrow arched so high it nearly collided with his hairline.

"That would be Julian Humboldt and his wife, sir. He runs the Badger 'n' Tentacle down in Hammersmith. They don't have any little ones of their own, but they love 'em just the same." He waited for the rest to respond, but when they didn't, he continued. "Look, it may sound like he's just a bloke what owns a pub, but his flat above it is rather posh. He's done rather well for himself. And he'd do anything for me. I'm the only one in the family that'll talk to him." He shrugged. "Of course, he's the only one that talks to me. But all the same. Please. Let me do this for the Chief. They can take care of her, at least until he figures out something more permanent." He pointed at the message. "Miss Llewellyn makes this sound serious, and I take anything she says very seriously. Sir."

"It might be dangerous," Pugh replied with wariness creeping into his voice. He studiously avoided looking at Gemma as he continued. "Brightman may try to interfere. And to borrow your phrasing, Mr. Humboldt, she's both talk *and* trousers."

Humboldt's smirk was unrestrained. "I don't know nothin' about any Brightman, but I bet my cousin's blokes will have a word or three to say about that. I'll tell Jules to take them with him. They'll teach anyone they meet a thing or two about interferin'. And he's used to taking risks. You know about his, erm, his back room? His, shall we say, midnight salon? Sir."

"Midnight salon?" asked Gemma, unsure if she liked the sound of that.

"I'm familiar with the owner of the Badger and Tentacle. I've had a fair few pints there," said the captain with a hint of a knowing smile. "But who are his blokes?"

"Oh, his chuckers-out. I'm sure you've seen 'em, sir. Big fellas that bounce out the riff-raff what gets too rough with the faux Martian at the bar. I've not been to an orphanage, myself, but some of those chaps grew up in 'em. They won't let anyone touch the babe what shouldn't."

The captain nodded. "Not a bad idea. That'll buy Mr. Davies a little breathing room. I have a few friends in that security office that owe me a favour or two. They can stand guard at the hospital until -- Julian, is it? -- can get there. I'll have to trust you on this one, Mr. Humboldt. How soon can you get a message routed to him? That may take some time."

"Oh, I know the wireless, sir. So does Jules. Has his own setup. Told you he was posh! Regular ham, he is. I can send a voice message straight to him, no routing necessary. If need be, I can use the one on the *Iron Wind*, so it's just us that knows about it. Jules doesn't use the military frequencies. Of course. Sir."

Christophe stood very, very still. His eyes fluttered closed for a moment. He appeared to Gemma to be listening to a voice that only he could hear, rather than simply thinking. He grunted softly, as if reaching a conclusion. After a few deep breaths, he spoke at last.

"Miss, does this meet with your approval, then?"

"I think it's the best we can do, with the time we have."

"That's the plan, then. Like the rest of us, Mr. Davies is sacrificing much for this mission. The least we can do is see that his child is safe. I'll go to the dropship with you, Mr. Humboldt. Let's keep this quiet. Oh, and Mr. Davies will have to send his own message to the hospital, or they won't know who to give the baby to! And, good heavens, someone find out what the child's name is. All ahead full on this, people. Dismissed."

Humboldt sped away from them. As Gemma turned to go back to the Gardens, Christophe plucked at her elbow. "Just a moment. Dr. Pugh, would you please escort our Miss Llewellyn back to Ladies' Country?"

Anger sparked behind Gemma's eyes. This was unexpected. "Ladies' Country? I won't be--"

"I am the captain, Miss Llewellyn. I will be obeyed in this." He leaned closer, so close she could smell the Men-T-Fresh on his breath and feel the warmth of his face on her forehead. He whispered, "If we do this, you may not be safe, even here."

She shot Dr. Pugh a harsh glare. "What makes you think--"

"No arguments, Gemma," Christophe said. "Despite the present state of our relationship, it is my duty to protect each and every member of my crew, and that's that. Go straight to your cabin and lock the door. Admit no one but Dr. Pugh, Frau Knopf, or myself. I will have her send you a tray. You're looking a bit peaked, Miss."

He shook his head at her next attempt to speak. She trembled a little at the sudden change in him, in spite of herself. The iron edge in his voice, which she had not heard since he had given the order to end Cervantes' suffering, was sharp.

"I'll come to you when I can. We must speak further on this, but not right now. You've done your bit. Now let us do ours. That's my direct order, Miss Llewellyn." He released her elbow. He swept his own long arm in front of him and gestured towards the lift. "Dr. Pugh, if you please."

As Christophe strode away after Humboldt, Gemma exhaled a strangled cry of frustration. She growled at Pugh as he put his hand on her shoulder and steered her in the direction of the lift.

"You told him. About me."

Pugh shrugged while a slight blush rippled across his face. "Just the barest of necessities. He doesn't *quite* know all the details of your Peculiar Occupation, so he's not ready to shove you out into the vacuum just yet. But, don't worry, the mission is still young."

Bollocks! Gemma screamed in her own mind with her anger roiling as she heard Pugh cackling at his own joke. *Despite the present state of our relationship, he says? Protection, he says? Arrest, more like.*

"He's right, you know," Pugh said in a more serious tone as the lift lowered them down to another deck. "You may not be Brightman's only representative on the ship."

She responded with a scowl and a stamp of her foot; but despite her indignation, she knew he was right. The message that Humboldt was researching for her proved it, but she kept that bit to herself. She had to maintain some control of the situation. Gemma continued to stew in her silence.

"Oh, ho!" Pugh guffawed at her lack of reply. "You wanted him to act like a captain, didn't you? Just not when it comes to you, apparently. How droll."

"And what is a *midnight salon*?" she shot back. "It sounds vulgar."

He laughed even harder. "Nothing you'd be interested in, I'm sure. Nothing that would harm the child."

"You're enjoying this far too much," Gemma snapped back.

"No, no," he chortled, pretending to wipe a tear away from the laugh lines around one eye, "I'm enjoying it just fine, thank you."

"Oh, shut it."

Pugh's laughter echoed around the lift. Gemma felt an odd jab underneath her ribs when she recalled the mention of Maggie, whoever she was. It made Gemma feel nauseous when she realized that it bothered her as much, if not more, than the fact that she probably had a target on her back.

Gemma tried to refocus her thoughts on her impending confinement, even if it was just to her own quarters and not the brig. Christophe's reaction was too calm, too composed, for someone who knew nothing about Brightman. He should not have suspected that she was in any danger. And yet, he knew. He knew, and there was only one way that he could know.

She should have known better than to trust Pugh. Now that she knew that Brightman had once worked for his mentor, she was doubly sure he could not be trusted. Something had happened between the two of them, of that she was certain. After reeling her in and gaining her trust -- which she had never, ever given to anyone save Philippa and her teacher -- Pugh was at last having his revenge on Brightman, if only through one of her students.

She had told herself when she had put her hand to the plow that she was ready for any consequences. But being prepared for consequences and then enduring the business end of them were two entirely different things. She had a feeling that she would have much more on her plate than burnt bacon.

Discovery was upon her.

CHRISTOPHE

The messages had been sent, and the minutes crawled by as they waited for responses. The arrangements had been made, and Humboldt's cousin was already on his way. It was all over but the waiting. This far away, waiting was all they could do.

Christophe had never been good at waiting. That was when his feet tended to have a mind of their own. He wandered to the bridge, where a message from Thorvaldson waited for him. This time, with the admiral's message in hand, his feet carried him to the Gun Control chamber, where a damage control detail repaired the damaged walls.

A swabbie scraped away at a stubborn stain near one corner. As Christophe approached it, he realized it was blood. He told the man to carry on, and the man took a moment to wipe his brow.

"I'm sorry this is taking so long, Captain. This is a rough job, if you take my meaning."

Christophe nodded and regarded the spots of his friend's blood on the wall in silence. He could feel the message from Thorvaldson in his hand, and he could remember what it said: condolences over their loss, approval of Mr. Pritchard's promotion to first mate, and a report on the situation back home. Russian warships were moving towards the straits around the Sea of Marmara, in a standoff over the TIA blockade. The TIA still refused to release any of their research. The French had completed their own walking machines and were positioning them in Alsace. No shots had been fired, not yet, but they wanted their territory back. And if they engaged the Germans over it, Thorvaldson feared what would happen next.

Christophe knew that even if he had been on Earth, there was little that he could do to prevent what the admiral could sense coming. He felt some solace that his crew was able to help someone back home, and he prayed that the keeper of the Badger and Tentacle made it on time. Prayer would have been Miguel's answer, and Christophe began to understand why. At the very least, it made him feel a tad less helpless when things were out of his hands. Christophe took a moment to indulge in one for his friend's soul.

"Leave it," Christophe said.

He traced some of the spatter with his index finger. Rather than revulsion, he felt an odd comfort in the wall's blemish. With it there, he could almost feel Miguel's presence in the chamber.

"Sir?"

"Yes, leave it as it is. Just bolt a new panel over it. We will deal with it when we get back to Earth."

The mate sighed with relief. "Aye, sir. Thank you, sir."

GEMMA

Gemma paced in her shrinking cage. Waiting was a slog through a deep sludge in which she never seemed to move forward. The captain did not come. Frau Knopf came and went with a tray, and still he did not come. Muddy time sucked at her ankles, and she strained her ears until she thought they would pop in listening for his footfalls.

No message. No crackle from the speaking tube. No hastily dashed missive on a scrap piece of paper. No frenetic whisper carried by a trusted crewmember. Nothing. The only thing she could feel was the eye of the unknown Watcher upon her, so close that the hairs on her neck stayed at attention. Her skin crawled with gooseflesh.

She did not know what she hoped for, really, except to know that Philippa's child was now safe. The strength she had felt in the captain's voice as he had given his orders had struck some chord deep within her, but she could not get her mind around the sound it made. Nothing beyond that bore thinking about.

Frau Knopf brought her another tray and escorted her to the head, but she had no news for her other than Mr. Humboldt's report that things were still in motion.

It was odd how the ship contracted and expanded around her. It was such a peculiar metal beast, all at once as tiny as an anthill or as large as the globe. At the moment, it was a single cabin with a very large engine. She thought she would go mad just thinking about it. She would rather face her Watcher head-on than suffer through this interminable limbo.

As she changed into some nightclothes, she discovered Nigel's watch in her pocket. She popped it open. Philippa was still inside it; she had not imagined it all.

Gemma pulled the lock of hair out of the watch and stroked it with the tips of her fingers. She could almost catch Philippa's scent in it. With trembling hands, she peeled off a few strands and set them aside. She opened her own locket and boiled with fury as she gazed at that stony face. In a frenzy, she scraped Brightman out of it with her fingernail. She bared her teeth at the ravaged face and fantasized spitting venom at the beast for separating her from the one she loved. She scratched away until her nail ripped, but by then most of the picture had been shredded.

Questions boiled in her mind and bubbled in every hidden nook of her heart. Had Philippa gone willingly? Or had she simply escaped a life that she no longer wanted? Had she missed Gemma? Had she sent some message, some secret code, along the way that Gemma had missed? How could Philippa have left her bereft, except at this monster's command?

Many satisfying minutes later, Gemma slipped the smaller lock of hair into the photograph's former home. She shut the locket with a sense of finality. Then she tucked the remainder of the hair back into Nigel's watch and closed it. She set the timepiece beside her pile of books to keep it safe until she could return it.

She tried to rest as ship's night rolled around on the cabin's clock, but sleep refused to come. She opened the Cyrus Smith journal. She was still furious with Pugh and not inclined to assist him, but research was better than boredom. The castaways of Lincoln Island were receiving assistance from some unseen benevolent being, much as she, unseen, was trying to aid a child out of her reach. Agitated by the similarities, she put it down and picked up the book that the captain had lent her. Even Twain's famous humour could not soothe her; after re-reading the same paragraph a dozen times, she put it down as well. The Lyell book lurked on her desk with an accusing stare. She stuffed it into the armoire and slammed the door. She then tried to read *Jane Eyre*, but the bits about the mad woman in the attic won it a spot with Lyell.

Night and morning blended into one another. Her internal clock had lost all sense of the sun. She gave up trying to sleep and wearily resumed her browns.

She examined her mirror and found grease pencil droppings wedged into the edges. As she dug them out, she noticed how pale her reflection was. It brought to mind what Frau Knopf had read at the Knitting Circle. The fate of the Lady was still a mystery to her, and the mystery made her think of Philippa's strange words about being half-sick of shadows. She wasn't sure she wanted to know how the poem ended.

A sudden rap on the door startled her.

"Fraulein?" a voice called through the door. "Almost time for the memorial service. The captain has asked me to escort you there."

Gemma opened the door to admit Frau Knopf, who bore a tray of tea, toast, and a side order of handmade black lace. Knopf placed it on the desk and studied Gemma's uniform with a critical eye. She strode over to the armoire, opened it, and examined the few dresses there.

"You did not pack any mourning clothes?" she asked. "How optimistic of you." She stepped back over to the desk. "Ah, I suppose it is just as well. Most of the others will be in uniform as well, so no harm done. They will have armbands, though. I made you this one," she said as she held up the length of intricate stitches. "Nice and ladylike, *ja*? House of Worth it is not, but it will do." She tied it around Gemma's upper arm with a firm hand. "You may keep it, Fraulein. No doubt you'll need it again."

Gemma had thought they would be going to the parlour, but Frau Knopf led her in the direction of the cargo bay. Frau Knopf moved with an economy that Gemma could appreciate, almost too swiftly to read the signs on the doors as they passed: "Atmospheric Control", "Orrery Gearage", and "Armoury", amongst others. Still, Gemma was relieved to enjoy the relative freedom of the corridors after her confinement.

They approached a growing cluster of crewmembers in front of a completely different sort of chamber. It was similar to the entrance they had used when they had first boarded the ship, but much smaller.

The crowd rustled in hushed whispers. They tugged on their black armbands as they watched a group inside the windowed room. Four men huddled over a man-shaped mass of shroud in the floor. They lifted it into a metal canister that gleamed in the bright light of the chamber.

Frau Knopf halted at the side of the gathering, and then the matron left her to seek out her husband. Gemma stared into the enclosure, the airlock that was the terminus of so many worries and the butt of so many jokes. No one was laughing now.

Humboldt emerged from the milling crowd and nodded at her. "It's all settled at last," he said quietly. "Jules and his Missus have the babe. Bar blokes managed to get her out of there without anyone following. At least, they think so. They're all a bit knackered at the moment, but honestly I think it all worked out for the best."

Gemma thanked him. She was glad for some good news. She just hoped that they had evaded the Watchers. She knew too well how quietly Brightman's people could slink about.

Humboldt struggled with his black armband. Gemma admonished him to stand still, and she adjusted it for him. He gave her a grateful look, and they stood side by side in silence to watch the others come in.

The captain passed by with Pugh and Wallace. Along with Alfieri, they stopped in front of the glass enclosure and turned to face the crew. There was a brief murmur as the chain of command asserted itself, and the crowd organized themselves into neat columns and rows.

Gemma, already on the edge of the crowd, stayed put next to the Booleans. Nigel was there with his crew, looking weary but lucid. As the Cohort entered, they collected around her. Hui and Bidarhalli actually seemed relieved to see her, and just as they were about to inquire about her health, the captain called for attention.

The command rippled down through the ranks. The captain's voice was measured and steady as he spoke. "We are gathered here today to pay our last respects to our comrade, First Mate Miguel Cervantes. Before we continue, however, Father Alfieri would like to say a few words."

The captain moved back into line with Dr. Pugh and Mr. Pritchard. The priest stepped forward and addressed the assembly.

"*Eros. Storge. Philia. Agape.* These are the names for love we have inherited from the ancient Greeks. There are many forms of love, and we have need of them all. Love for a sweetheart. Love of a parent for a child or the child for the parent. Love for a brother or sister. Love for our friends. Love for our fellow man and love for our Creator. All of these bring us here today. We are here to celebrate and honour the love that we have seen in Miguel Cervantes, our first mate, and Jennie Davies, beloved wife of Chief Nigel Davies and mother of his child.

"Each of them laid down their lives so that others might live. Cervantes' quick thinking saved the lives of the gun crew and possibly the entire ship. Jennie Davies yielded up her life so that a new life might come into this world. Our Lord tells us that there is no greater love than that."

As she listened to Alfieri's words, Gemma watched the reactions of the people around her reflected in the airlock window. It was much easier than staring into the knot in her own heart that tightened every time Alfieri mentioned Nigel's wife.

"We need this love. We need to see all the faces of love, especially now, with this great journey before us."

Humboldt had his eyes on the priest, but she could feel the corner of his eye catching her face every now and then. Rathbone and his crew were just beyond the Booleans, looking dark and worried.

"Love for our fellows binds us to one another, as gravity binds the Earth and Mars to the same sun, and allows them to influence one another, even at distances immeasurable to us."

Caroline and Nigel were on her other side, steady at attention. Caroline had a determined look on her face, as if to tell the world that all the Martians in the universe could not drag her away from her brother. Her fierceness was contagious, for Gemma decided, then and there, that she would think of Philippa as the winsome girl in Nigel's pocket watch and not a victim of Mrs. Brightman's scheming. She would never think of her as Philippa again. In her heart, she would only ever call her Jennie. There was little else she could do for Nigel, now, but she could do that, even if he never knew about it. The knot in her chest relaxed at the thought.

"Love heals us. Love transforms us. Love is the light that we carry with us into the darkness ahead."

Like a statue surrounded by water, the captain rose up from the pond of all those reflections. Christophe looked straight at her, straight into her. This was not the laughing lad on the gazebo bench. This was not even the spine-of-steel captain that dared confine her to quarters. Here was a complete stranger, with a veil across his eyes that concealed any sentiment concerning the figure in the cold and lonely chamber behind him. The inscrutability of his face disturbed her as she returned his gaze. She held his mute eyes, and he held hers, as Alfieri continued to speak.

"We never know where love will lead us. We never know to what heights of ecstasy we will rise or to what depths of sorrow we will sink along the way. But love, given its way, will lead us home in the end, even if not to the home that we expected."

Home, Gemma thought, as she turned her head away from the captain. She could bear that indecipherable stare no longer. *I no longer have one. If one could even call that place a home.*

"Never underestimate what love can accomplish, at whatever distance. We live and we love and we pass that spark forward -- through our children, through our ideals, our deeds and our courage.

"Whether for a lover, a friend, a parent, a brother or a sister, or for a complete stranger, or for the world entire... do not be limited in your love for yourself or for each other. Love is an inexhaustible resource. It feeds upon itself. Love fully. Love freely. And live."

Alfieri raised his hands in blessing.

"May the Lord be with us and show us mercy, as we show mercy to those we encounter in our travels."

He continued the service, but now he sounded a bit more official. She guessed that what he was performing now was some sort of Catholic ritual. She could never hope to comprehend such things. Mrs. Brightman was the head of her own form of religion; she would brook no other. Gemma fought to keep the boredom and frustration from her face. It might not mean anything to her, but it meant something to her new friends, and she would not take that away from them.

"Lord God, by the power of your Word you stilled the chaos of the primeval seas, you made the raging waters of the Flood subside, and calmed the storm on the sea of Galilee. As we commit the body of our brother Miguel Cervantes to the deep, grant him peace and tranquility until that day when he and all who believe in you will be raised to the glory of new life promised in the waters of baptism. We ask this through Christ our Lord."

Alfieri finally closed, and after his resounding "Amen", the captain barked a sharp "*Terra vigila!*"

"*Terra vigila!*" the crew cried back, and their chant echoed throughout the cargo bay.

The captain then turned to face the airlock doors and led them in a salute with a crisp command. Gemma watched the reflection of his face in the glass, and it never wavered as the outer doors opened. The canister was sucked away by the vacuum of space; it vanished in a blink, as if it had never been there. The knot in her chest convulsed again at the sight. Would it be that quiet and quick for a living person? She hoped she never found out.

Christophe lingered in his salute for a brief eternity. Being a civilian, Gemma did not have to salute, but she did notice the quivering of the aloft elbows around her. He finally gave the command to end the salute, and Gemma felt a silent sigh of relief wash through the room.

"Company, dismissed," the captain said, his voice devoid of emotion.

As the assembly broke up, Gemma whispered to Humboldt, "I wonder why the captain did not speak. He and Cervantes were old friends, were they not?"

Humboldt tugged at his armband. "I think he wanted to, Miss L. Seems the words might have just been too heavy to let go, just yet." He nodded at her. "I have to head back to Informatics. I have a little research I'd like to complete on your request. I will send word if I find anything. Good day, Miss L."

He touched her forearm with an absentminded pat and strolled away. The gathering wound down as crewmembers left by ones and twos. Caroline fussed over Nigel. Gemma paid her respects to them as she pressed Nigel's watch back into his hands. She could not bring herself to say much to him, not yet. He grasped her hands and choked on his words as he expressed his gratitude. He was not in any shape for conversation, so she let them be.

Gemma could not bear the thought of additional, possibly indefinite, confinement in her quarters. The captain was deep in conversation with Mr. Pritchard. She saw an opportunity, and she took it. She slipped out of the bay unseen. She thought Christophe might look for her in the Gardens first, so she headed for the orrery instead.

It was quiet there. The normal squeaks, rings, and roars that inhabited the corridors of the ship were a reassuring background rumble here, like far away thunder. All she could hear was the eternal grinding of the planets around the little sun, and again rotating themselves, showing day and night, night and day, season upon season, on each of the planets. There was the ever-present scribble-scrabble-skitter somewhere in the walls, but it no longer bothered her. She had been haunted by the Man from Shanghai for so long that another ghost would not matter.

She turned down the lights. As they dimmed, the model of the sun lit up like a roaring fire. It lit her way to the observation platform on the far side of the room. She wanted to open the shield door and have a look at what lay outside by herself.

With a trembling hand, she lowered the lever. The shield rumbled as it rolled back into the wall. She found no end to the stars that spilled across her view. She allowed her eyes to relax and go out of focus. One after another, more stars appeared. The more she looked, the more she saw, until the view filled her eyes with countless points of light. It was not just white light; every colour was there, from icy blue to fiery crimson, so many hues that she became giddy. The power and majesty of them all overcame her. Her knees gave way. She landed on the deck floor, but she barely noticed the frigid metal beneath her. She was enraptured. The stars beckoned her onward.

Never in London had she seen such a night sky. The street lamps there concealed the view in their closer light. Once, during her time in Sicily, she had had one brief night alone on a dark beach during a new moon, and she had swooned at the wash of light across the sky.

That glorious night on the beach paled next to this.

She had never known such beauty existed. She was filled with a sudden rage that Mrs. Brightman had kept her from this, not only from this beauty and grace, but from the very capacity for loving it. Out here in the wilds of the solar winds, there was nothing to hold her back. Not even her Watcher could restrain her now. She had severed her last anchor line to Earth, and she was ready to sail free.

She knew those lights were far away, mind-numbing numbers of miles and years away; but for the moment, she could touch them by only reaching out her hand. The stars did not care where she had been or what she had done. They only wanted her to soar among them. The Milky Way surged before her like a vast and deep ocean of night, with the light of the stars sparkling like the moon on the sea. She had never seen such pure beauty in all her life, even in her imagination. She had never had an inkling that it even existed.

What other wonders waited beyond Mars? Would she ever be able to go there? Her heart began to race with the possibility... could she just keep going, keep exploring? She felt she had finally found her heart, her purpose. It was a purpose far, far away from Mrs. Brightman.

She wished Jennie could have seen it. Jennie would have loved it, too. She should have come. She should have been there. The scar of her loss was reopened, and the pain was both fresh and sweet. She longed for some message, some reassurance, that her friend had still loved her at the end. But, other than that wish, nothing bound her to Earth.

For a brief moment, she forgot her anger at Brightman and her hatred of the Martians. She wanted to explore, like Drake, Magellan, and Raleigh, like so many others who had wandered the circumference of the Earth. She wanted to go farther, farther than Cabot, farther than Vespucci, farther than any of them ever dreamed that a human could. They had been to where the maps end. She had wandered off those maps entirely and was somewhere in the space Between Worlds. She felt the pull to go beyond that, as if there were some other form of gravity out there calling her towards it.

Brightman would never use her knowledge to plunder or murder again. There would be no more Men from Shanghai to haunt her dreams. She wanted to discover, not steal. She would be a pioneer, not a thief. She was determined that, no matter where her body might be, her heart would always be among the stars.

A sob of ecstasy escaped her as she pressed her palm into the window, and she wept tears of joy at the sight.

"So, you aren't so heartless after all."

She jerked her head towards the voice. Christophe stood at the bottom of the stairs that led up to the alcove. She was angry with herself for allowing anyone to sneak up on her. She had not been in the orrery that long; this must be the first place he searched for her. How could he have known?

She struggled to her feet and growled at him. "Just how long have you been standing there?"

"Long enough," he replied. "I only wanted to make sure you were alone. I thought perhaps you and Humboldt..." A smile crept through his voice as the words faded. She could only see a portion of him in the shadows, silhouetted in the light of the chamber's sun. "Well, I saw you standing together at the service."

"Oh!" Gemma was startled by his implication. "Of course we did. We are friends."

"I see," he said with a shade of satisfaction in his tone. He covered the stairs in two long strides. "I thought I might find you here. I wanted to come here for a moment, anyway. I could not think of what to say down at the airlock. The words... the words just wouldn't come. I'd rather be here and remember him." He swept his arm towards the window. The eerie veil that she had seen over him at the service fell away with every word he uttered. "This is what he lived for. The ship was part of him, you know. There were many times when I think he should have been the captain. He certainly deserved it more than I." He drew in a deep, slow breath, and held it for a long, stretched moment.

"I never had occasion to speak with him," Gemma said gently, "but he seemed a decent fellow. He certainly commanded the crew's respect. I am truly sorry for your loss. I hope we are able to discern the cause of the accident."

"My thanks," he replied. "I wanted to make sure you were safe. I also wanted to say I am sorry for not coming to you last night. For not updating you, that is. 'Twas a bit dicey there for a bit, but we did manage to get the infant to safety. From all reports, she is quite snug and safe with

Humboldt's cousin's wife."

"I'm -- I'm pleased to hear it," she stammered with relief. The news did not completely quell her irritation with him, but it did file the edge off it.

"I thought you might like to know that they named her 'Gemma'," he continued. "Apparently, they had that name picked out, if it were a girl, before we launched." He took a step forward. "Interesting coincidence, that."

A flutter of joy struck her heart, and she averted her gaze to her fidgeting fingers so that he could not see. *A message*, she thought. *She did send me a message. She did think of me.*

"Yes. Quite. Quite interesting," Gemma managed to say.

"Pugh said that this would cost you something. I only have a vague idea of what that cost is, but I am guessing that at the very least you will be, shall we say, sacked from your institute."

"Something like that."

"You might have a difficult time finding another employer, given your current location. Any plans?"

She had no answer for that. In her heady rush to rescue the baby -- little Gemma, she thought with a blush -- she had not thought beyond the moment. She had not expected to live long enough to make plans. She shook her head.

"I might be able to help with that," he said, taking another step closer. "But I'd have to know a little more about you, first. Who are you, Gemma Llewellyn? Who are you, really?"

"I don't know. I don't know who Gemma Llewellyn is," she said. "Without Brightman, I don't know who I am."

"I'll tell you what I know about her," he said. He used his long reach to give her shoulder a light squeeze. "She is brave. So very, very brave."

"Brave? I don't feel very brave."

"Oh, brave, and brilliant, and so much more. I am proud to have such a woman as a member of my crew. You just put your job -- and your life, I'll wager -- on the line to rescue someone millions of leagues away. Someone you have never met and someone whom you may never meet. Yet you did it. With that kind of pluck and moxie, you can be whomever you choose to be."

He closed the distance between them. He slid the hand on her shoulder around to her back and pulled her to him in a loose embrace. She had been here before, during the long-ago flare drill, but this time was different. It was not playful; there was something very serious about it. She could feel his warmth suffusing through the rough fabric of the uniforms that separated them.

"You inspire me, Miss Llewellyn," he whispered.

She did not know how to respond. She just breathed as steadily as she could manage, both fearing and hoping for what she could hear coming her direction.

"I might be able to help you, as I said," Christophe said. "No matter what happens with Brightman, you are still a member of my crew. That will not change. I promise you that. But in order to do that properly, there is something I need to know." He brushed his fingertips lightly against her hair. "Do you trust me?"

He hunched over, lowering his face towards hers. She shivered slightly as she thought, *Oh, crickets, here it comes.*

"Will you trust me?" he whispered.

His lips hovered just next to the sensitive skin around her mouth. She could feel the heat of him, the heat of the man that was both the captain of the *Fury* who had finally taken up the full reins of command and the innocent lad that devoured kiwis and cackled at Mark Twain. Like a cat seeking a ray of sunshine, in that moment she wanted nothing more than to sink into it.

This was the point where any other man would have gone ahead and kissed her, but he just hovered there, breathing, as if he were teetering on the edge of a fence, unsure of which way to jump. For once, for one fleeting mad moment, she anticipated it, wanted it. For once, she did not feel a choke of revulsion in her throat, as she always had if playing this particular role on a mission.

Why did he hesitate?

She shivered from the tautness inside her. The tiger that had paced in her mind for the past day coiled up for a pounce and made ready for the next move.

At long last, when she was about to tumble off the sharp knife-edge of frustration, he brushed his chin up the side of her face and rested his lips on her forehead, kissing it with the lightest of pressures, more like a kiss for a sister than a lover. He just held her in silence without making another move. She leaned into his chest and rested her face on it, trying to hear what wind was blowing in there. His breaths were tight and controlled, as if he were trapping the words that he wanted to say deep inside him and they were fighting their way out.

Christophe finally released a few of them. "I've lost a brother today, Gemma. I need to know--"

"Captain Moreau?" Humboldt's unmistakable voice floated through the darkness from behind them.

"Damn," Christophe swore softly as he released her, straightened his spine, and turned to the saluting Boolean in the doorway. Only a portion of his face was visible, but she could sense he was stifling a scowl. "Yes, Mr. Humboldt?"

"Begging your pardon, sir. Chief Rathbone asked me to find you. He has an urgent message for you from Admiral Thorvaldson. Priority one, he said. I think it may be about the, um, operation we just performed in London."

Under the cover of darkness, Christophe's spine sagged with a resigned exhalation only Gemma could hear. He took her elbow and guided her down the alcove's steps.

"I'll be on the bridge directly, Mr. Humboldt." He swung his gaze back to Gemma, and his eyes glimmered. "In the meantime, would you please escort Miss Llewellyn back to Ladies' Country? I think I can trust you to get her there safely."

Gemma shot the captain a smouldering look, but he only mouthed the word *later* at her before exchanging salutes with Humboldt and leaving them behind.

Gemma's insides were coiled tightly, and she trembled with the energy of it. She wasn't even sure if she could speak, and she certainly did not feel comfortable with Humboldt seeing her in this state.

"Mr. Humboldt," she began, "we--"

He held up one hand to stop her. "I don't have time for gossip just now, Miss L." He held forth a sheaf of paper. "I'll take you back to your cabin, like the captain ordered," he said, "but first I need to show you something."

They were still just inside the door of the darkened orrery. He tugged her over to a spot that was still inside the chamber but in the light of the corridor. He pulled a page to the front.

"It's your message, the one you wanted me to research," he said. "Try as I might, I could never find the archive copy. I've looked everywhere but under the hay bales on the stable deck. I don't think the wireless blokes ever gave it to us. That's regs, miss. They're not supposed to lose messages. But that's not the weirdest part. See this?" He pointed to the timestamps. "Here, you got your time they sent it and the time we got it. See how close they are?"

Gemma shook her head. "I don't understand. Do the electromagnetic waves not travel fast enough for them to be close in time?"

"When we're on or near Earth, I'd agree with you. They travel at the speed o'light, though. The farther out we get, the longer the delay. See here, look at other messages sent around the same time." He showed her the other messages in his hand. "The delay between send and receive on each one of 'em shows a lag time, except for yours. That can only mean one thing--"

A yelp of surprise cut Humboldt's thought short. He crumpled to the floor to reveal another man behind him, a man brandishing the length of pipe that had just collided with the Boolean's head.

"You've been a naughty girl, Artemis," growled the leering face of Rathbone.

Instinct blossomed in Gemma's brain. She kicked at the pipe to disarm him and missed. Rathbone leapt backwards with an astounding grace, as if they were dancing.

"Don't expect to repeat Shanghai here, love," he purred. "He wasn't ready for you. I am."

Watchers were silent. Invisible. There to Watch and Protect. Philippa would sometimes whisper to her at night, alone in their room, "If you ever see your Watcher, he'll be the last thing you ever see."

Her Watcher swung the pipe again with great force, but this time she blocked him with her arms crossed high. The impact jarred her smaller frame, but she absorbed the hit all the same. Gemma wrenched the pipe from his grasp and released the loudest scream she could muster. Any mere mortal, she could handle. But a Watcher? She would need help.

Rathbone slapped the pipe out of her hand, and it rolled out of the circle of light. It disappeared along with the echoes of her cry.

He lunged at her with a sneer. She tried to block him again, but his move was only a feint. He seized her arm and flung her to the deck as effortlessly as he would a rag doll. She rolled to her feet and scampered out of the light to catch her breath and think.

"Nowhere to run, love," he said as she dissolved into the darkness. Coiled like a panther ready to pounce, he planted himself between her and the chamber door. "Only one way out of here. All I have to do is turn on the lights, love, and you're all mine."

Then, an image came to her, unbidden and hazy, of another door, one marked "Gearage Chamber". And yet another vision followed, as she crawled along in the darkness, timing her movements with the slow groans of the orrery. It was the impression of a horse racing across a great rocky plain, with a gleaming red planet hovering just over its far horizon.

"All I have to do is turn over your messages," he jeered. "'I've decoded them,' I'll say. 'She's a spy,' they'll say. 'Out the airlock with her,' Cap'n'll say. Bad way to go, love, bad way to go. Not so quick a snuff as you might think. Might as well let me do it, love. I'll knock you out first, at least."

She hazarded a look back at the chamber door, but all she could see was Humboldt's crumpled form and the silhouette of the much closer Rathbone. She could not run that way. The impulse to flee was overpowering; it was even stronger than her instinct to fight. She looked to the only light in the room, the orrery's miniature sun, and a plan of action clicked into place.

The orrery covered two decks, pushing its way through a hole in the floor plates like a mammoth whirling tree. The model Mars crept its way around the outside of the railing with its two moons. That must be the Mars in her mysterious vision! This metal tree would have to be her path to safety. It would be tricky, but it was her only choice.

Rathbone could block her every move. He would wear her out. He would take her down. And it would be over. She had just found her life. She was not about to yield it up to the likes of him.

"What, running now?" he taunted. "I do believe you've gone soft, Llewellyn. Time was you'd stand and fight. You took down that fellow in Shanghai right sharp and proper, but since then you've been worse than useless."

Her heart pounded so hard that it threatened to burst out of her chest. She reined in her breathing as well as she could, gathering her strength as she crawled towards the Red Planet. She swallowed down the bitter lump of terror rising in her throat.

"Too bad you didn't know who it was you snuffed," he continued. She could hear his footsteps retreating in the dark. He preferred the advantage darkness gave him. "Might've given you a good turn if you did. But you've not been right in the head since, all the same. Botching the jobs. Leaving the best bits behind. Not skewing the tables enough to throw them off."

She remained silent, wishing for a fleeting moment that the Man from Shanghai was with her, for once. At least then she wouldn't feel so alone. Where was Christophe? Had he figured out Rathbone's trickery yet? There was still no movement at the door and no answer to her scream.

Where is everybody?

She edged forward, taking her time under the cover of shadows, with the edge of the strongest light yet before her.

"I think you've gone more than soft, though. You've gone positively daft out here. And for what? A baby? Or that failed experiment they call captain? Fallen in love, real love, I'll wager. I should have reckoned if we couldn't beat it out of your little Mrs. Davies, we'd never be able to beat it out of you."

The mention of her beloved friend wrenched a howl from her. She raced for Mars. She ran harder than ever in her life; her heart thundered. The pressure in her head urged her on and on, pushing her and pulling her; and like the swift current of a raging river, it was impossible to resist.

Rathbone caught her movement and gave chase, but she reached the railing first.

Mars rose before her. Mars was her only hope.

Rathbone shouted after her as she grasped the slick metal. She did not look back, and she did not stop.

As she vaulted the railing, she kicked out against the control levers. The orrery lurched from its plodding real-time stroll to a trot, and then that tiny park of celestial time burst into a full gallop. She fought to keep her balance on the narrow pole that revolved around the crimson globe like a merry-go-round. It was just wide enough for her narrow feet, and the hope beat wild in her breast that it would be far too small for her pursuer.

He called after her as she lurched across the narrow pole to the trunk that held Mars. Its whirling made her dizzy, but she did not let go.

"I've Watched you for a long time, girl. You were the best!" He followed her course around the tracks. "But Shanghai ruined you. Glad she got me into the Academy after that so I wouldn't be wastin' my time. That's why she sent you out here. Out to pasture. She was done with you before you even launched, girl. She just sent you on one last mission, hoping to squeeze one last drop of worth out of you. But you mucked that up, too."

He pursued the sphere with surprising grace and speed as he spoke again. "Finding Orion is my job, now." Rathbone the warrant officer shed his skin, and the Watcher emerged at last. "Brightman wants it. Brightman needs it. And I'm going to get it for her."

She took a leap of faith from the pole of Mars and just managed to miss a collision with the edge of the track. She landed on the topmost gear beneath the crimson globe. Her knees and ankles protested the shock. Ignoring his mockery, she peered over the side to find the next step down. She couldn't see the bottom of the pit, but it had to be down there, somewhere. The floor of the gearage chamber was lost in a sea of deep shadows. The ship was not bottomless, though, so she was able to fight down the surge of panic in her belly. The gear kept moving beneath her. She was a branch carried along in a swift stream that had curled into an eddy. She would have to time her jumps carefully. He was coming, he was coming, and there was no time to waste.

She could only jump down to the next visible gear, which was as far as she could go without tumbling to her death to the unseen floor below or between the crushing gears. They no longer sang the relentless song of ocean surf; they roared with the rage of a mighty waterfall.

She had to get down. Somehow, she had to get down to the deck below. The images flooded her mind, images that whispered "home" to her, even though the concept of "home" was as foreign to her as the Red Planet. One image, like some dusty memory just now recalled, told her that the floor was shelter. The floor was safe harbour. If only she could get there, she would be safe. Somehow, she would be safe.

She jumped down again, but she landed in a heap and nearly tumbled off into the darkness. Gasping sharply to catch her wind again, she peered around at the platform that had caught her. It was a hidden track that the gear she had just escaped trundled along. Her overestimation of the height had caused her bumpy touchdown. She could not tell how long it would be before the gear swept around again.

The gears were whirring faster, and still faster; Rathbone must have mucked with the controls. She could sense him moving above her, having gotten past Mars at last. Her reserves were running low; but still the drive to get to the floor, no matter the cost, seared her brain. Rathbone was fumbling his own way through the strange maze, but he was learning fast and closing in.

Bruises from their bout blossomed across Gemma's body, and they screamed for relief. Panting with fatigue, she eyed Rathbone's silhouette, only to find him not on his gear but hurtling towards her, aiming at her, and she could no longer move fast enough to escape him. They fell, locked together, off the side of the circle, and plummeted to the floor.

They sang a chorus of pain as they landed in a heap. Gemma's skull bounced off the hard deck. Before she could recover her wits enough to scuttle away, Rathbone pinned her to the floor. He straddled her and squashed her beneath him. He was so much taller than she was that her legs could not get purchase behind him. Squeezing her sides between his bony legs, Rathbone wrapped his long fingers around her slender throat, pushing into the tender flesh there so deeply that she thought he would rip right through her skin.

"You'll follow Cervantes out the airlock," he growled as he pressed down upon her like a boulder. What little air made it past his fingers squeaked and squealed in her throat. Screaming was beyond her power now. "You and that Humboldt. She wants you both gone. You'll all be gone, before too long. But she wants you first, you little minx. She wants Pugh to hurt, hurt bad, before it's all over, and taking you out first will pierce him right through. Orion's mine to find, now, and they'll be too busy looking for you to worry about who's looking for some stupid file."

He was pressing the very life out of her. She writhed beneath him, but in his frenzy, he was much too strong for her. She could not move. Her ribs could not expand enough for her to inhale. The space around her grew ever dimmer as Rathbone's words descended into something akin to madness.

"We were supposed to find Orion," he snarled through his clenched teeth. "I had the wireless. You had the scientists." He leaned low, nose brushing her forehead and sweat dripping onto her, choking off any last hope of another breath. "There's something here, something more than this stupid ship. When we launched we had plenty of time to find it, but now, time's out. Time's out for everybody. I've got to find it and get out before--"

A primal screech cut him off. Some dark and solid mass collided with him and ripped him off Gemma's body. She rolled over twice from the force of it. It landed on top of him several yards away. She wheezed and gasped, trying to breathe past the burning in her side, like a drowning woman who had broken the surface of the sea at last.

The last thing she saw, before the world went completely black, in the dim light filtering down from the orrery above, was the giant squid from her nightmares, pinioning a shrieking Rathbone beneath its meaty tentacles.

CHRISTOPHE

Christophe fumed his way to the command deck, searching for Mr. Rathbone. He was irritated at the man's interruption, but he stuffed the feeling down into a dark corner of his brain. He had commanded enough ships to know that captains rarely enjoyed a moment's peace.

The warrant officer was not there. Christophe caught the eye of Mr. Adebayo and fired off an inquiry.

"Sir, we haven't seen him," the midshipman replied. "Not since the memorial service. He didn't leave any sort of message for you. He's supposed to be back on duty in half an hour, though."

Christophe shook his head in puzzlement, about to answer, when a sudden buzzing sounded in his head.

"Humboldt, you rake," he hissed to himself.

A queasy wave rolled through his stomach, and he felt the urgent need to locate Gemma. He was not sure whether to run to the orrery or Ladies' Country first, but he had to start somewhere. He reached for the speaking tube when he received a sudden flash in his head from Maggie. Maggie called to him, called to him the way she did when words were not fast enough.

The sense of a man getting between a bear and her cub flooded him, as well as the image of colossal gears grinding away in the darkness. In his mind's eye, he saw two figures locked in a frantic battle as they leaped through the shadowy spaces between revolving brass plates. He saw them through a dim red haze, like a dusty memory just recalled. But this was no memory; it was happening now, now, and Maggie was witnessing it. She was screaming for him to come and to bring help.

"Mr. Adebayo," he barked, "Call Dr. Pugh over the pipephone in his office and send him, and only him, to the orrery gearage chamber, smartly!"

He could not wait on the lumbering lift. Christophe charged down the corridor, leaving the startled junior officer in his wake. He plowed his way to the Ready Room.

After securing the door, he traced the opening combination on the wooden mural and slipped into the dim corridor behind it. After he pushed the lever to close the panel, he snatched a charged Leyden pistol in its holster from the hidden rack and clipped it to his belt. He then barreled full-speed down a gradual slope, faster than he had ever run in his life, cutting down the side of the ship, passing deck after deck and sending the image of his location to Maggie the whole way down.

I'm coming, Maggie. He pushed the words out to her in his mind, but the primal shrieks in his head grew ever shriller. *Protect her. I'm coming.*

Down, down, and down he ran, so swiftly he nearly missed the exit to the gearage chamber. Maggie had stopped sending him images; he could only feel her rage thrashing around his brain. Christophe could hear a man screaming on the other side of the door.

"Humboldt! Damn you!"

A cacophony assaulted his senses as he burst through the opening. The giant gears rolled in and out of the light at breakneck speed, and the howling of it nearly overwhelmed him.

His frantic eyes pierced the shadows, searching for movement. The gears' shadows slithered along the floor; their grinding was as relentless as a waterfall, one in which he felt he would drown.

Christophe shut his eyes and waited for the man's screams to rise above the clattering once more. He looked in that direction and found what he was looking for: a writhing, pulsing mass pinning down the shadow of a man. The oily grey of its flesh rippled in and out of the scant light that shone down from the orrery's sun, and the captain could see tiny flashes of a slick beak as the being wiggled on top of its quarry and pressed the man down into the floor. Christophe rushed towards them with a roar. As he approached, one sinuous limb stretched out to him, a great meaty serpent slithering away from a nest of its fellows. It curled into a slight spiral as the limbs left behind grasped their prey ever tighter.

"Martians, Martians!" the man gurgled. "It's the end!"

The lump of grey pulsed and shifted to cover its prisoner even more and muffled his moans. The tip of the single free tentacle flicked at Christophe. He raised his hand to it and brushed the edge of it with his fingertips.

"Maggie," Christophe addressed it as the delicate end wrapped itself around his fingers and held them. "Maggie, hold him fast!" He peered around them, eyes still adjusting to the lack of light. He ignored the whimpers creeping out from underneath her. "Show me, show me! Where is she?"

The snake released his hand and pointed away from them. Christophe followed its trajectory and nearly tripped over a crumpled Gemma at its end. Kneeling by her side, he took no time in folding back her collar and checking her pulse. It was rapid and shallow, but it was there. Alive. He had made it in time, thanks to Maggie's warning. He trembled with relief. He felt her limbs, checking for injuries, wincing as she moaned when he touched her ribs.

His hands eased underneath Gemma's tiny form and separated it from the icy floor. He cradled her against his chest and marveled at how small she was.

He placed a firm kiss on her forehead. He remembered the brief warmth that they had shared not an hour ago, and he rested his cheek against hers in hopes to feel it again. He closed his eyes tightly for just a moment, as if he could drag her back to consciousness by force of will the same way he could talk to Maggie.

"Breathe, Gemma. Breathe!" he urged her, ordered her, but her only response was a fit of coughing that vibrated right through him. As his vision adjusted to the semidarkness, he detected bruises forming on her face and around her open collar. Rage crept into the edges of his vision. There was no mistaking what this was. It was no accident. One member of his crew had tried to murder another.

I am the captain, damn it.

They should be fighting the Martians, not each other. He should have known, had known, after listening to Pugh's story, that Gemma was in danger from someone on the ship. He should have stayed with her, should have taken her back to her cabin himself.

"No more!" he howled to the cool and unsympathetic walls surrounding them.

He had lost the man that was his brother to this hollow beast, this metal monstrosity that plowed through empty skies. He was not about to lose another piece of himself to her.

"Not my crew! Not my people! Not her! Not again, you soulless creature! *Fury!* You iron whore! No more!"

Gemma struggled mutely in his grasp. As she gasped for air, he could feel Maggie reaching into his mind as easily as she had reached out for his hand. A veil of calm settled around him, and the edge of his anger faded for a moment. He directed his attention back to Gemma as she coughed and sputtered without opening her eyes.

"Stay with me now," he said as he stroked her cheek. "Stay with me. That's an order. Listen to my voice, Gemma. Follow my voice." He shook her, just a little. She coughed and twitched. "I am your captain, Gemma. I will be obeyed in this. You will stay with us. With me."

Dr. Pugh emerged from the darkness near the hidden entrance. He crossed the room in a few long strides.

"Hold the man for us, Maggie," he said to the great lump. He paused for a moment and stared at the strange pile of flesh. Then he left it behind and went to the entrance proper. He pulled at the control levers. Time ground to a halt as the gears rolled to a stop. The resulting quiet pressed in on Christophe's ears like an avalanche of silence.

The man trapped beneath the tentacled creature sighed one last "Martians!" before he lapsed into unconsciousness.

Pugh stood over Christophe and rested a hand on the younger man's shoulder.

"How is she, son?"

"Alive," he said. The word barely made it out of his mouth. He could not disguise the tremor in his voice. "But just. Maggie saved her, Elias. Humboldt was choking her. Choking her! Bastard! It's my fault. I trusted the wrong man. Maggie has him, though. We need the doctor."

"That's not Humboldt," Pugh replied as he pointed to the figure underneath Maggie. "She has your wireless officer. Rathbone."

"Rathbone?" Christophe asked as Gemma's eyelids fluttered open. He gasped in relief. "Good Lord! Then where's Humboldt? They were at the orrery door when I left them."

Gemma finally rasped, "Humboldt... up there... door... please... please..."

"Gemma," Christophe said, choked with relief.

Her consciousness faded as he said her name, and an iron fist closed around his heart.

"Elias," he said as he fought to stand up with Gemma in his arms, "we've got to get her to sick bay. She's alive. She is alive, thank God, thank God! But she is so very weak."

"Take her on, son. I will handle things here and check in on Humboldt upstairs. Have Hansard send some orderlies to the orrery door to assist me. Maggie?"

Maggie screeched and chirped in response, and Dr. Pugh answered her unvoiced question.

"Take this ruffian down the passage to the brig door and wait for me there. Keep him quiet if you can, m'dear. I'll be there directly." He shook his head. "Pah! Martians on the ship, indeed! What rubbish."

GEMMA

"Whatever shall we tell the crew?" asked the Man from Shanghai. "I'm sure the rumours are flying even now."

No, no, Gemma thought in the midst of a haze of pain. *That is not right. He doesn't speak. He never speaks. I never hear his voice.*

Even the act of thinking was a Herculean task. The spike of agony in the side of her skull drove even deeper into her brain. She could hear voices, but their words made no sense.

"No matter what we tell the crew," the other voice replied, sounding much like Dr. Pugh, "we will have to tell her. And what to do with Rathbone? He has seen even more than she has."

Frozen hailstones disguised as words plummeted onto her eardrums, and she winced as each one bounced around in her skull. Lost in a fog of them, she could not recall anything but the searing pain in her head, her neck, her sides...

Broken, she thought again. *Ribs broken. Rathbone. Rathbone broke them.*

She was still alive. The last thing she remembered was the weight of Rathbone crushing the life out of her. *The airlock.* He was going to chuck her out the airlock, along with Humboldt.

Now all she knew was that it hurt to breathe, even to think, but at least she could do both now. She had blacked out. How long had she been insensible? What secrets had she spilled? She hated being out of control, even for a moment.

Control. She had been under Rathbone's control, struggling for breath. That was her last memory. What had happened next? She had seen, or thought she had seen, a writhing mass of snakes ripping the man away from her.

No, no, she thought, *not snakes. A Martian.* But that vision had to be a hallucination, an artifact of asphyxiation. *A Martian on board?* The Invaders were no more than preserved specimens.

Her eyelids were heavy, so heavy, and she could not yet open them. She shifted her body in a vain hope of finding a comfortable spot, and a groan escaped her from the effort.

"She's coming round," cried a voice that definitely belonged to Christophe.

Sudden warmth pressed against her cheek, the one that was not throbbing. The heat of it solidified into a hand that cradled half her face. Her eyelids finally yielded to her will and opened. The world was a blur, entirely occupied by a single face. Gemma blinked, slowly, to allow her eyes time to focus. They finally decided to get to work and revealed Christophe's face, steeped in a mixture of relief and concern. Repelled by the shower of anxiety falling over her, she shrank back into the pillow. His other hand followed her, and he brushed a stray lock of hair from her forehead. He winced at her act of revulsion, and one side of his mouth twisted down as her face clenched in pain.

"Gemma," he murmured, "sweet Gemma. I was so worried--"

"Where... where am I?" she asked, shifting her shoulders a little. She could see little except for a soft white glow beyond Christophe's face.

"Safe. In a nest, of sorts." When she started to speak again, he shushed her with great gentleness, brushing the unbruised side of her face with the back of his hand. "Rest, rest, my dear. Rathbone's in the brig. You're safe."

She could feel fabric brushing her skin as she tried to move. Tight bandages swaddled her ribs, and some other soft cloth -- not the rough wool of her scientist's uniform -- kissed her upper limbs. She glanced down and saw that she was wearing a very loose shirt of Egyptian cotton. She could also tell that beneath the blankets that warmed her from her waist down she wore very little else. The laces down its front were slightly loose; for a brief moment, she thought she was hallucinating that the *Fury* was a pirate ship of old. She narrowed her eyes in irritation as she realised that someone had to have undressed her.

As Christophe retreated from her curled lip, a shadow crept up over his head and curled around his shoulder. A grey mass waggled in the air, like one of Medusa's wilder curls. For a moment, Gemma thought she was hallucinating yet again. She gasped as the strange reptile slithered over his shoulder and up the side of his face. Gemma choked back a shriek as it caressed the edge of his ear.

He turned at the touch. Gemma expected him to scream. He should have screamed, struck out, clawed at the serpentine limb with vengeance in his heart. Instead, he gazed at it with great affection. He turned his eyes back to Gemma, and an open-mouthed grin spread across his beaming face. That expectant, hopeful smile reached from his chin through his clear green eyes and across his forehead all the way up to his high hairline. The warning cry that was tearing a path out of her chest screeched to a silent halt.

"Have I gone mad?" Gemma demanded. Some of her restrained shrillness leaked out with the question. "Or have you?"

"Oh, neither," said the voice of Pugh from somewhere beyond Christophe. "At least, not because of this. Miss Llewellyn, may I present to you someone who is very eager to make your acquaintance. This is Maggie."

The sinuous tip was eclipsed as another, greater, shadow rose up behind Christophe's grin.

"Try not to scream, my dear child," Pugh said. "We don't want to upset Maggie."

The greyness grew and grew, until it nearly touched the ceiling. A sharp beak glistened in the midst of the rolling flesh as the fiend loomed over the comically grinning Christophe, who only emitted a squeaky "ha" as Maggie reared up over him.

"Upset *her*?" Gemma asked, fighting the panic rising in her aching chest.

The beak clicked twice in response, and the round blue eyes above it blinked. In Gemma's mind, she thought she heard the Man from Shanghai whisper, "Yes."

Pugh walked between her and the creature he called "Maggie" and continued in a gentle voice. "Don't worry about your change of togs. We did not watch! Maggie handled that for us. She thought that one of Christophe's old sailing shirts might be more comfortable than that scratchy old jacket. Especially with those bandages." Embarrassment coloured his laugh as he witnessed disgust and horror spread across her face. "Not to worry, Llewellyn. She was very careful to avoid injuring you further. Trust me, if she can dress a squirming two-year-old," he said as he cast a meaningful nod at Christophe, "she can handle an unconscious patient. She's quite good at it, actually."

"Maggie," Gemma managed to stammer. She swallowed twice before she could speak again. "This *thing*, this Martian, is Maggie? This is your other assistant?"

Maggie squealed and rolled away to the far side of the room and sagged into the floor, like a lump of sad pudding. Gemma blinked again, but the alien was still there.

"Please don't call her a thing," Christophe said softly. He leaned closer and whispered, "She's very sensitive."

"Impossible," Gemma whispered.

The Invaders were all dead. They could not survive contact with humans for long; that was the gospel of the *Invasion Chronicle*. What, then, was this creature that sulked in the corner?

She stumbled over her words. "Th-that Martian..."

The monster gurgled as Gemma spoke and huddled even more into the corner, if that were possible for such a brute.

"She saved you," Christophe said with more than a twinge of indignation in his voice, as if she had called his mother a warthog. He leaned back into the chair beside her low bed. "She pulled Rathbone off you before-- well, before. You should be grateful to her."

"*Saved* me? *Grateful?*" she cried. "To an enemy? Christophe, these -- these demons -- they killed my parents! Cervantes' parents! Brightman did this--"

"No, no, no, love," Christophe cooed as he took her waving hands into his own, "the *Martians* did that. This is *Maggie*. She's one of us. She's Terran."

She could not bear the hope shining in his eyes. Her gaze trailed down to his hands, which seemed to swallow up her own smaller ones between them. If he had stated that dragons had taken up gardening at Windsor castle, she would not have been more stunned. Despite the throbbing behind her own eyes, she sat up, hands still caged within the captain's, and turned her attention back to Pugh.

"Where is Rathbone?" Gemma demanded.

Pugh shook his head as he replied, "The brig. He needed some rest. The poor fellow kept blathering on about Martians on the ship."

"Well, aren't there?" She yanked her hands away from the captain and pointed a quivering finger at the alien in the corner.

The elderly scientist folded his arms over his chest and leaned back against the wall near the moping Maggie. Pugh sighed, as if he were repeating a formula to a lazy student for the forty-fifth time. "Maggie is just as Terran as you or I, Gemma. She's simply not human."

"Terran? Human? What's the difference?" she sputtered.

"A great deal, I'm afraid," Pugh answered.

Gemma pursed her lips as she realized that something did not add up. "You and I are human, you said. What about Christophe?"

Pugh spread his hands in a helpless gesture. Christophe just beamed at her with that ridiculous, toothy, full-faced, open-mouthed raised-eyebrow grin of his.

"Well?"

"Well, I am Terran," Christophe admitted. "Close enough."

Gemma sank back into the pillows. His face crumpled as she recoiled from him, but she could not help it. All the wind had blown out of her sails at last. She focused her attention on Pugh, instead, so that she could not see the agony bubbling up on the captain's face. Hysteria jousted with Curiosity deep in her mind.

This cannot be, she thought.

She had often mocked this young man in her thoughts for being not quite real. She had had no clue that she was right.

Curiosity won.

"You're going to have to explain that," she said at last, unable to disguise the weariness in her voice.

"Maggie is not the only one of her kind," Pugh said. "There are several second-generations. Remember that crash on Mount Cook I mentioned on your first day? The victims weren't human. That's why it wasn't in the papers."

"There are others?"

"Most of them are in the custody of other departments. Who do you think did most of the construction work in orbit before Shackleton Station was finished? The poor brutes." Dr. Pugh sniffed. "Well, our Martians are better than their Martians, of course."

Maggie gurgled. Pugh turned to her and said, "Yes, yes, I am sorry, Maggie, you are still Terran. I was simply making a point. Give the girl time."

"I don't understand. Where did she come from? The *Chronicle* said--"

"The *Invasion Chronicle* only told part of the story. Not all of the Invasion Orphans were human, Gemma," Pugh explained. "The Martians 'bud off' without sexual recombination, thereby creating a perfect copy of themselves. They are especially prone to do this if they sense death is near. We know this because we have witnessed it. Several of the Invaders managed to bud off after they had fed and before they had perished of disease.

"They left their children behind. Living children. Children nearly identical to the parent, with one major exception. Apparently, they have the ability to control what Code the copy receives, as long as they have that Code in them. Do you remember their means of nourishment?"

"They drink blood! How could I forget?"

"Yes. To them, though, the consumption of blood is far more than sustenance. It is the collection of data, of Code. Once a Martian consumes blood, it seems, the Code within is available for use. These particular Martians managed to mix enough human Code with their own, and enough of their victims' antibodies, to give their progeny human immunities. Therefore, their children did not die from our diseases. Maggie is one of those children. But something went horribly wrong with her, at least from a Martian point of view. She has far more of the human touch than they expected. She is hardly, as the *Chronicle* would say, 'cool and unsympathetic'. She has the heart of a lioness, and she protects her cubs. She loves. She understands."

Maggie purred her way through the end of Pugh's speech. Gemma felt as if she would vomit, and she had to work hard to ignore Christophe as he fidgeted next to her.

"So, she is partly human? And her children will have her immunity? Can she--"

"Species is no object," Pugh said. "Naturally, we feed her from livestock and not from people. She has budded off several times and produced a variety of other creatures." Gemma could not help but notice his slight glance in Christophe's direction.

"I think we should tell her all of it," Christophe said. "We've gone this far."

"What else is there?" Gemma asked. "What makes you *just* Terran?"

Dr. Pugh rested his hand on Christophe's shoulder. "As I said, species is no object. And it doesn't take much of a sample to capture a Code, if that is all one wants. A crumb is sufficient, instead of the cake entire, if one is not hungry, to get the job done. We don't have to kill to copy."

Gemma's thoughts froze. Comprehension escaped her, or at least, she wished that it had. She looked from Christophe to Pugh, then to Maggie, then to Pugh and back again to the young man in front of her.

"Dr. Pugh," she asked, unsure of how much longer she could remain so calm in this tiny spot of insanity, "h-how much blood did you have to give to Maggie? I know there is some of you in there somewhere." Christophe looked shocked at her conclusion, but Pugh simply smiled at her as she stammered on. "I've heard you call him 'son'. Don't deny it. I am a trained observer, Dr. Pugh. You have only sharpened that knife in my time with you. You are his father!"

Pugh laughed. "That's my Llewellyn. I knew you would figure it out eventually. Yes, yes, I am his father. Well, after a fashion. But I'm not the only one." At Gemma's puzzled look, he added, "Later. You are a tad weak for the whole story just yet, child. Suffice it to say, long ago, we gave Maggie some Code samples. We asked her to use them to create a commander for us. We needed a leader for this mission. She budded off. That bud now sits before you."

Gemma stared at Christophe in a state of utter shock. She had seen no sign, no evidence, that he was anything other than a randy, red-blooded human male. He offered her only another of his nervous chuckles in response. Rathbone's remark about "that failed experiment they call captain" crept out of her memory and leered at her. She had been about to die at Rathbone's hands; his intimation was likely true. Why would he lie at a time like that? No, no, they had not told her everything. Not yet.

"But you're not... y-you don't have any--"

Dr. Pugh. "I assure you, child, that many members of the fairer sex have examined him thoroughly and confirmed that he is completely normal. The tests were repeated and redundant, and the results were always consistent."

Christophe did not even have the decency to blush at that, although he did chuckle. He merely said, "Elias, I think we should tell her everything. There is yet another thing, Gemma. Dear, dear Gemma. There is a chance you could be--"

"Let's stick with what we know, Christophe. For now, the facts only. There are other things we need to ask her first."

"I think I've heard enough for the moment," she said. Curiosity screamed in the back of her head, hungry for more, but her Hysteria informed her that it was quite full, for now.

"You do need to rest," Pugh said. "Dr. Hansard was quite put out that we removed you from sick bay. However, we could not speak openly to you there, once you were out of the worst danger. As for your ribs, you are deeply bruised but unbroken. You are now part of a very small circle that knows of Maggie's existence, Gemma. It is your turn to speak frankly to us, and then we'll let you rest a bit. I have a notion about why Rathbone attacked you, but I need to hear it from you. And so, I think, does your captain."

Gemma did not answer.

"He was your Watcher, was he not?" Pugh demanded. "I know Brightman's methods. And you know I know."

"Watcher?" asked Christophe. He did not seem as surprised as he should be. "Brightman smuggled one of her Boys on board after all?"

Gemma stared daggers at Pugh. "How much have you told him?"

"You are here and not in the brig, child. I told him enough. That man tried to kill you. He very nearly succeeded. Out with it."

"Yes," she admitted. "At least, he said he was my Watcher. I did not know she'd managed to get one on the ship, not until he--"

She hesitated. Memories of Rathbone gave way to images of Humboldt's face just before he had crumpled to the floor. "What is Mr. Humboldt's condition?"

"Alive," said Pugh. "Unconscious, last we saw him, but alive. Still in sick bay, since he didn't see Maggie. Don't change the subject."

"Gemma," Christophe interrupted. "We need to know why he revealed himself. There had to be a reason. Why did Brightman send the pair of you here?"

He reached for her hands again; when she flinched, he held his hands up in a gesture of resignation and then let them hang limp at his sides.

"Please," he said. "Please, tell me. As the captain of this ship, I can protect you, but I need to know what the danger is. What were you looking for? Did Brightman send anyone else?"

She clenched her eyes shut. At this point, there was no reason not to fill in the gaps. She had been Discovered. This man -- if she could call him that -- knew the worst parts of it already. The Man from Shanghai stirred in the back of her mind, and she corrected herself. He knew the second-worst parts.

"I was not even sure there was a Watcher aboard, until he attacked," she recalled, eyes still fast shut, leaving the memory of Humboldt's research in the vault of her heart. "My task was to search for something called 'Orion'." She opened her eyes to see their reaction, and the look that passed between Pugh and the captain did not escape her notice. "But I have no inkling of what that is. She gave me no details. Just the orders to search for it. He was here, I think, to make sure I found it. He was angry over what happened with Nigel's child. We stole her from Brightman. I honestly have no knowledge of anyone else. But--"

"Yes?" the two men asked at once.

"Rathbone said something else." The throbbing in her head raged now, and the noise of it made it difficult to think. She pushed past the agony of it and pulled Rathbone's words out of the haze. "Something I just now recall. 'Time's out. Time's out for everybody. I've got to find it and get out *before*.'"

"Before what?" asked Pugh.

"That is when Maggie struck," she replied. "She cut him off. He seemed most urgent about it, though, as if some disaster were imminent. I got the impression that he might not have revealed himself otherwise. He had decided to take over my task because time was running out. But what the danger was, he did not say."

Christophe stood, his brow furrowed and his jaw set. "Elias, we must interrogate him. Immediately. The rest can wait. If there is a danger to the crew, we have to know." He looked down at Gemma, every trace of warmth drained from his face. "I leave you here in Maggie's care. I assure you, you could have no better Protector. Rest. That's an order." His eyes softened, ever so slightly. "When we return, if you are up to it, I will take you to see Mr. Humboldt myself. I am certain you would do wonders for each other."

Before she could protest, Christophe swept Dr. Pugh out of the room through a door that revealed a narrow, dimly lit tunnel. It looked like nothing else she had seen on the ship.

As the door shut, Gemma locked her gaze onto the gruesome brute skulking in the corner of the chamber, unsure of which of them was the most afraid.

CHRISTOPHE

"She'll come round."

He could hear Elias behind him, huffing and puffing his way along the corridor. Christophe did not answer. There was too much that he needed to say, and too much that he did not want to.

She was no lady. She was a thief. *Thieves.* There were thieves among his gallant crew, thieves bent on murdering each other. Pugh had tried to warn him, and he hadn't listened. The knowledge burned him. He could not have it. He would not have it.

"Think, son. Gemma's in shock," Pugh continued. "She's injured. I'm certain she's not thinking straight. Forgive her! We did throw a lot at her at once. She's just not used to the idea." His words came in ragged spurts. "Remember, she could--"

"I need to get to the bridge first," Christophe barked. "I need to check in with Pritchard. I want to know the ship is safe before I start with Rathbone."

"Christophe! Stop! Look at me!"

Christophe whirled upon the other man. His face was a chunk of stone, as if some gorgon had slithered out of the wall and pinned him with its stare.

"Please, son, listen to me," Pugh said, bent over, hands on his knees, gasping for air. He grunted a few times before he continued. "She was not ready. You grew up with this. Miguel grew up with this. She did not. Something that is normal and humdrum to us is, well, is miraculous to others!"

Christophe growled, "I have no time for this nonsense." He turned on his heel and continued his course up the slope. "Go on to the brig and tell the master-at-arms to have Rathbone ready. I'll be there directly."

"What are you going to do?" The elderly man's words echoed in the narrow corridor. "Please, please tell me."

"You can't protect me forever, Elias," Christophe replied. He didn't look back, and he didn't wait.

He arrived at the Ready Room exit. The terror he had felt last time he had passed through it, and the reason behind that terror, came back to him in a rush, and he had to pause for a heartbeat or two. Was that reason still there? All he could see now, when he thought of Gemma, was her face twisted into a knot of revulsion. It was etched into his mind's eye with absolute clarity, a part of his redundant memory whether he willed it nor not. For once, he cursed his perfect recall.

He pushed his dark thoughts aside as he emerged onto the bridge. Mr. Pritchard towered over the back of the captain's chair. Christophe paused at the door to catch his breath. He watched his new first mate as the man slowly turned this way and that, reading the glass panels and calling to the various stations for reports, then conferring with Mr. Adebayo and Mr. Goldman. The responses were smooth and rapid. It felt odd, watching it from the outside.

One of the officers looked up from his station and called out, "Captain on the bridge!"

"As you were," Christophe responded. "Mr. Pritchard, a word, if you please."

The first mate nodded and joined him by the door. Christophe took him by the elbow and turned the man so that the crew could not see his face.

"Things sound well in hand, here, Mr. Pritchard," Christophe said in a low voice. "I'm just checking in. Anything unusual?"

Pritchard chuckled. "'Unusual' is relative these days, Captain, but we seem to be flying straight. A few wireless messages have come in, but they were all for Mr. Wallace. They've kept him out of our hair."

"Anything from Thorvaldson?"

"Not since this morning. Mighty quiet on that front." Pritchard cleared his throat. "Begging your pardon, sir, but may I inquire as to Miss Llewellyn's condition? Scuttlebutt has it that Rathbone and Humboldt tussled over her down in the orrery and that all three of 'em got hurt. I do hope the little lady's going to be all right. We're all worried about her up here. We can't get word on her since she's not in sick bay."

"How do you--"

"Orderlies. They're worse than a henhouse, sir."

"Of course. Put your mind at ease, Mr. Pritchard. She is recovering. Safe as houses down in Ladies' Country. Away from the hens."

Mr. Pritchard nodded. "Good to know. Begging your pardon, sir, but why'd they get all rowdy, you think? Seems mighty strange to me. Fights always starting 'round her. That don't sit right with me. I'm thinkin' about having a comin' to Jesus meetin' with a few of these boys. They need to keep their hands off the ladies. Sir."

Christophe could not help but smile at that. "It certainly seems that way, doesn't it? I'm on my way to ascertain exactly what happened. I'll be in the brig. Contact me right away if anything, anything at all, seems out of line, all right? You have the conn, Mr. Pritchard."

GEMMA

The Thing was staring at her. Gemma could feel it.

The chamber was cozy, or as cozy as such a brute's nest could be. It was just a bit larger than Dr. Pugh's office. With only a short distance between the two of them, it would take a scant moment for "Maggie" to reach out with her tentacles and drain her dry of blood.

Gemma tried to shake off the notion as her long years of training took over. She took her eyes off the creature and studied her surroundings. Strange symbols sprawled across the otherwise white walls. The walls shone, reflecting the light from the ceiling in bright spots, and she realized that glass panels floated over the bulkheads. Maggie moved slowly, picking up three of the grease pencils that littered the floor, and scribbled more symbols in three directions on a relatively blank portion of the wall.

A movement at the door made them both pause. Gemma shut her eyes and pretended to be asleep. Instead of Christophe's long strides, she heard the determined march of Frau Knopf, accompanied by the alluring scent of fried pork. Gemma risked cracking open one eye to watch the matron set down a tray and a folded bundle of cloth on the table at the head of the bed. She hummed her way across the room to Maggie, who stretched out a free tentacle to her.

"And how are you today, *Liebchen*?" Frau Knopf asked Maggie as she scratched the limb as one would a cat's ears. "Is the Fraulein being a good girl and getting some rest?"

At that last question, she turned to look at Gemma, who gave up the game and returned her gaze.

Gemma grimaced. The sight of the proper matron cooing over that squirming mass made her queasy. Finally, she managed to say, "You are the last person that I would expect to pet a Martian."

"A Martian?" Frau Knopf blinked. "On this ship? *Ausgeschlossen!* Don't be ridiculous. Maggie would be the first to let us know if we had been boarded. Do not worry. You are safe here, Fraulein." She tickled the underside of the tentacle, and Maggie fairly trilled at the touch. "Isn't she, *Liebling*?"

"H-how long have you known? About Maggie, I mean."

"Oh, I have always known, Fraulein. Why else do you think I am here? I have been with Dr. Pugh for many years. I have cared for Maggie since she was smaller than a kitten. She trusts me." She marched back over to Gemma's bed. "*Essen!* Eat, eat! I brought your favourites. We had some fat rascals left from tea, as well. You need your strength to heal." She pointed to the tumbler next to the plate. "And that will help you sleep."

Gemma recognized the scent, the same evergreen and cinnamon blend that Knopf had enjoyed at the Knitting Circle. "What is it?"

"Gin. My husband's secret recipe. He is a bit of a scientist, himself! Why else have juniper trees on a space ship? It goes down better with some blues, but we will have to make do for now." She poked around the room for a moment, straightening this and tidying that. "Can you believe some people wanted to outlaw such spirits? Fortunately, the TIA is made up of more than just steel tycoons. The major breweries would not stand for it."

She snatched up the pile of fabric at the foot of the bed. "Your uniform!" She clucked her tongue at the sight. "Such a tragedy here. A real villain, that Rathbone, more than just a *Funkmeister*! Perhaps we can get some of this grease off. Bah! The sleeve is torn! You cannot wear this! I brought you some fresh clothes." She pointed at the bundle she had brought in with the tray. "Eat and rest. Have Maggie fetch me if you need anything."

With that, she swept out of the room before Gemma could utter another word, leaving the two to stare at each other once more.

Gemma reached for the tray and immediately collapsed back into the mattress. The plate with the tantalizing smell was just out of reach, and stretching was pure torture. At her moaning, Maggie stirred. She dropped her grease pencils and rolled across the room. Gemma was certain it was all over now, but Maggie simply pushed the tray closer to her with the tip of her smallest tentacle. She barked out one high-pitched squeal.

Somewhere in the depths of Gemma's brain, a foggy image of the Man from Shanghai emerged. This time, he was whole and unharmed, without a wrinkle in his tweed suit. He adjusted his cravat and remarked in a deep voice, "I mean you no harm. And I do regret the damage to the cabbages."

Gemma bit her lip as she looked from the tray to Maggie and back again. She reached for the bacon again (unburnt, she noted) and grasped a strip between her thumb and index finger.

"If I really am dead," she muttered between nibbles, "this is a very strange sort of hell."

CHRISTOPHE

Rathbone rested on the edge of the narrow cot anchored to the wall of his cell. Sweat glistened on his brow, and a nasty half-grin slithered across his mouth.

"So, the abomination comes out at last," he said.

Christophe did not flinch at the taunt. He had expected no less from this ruffian. "I am still the captain of this ship. You will address me as such."

"Oh, *Captain* Abomination, then. Pardon me. So the monster is your pet, I see. Taking her back home, are you?"

"You must be mad, Rathbone," Pugh replied. "There are only Terrans on this ship. Terrans and a traitor."

"Ah, traitor. Now you come to it. A traitor, you got that right, but it's not me. 'Traitor' implies I was on your side at some point. I never was. No, no, no. 'Mole'. That word fits much better, don't you think? Gemma? Now, *she's* a traitor, but not to you, so she don't count here. No, no, you have a traitor of your own."

"Who, then? And what proof do you have?"

"Knowledge has its price."

"You're the prisoner here, Rathbone. You are in no position to negotiate."

"That's what you think. Look, I know the regs as well as anyone on this ship. I know what's in store for someone like me. I want immunity!" He stood up from the cot and stepped up behind the bars, just out of Christophe's reach. "If I say nothing, I got nothing to lose! If I don't tell you, we all die. If I tell you what I know without something in return, I die alone. I'd prefer to have some company."

"Immunity? You are mad! Do you honestly think we'd let you loose inside this ship after what you did to Miss Llewellyn?"

"Ha-ha, oh, no, no, my Lord Monster! Of course not. Why I went after her ain't important, anyway. Just don't let me loose *outside* the ship. Anything else is negotiable. Guarantee that I won't get the premature Cervantes treatment, and I'll give you the secrets of the ages." Rathbone's voice dropped to a husky growl as his lip curled in a mixture of distaste and amusement. "I'll tell you all about our little Miss Llewellyn. You want to keep that little tart alive, don't you? Smart lass, that one. Almost as smart as her old man!"

Rathbone spit in Dr. Pugh's direction. Christophe heard the old man's gasp, but he never took his eyes off Rathbone.

The prisoner wiped his mouth with the back of his hand and continued. "Grant me immunity and oh, she won't have anything to fear from me. But she might be afraid of you when I tell you all about her. About the secrets she's stolen. The hearts she's broken and the lives she's left in ruin. The men she's seduced. The man I watched her kill. When you know you might not want her any--"

The impact of his face upon the bars cut off his speech. Christophe's reach was longer than Rathbone had calculated. Rathbone simply hooted, as if he had received a mere tickle, at least until Christophe's other arm snaked through the bars and helped the other one slam him into the bars again, over and over, until they were slick with spit and blood, until Pugh called for the master-at-arms to pull Christophe off him. Rathbone's breath rattled in his throat as he spit out a broken tooth. He shuffled back to the cot and wiped his mouth on the edge of a blanket.

Pugh's hand rested on Christophe's shoulder, which was shaking from the aftermath of his attack. "Perhaps we should contact the--"

"Contact whom, exactly?" Rathbone asked. "Headquarters? Why would they give you permission to discover one of their own? Admiral Thorvaldson? Old Artur hasn't got the foggiest idea what's happening under his nose." A bit of blood dribbled off his lips.

"Their own?" Christophe shook Pugh's hand off his shoulder. His carefully ordered world crumbled with every word that Rathbone fired at him.

The prisoner gurgled for a second, speaking through bleeding gums. "The TIA has Watchers of their own. A Watcher that could be anyone, from the lowliest swabbie on up the chain."

"Who, then?"

"Promises, Captain. Promises."

Pugh said, "Christophe, the regulations! On your own you can't--"

"I can do what I need to do to protect my ship," Christophe snarled without looking at him. "This is my decision, Elias. On my own head be it. If our own people are trying to kill us, I'm not concerned about disobeying orders! Very well, Rathbone. You are granted immunity. From execution.

But not from confinement. You'll stay in the brig for the duration. I can't let you talk to anyone else. Not after what you've seen. We'll give it out that you had a nervous breakdown, just in case you do start talking to someone. When we get back to Shackleton Station... well, we'll see."

"And your pet?"

"I can't guarantee Maggie's behaviour. But I'll order her to stay out of the brig," he said. He straightened his spine and his jacket. He had to keep this from being a doomed ship. "This is all contingent, of course, upon verification. You're leveling a very serious charge at a member of my crew."

"Well, he's not as much a member of your crew as you think. D'you really need a Cultural Officer, anyway?"

"Wallace?" Christophe asked, incredulous.

"You're certain of this?" Pugh demanded.

"Positive. You can verify it with the message archives. Been readin' his messages since I cracked his code. Long ones. Detailed ones. He's none too fond of you, Dr. Pugh, I can tell you that. I found most of Orion in his messages, what it was, at least. About the captain being, shall we say, custom ordered. Not the how. That's what I was needin'. How Frankenstein put together this particular creature."

"What's Wallace going to do? I hardly believe he would want to martyr himself as well."

"Don't reckon that was in his plans. Go have a look at the *Iron Wind*, Captain. Do an inventory of the ship's stores. You might find some missing items in its hold. Don't know exactly what he meant to do to the ship. He was smart enough to leave that out of his messages. But one thing is for sure. He's going to do something. He's going to do it soon. And he doesn't expect to hang around to admire his handiwork."

"How do you--"

"It's what I would do."

"Sinister minds think alike, I suppose," said Dr. Pugh. "I'll work with the Booleans to verify his claim. We need to know before we act. Can we distract him until then?"

"Oh, you'll need more than the messages, Captain. You'll need his code to read them. It's a doozy, that one. Took me forever to crack. Been workin' on it ever since we launched."

"Wallace!" Christophe punched the wall of the chamber and let loose a string of curses. "Our own people! We'll never make it to Mars if we keep fighting each other! We'll never make it anywhere!"

"That's what you don't understand," Rathbone answered with a frozen laugh, one devoid of mirth. "That's what his messages were about. You weren't meant to make it to Mars. Fighting the Martians is not the point. Not the point at all."

"Then what is the point of all this? Why go to all this trouble, all this expense--"

"Most of the people what funded it aren't in on it. Wallace is using what others have built for his own ends. He isn't trying to continue a war, you fool. He's trying to prevent one. On Earth."

"Prevent one?"

"Don't be such a prat. Anyone that can read a newspaper should guess that half of Europe is chomping at the bit to get back to business as usual now that the post-Invasion love-festival is fading out. And what else is our business, but to fight each other? I'm sure Pugh here taught you some history. Humans have never been nice to each other without some profit in it. We'd rather fight it out any old day, no matter what we signed at the Invasion Conference. It would've been messy enough with what we can cook up on our own. Then the Martians dropped by for a visit and left their toys behind: Black Smoke, walking machines, heat rays, Red Weed. Imagine what we can do to each other now! We can finish what the tentacle-heads started! Wallace and his fellows want to hold that off as long as they can. At least, until they can get the worst of the leftovers under their own control and they can wring some profit from it. Then they can dictate who is in charge of it all."

"But what does that have to do with us?" Pugh asked.

"Martyrs. Wallace needs martyrs, not victors. If we lose a crew to the Martians, it buys them some time." He rubbed his hands together, almost enjoying his revelations. "Oh, once I broke his codes -- and there ain't a code I can't break -- I read more than I cared to, more than even Brightman had told me. Bit of a nasty shock to find out who they were trying to bring back to life. Ha! A daft idea, maybe even more daft than going to Mars in the first place. And instead of the grand hero, they got you. They found the best possible use for their failure. A kind of success, I reckon." He spat on the floor again. "Your mission is to die, you freak. All of you. Die here in space. A little disaster for the folks back home, so they'll hold off killing each other for just a little bit longer. Maybe they'll say, oh, the engines went bad. Maybe they'll say, oh, the Martians outgunned 'em. The story doesn't really matter, does it? As long as they have martyrs. You're fodder. Your face on all those little cards. That's what they want. Like all the Sophie the Steamfitter smut. It's to stir people up, get them all on one side. The TIA's side. For just a little while longer."

Christophe ground his teeth. He had never trusted Wallace, true, but he had never fathomed anything like this. He had to find the man, he had to find the truth, find--

The harsh lights of the cell sputtered and died, leaving them in darkness for a heartbeat until the dimmer emergency illumination flickered on. Christophe glanced at the brig's monitor, and it glared back at him with one baleful red eye. Christophe had not seen the red one lit since the lunar voyage.

"We're on batteries only," Christophe said as he held his hand out to steady Pugh, who had stumbled in the darkness. "Power's out."

"Looks like he's already set to go," said Rathbone.

GEMMA

The glass walls shimmered in the light of Maggie's "nest". Gemma examined her new cell as she nibbled bacon and tried to ignore the purring Martian in the corner. It was far easier to focus on the walls and the strange symbols that marched across them.

"You've been a busy little squid, haven't you?" she asked in a dry voice. She felt that if this creature were going to harm her, it would have already. An annoyance at her own fear crept over her.

"Please don't call me that," she heard the Man from Shanghai say in her head. "My name is Maggie."

Rather than answer, Gemma kept one wary eye on the beast as she tore into some of the other items from the tray and felt her strength return. There was very little, it seemed, that bacon could not cure. She washed the salty taste down with the gin.

Gemma recognized Dr. Pugh's scrawl peeking out here and there from the forest of letters. After her tenure as his pupil, she could decipher most of it. Notes on the Code of Life coated the room like blood cells on a microscope slide. His notes could act as a Rosetta stone for this new jungle of information.

Her mission was dead, but her curiosity was not. Gemma had enjoyed the learning, albeit after the fact. She hungered for more, despite her current discomfort.

Not to mention, the notes also distracted her from thinking about Christophe.

Had she felt something for the captain? She had felt something, to be sure, but she was at a loss to name it. She could not call it love, as it was as unfamiliar to her as the landscape of Mars. Despite Father Alfieri's sermon, she could not compare that celebrated sentiment with the tangled feelings bouncing around in her head.

For most of the trip, she had felt annoyance where he was concerned. But there in the Gardens, when they had both let their guard down, she had felt something else. The feeling had been close cousin to what she had felt for her Philippa, her Jennie, and it had warmed her. During that time, she had enjoyed his company, and he had treated her as an equal.

Her computer's mind shifted gears. Could she use what she had felt for Jennie as a Rosetta stone, as well? Could one form of love help her understand the others that Alfieri had mentioned? Could it be that her love for Jennie was what she felt for Christophe?

She had wanted the man to kiss her. She had wanted that kiss, in that moment. But a desire for a kiss did not encompass what Alfieri had said about love. Did she even want that kiss now?

She had recoiled from Christophe -- as she had on the inside from every other man -- when she had discovered what he was. But now? Having been fed bacon by a purring creature that was basically his mother, having rested a little and imbibed a little liquid courage, she wasn't so repelled. She wasn't even sure how to name what he was. But there was one thing she was sure of: something still stirred deep inside her when she remembered that almost-kiss.

That very moment, which had been so fuzzy for the past hour, was coming back to her now as her headache receded. He had been about to ask her something. He needed to know something. "Do you trust me?" he had asked. What did he need to know? What had he been about to ask, if not the old standard "do you love me" tripe found in the penny dreadfuls? What else could it have been? She scowled at the walls again, wishing she could find the answer written there.

"Maggie," she mused aloud, "I think the Code of Life will be easier to decode than men ever will be."

Maggie squealed in what might have been agreement. She tapped a section of the wall with a tentacle so urgently that Gemma turned her attention to the diagrams there.

Pugh had described Maggie as a researcher. Gemma no longer needed to question how Pugh had analyzed the Code of Life. He needed neither machine, nor microscope, nor analytical engine to analyze Codes; there was no algorithm to steal. There was no secret formula to encode in a furtive frenzy and hurl through space over the wireless to a waiting Mrs. Brightman, even if Gemma had still been so inclined.

There was just Maggie.

Maggie was the true author of this research. Pugh and his team had taken all the credit and left the real creator none.

"Typical," Gemma said with a snort. "And Pugh said he didn't use computers."

"He has his reasons," came the reply. The words slipped into Gemma's brain so easily, so painlessly, like a voice buried deep in her memory, though she had never heard it out loud before. "I doubt the Royal Society dinners could accommodate my dietary requirements, anyway."

As Maggie "spoke", Curiosity and Hysteria were at it again. Curiosity won this round and stuffed Hysteria into a mental corner in the back of her head. Gemma could sense no malice in Maggie's movements or unique method of speech, and she began to relax a little more (perhaps it was the gin talking) and watched the researcher continue her work. Two chains of Code appeared in impossibly tiny hand -- or tentacle, as the case might be. Each was labeled, but she could not discern the letters printed there. Arrows pointed from the set to a third chain. As she looked more closely, she saw that the last chain seemed to contain a very specific blend of the codes above. It was labeled clearly as "C. Moreau".

He was a bespoke hero, after all.

She gritted her teeth as she sat up to read the labels on the other chains. The leftmost of the top two bore the label "E. Pugh". That confirmed it; Pugh was his father, after a fashion. That was no surprise.

The second was labeled "Nobody". That wasn't a proper name in any language that she knew. Was it a label for an unknown person? But why would they use Code from someone they didn't know? No, knowing Dr. Pugh, that was not the case. Perhaps Maggie was not given the person's name. Or it was an alias, then, for a secret within a secret, Christophe's mysterious "other father". Or, perhaps, another mother? Or to partially "blind" the process?

She looked at Maggie, as if to ask her a question, when she noticed that the creature had put down the grease pencils and had picked up, of all things, a pair of knitting needles. They were longer than normal, probably to accommodate her longer limbs, but they were, for all intents and purposes, knitting needles. The makings of a woolen scarf tumbled from them, and the letter "M" scrolled out from the end. Was the Martian knitting a scarf for her "son"? The sight of it was so absurd that Gemma could not help but laugh, even though her ribs screamed as she did so.

"So, even you could not escape the Knitting Circle of Doom, eh?" Gemma remarked with a chuckle.

Maggie gurgled at her in what Gemma assumed must be her version of a laugh.

"Space is cold," the voice in her head said again. "I must keep my little bud warm."

Gemma gazed at the creature for a moment in a mixture of amusement and befuddlement. The warmth of the last drops of gin glowed within her as she drank them. Only the pressing pain in her ribs kept her from guffawing at the thought of the tall, lanky Christophe as an infant cradled in

Maggie's tentacles. The mental image was far too ridiculous to hold any terror or disgust in it.

Gemma had nothing to fear here.

This is why she could not find Orion, no matter how hard she had searched through Pugh's office. Orion was not some formula, or a file, or anything so mundane. Orion was flesh. Orion was alive. Orion was Christophe Moreau, the master and commander of the *Thunder Child's Fury*. That infuriating man, the one who had made her laugh, the one that earlier today she had so wanted to kiss. They were one and the same. Orion had been in front of her, all along.

And just when she didn't need to find it, it had presented itself to her. But there was something more to it than just churning out people like fabric from a jacquard loom. Why would Brightman be interested in that? Had her former mistress even understood enough about Orion to know what she really wanted? Had she known that a Maggie was required to carry it out? Without a Martian, this knowledge was useless.

A new thought left her cold. She knew what happened to the older students, now. Was this how she planned to continue her work when the first ones aged out? Create fresh ones out of the old?

She could not let it go. Gemma set her computer's mind to work on the problem. There was nothing else to do but moan or watch Maggie stitch more rows on the scarf.

"Where else have I heard that name, Maggie?" she mused aloud. "Orion. Orion. Oh, it's as bothersome as 'Moreau'! Must have been back during that astronomy job last year at Oxford. What did the professor say? The constellation of Orion was associated with Osiris? That Egyptian fellow?"

"Yes," the voice replied. "Pugh told me the story. His wife, Isis, brought Osiris back to life after his brother killed him."

Gemma remained silent as she ran through the possibilities. Rathbone, for all his insanity and anger, was right. The greatest wonder out here was not the ship. The *Fury* was just a vehicle. It was going to wondrous places, yes, and it was terribly complicated; but it was still only a horseless carriage on a different road. This was something altogether different, something orders of magnitude greater.

One could do more with this than create new people. One could copy a person.

One could bring the dead back to life.

One could be a god.

And that's when the lights went out.

CHRISTOPHE

"Damn that Wallace!" Christophe spat into the yawning darkness of the Oberth deck. "Damn him, damn, damn, damn him! Five more, five!"

Christophe seethed as he held the lifeless body of Chief Nesbitt. The engineer's uniform was soaked in the blood that poured from the gash in his throat. The poor fellow hadn't even had time to cry out. Christophe screamed for him, another crewmember lost to a useless and brutal death. And if the power was not back online soon, he would lose the rest of them.

He had to find Wallace. He had to find Wallace and end this madness.

Pugh called from one dark corner. "Christophe! A live one! Over here! Call Hansard!"

Nearly blind with fury, Christophe made his way to the pipephone and called sick bay.

As he hung up, Pugh said, "I think he got all the on-duty engineers. Where is that bastard?"

"There's only one place he could be," Christophe replied as he jogged towards the corridor. "Elias, have the master-at-arms and his men meet me at the *Iron Wind*. They're already closer than we are."

"Can't Pritchard just stop him from the bridge?"

"No! It's designed to launch independently! Get Pritchard and the off-duty engineers down here to look at the Oberths. I'm for Wallace."

"Are you armed?"

"Leyden pistol's been on me ever since before the Rathbone incident," Christophe called behind him as he patted the holster at his side.

He broke into a full run, his long legs like pistons driving him towards whatever awaited him.

GEMMA

Maggie jolted when the lights flickered back on at half-strength, as if she had been bitten by a snake. Her knitting soared across the room and smashed into the wall.

"What is it?" Gemma asked aloud.

"Christophe!" Maggie's manly voice said in her mind. "There is danger. Someone has harmed the ship." She rolled towards the door into the mysterious corridor. "I have to go help him. Stay here, where you are safe."

Gemma stirred in the bedclothes and attempted to stand. "Is it Rathbone? I should go with you."

"No, no, it isn't," Maggie protested with raised tentacles as she opened the door. "It's someone I didn't expect. Please stay, child. Rest. I do not fear him."

Maggie latched the door behind her, leaving Gemma alone in the dimly lit chamber. The room felt all the emptier for the alien's absence, much to Gemma's surprise. She could hear the creature rolling herself down the hall. The skittering sound of her movement through the corridor was unmistakable.

Here, here was Caroline's ghost! Here were the eyes that had watched her in the hallway and followed her through the ship! And thankfully so, Gemma thought, for that had enabled the creature to save her from Rathbone.

She had to find out. She had to find out why Maggie would save her, a stranger, one who reviled her kind more than any other thing in the universe. Why would Maggie protect her more than any Watcher ever had and risk exposing herself to the crew of the *Fury* in the process? Gemma had to know. Her instincts told her that if she did not help Maggie now, she would never have the chance to find out.

The insect sound of Maggie's movement was louder than ever; the background hum of the engines had faded into an eerie silence. She had grown so used to the ever-present drone that she had learned to tune it out. Now the lack of it was louder than thunder.

She struggled to stand and yelped at the coldness of the floor when her bare feet landed on it. Every muscle protested as loudly as Maggie had as she reached for the clothing that Frau Knopf had left. Grimacing all the while, she discovered that it was a pair of trousers instead of her usual skirt. It took her a few minutes to wrestle herself into them, but she managed it.

She rummaged about for her shoes and stockings and fumbled her frozen feet into them. There was a cool edge to the air. Gemma snatched up one of the smaller blankets and draped it over the loose shirt as she shuffled out the door and into the unknown country of the corridor.

It was smaller and darker than any other passageway she had seen so far. It was wide enough to allow something of Maggie's size to move about, but no more than that. The door to Maggie's nest was in the lower portion of a gentle slope that crossed the decks above and below it. Gemma could not recall seeing anything like it on the schematics and was unsure of which direction to take. She cocked her head from side to side until she heard the familiar skittering and scratching. Otherwise, the narrow tunnel was empty, with neither sailor nor map to point the way. Not even a spider troubled the cold shadows that draped across the space at odd angles.

Gemma, slipping between pools of faint light, padded towards the sound of Maggie's path. Breathing was a chore through her tender ribs, and she limped up the course with cantankerous knees that were keen on getting back to bed. She passed door after unmarked door underneath the snaking tracks of what appeared to be the hidden network of pneumatic tubes. She could still hear Maggie in the distance, but she could not see her. The occasional cross-corridor -- possibly in the area between decks -- interrupted her path. Gemma felt that Maggie may have turned down one of those, but she still heard the sound down the long hall, though it grew ever fainter. Maggie did not dawdle.

Racks of tools and weapons decked the walls. One happened to be in the light as she loped by it, and she could see firearms hanging from it. Their odd appearance stopped her in her tracks. Dull matte black rectangles hung in the place of conventional revolvers. Except for their triggers, they did not resemble anything that Gemma had ever seen before, not even when she had assisted a weapons development specialist three years before.

One of the slots was empty.

As she gazed at the spot where it should have been, her foot slipped on something in the floor. She held her breath as she stooped to pick up the scrap of paper that was so out of place in this otherwise scrupulously clean back alley of the ship.

Jagged and creased as it was, she could make out the undeniable lower half of Sophie the Steamfitter, the mate to the scrap she had found in the wreckage of the heat ray. Goose pimples raced across her scalp as fury rose in her throat. She could almost taste her anger.

"Accident, my arse," she swore. "Is anyone on this bloody ship an actual *sailor*?"

She stuffed the card into the pocket of her trousers and hobbled on, as Maggie's version of footsteps had almost faded entirely.

"Crickets!" she muttered. "I'm rescuing a Martian. Will wonders never cease?"

Muffled voices in the space ahead spurred her on, but she saw no one. She only found the odd vent here and there in the wall that showed glimpses of the main corridors through tiny slits. She heard sailors' voices filtering through the registers, and apprehension skulked behind their words. They talked of sheltering in the head.

Has there been a solar flare? Gemma asked herself. *Am I safe here?*

The corridor stretched on forever, but a commotion around the corner ahead drove her forward. She could hear an unearthly screech echoing down the cold and empty metal tunnel, reaching for her like the Man from Shanghai had, and then she felt it searing her thoughts.

Maggie was screaming.

The force of her suffering nearly knocked Gemma down to the floor. Maggie wasn't just screaming. She was in agony.

Gemma willed herself into a lurching, running, hurtling pell-mell around the corner and into the cross-corridor. At the end of it was an open door, and beyond it the cavern of the cargo bay. Silhouetted in the opening was a man bent over a boneless grey mass. He placed one of the strange weapons she had seen a moment before on a rack just inside the door.

Maggie's tentacles convulsed and seized, and her beak clacked loudly with her twitches. Icy claws tore at Gemma's pounding heart; she was too late, too late to help Maggie. With a howl of fury, Gemma seized the first tool she could reach from the rack and launched herself at the man.

The next few moments blurred into a haze of pain. The promise that the stars had made to her seemed so far away. She would have to kill again, after all.

CHRISTOPHE

The trek across the ship took ages, but Christophe finally arrived at the cavernous cargo bay that housed the *Iron Wind*. He slipped into the chamber and stole over to where the vessel hung suspended over its own airlock. The black Leyden pistol felt heavy in his hand as he crept through the shadows of the towering crates. The sudden eruption of the slaps and thuds of harsh blows urged him forward.

A shocking sight met him as he rounded the last stack of containers. Wallace was there, pinned beneath the last person he expected to see. Despite her injuries, Gemma clutched a hammer in her hands, held high above them both. She was an angry succubus, ready to bash in the head of her unconscious victim. Her face was a harpy's mask of twisted fury, and her loose hair was a mass of pure bedlam about her head. Her forehead shone with a mixture of sweat and blood trickling down from her scalp.

"Gemma!" Christophe roared as he ran closer to them. Her rising arms froze at his call. "No! We need him alive!"

"No, we don't!" she snarled back. Wallace was limp and still beneath her. Christophe could not tell if the man was still breathing. "Do you know what he's done? This bastard killed Cervantes! And Maggie!"

"Llewellyn! No!" He bellowed at her as he continued to close the distance between them. He could still feel the pressure of Maggie in his head, even though it was silent. "Maggie's alive! Just hurt!"

She froze, but she did not look up.

"I know what he's done," Christophe said. "If he dies, we all die! Let him go! That's an order!"

"Shove your orders! Shove me out the airlock! It would be a mercy! I've had enough!"

The hammer rose even higher.

Christophe squeezed the trigger of the Leyden pistol without further hesitation. Tiny balls of light shot across the remaining distance and struck Gemma in her already battered ribs. With a sharp shuddering twitch, she collapsed, the wooden shaft of the hammer still grasped in her right hand. Her fists clenched; waves of spasms washed over her muscles as the electricity carried by the steel-encased glass arced through her body and down into the man beneath her. Wallace, unconscious and unfeeling, twitched just as madly.

Christophe crossed the floor and loomed over her. He watched the seizure ripple through the fallen woman without touching her. His mouth was a hard, grim line as he watched the familiar stages of the Leyden Effect play out. Gemma's eyes rolled back in her head. He watched the agonized contractions on her face and her rapid intakes of breath until both she and Wallace were still.

He had exorcised the demon, for the moment.

He knelt down and pressed his fingers into her neck. A ragged pulse still beat there. He checked Wallace next. He sighed in relief as he felt the man's heartbeat. Bruises covered the man's face, and a thin stream of blood trickled from his nose. Bile rose in Christophe's throat as he realized that he had rescued the villain in distress from the damsel.

He studied the crumpled figure next to him. This fallen form was not the Gemma Llewellyn that he had come to know. She was not the bold woman that had put everything on the line to rescue a child. The beastly snarl that had defied him was not the soft smile from the gazebo. The person curled up on the cold deck was a complete stranger.

As he heard the clatter of the master-at-arms in the distance, he wondered if the Gemma he knew even existed. He pulled out his pocketknife, unfolded it, and sawed off a lock of her hair. He stuffed the bundle into his pocket before the master-at-arms could see him.

One limp tentacle peeked out from behind a stack of crates. Christophe holstered his pistol as he ran to Maggie and pulled the limb out of sight of the incoming crew. Her beak clicked at him; she was coming around quickly. He looked down at his jacket and saw the stains left by Nesbitt's blood leering at him.

"You've had enough," he growled into the forest of shadows. "So have I."

GEMMA

"Thank you for rescuing me," said the Man from Shanghai.

Gemma started awake at the ghost's voice. *Rescue?* she thought.

"Not to worry," continued the whisper as it faded, "Wallace is with me. Pritchard is on the job. We'll save the ship, as you saved me."

"Maggie?" Gemma mumbled as she opened her eyes, expecting to see the hieroglyph-splashed walls of the Martian's nest once more. Instead, the bandaged visage of Mr. Humboldt greeted her.

"Maggie?" he asked. "Who's Maggie?"

"Ahhh!" she shrieked.

"Oh, no, it's just me, Miss L," Humboldt said as he patted her hand. "You're in sick bay, love. You look like something the Martians dragged in. Decided to fight them all on your own?"

Every single joint ached. The pain she had felt upon her last waking was nothing compared to this. Her bruised ribs throbbed and screamed. This was becoming far too common. She struggled to remember what had happened to her this time. The last few hours were a fog in her brain. A fleeting image of a furious Christophe came to mind.

She had to invent an answer that the Boolean could comprehend. She doubted he would understand that his bastard of a captain had shot her with some unknown weapon as she defended the ship's resident ghost.

Gemma looked past him at the crewmen milling around the chamber. Some were injured and in various stages of treatment. Father Alfieri ambled among them, distributing prayers and pats on the shoulder. Humboldt followed her gaze.

"Power conservation protocol. Everyone not on a vital task has to take shelter in a warm area, so's we can make the batteries last longer. Looks like we're stuck with the Sick Bay Brigade."

She answered him a questioning look.

"Oh, never mind this," he said as he pointed to the strip of gauze wrapped around his head. "Old Rathbone isn't as strong as he thinks. Still, doesn't give him the right to hit on the ladies. Any word on what that was all about? Can you talk, love?"

Her throat felt dry and raw, and it hurt to breathe deeply. Her voice rattled as she answered. "Still... a bit... weak."

"I'll fetch you some water. If you think you can eat, we have some of the emergency rations here. They're a bit manky, if you ask me, but they'll keep a body going. You look a bit puny."

He wandered away and returned with a cup of water and a ration pack. He helped her to sit up and sip the liquid. To her relief, his brief touches were gentle and unobtrusive. The bored crewmen in the chamber stared at the pair. Humboldt pulled one of the unused screens over to block their view.

"Not trying any funny business, love," he explained. "It's just hard to rest around this lot. Too bad Caroline and Nigel are stuck in the Gardens. But, at least we're not on the stable deck like the Cohort. Phew, imagine being in there if the manufactured gravity goes out. Lucky that you're injured." He gave her another sip. "What d'you reckon about all this happening at once? The funeral, then Rathbone jumping the two of us, then the power outage? Crew's all cattywumpus. We hear from the other parts of the ship on the pipephone every now and then. They still work since they run on voice power, not the batteries. Wish the rest of the ship did. I could power us all the way to Mars and back!" He cackled. "Cap'n's on the Oberth deck with Pugh and Pritchard trying to get the power back on. Not sure why Pritchard's there when Nesbitt's the real genius, though. You ask me, things aren't cricket. Something's happened to the engineer, but they're not telling us what."

"What about Wallace?"

"Yeah, he's there, too, but I'm not sure why. Is there a proper way to hold one's pinky whilst turning a wrench?"

She managed a watery smile at the thought. She was sure she knew why Pritchard was on the Oberth deck in Nesbitt's place; Wallace's trail of blood had surpassed her own. She decided to let Christophe be the one to break the news of Wallace's treachery to the crew.

Humboldt retrieved a packet from the small bedside table and placed it on the bed beside her.

"Frau Knopf sent this to you, in case you get bored. It might help while away the time."

Gemma pulled some books from the packet. One was the Aronnax journal. Humboldt scanned it as she turned through its pages.

"Why do they have you reading up on old Captain Nobody?" he asked.

"'Nobody'?" she asked as she held up the other book and discovered it was the Smith journal.

He laughed. "'Nemo' is just a bit of Latin, love. Means 'nobody'. Didn't you do any Latin in your school days?"

"Enough for science," she replied, "but not much else. My instructors had other priorities. How do you--"

"Winchester. One of the few posh schools left after the Invasion. Would've been Head Boy if I'd kept me nose clean, but you know me. More lager and pig Latin than Plutarch and Homer. But it does come in handy every so often."

A certain notation on Maggie's wall flared up in her mind's eye. Mr. Humboldt was proving to come in handy.

He winced his way through a smile of his own. "Speakin' of which, haven't had any lager since we passed the moon." He sighed wistfully, then said, "If you don't mind, Miss L, I think I'll have a bit of a lie-down meself." He pointed at his bandaged head. "Headache."

She nodded at him and watched him settle in to the cot next to hers.

That's what Maggie was trying to show me, she concluded as Humboldt's snores reached her ears. She allowed herself one small smirk in spite of the full-body ache that would not leave her in peace. *That son of a bitch is a son of a Nemo. Why am I not surprised?*

CHRISTOPHE

"Captain," said Mr. Pritchard, "here's where we stand. The tralphium reactor is still going, so that's good. Carter's checked out the radio wave transmitter and the Oberths, and they appear undamaged. So that's good. Looks like that weasel -- begging your pardon, sir, Wallace -- did the most damage he could by himself in just a couple of minutes. In a pretty low-tech way, too. He took a fire-axe to the power converter. All the parts of the system are working, but without the converter, they can't talk to each other. We can't funnel power from the reactor to the Oberths and the flywheel batteries."

Christophe fought to hold his face steady. "Can we repair it?"

"I think so. We've got the extra parts and the people. Thank God Carter and Vemuri were off-duty! Question is, can we get it done before the batteries wind down? This could take a day or so, and we've only got a few hours on the flywheels. If we can't fix it before then, then we'll be the first *Flying Dutchman* in space."

"Understood. Crack on, then. Focus on the converter. Let us handle the batteries. I know a few tricks. Work as fast as you can, Pritchard. When we're done, first round of lager is on me."

As Pritchard left to organize his crew, Pugh said, "Some manual cranking on the flywheels might buy us a little time. It'd give the off-duty crew some occupation. It might keep them warm when we have to reduce the heat again."

Christophe nodded. "We'll see to it, then. The able-bodied can take it in shifts, starting with those taking shelter in here. It is a rather chilly space. The cranks are stored under the flywheels. Cunningham can organize it. It's not much, but Pritchard needs every minute we can give him."

"And what about you, son?"

Christophe stalked away towards the deck's head without another word.

"That's what I thought," Pugh growled.

Wallace -- what Miss Llewellyn had left of him -- lay cuffed to one of the exposed pipes. A hissing Maggie stood guard over him from the head's secret entrance to the hidden auxiliary corridor. His left eye was swollen shut, and he squinted with his right. His pince-nez was in a million pieces back in the cargo bay. Blood dribbled over his bottom lip; more than a few teeth had escaped from his mouth.

"Pritchard's confirmed what you told me," Christophe said as he latched and bolted the chamber's door. "Pretty efficient destruction, that. Any other damage? Besides the men you've already killed?"

Wallace attempted to get to his feet, but Maggie reached out with her tentacles and yanked him back down onto the frigid floor. The move knocked the wind out of him, and it took a moment for him to gather enough breath to speak.

"We have to get Maggie back to the *Iron Wind*," Wallace managed to wheeze between gasps. He exhaled mist into the cooling air, and his voice sounded huffy as it escaped his mangled mouth. "Now. Let me go."

"Let you go? Let you go?" Christophe snarled. "After you've murdered members of my crew, tried to abduct my mother, and endangered the ship?"

"Because you want to save her. Save Maggie."

"Save her? That's hardly saving her. Even if you could get her back to Earth, I'd rather see her dead than with you. I know how the other departments treat their second generations! No, no, Wallace. No matter what happens now, you will share our fate, so you'd better hope we can fix what you did before the flywheels wind down. If we can't, I'll feed you to Miss Llewellyn."

Maggie sputtered and reared up on her tentacles, ready to strike, as Christophe spoke. Wallace rattled the handcuffs against the pipe as he tried to crawl away from her.

"Let me go," he repeated. "At least this way you'll go out with dignity. If you make it back now, you'll go to the gallows." He pointed to the restraint with his other hand. "You know this is against regulations."

"Against regulations?" Christophe's choppy laugh blended disgust and disbelief. "Against regulations? And destroying the power converter isn't? And murdering engineers isn't? You changed the game when you did that, Wallace. You changed all of it. The question is, why?"

"I told you when Cervantes died, boy," Wallace spat. "You just didn't listen. We don't need victors. We need *martyrs*. We have nothing to gain by killing Martians. But we can prevent another war on Earth by creating *heroes*. Heroes that died for their cause."

"Heroes? Leaving the planet isn't heroic enough? Isn't space travel Herculean enough on its own? We might die anyway! A million different things could destroy us before we even get to Mars. We don't need any help in that department."

"No, it's not enough. It was never enough. Enough Directors felt that you had enough of a shot to fund the mission, but the rest of us knew that there was no chance in hell that the mission would succeed. You're a failure, Christophe. I've known that from the start, even if Pugh and the rest refuse to admit it. You're nothing. A figurehead. You have none of the memories, none of the skill, that we need to defeat the Martians. But Maggie! Maggie is a masterpiece. She's the only one of our second-generation Martians to have the Code of Life that we need. To try again. To get the leader that we deserve. You? You're just a mistake. An aberration. It would have been better if it had been you in the fire. Cervantes would have made a far better captain."

"Cervantes," Christophe repeated. Gemma had accused Wallace during her rant. He decided to press the point. "Was it -- was that you? Did you sabotage the heat ray?"

Wallace howled with laughter. "No, oh no, no, no. I didn't kill him. I just took the ray out of commission. He wasn't a specific target. That poor devil just got in the way. You're the one that signed his death warrant, *Captain.*"

Christophe clenched his jaw so tightly that he thought it would snap. "And you've signed all of ours! Including your own, Wallace. Don't you understand? We cannot accelerate. We cannot navigate. We cannot avoid the growlers. We barely have enough power for the navigational shields. One good-sized chunk of rock can finish the job you started. And that's *before* we run out of heat and air. You already have the blood of Cervantes, Nesbitt, and four other men on your hands. Why do you crave more? Just to destroy me? It makes no sense. Why would you disable the heat ray when you were planning to do this?" With a curl of his lip, he snarled, "I should have let Llewellyn finish you off."

Wallace remained silent.

"You weren't thinking, were you, Wallace? You're a font of knowledge with intrigue and regulations, but you are an absolute dunce when it comes to the basics of space travel. Despite my apparent lack of inherited knowledge, I have managed to learn a few things along the way. The *Iron Wind* is just a shuttle, you fool, not a starship. Its engines aren't strong enough to get you back home. You would have died out there, and Maggie with you! Eventually the TIA will have a fleet that might be able to rescue ships in distress, but now there are no other ships--"

The venomous snake of a smile that slithered across Wallace's blood-encrusted face made Christophe's blood run cold.

No, oh no, he thought. *Sweet mother of mercy, no.*

"Let me go," Wallace hissed through his broken mouth. "Let me go,

Moreau, or they will board you and finish the job. I'll make sure you go down in history as the rogue captain that we had to hunt down. That will still be enough to capture the world's attention. But if you let me go, you'll all die with dignity."

"Not when I wire back--"

"No one will listen to you now, Moreau. I've already received word. Thorvaldson is no longer in control. My people have taken over. If you turn around, you'll be blown out of the sky. Even if you make it back to Earth, Shackleton won't let you dock. There's nothing for you to go back to." He spit a gob of blood onto the floor. "The memorial CDVs are already on the presses. People will trade your death over lager and chips. The news stories and the memorial speeches are in the wings, waiting for the curtain to fall. You're already dead. You just don't know it yet."

"I don't believe you."

"Have you received any messages from him in the past few hours? Thorvaldson is not in a position to help you."

"Did he know? Did he know about the second ship?"

"It was under another admiral's supervision. Thorvaldson is as lost as you are."

"Another admiral? Who?" Christophe asked. When he received no answer, he went on. "If that is truly the case, then you're dead, too. Before they find us, I'll let my crew use you for a piñata. And they will, when they know you are responsible for Cervantes! If your friends board us, there won't be anything left of you to rescue."

"Temper, temper! Think of history, Moreau."

Christophe slipped a hand into his pocket and fingered the key to Wallace's cuffs as he listened to Maggie's growling. It was a menacing sound that he had never heard from her before. *No*, the growl told him, Maggie would refuse to go with Wallace, no matter what. In his mind's eye, he saw his *Kiwi Clipper* in flames; the life he had hoped to see again dissolved into the imaginary smoke. He thought of Chief Davies' little daughter and all the other things his people would lose if this weasel were somehow uttering the truth.

Something brushed his hand as he fumbled in his pocket. He pinched it, and he remembered the lock of hair that he had taken from Gemma. He thought of Pugh. If they were about to snuff it, the old man deserved some peace first. No matter how Christophe felt, and even if she were about to die with them, Pugh needed to know if he had found his daughter at last. Wallace would not take that from him, at least.

"Hang your dignity, Wallace," Christophe said at last. "If we go down, then you go down with us. Our fate is your fate."

Christophe turned to Maggie. He held the lock of hair to her beak and whispered, "Maggie, decode this, please. This is from Gemma."

Maggie warbled at him with a shade of chastisement in her tone.

"Yes, I know, I know. She won't be very happy with me for this, either. I did shoot her, after all. I didn't have much choice." The Martian opened her beak and allowed him to drop in the lock. "Compare it to the other codes you have. Tell me if anything is familiar. Don't tell Elias what you find, just yet, not until you've talked to me."

Maggie chirped a question back at him as she nibbled the hair. Christophe turned back to his prisoner.

"Maggie has a point. Is the other ship armed? How far away is it? How much time do we have?"

Wallace fell silent again. His only answer was to stare daggers at Maggie, who had settled down into a nest of her own tentacles, with only the occasional rumble emerging from deep within her.

"I leave you in her tender care," Christophe growled. "Maggie, bar the door."

He made his way back to the batteries, where a host of crewmen cranked away at the flywheels. Dr. Pugh puffed away at one of his own, moving at a quarter of the speed of the others. He paused, panting, as Christophe approached him.

"Doing your part, I see," Christophe observed.

"They've had to break out the overcoats in the other shelters, but we're managing. We'll need to swap people out soon." Pugh spoke between ragged gasps in the cooling air. He withdrew a kerchief from his pocket and wiped sweat from his brow. "Did you manage to get anything out of him?"

Christophe pulled him away from the bank of batteries towards the unmanned Oberth control panel. He helped the elderly man sink down into one of the chairs before he spoke.

"Yes," he replied. "It's as he said when Cervantes died -- someone in the TIA wants martyrs. Except they want all of us on the altar."

"Hrmph," Pugh said with a cough. "Explains why they only sent the *Fury* instead of a fleet. Especially one without a functioning weapon. It never made sense. Not really."

"I'm afraid we're falling even deeper into the fire, Elias. There is another ship."

Pugh's face turned pale. "Another ship? Are you sure? But how could--"

"He was mum on the particulars, but it's the only way his attempt to steal the *Iron Wind* makes sense. He was expecting them to pick him up, presumably after the rest of us had moved on."

"I knew there was a faction that protested the mission, but I had no idea--"

"I believe that faction has taken over. Completely. He indicated that his people have usurped the Admiralty, that Thorvaldson is no longer in command. I'd like to confirm that, but I'm not sure how our wireless messages will be received, if what he says is true. If they've had a coup, I don't know who is in charge."

"A coup?" Pugh snorted. "Only of the boardroom variety. The TIA is not a state unto itself, as much as it might dream of such things. As far as the rest of the world goes, it's just a change of directorship, I'm sure." He twisted his lip in thought. "But to the immediate concern, what if the other ship discovers Wallace didn't escape?"

"I assume that they'll board us in an attempt to retrieve both Wallace and Maggie. He hinted at that, anyway. He's responsible for the heat ray disaster, too, probably in anticipation of something like this."

Pugh nodded. "I knew he wasn't just the ship's *arbiter elegantiae*. But this! Oh, poor Miguel! Our poor crew! Even if we live long enough to get back home, can we?" He shook his head and stared down at the scuffs on his shoes. He sniffed, wiped his nose with his sleeve, and looked back at Christophe with hard eyes. "Any other details? What should we tell the crew? How much time do we have? Will the batteries even last until then?"

"I don't know. I don't want to stress the crew any more, but we have to prepare them to defend themselves. I know my people. They deserve the truth. They deserve a chance to serve the mission they signed on for." He pounded his fist against the console. "I can't believe we'll have to fight our own people. The Martians are honest enemies, at least. They never pretended to be on our side."

"I agree. Wallace has to have been in communication with the other ship at some point. Especially if they are close enough to pick him up in a reasonable amount of time! They would have to be traveling at an incredible velocity to catch up with us."

"Depending on when they left, yes."

"Can we read some of his archived messages? If Humboldt's awake, he's the one you want. Perhaps they could give us a notion."

"They are certain to be in code, Elias. I'm not sure we have the time to crack it ourselves. Rathbone did say he had broken it, but I don't trust him to decode them for us."

"Well," Pugh said, "he has as much to lose as the rest of us, so perhaps we can trust his desire to live. If not, perhaps Miss Llewellyn can be of assistance."

Christophe frowned. "After our last encounter, I don't think she'll be very keen to help me."

"She may seem a wild creature, Christophe, but she's no fool. She'll certainly do it to help herself. And no matter what you may think of her, she does care about the people on this ship. Look at what she did for Chief Davies! And for Maggie. She kept Wallace from getting away. Even if she did try to kill him, she's the reason we know what is happening to us. Rathbone exposed him, and Rathbone was here because she was here. Oh, the irony!" He shook his head. "She knows how to use ciphers. Let's see if she can break them. We lose nothing by trying. I'll see to it, if you wish."

Christophe chewed the inside of his cheek, lost in thought. "I've got to face her sometime," he concluded. "Might as well be now. Stay here with Wallace and Maggie. See if he'll talk to you. Keep me apprised. I'm off to sick bay. Use the pipephone to call around and have the Booleans meet me there. Let's include Hui as well." He sighed. "I should deal with this in person. If she reacts badly, at least Dr. Hansard will be handy to patch me back together."

GEMMA

Gemma looked around Hansard's desk at the Booleans sitting across from her. She could have sliced through the stunned silence with a butter knife.

"This cannot leave the room, at least not yet," Christophe said. "I should be the one to deliver the news to the rest of the crew. And I will tell them. I just want to know what the truth is before I do."

He rubbed the back of his neck and watched their silent nods of assent. He continued, "If what Wallace says is true, and we manage to survive the next day or so, we'll be renegades. Even if we make it home, the faction in control of the Admiralty will not welcome us with open arms."

Confusion and anger mixed on Nigel's exhausted face. "Is there anything we can do to help Admiral Thorvaldson? Any way we can change this?"

"From here, from so far away, I just don't know. Let's take this one crisis at a time. Pritchard is making progress on the power restoration. I need this group to deal with the next predicament. We need to know everything Wallace knows. Is there another ship? If so, how far away is it? Will they be able to catch up with us?"

Humboldt blinked and spoke slowly. He looked in desperate need of another nap. "I know Wallace spent a lot of time on the wireless. He didn't bother to hide his messages, though, since they're all in code. Hiding them would have gotten our attention. I can pull them up from the archives." He tugged at the bandage that threatened to slip off his head. "As for the Admiral, I might be able to get some news out of Jules on the wireless."

"Forgive me, Mr. Humboldt, but what could he know about that?"

"Jules is a barkeep, sir. He keeps his ear to the ground. You'd be surprised at the people that pass through the Badger and Tentacle and the loose lips that his ale can engender. Not to mention, if we need anybody to get the truth about us out, he's the way to go. You don't mess with bartenders. Or their cousins."

Christophe nodded at him. "All right. See what rumours he's heard and in turn let him know we are fine. Hold off on the rest until I give you the go-ahead. It will be useful to have someone back home know that we're still out here." He turned to Gemma. "Any chance you can break his code?"

If her eyes had been heat rays, she would have melted him on the spot. So much for keeping her Peculiar Occupation a secret.

He seemed to notice the Booleans staring at him and added, "With your background as a computer, I'm sure you can work with Chief Davies and his crew on it."

She shifted in the harsh wooden chair, searching for a comfortable spot. "I cannot tell until I see it, Captain."

"But will you try?"

She looked around the table, into the eyes of Caroline, Nigel, and Humboldt. She thought of Pugh and Nigel's little Gemma back on Earth. She looked up at Christophe and caught her own rough reflection in the door's window. She was a mass of shawls and blankets, and her hair was an unholy halo floating about her head.

"If you promise not to shoot me again," she replied, her voice dry and rough. Her statement startled the Booleans; apparently, they did not know the entire history of her injuries. She cleared her throat and continued. "I can guarantee nothing, Captain, as these things take time, and that is one thing we don't have. But I will try."

"That is all I can ask of you, Miss Llewellyn," he replied gently. "Very well. I will be on the bridge. Contact me there when you have something. Dismissed."

"Get some rest, Miss L," Humboldt said to her. "It'll take a while to retrieve those messages. Might have to burn some midnight oil on this one."

"It's all midnight oil out here, isn't it, Mr. Humboldt?" she replied softly.

The Boolean patted her shoulder as he passed her chair and followed the others out of the room. He secured the door behind him.

Gemma took a long moment to stand up, shrugging off Christophe's proffered hand. She did not look at him as she struggled, but she could sense him backing away a step when she made it to her feet.

"Miss Llewellyn, it is good to see you up and--"

A sharp slap from Gemma's hand cut him off.

"Ow," she yelped. She clutched at her screaming ribs, and her face twisted into a grimace. "That's for shooting me."

He touched his face, where her hand had left an angry mark across his cheek. "It was just the Leyden pistol. It's not lethal."

Her teeth chattered in the cold and broke up her reply. "It may not be lethal, but it is painful nonetheless."

"For your pain, I am indeed sorry," he said as he pulled a blanket down from a shelf beside the door. "But you brought it on yourself. Next time, listen to me. But Humboldt is right. You should get some rest while they work."

He unfolded the fabric and stepped closer to her again, lifting it to her shoulders. She jerked away from him, and it tumbled to the floor.

"Don't touch me," she hissed. "I don't want you to touch me. I don't want Humboldt to touch me. I don't want anyone touching me."

"Gemma," Christophe replied, "you heard what I said. You know what's happening. We may not have much time. Don't you need some kind of human warmth or comfort? I know there are... barriers... between us. Don't you need to... to spend time with someone, even for just a little while, if this is the end?"

"Need? Who are you to know what I need?" she asked. "Who said I need to be with anybody? I'd rather spend my time figuring out how to survive this, thank you very much."

She stomped her foot at him, and the action jarred her from head to toe. She groaned yet again and scowled at his stunned silence.

"What I need is to be left alone! I am tired of men pawing at me," she said. "I am tired of Brightman. I am free of her, but I am not free of what I am: a thief that happens to be good with numbers. A thief and a trained killer, Captain. That's all I'll ever be. I even thought, for a fleeting moment in the orrery, that I could be something else. But no. No. Wallace brought it back. He brought it all back. I'm sick of shadows. I'm sick to death of death. But I track it with me everywhere I go, like tar stuck to my soles."

"Then Rathbone was telling the truth? You have--"

"Yes, Captain. Yes, I have done many, many things in Brightman's name. Make of that what you will." She touched the latch. "You once asked me who I was. This is it. This is who I am. A heartless beast." She opened the door and slipped through it. As she latched it behind her, she whispered, "Maggie isn't the monster on your ship, Captain. I am."

Gemma's agitated mind, the shuffling of the crewmen, and the antiseptic smell of the chamber would not let her rest. The stunned expression on Christophe's face as he had left sick bay haunted her. In a pretense at distraction, she rifled through the Smith journal. Frustrated, she flipped to the last pages to see how it ended, since she might not get another chance.

Smith and his crew were exploring a watery cavern in a canoe provided by their mysterious benefactor. They had just encountered a vessel with a terribly familiar description when Smith guessed at their angel's identity: *Nemo*.

Gemma frowned. Smith's journal stated that the date of that encounter was October of 1868. She flipped back to the end of Aronnax's journal and read the date of the maelstrom: June 1868. Nemo had died the day after Smith's men found him, even though he had been on the island for their entire sojourn. He had perished of nothing worse than illness and old age. The *Nautilus* had served as his sarcophagus when Smith followed the old captain's wishes and scuttled the submarine, never to be seen again by the eyes of man.

She flipped back and forth between the two journals. She was beginning to see what Pugh found so fascinating here: Nemo seemed to be in two places at once, with Aronnax between 1867 and 1868, yet also with Smith on the island from 1865 until 1868. To make matters worse, Smith claimed to Nemo that he had already read of Aronnax's adventures. Her inner scientist nagged at her. Smith would have to have read it before landing on the island in 1865, although another two years would pass before Aronnax and Nemo met. It had not been written yet.

She sat back, stunned, her exhausted mind unable to absorb the overdose of oddity. She closed both of the books and hoped to read them again when she had recovered her faculties. Perhaps her addled brain had read the dates incorrectly.

It was all in the past. It could wait.

At the bottom of the stack, she found the slim volume that the good Frau Knopf had read aloud during the Knitting Circle, *The Lady of Shalott*. Bored and mildly curious about its ending -- and thinking she may never get another chance to do so -- she opened the book and read the verses.

Heard a carol, mournful, holy,
Chanted loudly, chanted lowly,
Till her blood was frozen slowly,
And her eyes were darken'd wholly,
Turn'd to tower'd Camelot;
For ere she reach'd upon the tide
The first house by the water-side,
Singing in her song she died,
The Lady of Shalott.

"She dies," Gemma grumbled. She flung the book to the end of the bed without bothering with the last lines. "All that, and she dies. For what, a broken heart? What a disgusting notion."

"But people do die of broken hearts, little jewel. It happens all the time. What would you have done?"

Gemma felt Maggie tugging at her mind again, from wherever she was in the ship, with the voice of the Man from Shanghai. Gemma closed her eyes to listen, and she could see the Man as well.

"I would have tracked down the source of the curse and eradicated it. Permanently."

She could almost feel Maggie's smile in her head as she replied, "I thought as much."

"Why him? Why are you always *that man* when you talk to me?" Gemma thought, addressing the apparition in her head.

"I needed an image from your past. I didn't think you'd accept me in my true form," Maggie said.

"Point taken," Gemma replied. "I think I have graduated to seeing you as you are. I am becoming accustomed to it."

The Man from Shanghai smiled at her before the mental image of him shimmered and dissolved, and the wriggling form of Maggie took his place. His voice still rang in her head, though.

"I am not sure of my voice," Maggie said, "as I do not actually have one of my own. Your teacher's, perhaps?"

Gemma was certain that her cringe was visible to the others in sick bay. "Oh, please, let's not. Frau Knopf?"

"I love her dearly, but her accent is rather difficult. What about your friend?"

Gemma thought about that for a moment. "Caroline? Or do you mean Jennie?"

"Yes, Jennie," Maggie said, with a dreamlike timbre that resembled her memory of Jennie's voice. It was oddly comforting.

"Strange to say, but that is better," Gemma replied.

She looked up and noticed Caroline shuffling through the main door of sick bay with a bulky box in her hands. She glanced at Gemma before waddling over to Hansard's office. She gave the closed door a helpless look. Gemma groaned, creaked her way off the cot, and opened the door for the Boolean.

"Nigel is on his way," Caroline said as she struggled through the door with the box, which was packed to the gills with cards. "He's bringing a portable reader down from Informatics. It's a bit heavier than this. Won't fit in the pneumatics. Perhaps it's a good thing the gravity plates are losing power in the corridors."

Stumbling with fatigue, Caroline tripped and lost hold of the box. Punchcards flowed across the table, along with quite a few CDVs.

"Bugger!" Caroline yelped. She shook with frustration. "And that's Humboldt's collection, too. He asked me to bring 'em down for him."

Gemma picked up one of the punchcards and noted the preprinted number in its corner. "Do you use these in order, Caroline?"

"Yeah," she replied, "Should be able to put them back in sequence so we can read 'em, but I'm so tired that the numbers are blurry."

Gemma pointed to the chair next to her. "Sit, then. I can do this while you rest a moment. I can see well enough."

As Caroline pulled out the chair and plopped down into it, Gemma sorted through the cards. The CDVs were nearly their twins in size and shape, and she silently commented on them to Maggie.

"There is a difference?" Maggie asked.

"Mostly the CDVs are just a way to pass the time," Gemma replied as she continued to sort through the pile. She discovered a rather naughty one of Sophie the Steamfitter and grimaced. "Some more disgusting than others."

She spoke aloud to Caroline. "Would you like some cold ration?"

She only received a soft snore in return. Gemma smiled softly at the mass of brown hair buried in a set of crossed arms. She let the Boolean be. The poor girl was exhausted, and there was really nothing for her to do until Nigel arrived with the card reader.

Gemma continued to work, grateful for something to occupy her thoughts. She set Humboldt's CDVs aside in their own pile as she found them, noting the variety of pubs and actresses. She tucked the saucier ones into the bottom of the pile; she wondered how Caroline had reacted to seeing her beloved heroine in that state of undress.

Still, Gemma felt the need to talk to someone. The slight pressure in her head she felt when Maggie spoke was still there. She focused on that pressure and sent a thought along it, hoping Maggie would hear her. Gemma was still unsure of the alien's location. Her Curiosity was hungry, though, and the punchcards had offered up a question.

"How do you do it?" Gemma asked. "Exchange information, I mean."

She was pleased to hear Maggie reply, "I believe other second-gens send data directly from their minds, much like I am talking to you, but in Code instead of words."

"You mean, like the wireless?"

"Yes. Alas, something happened with me. Perhaps it is my human Code. I can only talk to humans this way. It works well, though. I can talk to you from anywhere on the ship, like I am now."

"Like a wireless pipephone in our heads?"

"Precisely. I cannot communicate with any of the other second-gens except in person, by other means. That has only happened twice."

"Do you get on?"

"As well as could be expected. They have no sense of humour."

Gemma chuckled aloud, but the noise did not wake Caroline. "Do you have any memories of Mars? From your parent?"

"Sadly, no. I hope to acquire some memories, good memories, when we are there, if we do not have to battle. I rather agree with the priest. I hope we do not have to fight."

"I am not sure we will be in any shape to fight, at this rate. I suppose

Christophe has no memories of Mars, either?"

"You cannot copy what is not there, my little gem."

Humboldt's voice came to her; he had said much the same thing about the analytical engine. That led to another question.

"Do you store your memories in your Code of Life?" Gemma asked.

"In a manner of speaking. Elias believes my parent was already dying as I formed, and that affected the copy process. I received more human Code in my life Code than I should have. I think it overwrote my memory Code. But I've been writing new memory Code as I go. I was very young when Christophe budded, so he did not inherit many memories from me. However, if I choose to bud again, that bud will have many memories. It will know you."

"So that's the extra Code that Pugh was studying," Gemma replied. She chewed that thought over. "Wait. You would have told him that already, correct? He already knew, didn't he?"

"Perhaps he wanted you to work it out on your own. He does that sort of thing. I think he was preparing you to meet me, eventually. I don't think he anticipated our early encounter."

"No one did. Do you remember your parent at all?"

"No. For the most part, Elias and Frau Knopf cared for me until I could manage on my own. That did not take long, though. We mature quickly. Instead of treating me like a specimen, though, Elias made me part of his family. He *is* my family, as is Christophe. As now are you."

Gemma allowed herself a faint smile at that and said, "I do not remember my family at all. I was just an infant during the Invasion."

"With all your skills, you did not try to find them? At least their names? I am certain you could have found their names, and rather easily. It is just a matter of matching Codes."

"You make it sound so simple! Brightman discouraged us from even thinking about our parents, let alone searching for them. And I knew nothing about Codes until now. I had no Code samples to work from. And I certainly had no way of analyzing them!" Gemma paused, remembering her discussion with Alfieri, about seeing into the past from a distance. She continued, "But, now that I can think about them, now that I can think about anything at all, I can't help but wonder if my life would have been different if my parents had not died in the Invasion. Would I have been *this*?"

The image in Gemma's mind paused its tentacles in the air. Maggie simply froze for a moment, whether in sadness or contemplation, Gemma could not tell.

"But, my darling jewel," Maggie said at last, "your parents did not die in the Invasion."

CHRISTOPHE

On the bridge, Christophe scratched his chin and felt the scraggly beginnings of an emerging beard. He had barely paused to eat in the rapid fire of events since Cervantes' memorial service, let alone shave. He looked at his pocket watch to check the time, but he wasn't sure if it was time for breakfast or tea. He could hear the noise of Booleans working through the open window, and he could hear the tap-tap-tappity-tap of Humboldt talking to his cousin back at the Badger and Tentacle. With Wallace under guard, he felt safe working from the command deck.

Christophe was tired, so very tired. He pinched the bridge of his nose and rubbed his closed eyes with the tips of his fingers. Exhaustion settled into his joints; he ached with it. The world was upside-down, and if they did not fix the power soon, it would be unanchored entirely.

There was no protocol for this. He had never anticipated getting his most reliable news from a public-house barkeep, but then again he had never anticipated fighting his own command. He was truly flying without a net now. If he were on the *Kiwi*, he would know what to do: find some remote and exotic island and tell the rest of the world to go hang themselves. What could he do here, in space? The endless sky around them bound him to a narrow set of options.

He could not stop now, even as he heard the siren call of his hammock, not until he knew his crew could rest in safety. They were all weary. Fatigue crept into the corners of his vision, and his stomach growled from inattention.

A pile of cold rations waited on one of the panels for the busy bridge crew. He opened one of the wrapped bars, tore off a corner with his teeth, and swallowed it as quickly as he could manage with a straight face. As tasteless as it was, it took the edge off his hunger while he mulled over the

249

next problem, the one that would need resolution as soon as the current crises were over.

It wasn't Wallace. It wasn't Rathbone. They were safe enough where they were. It wasn't even the conundrum that was Miss Llewellyn. She was injured, and she might even hate him now, but she was safe. It wasn't even the possibility of another ship looming over his shoulder.

Should they go on to Mars or return to Earth? *Could* they go back now? That was the real question. He did not have enough information to make the call. It would be all he could do to keep them alive long enough to decide. In all his training, in all those years, no one had ever posed that question: *what do you do when your command turns against you?*

He shivered in the growing chill; the cold was just another reminder of how far away he was from the South Pacific. Even with the engines down, the ship's momentum took him farther and farther away from his beloved sea. Without acceleration, the time it would take to return stretched out endlessly.

Even the heated portions of the ship were cold. The walk back from sick bay had turned his fingernails blue. The bounce in his step along the way disturbed him. He wasn't sure how much longer the manufactured gravity would hold out. He was saving the majority of power for the most basic life support and for the Gardens. If they made it to Mars, they would need the food it provided in the future, not to mention its contribution to the air recycling. The animals in the stable could stand cold better than the vegetation -- even if the stable deck would be rather messy if things started floating about there -- but if they couldn't get the power up soon, they wouldn't have to worry about cabbages or goat manure or anything else.

A crewman's voice broke into his thoughts: "Captain? Dr. Pugh on the pipephone for you, sir."

Christophe nodded at him and picked up the handset. "A little heat would be nice, Elias," he said into it, trying to still the chatter in his teeth.

"So would a cup of tea, a side of bacon, and a fat rascal or three," replied the tinny voice of Pugh. "Not sure we'll get any for a bit. It's touch and go on the power, lad. We think it will be at least several more hours. Pritchard is a real trooper, though, and he is charging through. One would almost think he had a bit of Martian in him. I'm not sure if he is a better engineer or first mate. Either way, he is due a promotion."

Christophe allowed himself a faint smile. "Another one. To captain, even. Once everything else is working, we will be able to solve that bit at our leisure. A problem that simple would be a luxury."

"How are you holding up, son?"

Christophe faced the wall so that the bridge crew could not see his yawn. They were all going to have to get some rest, and soon.

"I am hanging on," Christophe replied as he fought the urge to lean on the panel. "I need to swap out the bridge crew. We're losing focus up here."

"You need rest, too. Even you need sleep."

"I will when everyone else can. Occupational hazard of captaincy. It is probably time to swap out the cranking crews as well, and see if we can get the batteries to last a little longer. How is our friend?"

"Wallace? Oh, Maggie is keeping a close watch on him, don't you worry. He's not going anywhere."

"Has she... has she said anything to you? I have not heard from her in a bit."

"Not a peep. I think she is focused on something."

Oh, she's focused, all right, Christophe thought. He hoped that her analysis of Gemma's Code would be complete before it was too late to give the man a little comfort. He heard a gasp from the direction of the wireless room.

"I'm needed here. Keep me informed."

"Take care, son."

"You, too, Da," Christophe replied softly.

He hung up the pipephone and turned on his heel to investigate the noise, almost grateful for any distraction from the impossible decisions that kept rearing up in his path.

Humboldt stood up from his chair at the wireless machine. With a moon-pale face, he stumbled his way over to the window that separated him from the bridge.

"What is it, Humboldt? What news?"

The man swallowed hard as he tried to still his trembling hands.

"It was all for nothing," he stammered. A sob escaped the man. "Oh, Captain! It was for nothing, nothing at all. Cervantes. Nesbitt. Wallace. The *Fury*. We're all going to die for nothing."

"What do you mean? What's happened?"

"The war, Captain. The one Wallace said he wanted to prevent. It's started. The world has declared war on the TIA."

GEMMA

"That cannot be!" Gemma exclaimed.

Her yelp jolted Caroline from her slumber. The Boolean, eyes heavy with sleep and confusion, blinked at Gemma in the dim light of Hansard's office.

"Wha'?" she mumbled. "Nigel here?"

"Not yet, Caroline. Rest, dear."

"Yessum," she said and was fast asleep at once.

Gemma sorted the cards with trembling hands into jumbled piles. In her mind, she said, "That cannot be. Mrs. Brightman said--"

"Why would you believe anything that woman says?" Maggie replied. "She lied to you about Jennie. That was not her only lie."

"How do you know this? How long have you known?"

"I made the discovery just a few moments ago. Your Code, like all Code, takes time to examine."

"How did you--"

"You must forgive Christophe, my dear. He had his reasons, but you must ask him what they are."

Gemma growled in her throat as she examined her mass of hair. She had thought there was a bit missing, but she had chalked it up to her fight with Wallace.

"You said my parents are still alive. Who? Where?"

"No, my little gem, I said they did not die in the Invasion. Your father, alas, died before it happened. Sadly, that meant I also had no chance of knowing him. However, I must say, you come by your scientific talents honestly."

Gemma's mind whirled. If Maggie could identify the man personally, then she had had access to his Code. The hair on her neck stood on end as a chill deeper than the one on the slowly freezing ship crawled across her skin.

"Who?"

"Our Elias' beloved mentor."

Gemma rested one hand on the journal that had followed her around the ship like a shadow. Her eyes were wide and wet with wonder. The man that had written this diary, had traveled with Nemo, and had taught the man that had fought so hard to save her from herself, was her father.

Her father had written these words.

"Aronnax," Gemma replied, and the name barely slipped out of her throat into the room. "My father is Pierre Aronnax."

"Yes. As he was a confirmed bachelor, he had no other family save Pugh to handle his affairs. Pugh keeps a lock of his hair in a mourning locket. When I came along after the Invasion, they gave me a few strands of it. They were trying to collect as much Code as possible, you see. I have not used his Code otherwise, but it seems that someone else did."

"Someone else."

She choked back a shriek as she re-opened the back flap of the journal and re-read the list of computers there, the list that she had seen earlier. Brightman's alias fairly floated off the page. She marked the date and worked figures in her head.

"Oh."

"Do you see the connection?"

"I am a computer, Maggie," Gemma said, her veins seizing up from the ice forming in them. "I can do the calculations. I came by my other talents honestly as well, it seems."

She studied the last few pages of the journal, the ones describing the late professor's last research project. These pages came after his adventurous tale, and they had not been included in his published account.

They contained, in the loftiest of terms, a plan for researching the Code of Life and how to manipulate it, and how mankind might benefit from the artificial insertion of superior genes into existing Code. There were older, long-standing, time-tested names for this sort of research. It was the sort of research that filled Brightman's hidden office to overflowing.

Selective Breeding. Animal Husbandry. Eugenics.

Gemma concluded, "Brightman took more than Aronnax's research. She took a secret of her own. She took life with her." She slowly, gently, closed the file and pushed it away from her. "My life."

She numbly gazed at Caroline's hunched-over form and wished she could join her in rest, but she thought it would be a very long time before she would sleep in peace again. The word *mother* floated in her mind, cut free from any true significance or sentiment. It was just a cold fact, as cold as the woman who had raised her. She could feel a young Brightman's train of thought pulling into the station. After exposure to such ideas, it seemed that the lady had performed her own version of Code engineering to combine her genius with that of Aronnax.

Jennie. Gemma realized with an inner growl that Brightman had tried again, this time with the Code of a brilliant young Boolean named Nigel Davies. Brightman's keen interest in the infant made perfect sense in this light. That, then, was to be the source of the next generation of Brightman Girls and Watchers. Had her friend been aware of the plan, or had she been a willing participant?

She looked down at the next card in her shaking hand. It was a painted CDV depicting an armoured Christophe kneeling to a queenly Sophie the Steamfitter, who was knighting him with her welding torch. She had a tawdry smile on her face, as if she anticipated a roll in the hay afterwards. The world saw him as the pinnacle of strength and daring, the hero's hero; everyone but Gemma seemed to want a piece of him.

Did her mission mirror Jennie's? To capture Christophe's Code in the same fashion? Had that been Brightman's plan all along? One that even an eternally grateful Gemma might have refused if she had known it beforehand? Gemma had cut off communications with her before things had become clear.

She didn't need a Maggie to capture Moreau's Code, Gemma thought. *All she needed was me.*

She thought of Mary Shelley's Frankenstein and his patchwork monster, stitched together from bits salvaged from the dead. She thought about Aronnax and science, about theft and heartbreak, and about the vicious spiral of history. The bizarre origins of Captain Moreau swirled about her, and she realized she had more in common with him than she had ever dreamt possible. She clutched the edges of her shawl to her, but she could not get warm.

She said aloud, in the barest of whispers, "Like Christophe, I am bespoke."

CHRISTOPHE

"Who has declared war on the TIA?" Christophe demanded.

"Everyone," Humboldt replied, choking on the words. "Russian warships are firing on the blockade of the Bosphorous. France and Germany are invading and claiming their own quarters. Luxembourg City's in flames."

"And London?"

"Jules don't know, sir. London's quiet. Parliament's still meeting -- oh, it's chaos down there. That's all I know. But he'll try to find out."

"All right. One crisis at a time. At the moment, we can only help ourselves. Humboldt, stay by the radio and find out all you can. In the meantime," he said, raising his voice for the entire bridge crew to hear, "this news doesn't go outside the bridge until the power--"

"My son," Maggie broke into his brain, "come to us. Elias is ill."

"What happened?" he asked her, picturing the dear old man keeled over from cranking the flywheels.

"I am afraid he fainted when I gave him some rather startling news."

Christophe lowered his eyes as his heart rolled over. *Sister*, it whispered to him in the middle of the fury that bloomed like a fiery rose in his chest.

"I told you to wait and tell me first," he thought as loudly as he could. "I wanted to be the one--"

"I can see him by the flywheels. He is not waking! I go to his aid!" Maggie declared.

"No, Maggie, wait, you'll be seen! They don't know you! Wait for me!"

There was no answer.

"Maggie?"

Still there was no answer. Without a word to Humboldt, Christophe dove for the pipephone and attempted to call the Oberth deck. No one picked up. The hairs on the back of his neck stood at attention. He shivered even harder, and he knew this time it had nothing to do with the bridge's temperature.

"Mr. Humboldt," Christophe said, "stay by the wireless and inform me the moment you hear from your contact. I'm needed in the engine room -- Pritchard is -- Pugh is -- Mr. Goldman, you have the conn!"

The bridge had been a balmy paradise compared to the icy cave of the auxiliary corridor. Christophe re-armed himself with two of the Leyden pistols as he passed through the hidden tunnel.

As fast as he went, he could not outrun the darkness that enveloped the tunnel as the conservation protocols shut off power to still more sections of the ship. He felt his way along the bone-chillingly cold walls, counting the exits down the path to the Oberths and cursing himself for not picking up an electric torch along with the Leydens.

"I'm coming, Maggie," he thought as loudly as he could.

The only answer was the echo of his feet against the slowly freezing blackness.

GEMMA

Gemma watched as Nigel set up the portable card reader on Hansard's office table. Her teeth chattered from more than just the growing cold in the room. Maggie had been silent for a few minutes, probably leaving Gemma alone to absorb her news in peace. Everything seemed off-kilter. Her entire life had been spent in acts of gratitude to Brightman. From twenty million leagues away, Gemma had a completely different perspective of her mistress.

Was she the only one? Had Brightman "engineered" other Girls? Gemma had been born before the Invasion, planned before anyone even knew Martians existed. Her trajectory had been set before the first cylinder had launched. Perhaps some of the other Girls would have had their real parents, their real lives, if the Invasion had not happened. Caroline and Nigel might have avoided the factory life. So many others -- Mr. Pritchard, Frau Knopf -- would have known a completely different history. But Gemma? She had been damned to her course, Martians or no Martians.

Unvoiced words pierced her thoughts. "I can see him by the flywheels. He is not waking! I go to his aid!"

"No, Maggie, wait, you'll be seen!" cried another voice, one she knew but had never heard in her head before. "They don't know you! Wait for me!"

"Christophe!" Gemma cried aloud.

"Are you all right, Gemma?" asked Caroline.

"No, no, I'm not," she replied, the words tumbling from her. "Something's wrong. Something's wrong on the Oberth deck. I have to get down there."

Nigel looked up from the card reader. "Beggin' your pardon, Gemma, but what in the world would they need a geologist for right now? You're overwrought, that's all."

"And how d'ye know, anyway?" Caroline asked, her face twisted in confusion.

"Call it feminine intuition."

Her breath came in rapid spurts. She could no longer hear their voices, but she could feel the combined fear of Maggie and Christophe writhing in her head. She had to get there. Now.

She waddled towards the door, shedding blankets as she went to reduce the bulk that she had to move. Caroline grabbed her arm as she passed by, but Gemma shrugged her off.

"I have to go, Caroline," she said. "The captain is in danger!"

Nigel said, "But the decoding -- the other ship--"

"This is more urgent," Gemma replied.

She opened the door in the face of bedlam. She stared at the gauntlet of frenzy before her. The crewmen, who had moments before been milling about in a state of ennui, were turning sick bay upside down, pulling mattresses off the beds and wrenching iron crossbars from them. Loose papers and books sailed around the room. Bile rose in her throat; she knew impromptu weapons when she saw them. One man was shouting down the pipephone handset by the door, with the words "boarded" and "Martians" springing from his lips.

"What the bloody hell is going on?" Caroline shouted.

"I don't know, ladies," said Nigel behind her, "but if you are determined to go, I won't let you move through that mess alone. Caroline, take her other side."

The Booleans formed a protective guard around her, and they moved through the crowd, which was so hysterical by now that the trio might as well have been invisible. Alfieri stood on a bed at one end, shouting for order and calm; but he, too, was unseen. As they reached the corridor, Nigel tugged them to the left.

"We daren't use the lifts now," he said as they rolled down the hallway. "Even if they were working, we might get trapped on our way. Best take the ladders, if you can manage, Gemma."

"Whatever it takes," she replied through clenched teeth.

Without her blankets, Gemma felt the cold keenly in the long corridor. Here and there the gravity plates were taking a tea break, as they bounced every few steps until they made it to the ladder shaft.

Nigel helped her lean into the shaft and wrap her shaking hands around the first rung. She might as well have been palming ice. She leaned back, almost into him, and pulled the loose sleeves of the linen shirt down over her palms. She leaned in again, and he came with her, taking the rung above hers.

"Pardon my being forward, but I'd rather you not fall. You might slip your grip, in this condition."

She nodded, and they placed their feet on the ladder together, his one rung below hers. They began their climb down, like a turtle with a Boolean shell. Caroline followed them a moment later.

Gemma was grateful for the awkward arrangement when she missed a step a few yards down. Nigel braced and caught her, giving her a moment to breathe and set her feet aright. Her heart hammered against her screaming ribs as she prayed to Alfieri's God that they weren't too late.

Their progress was slow. The lights flickered like strobes of continuous lightning as they descended. More than once, they went out completely. They were sinking into a cave deep into the ship, and during those frightful moments it was darker than space itself in that cramped vertical corridor. At least outside the ship they would have had the stars to navigate by. In here, they had to see with their feet. The moments drug by, heartbeat by heartbeat and step by step on that long ladder. Despite the blossoming chill, drops of sweat poured off her brow with every movement she forced her throbbing muscles to take. Just a few hours ago the ship had seemed too small; how could it have grown so large again?

She could not hear any voices in her mind now, and that inner silence was worse than any scream. That silence shoved her down through the agony of the climb. All three of them were breathing hard out of a mixture of effort and fear, and she could feel the knocking of Nigel's heart against her back. The air in the tube was stale and tasted of oil and metal.

She stumbled once, twice, and each time Nigel caught her, preventing a wild plunge down into the unseen depths below them. She had not guessed that he was so strong, but he held on for both of them. The normal roar of the engines had died out hours ago, but as they neared the Oberth deck, they could hear another sort of roar: that of a howling mob.

Breathless, they dismounted the ladder and nearly collapsed onto the deck. Gemma drove herself towards the yawning cavern of the engine room with the panting Booleans close behind.

Maggie was not on the floor, and Pugh was nowhere in sight. Gemma's eyes followed the target of the mob's rage up, up, up the pipes that climbed the far side of the chamber. High in the shadows near the ceiling, tentacles fluttered in and out of the light. Shrill whirrs and shrieks pierced the air and ricocheted off the walls, and mist poured out of Maggie's beak as it clicked in the chilly air.

Gemma knew what the crewmen saw: a hideous alien, a snarling Martian, an intruder. They saw the tentacled beast that stalked the dark crannies of their minds, the one that had murdered their families and altered their world forever. She knew they heard Maggie's howls as threats and feared for their lives. She knew they craved revenge against the one Martian within reach.

Fully extended, tentacles grasping, beak clicking, skin glistening, Maggie was truly terrifying. In fact, Gemma had forgotten in a short time how fearsome the alien's appearance could be. In her own eyes, all she could see was Maggie: her rescuer, the scientist, Christophe's mother, the loyal Terran. That was something she could not unsee. Gemma could hear her now. She heard in her heart the terrified screams of a hurt and hunted friend, one who screamed in Jennie's voice; she could not unhear them. Gemma pressed forward into the fray.

"Stop!" she cried, fighting to be heard above the din. "Leave her alone! She's one of us!"

"Have you gone barmy?" Caroline shrieked as she picked up a crowbar someone had dropped and shook it in Maggie's direction. "Bloody hell, we've been boarded!"

Gemma pushed the Boolean's arm down. "How? From where? We haven't met any cylinders! Think, Caroline! Use your brain! She is with us!"

"With us?" Nigel cut in, snatching up a massive wrench in his white-hot fist. "Did Rathbone damage your noggin?"

"Listen to me! Listen!" Gemma screeched as she pulled them both away from the throng. She could barely hear herself above the roar of the crewmen and Maggie screaming in her mind in terror for help. The crowd grew of its own accord, like a thing alive, like an amoeba dividing itself beyond control. People poured in as word got around the ship. Where was Christophe?

Clipboards and tools sailed through the air, but they all fell short of Maggie's perch. They took their time falling back to the deck, almost fluttering like metallic feathers in the diminished gravity. Some shouted for a Leyden pistol, others for a pitchfork from the stable deck. Gemma shuddered; she had lived in danger and violence all her life, but it had all been singular, one on one, nothing at all like this howling whirlwind of madness and hate.

She returned her gaze to Maggie, and for the first time she saw a limp Dr. Pugh cradled in her tentacles. He was safe from the trampling of this wild herd, but Gemma still feared the flying missiles. One would eventually find its mark.

"I am afraid," she heard Maggie's voice say in her head. "Why do they fear me? I mean them no harm. Where is my bud? I don't want to hurt them! Where is Christophe?"

Gemma's ribs berated her as she projected her voice again into the furor. "Listen! Stop! Don't!"

But she might as well have screamed at the stars, for all she was heard. Slapping makeshift weapons from angry hands, Gemma hurled herself into the fray. She shoved and elbowed her way through a sea of navy blue coats and howling faces to the wall that Maggie clung to, with Caroline and Nigel in her wake. One sailor began to scale the web of pipes towards Maggie.

Gemma scrambled to reach his ankles and bellowed for him to come down. "Stop!"

A thunderclap of a voice boomed over the speakers. The uproar paused, as if a needle had been scraped away from a gramophone record of the sounds of war. The single word echoed off the walls of the vast Oberth chamber.

"This is your Captain. Put your weapons down and come to attention," the voice commanded. Hands released hammers and wrenches, which took their time falling to the floor, as if they were sinking in molasses. The crew faced the speaking tube by the engine control panel, where a glowering Captain fixed them with his eyes.

"Better," he said.

He marched toward the mass, but as he neared them he bounced. Gemma found her own stance on the deck was rather tenuous, and the darkness grew around them, shade by shade.

In the sudden silence, one sound hovered over them: the echo of a wrench turning a bolt to the tune of Pritchard's swearing in the distance.

"Y'all pipe down, now," Mr. Pritchard muttered. "Man's tryin' to work over here."

Christophe gazed up into the darkness and said, "You can come down now, Maggie."

Cries of "Maggie?" and "It has a name?" rang through the chamber until Christophe called the crew back to attention. Some of them struggled to stand still as Maggie made her way down the network of pipes. Gemma watched her as she deftly navigated the steel web whilst keeping the unconscious Dr. Pugh steady and safe in a nest of rubbery limbs. Gemma felt someone's gaze upon her, but Caroline and Nigel were staring straight ahead. It was the captain who was studying her. She nodded at him, sharing what she knew was his relief that Maggie was unhurt -- and that Gemma herself was not more injured than she already was.

Maggie crossed the cold deck using two free tentacles as makeshift legs, holding both her body and Dr. Pugh up as she moved. She stopped next to Christophe in full view of the barely restrained mob.

Gemma could almost hear their thoughts: had the Captain repeated the failure of the maiden lunar voyage? Had they been boarded? Or worse, had they been betrayed by the captain? A tear of frustration escaped down Caroline's cheek; seeing her beloved Captain Moreau defending one of those creatures was almost too much for the Boolean to bear. But, to her credit, she held her ground and neither buckled nor ran.

Christophe cleared his throat. "As you can see, we are in no danger. We have not been boarded. You have not met the Enemy. You have, rather, just met the ship's ghost."

A murmur rolled through the assembly.

"Silence!" Christophe bellowed. "Maggie is as much a member of this crew as Dr. Pugh or Miss Llewellyn. She even designed parts of the ship! I promise you all, I will give you more details when the present crisis is -- I said, stand at attention!"

But the command was impossible to obey, as their feet had just left the deck entirely. They all floated -- even Maggie -- like newly-deceased spirits as the gravity plates finally gave out. The lights dimmed a little more, and it was fully night on the Oberth deck. The few active flywheels, one by one, wound down like exhausted watches.

The crew's terror was tangible, a living thing on its own. Many of them cried out in shock, knowing they could not simply open a hatch to let in the light and warmth of the sun. Gemma reached out for Nigel and Caroline, gripping her friends' hands as if she would never let go.

"Hold on to something," she called out.

Maggie stirred again, moving gracefully with her great bulk, almost swimming in the frigid air. Christophe held on to the end of one waggling limb. Without a word spoken between them, Maggie passed Dr. Pugh to his free hand. She reached for another floating crewman, who squealed at her nearness and beat at the air between them.

Christophe barked at the man. "Yeoman, take her tentacle!"

A frisson rippled down Gemma's spine at the steel in his voice.

This is it, she thought.

This was when Captain Moreau would be made or broken. It did not matter if they made it to Mars; it only mattered that his crew finally, fully, trusted him in this awful moment. It only mattered that they had the blind faith Nemo's crew had had in their commander. It was the only kind of faith one could have out here in the deep black. Would they trust him, or would they run wild in their terror? Would the sailor obey, or would he give in to madness?

"Not touchin' a bloody Martian!" the man shrieked. "Never!"

"There are no Martians on this ship!" Gemma cried, loud enough that Pritchard poked his head up over the power station door to gawk at them. "Just us Terrans! She was born on Earth, like the rest of us!"

Christophe said, "Take Maggie's limb, Yeoman. That's a direct order."

The man cringed. He swallowed. Hard. Twice. He reached out, hesitating and shaking, as one would when reaching through fire to flip a switch that would extinguish the flames. Finally, he took the end of the tentacle with both hands, eyes closed, waiting for the attack that Gemma knew would never come.

"Free one hand, Yeoman," Christophe said, gently this time. "Get ready to pick up the next one."

The man peeled open one wary eye and gazed down at his body, then up at Maggie. Seeing that he was still in possession of all his limbs, he obeyed and reached out for the next floater. They continued in that fashion for some minutes, adding sailors one hand at a time. The only sounds were Pritchard's accelerated cursing over at the power station. The great chain of people, with Gemma and her friends at the bottom, made its way to Maggie's former haven on the pipes.

"Everyone grab one," Christophe ordered. "Hold on! When the power comes back on, we don't want anyone falling!"

"Won't be on at this rate." Pritchard's grumble rambled across the deck.

"What's that, Pritchard?"

"Begging your pardon, Cap'n," he replied, "but I could really use a hand or three over here. My tools are all over, I can't see worth a damn, and I can't get any torque 'cause I can't stand up. And, dagnabbit, I'm a hair's breadth of bein' done with the fool thing!"

"Mind if Maggie helps?"

"Hell, I don't care if she's from Mars, Jupiter, or the Rational Dress Society. Long as she can hold me still! If Miss Gemma says she's okay, then she's okay. Send her on over!"

With a joyous trill, Maggie made her way across the deck at a speed that astonished Gemma. Maggie had never moved with such grace and swiftness in the short time she had known her. She was like a penguin that waddled on land but soared like an eagle beneath the waves. The scientist in Gemma asked: why would such beings even need gravity plates in their ship designs?

The question rang in her head like the peals of a bell as Maggie wrangled Pritchard's wayward tools for him. She grasped the power station with two tentacles and wrapped another around the tall man's waist. In her remaining limbs, she held his tools, including an electric torch to give him the light he so desperately needed. She handed him each tool as he called for it, like a nurse assisting a very exhausted surgeon.

"Now that's what I'm talkin' about," Pritchard said. "Good help is so hard to find, y'know."

"The captain's got some explaining to do," Nigel said, his voice tinged with the same steel as Christophe's. She could barely see the Boolean in the darkness. Shadows veiled his face. "And if you knew about this, so do you."

Caroline grasped Gemma's hand and squeezed her fingers. "Oh, it's one of them top science secrets, ain't it? She's nice, ain't she, Gemma? She won't hurt Ron? You promise?"

Gemma squeezed back with some warmth, remembering her own initial meeting with Maggie. "'Twill be all right, Caroline. I promise."

"I think it would be best if we all came clean," said Dr. Pugh.

Gemma watched the elderly scientist as he rested his gnarled hand against his chest. Dr. Hansard had just departed the cabin after leaving many admonishments for those that Pugh now addressed: Christophe, Maggie, and Gemma. Christophe perched on a stool next to the bed. Maggie rested on the floor beside him with one tentacle draped over the captain's shoulder and another one holding Dr. Pugh's other hand. Yet another one trailed through the air and waved in Gemma's direction. Every few minutes it would reach over and caress her knuckles.

Gemma shed the last blanket from her shoulders. They all blinked in the bright lights that had finally popped back on; Christophe was already sweating from the rekindled heat. After the power had been restored, they had lost no time in getting the unconscious scientist to sick bay, where he was treated along with others that had suffered minor injuries with the sudden reappearance of gravity.

While Gemma and Maggie hovered over the ailing scientist, Christophe had seen to the organization of the rest of the crew, giving orders and delegating tasks to damage control teams. Still without rest, he had reconvened with them in Pugh's cabin to check on his condition. Gemma wondered if the young man ever slept.

"It wasn't just Brightman that got you onto this ship," Dr. Pugh said. "I had a hand in it, too. I am rather sorry for putting you in harm's way, Gemma, but in all honesty, even with all that's happened, I think you are far safer here than anywhere on Earth as long as Petunia is creeping about."

"You got me on board? Why? How? And how did you even know I existed?" Gemma asked.

Pugh released Maggie's tentacle and retrieved his pocket watch from the night table. He clasped it between his hands, as if warming it. He finally popped it open and placed it in Gemma's hands.

"Because of them," he replied.

She looked down at the image inside the watch and found a woman and child staring back at her.

Dr. Pugh continued, "My wife and daughter. Before the Invasion. Elizabeth died during the initial attack on Woking, but my daughter--"

He halted, choking for a moment, never uttering the girl's name.

Gemma picked up the dangling thread of his thoughts. "You thought Brightman had taken her."

"Once I discovered what my mentor's former assistant was up to, yes. It took years to even discover that much, that Brightman had abducted so many survivors."

Christophe added, "I didn't know of any connection between you two until we were under way."

"But you knew later," Gemma said in as neutral tone as she could manage.

"Yes," he said, "but--"

"I asked him to say nothing," said Pugh. "I wanted to know for certain before I troubled you with the knowledge. I wanted to be the one to tell you, and I wanted to make sure that you were ready to hear it."

"And if you turned out to be wrong, and I was just another Brightman Girl, what would you have done with me?"

He stared down at his hands. "I don't know," he said gently. "I didn't know you then. I only had hope, a desperate hope, that I had found my girl at last. At the very least, I would have known you were still a victim of Brightman's schemes. Still somebody's lost child. I hope I would have done what I have already done: accepted you as part of my family."

"Even if I were not your child? Or Aronnax's child?"

"That is my hope."

She turned to Christophe. "So, that is why you tested my hair?"

"Yes," he said. "I know I should have allowed Elias to test you in his own time, as he had intended. But things were getting a bit dodgy--"

"Dodgy enough to shoot me," she growled.

"You got better!" he retorted. "Well, we did cut it close. I wanted Elias to know something for certain before we all snuffed it."

"You wanted to make sure you hadn't tried to kiss your sister, you mean," Gemma growled again, but this time it emerged through a playful curl in her lips.

"That, too."

"Kiss?" asked Pugh.

"But why me? Why did you gamble on it being me? There are many other Girls--"

"I had eliminated all but two from the list, either because they were the wrong age or because their Codes did not match. I hired a Mr. Chapman to collect Code -- however he could -- from the ones I thought might be a match. He managed to narrow it down to two. One, by all reports, was deceased already, with the location of her grave unknown. There was nothing available to test." Images of her friend, once Philippa, now Jennie, flitted across her mind as he then said, "The other was you, my dear."

She knew the rest of this tale. Could she bear to hear it fall from his lips? Could she -- should she -- tell him her truth?

"The last time I saw him, he was departing for Shanghai, to search you out. But someone killed him before he reported back. Getting access to you after that was well nigh impossible. But when I discovered that Brightman was trying to plant one of her people on the *Fury*, I saw my chance. And I took it."

"His name was Chapman," Gemma replied in a quiet voice.

The ghost that had haunted her for years had a name. Would he leave her in peace now, if she confessed? Even if that peace was short-lived?

She heard Christophe's sharp intake of breath. He knew. She had told him before that she was a monster, and now he had put the pieces together. Even though he now regarded her with sadness and pity in his eyes, there was no way he could tell her she was anything else now.

Maggie rolled over to her and wrapped a couple of tentacles around her in a gentle embrace. Gemma felt a coolness on her face; she touched her cheek and stared at the tears dancing on the tips of her fingers.

There was no thunder here, no rain outside a gray window to weep for her. The storm had broken loose inside of her at last.

"Did you see him, child?"

"I thought he was there to kill me," she said with a crack in her voice.

With every heartbeat, she could feel the promise of the stars slipping away with her confession. She could not look at him, at that kindly face. She stared at the wall instead. It was covered with images of a younger Pugh with his mentor, a man she now knew to be her father, a man known to her only through her reading of his journals. She tore herself away from that kindly stranger's gaze as well. Surely Pugh would loathe her after this, no matter who her father had been. Any hope that she had had of making a true life for herself out here was slipping like sand through her fingers.

"It was in a dark alley. I thought I was alone until he came upon me. He got too close. I reacted. It was instinct. He was dead before he could speak. If I had known--"

"Oh, my dear child," Dr. Pugh sobbed. "I warned Chapman to be careful. I warned him how Petunia had *brutalized* her pupils. I warned him not to approach you so directly. Hair strands stolen from a brush would have done. But he was stubborn. I should have guessed."

He passed a shaking hand across his eyes; she was not the only one weeping. "Oh, Gemma. My darling little Gemma. That I sent him, that I pushed you into such a corner. That you endured that burden alone! I should have gone myself, instead of sending a stranger. Oh, can you ever forgive me?"

"Forgive *you?*" she stammered. This was more surreal than meeting Maggie. "How could you forgive *me?*"

"It was self-defence," Christophe broke in. He tried to reach for her, and then something in him forced him to withdraw and sit back down. "How were you to know any differently, with a strange man coming upon you, in the dark, alone and so far from home?" He turned to Dr. Pugh, and a sense of relief flooded his voice. "Elias, you would have been as much a stranger to her as Chapman."

"But I would have been more careful with her," Pugh said. "I would not have ambushed someone who was trained to--"

A knock at the door made them all jump. At Pugh's word, it opened to reveal the weary visage of Ron Pritchard.

"Pardon the intrusion, Cap'n, ladies," he said as he flashed a wide smile at Maggie. "Dr. Pugh. Thought I'd check in with you."

"Of course, Mr. Pritchard," Christophe replied as he got to his feet. "What's our status?"

"Power's back up in all sections and has been stable for a few hours now. Engines don't look any worse for wear and should be fine when we restart 'em. Dr. Bidarhalli is crankin' through the calculations to see when we should fire 'em up. Because we're a little off our acceleration schedule, we'll have to adjust Braking Day. He figures we should just cruise along as we are for a while and then just fire 'em up for braking to begin, instead of speedin' up to just slow down again. We're behind, but not by too much."

"And has everyone reported in about how the power outage affected their systems? How about our provisions?"

"Oh, I think Frau Knopf has that well in hand, sir. Herr Knopf reported that there's some frost damage in the Gardens, not to mention the mess created when the artificial gravity gave out. Thankfully, a lot of stuff in there is pretty well nailed down, but not everything. He sure was cussin'. Stable deck is a disaster, though. There'll be no shortage of cleanup details 'round here, I'm thinking."

Christophe chuckled. "Well, I know exactly who to assign to that. I'm sure Rathbone and Wallace would love to get out of their cells for a while. Under guard, of course." He stroked one of Maggie's outstretched limbs. "What is the crew saying about their new member?"

"Well, sir, I've not heard anything out of line, but I do have to say that they all know better than to disrespect Miss Maggie 'round Hieronymus Pritchard. She saved the ship, and that's good enough for me. Though I do admit to some curiosity as to how she got onto the roster."

Christophe rubbed his knees. "I'm sure you are not the only curious one. Perhaps I should address the crew, now that things are calming down a bit. We have several matters to attend to." He stood and straightened his jacket, a futile operation considering how rumpled and soiled it was. "You have my gratitude, Mr. Pritchard. Your steadiness, perseverance, and good sense saved us. And you deserve some sleep, for heaven's sake! Your next post is your pillow, my good fellow!"

"Yes, sir," he said with a deep thunderous laugh. "But I think Frau Knopf has a plate of bacon with my name on it, first."

"Far be it from me to stand between a man and his bacon," Christophe chuckled.

As the door closed behind the departing first mate, Pugh tugged at his blanket. "I would suggest addressing the crew sooner rather than later, son. I am sure that Maggie's sudden appearance was quite a nasty shock for some of them."

"They frightened the dickens out of me," Maggie said. "I am not very fond of crowds."

The captain rubbed his chin again, grimacing as he re-discovered the rough scrub lurking there. "Well, without a bath and a shave, I don't believe the crowd will fancy me, either. Let's get everyone fed and down for a nap before we read them in. Perhaps 'twill be easier to take on a full stomach."

"Especially if Frau Knopf has anything to say about it," replied Gemma. The interruption had given her some time to pull herself together. She felt shaken, still, but she could breathe again. Maggie steadied her as she rose from her seat. "My ribs remind me that I could use some rest as well." She bowed her head at the scientist. "Good night, Dr. Pugh."

He took her hand in his and kissed it lightly. "Elias, please, my dear Gemma Aronnax."

"I will stay with him," Maggie said. "Rest well, my children."

Christophe followed Gemma across the room and out of the cabin. He closed the door behind them.

"Where are you headed?" he asked. "I mean, really? You seem too overwrought for sleep."

"Back to Dr. Hansard's office. I still have a code to crack. There's another ship out there, remember? Or so Wallace claims."

He winced, as if just then recalling the next crisis on the list. "Well, I'm certainly glad you're on the job. I can barely remember my own name at this point. Wallace is safely ensconced in the brig for the moment, so don't worry about him just now."

A tense silence drew out between them as they waited by the lifts, which had finally ground their way back to life. They entered an empty one and directed it to the deck for sick bay.

"Gemma," he said now that they were assured of privacy, "I believe it's best if we keep my, shall we say, rather special relationship with Maggie private. At least for now."

Gemma nodded. "As you are fond of saying, 'one crisis at a time'. I believe I can keep a secret."

With a ghost of a smile, he said in a quiet voice, "Thank you."

"For what?"

"For trying to save Maggie. For... for befriending her."

"I failed to stop them."

"But you did stall things a bit. You gave me time to get there. The poor blokes. They were all so afraid! It could have taken a very bad turn without you. And they did calm down when you showed them your support for her. No order of mine could have done that. I think they will accept her more readily when they see you two are thick as thieves! They respect you."

They exited the lift and entered an empty corridor. He stopped mid-stride and regarded her with the same inscrutable look that he had used at Cervantes' memorial service.

"And so do I." He reached for her hand. "With your kind permission."

She inclined her head at him, as she had at Dr. Pugh. He brushed his lips against her knuckles with the same tenderness his father had used. It was in that moment that she saw Elias Pugh in his face. No matter what other Code had been used in creating him, he was his father's son.

He straightened up, still holding her hand loosely by the fingers. "Awfully sorry about the shooting bit, old girl. I solemnly swear not to do it again, if you promise not to use Wallace as a punching bag. Or Rathbone, for that matter. Pax?"

"Pax," she replied. She grasped the hand that held hers firmly and pulled it down into a firm handshake. "Now, get us to Mars, Captain!"

He brayed with laughter. Without releasing her hand, he leaned in and said with a conspirator's whisper, "And after that, we'll figure out what we'll do once we get back to Earth. I believe we've all been sacked."

She tilted her head at him and said, "Well, you could always turn pirate. You certainly have the wardrobe for it. Instead of a *Flying Dutchman*, we'd have a *Queen Anne's Revenge*." She plucked at the wide flounces of his linen shirt that she still wore. "Then you might actually be interesting."

He seemed so very young in that moment. The glint she had seen in his eyes when she had first met him -- the one that had faded with the death of Cervantes -- had returned. They all seemed so young, too young, to venture so far from home. Even ancient Dr. Pugh seemed too much of a fledgling for the unknown wilds of space. But they would have to make do.

He squeezed her fingers warmly and released her. He re-entered the lift alone. As the door closed, he said, "Miss Aronnax, you slay me with hope."

She turned away from the doors and trudged to sick bay. Somehow even her toes knew that in Hansard's office, Caroline was already at work sorting the last of the punchcards. Nigel was nowhere to be seen.

Caroline embraced her with care and greeted her in sleepy tones. "Oh, what a day! What a day! I'm too tired to sleep!"

Caroline had already re-sorted the punchcards (shuffled out of order by the gravity failure) and stacked them on the table. She plucked the first one off the top and fed it into the portable reader. The keys on the adapted typewriter moved of their own accord, like some phantom secretary composing a cryptic message from the Beyond.

The two women watched the information flow from the carriage onto the paper. First was the header information, which was plain enough if one knew how to read it. Then, as expected, sets of numbers appeared, still concealing the true message within them.

"It's a book cipher, I'll wager," Gemma observed.

"How can you tell?"

"See the pattern of numbers here? The triplets? That pattern is used in a book cipher. See, this first number is a page number of a specific book. The second is a line number on that page, and the third is the letter on that line.

Record each letter as you go, and you have your message. Assuming, of course, you have the corresponding book."

"Sounds tedious," replied Caroline. "And you do this by hand when you get your messages from your institute?"

"Yes."

"Didn't know geology was so top-secret! It would be faster with an engine, though. If you had the right book set up on punchcards, that is." She paused and studied the many titles on Dr. Hansard's shelves. "Question is, which book did they use?"

"That is the real trick. The person who sent the message could have used any book. To read the message, you'd have to have the same book, down to the same edition, to make sure everything matched up. One bit of good news, though, is that it might be easier to locate that book on an isolated ship than it would be back home. We're limited to what is actually on hand."

Caroline frowned. "There's plenty of books on this ship, though. Why, there are scores between the parlour and the science lab alone!"

Gemma chewed her lip. "It might be amongst Wallace's things, in his cabin. He would need privacy for this. And he'd have to get rid of his decrypted messages, if he wrote them down."

"Wouldn't be easy, unless he fed them to the goats or something," Caroline observed. "Rathbone would need to have the same book. He said he'd broken Wallace's code. He'd have to have another copy, most likely, or Wallace might've figured out what he was up to."

Gemma grabbed the Boolean's hand in her excitement. "Yes, you have it! How can we enter their cabins?"

"Well, they're both in Gent's Country. I don't feel right going there without--"

"I just left Pugh's cabin there, and no one objected."

"But you were with the Cap'n." Caroline shook her head. "We shouldn't bother him with this. He has a lot to do! This is our job, and Nigel should be helping. I'll get him--"

"Where is he? I can tell him what to look for."

Caroline shuffled her feet. "I think I'd best talk to him, just now."

"Whatever for?"

"He's still getting used to the idea of, um, Maggie. I understand why you science lot may have wanted to keep it hush-hush, but Nigel? He's not one for secrets."

"And I kept a huge one from him."

"Something like that, yeah."

"All right. I trust your judgment, Caroline. You've known him far longer than I have." She snatched a pencil and a blank sheet of paper from the many stacks on the table and scribbled down a few words. She handed it to

Caroline. "He should compare the books they both have, but look for this one especially."

Caroline skimmed over the note. "I thought this might be the one you wanted," she said as she tapped the side of her nose with her finger. "I'll be a while. Why don't you try to catch a few winks while I'm gone?"

Alone again, Gemma slumped into a chair. Her ribs whined as she leaned towards the reader, still cranking away at the first message. The numbers blurred together, and she felt weariness wash over her once more.

Codes. Codes for messages. Codes for engines. Codes for Life. Even bloody codes for bloody knitting patterns. They were everywhere.

Even with all of her experience in and around science, Gemma found it extraordinary that one could connect two people by just comparing sequences of their Code, Code taken from strands of hair. Her fingers strayed to her locket. She stroked it and lost herself in memories of the owner of the hair hidden there. So much had happened in the past few days, and she ached to tell her lost friend everything that had transpired. Gemma wished that Jennie had been able to join Nigel on the ship. A mist formed over her eyes as she imagined it. What a joyous reunion it would have been!

The office felt emptier without Nigel there. Would he ever forgive their secrecy? Would she ever meet her namesake, her dearest friend's daughter? Would she ever tell Nigel an even darker secret, tell him that his wife had been a thief, like her? What did he already know? By now he surely suspected something. It would be difficult to rest easy with this new spectre hovering over her.

"Dr. Pugh said we should come clean," she mused aloud. "Perhaps I should--"

Her train of thought froze in its tracks as the rest of that conversation clacked through her memory as precisely as the reader consumed the holes in the punchcards. She gripped the locket tightly in her fist.

Pugh had said that there had been no way to check the Code of the last Brightman Girl, the one Chapman could not find because she rested in an unknown grave.

Gemma opened the locket and touched the hair within. Perhaps the grave was not unknown; perhaps that daughter was not lost. There was one last test to perform; there was one last Code to crack.

She reached out to the now-familiar mental connection with her newest friend.

"Maggie, can you do me a favour?"

CHRISTOPHE

Christophe, standing tall on the front table of the mess hall, stared out across the sea of sailors as they settled into their seats. He was unsure if there was enough sleep in the world to let him catch up on his rest. He had, however, taken great pains to make sure that the crew had, especially Mr. Pritchard.

He clenched his fist behind his back, forcing the nervousness into his knuckles. This felt so very different from his brave speech at the beginning of their voyage. He hoped the right words would come. He could sense ripples of sentiment flowing through the people arrayed before him: bewilderment, anxiety, anger, frustration, exhaustion, and a teasing hint of curiosity. He could order an end to violence, but not an end to fear. It was there, slithering through the waves of his brave people and caressing them with its scales. He could see the dread in their eyes as he used to foresee a storm in streaks of grey and jagged flashes of light on the horizon. There was a squall ahead, on a different horizon, and there was nothing for it but to reef the sails and push through it.

Despite himself, he searched for those familiar faces that he knew were no longer there. Cervantes had always been there, close by, and Christophe could sense the hole that he left behind. His eyes then settled on a face that was new to the crowd.

Maggie, in an attempt to appear less menacing, had piled herself into the floor next to Gemma's seat on the front row. The young lady held the end of one of Maggie's limbs in one hand upon her lap as she sipped a steaming cup of tea. The knot in his middle relaxed as he rested his gaze on the two ladies. Several of Maggie's other limbs twitched the way they did when she had the itch to knit but couldn't get to her needles. Expressions in miniature crossed Gemma's face, from a half-smile to a rise of the eyebrows. Christophe fought to suppress a grin of his own as he recognized the hallmarks of an internal conversation with Maggie.

Suddenly he was very glad that Gemma was most definitely not his sister.

The remainder of the Cohort occupied the rest of the table, in a rare show of solidarity. Dr. Hansard sat with them in Pugh's place, as he was still resting in his cabin. The medical officer chewed the end of his unlit pipe with vigour as he kept an eye on everyone else. Father Alfieri was there as well, beaming at Maggie. His sermon on love was about to be put to the test.

There was a glaring no-man's-land of empty tables between the Cohort and the rest of the crew. The back walls were lined with people that had chosen to stand instead of sit near that particular table. Mutterings of "Martians" and "secrets" and "ghosts" slinked through their conversations like serpents in tall grass; murmurs with an edge of alarm had supplanted the old whispers about treasure.

Maggie's voice slipped into his head. "Are you certain they are ready for this? I am not sure I am."

"They are my crew, Maggie," he thought back at her. "I trust them. All will be well."

Christophe cleared his throat and waited for the silence, which took longer than usual to settle over the group. He nodded to the waiting Mr. Pritchard, who bellowed at them to come to attention.

The reaction was immediate, sharp, and crisp as the entire hall -- even the Cohort, which didn't have to -- stood at attention. Long discipline could still tamp down fear, even if only for a short time. He let them stand in silence for a moment, partly to gather his own strength and partly for them to get used to the idea of sharing space with Maggie.

At long last, when the shuffling and scraping and inevitable coughs had died out, leaving only silence behind, he said, "Be seated."

He took a deep breath and unfurled his thoughts before them. "The last few days have seasoned us a bit. We are becoming true spacefarers! There are always storms ahead when one sets sail. This was one of ours. The explorers of old often faced such terrors and lost crew on their way. We have not been spared that fate.

"Every crew, no matter the sea, suffers loss along the way. One hopes that at the very least, it will be a terror from without, and not one from within. We did not escape that fate, either. We have left our home behind us, but not ourselves. We packed our imperfections and carried them with us like luggage that refuses to remain behind. At the same time, we have also brought our courage, our fortitude, and our perseverance, as all of you demonstrated during these many anxious hours. I congratulate you. I thank you. Because you give me hope. Hope that another virtue -- curiosity -- will prevail as we face our next adventure on this odyssey. Some of you are already very familiar with a certain member of our crew. Others of you only met her the other day as she assisted our Mr. Pritchard on the Oberth deck. The rest of you only know her via rumour. And that we are about to remedy.

"It is my pleasure to introduce you to a very important member of the Scientific Cohort: Maggie. Many of you have already called her 'the ship's ghost'. Crew of the *Fury*, this is Maggie. Maggie, meet the crew."

He had hoped that she would say something, but she simply hunkered down next to Gemma, trying and failing to make herself smaller. He had never known her to be so shy, but then again this was her first time in such a crowd.

"What does it... eat?" asked one of Dr. Hansard's orderlies.

"*She*, not *it*. Like her progenitors, she subsists on blood." He had to shout over the worried murmurs that rolled through the crowd in a swift current. "But not human blood. Honestly, she doesn't like the taste. She lives off the animals on the stable deck. We store their blood for her during normal slaughter operations. They are not just our food supply. They are hers."

One of the wireless operators stood up. "But... wasn't she part of the Invasion? She seems... friendly enough, I s'pose... but ain't this fraternizin' with the enemy?"

"No. She is a loyal Terran, just like you, even if she is not human. Maggie did not take part in the Invasion. In fact, she was born just as the war ended. Her progenitor died in the process. She is as much an Orphan of the Invasion as many of you are. She has never harmed anyone."

"But what about Rathbone?" the operator asked.

"She was defending Miss Llewellyn at the time. If Rathbone had never attacked her, he would have been safe as houses. I am certain any of you would have done the same if you had been there. She will not harm you, but she will defend herself and anyone else in harm's way. She will defend this ship. Many of you bore witness to how she assisted Mr. Pritchard in finishing his work to bring the power back online.

"She has been an excellent friend to Dr. Pugh and myself these many years. My hope is that she will make many more friends among you. And, even if you choose not to associate with her outside of your duties -- as is your right -- I expect all of you to show her the same courtesy that you would show Dr. Pugh. Her name is Maggie, and you will refer to her as such. Not 'the Martian'. Not 'Tentacle-Head'. Not 'It'."

Frau Knopf stood and turned to the crowd with a stern face. "And if I hear of any one saying bad things about my Maggie, well, then, no bacon for you!"

Christophe swallowed a chuckle at the sudden sharp intakes of breath. Frau Knopf did not threaten. She never simply threatened. He could feel the crew wrestling with the promise of a baconless existence versus their fear of the unknown. Would the bacon win?

Mr. Pritchard stood up with a smile. "I've had the pleasure of meetin' Miss Maggie up close and personal. Does the lady have a surname, or is it just Maggie?"

"Just Maggie," Christophe replied, grateful for the levity in the man's manner. "We tried to call her Professor Maggie once upon a time, but she wasn't very keen."

"How does she communicate?" Mr. Holomek, one of the midshipmen, asked. "Does she speak the King's?"

"She can hear you if you speak normally. She understands German and a smattering of French as well. As for her speech... Maggie, say hello to the crew."

"Um... hello," said Maggie's nervous voice in his head.

A shiver ran through the crowd as they touched their ears and heads, and twitters of "did you hear that" floated towards the ceiling.

It always astounded Christophe that anyone would find this unusual. Her voice had always been with him, since before he knew what a voice was. Before he had understood her words, he had understood how she felt. She was comfort; she was home. It was difficult for him to comprehend how some people had never had such love. He had never been an Orphan. He had always had her.

He glanced at Gemma, and he felt sorrow for anyone who had not had that gentle benevolent presence since childhood. The tentacle intertwined with Gemma's tapered fingers made him happy. At least, Gemma was starting to feel such a steady presence now, even if it was Maggie's and not his.

"She does not have human vocal cords," he assured them. "Instead, she can speak directly into your mind. It may feel strange at first, but you will grow used to it."

Yeoman McLure jumped up onto her seat and added, "It's just like in them scientific romances, lads! We're living in one!"

One of the remaining engineer's mates got to his feet. "That's all well and good. So long as she keeps to her knittin' and we keep to ours, I reckon we'll get on just fine. I'm more concerned with Mr. Nesbitt and the others what Mr. Wallace killed."

"Yeah," shouted another one, "what about Wallace? He's more dangerous than she is. He's the one what killed somebody. We gonna space him?"

Christophe held his hands up in a reassuring gesture. "Our fallen comrades will be remembered in a memorial service tomorrow evening. Maggie will be present. She is free to attend any shipwide events she wishes, like the rest of us. As for Wallace, I think enough blood has been spilt on this voyage as it is. We will keep him under lock and key until we return to Earth. He will be tried by an appropriate court and jury, and they will determine his fate."

"But what if there ain't no court?" someone else asked. "We've had no communication with the Admiralty. What if the TIA ain't there when we get back? What do we do then? What do we do now? Should we even go to Mars?"

"All very good questions. It is true that the Admiralty is in an uncertain state. We have attempted to send messages to Admiral Thorvaldson and have yet to receive an answer. What news we have been able to get says that the very Treaty that created the TIA is in danger of being dissolved."

He allowed that to sink in, but before the full impact of it stole their attention, he continued. "For the moment, we have to answer for ourselves. No matter what is going on back home, no matter what individual factions may be at war, one thing has not changed: we still have a mission. We are too far away to make any difference back there, except for the fact that we can investigate this danger. So, we will do our job, with or without the Admiralty or the TIA or whomever replaces them. We are one crew. We are for Earth! *Terra vigila!*"

A tepid war cry rippled through the crowd and faded out.

"Listen to me," he continued. He didn't have them. Not yet. "We are drawn from many nations, many backgrounds, many religions, and races. Even different species!" He gestured at Maggie, who trilled back at him. "But we all have one thing in common: we all want to protect Earth! Are you with me?"

"*Terra Vigila!*" Louder this time.

"Will you stand with me?"

And they shouted back in throaty unison, so loud that the walls shook: "*Terra Vigila!*"

GEMMA

"Blimey, this is taking a bleeding eternity," Caroline said.

Seated at the desk in Gemma's stateroom, she typed away on the portable card machine. She had propped Rathbone's *The Riddle of the Sands* -- nicked from the parlour, as Gemma had suspected -- upon the desk, on top of Gemma's copy of Lyell.

"It will be worth it in the end," Gemma said from her bed, where she nursed her bruises and nibbled on pastries from the tray brought to them by Frau Knopf.

Dr. Hansard had shooed them out of his office, for he wanted to neaten up the disaster that the gravity outage had made sick bay. Fortunately, most of the poisons and medicines had been locked down, or they would truly have had a mess on their hands.

Gemma glanced over the first decoded messages again. There were so many of them, both coming and going. Wallace had kept the wireless very busy, indeed. They had decoded the last message first, and Gemma read over it again with great satisfaction. The other ship, the *Orestes*, had encountered engine trouble not far into their own voyage. As of their last message, they were currently in orbit around the moon and were desperately trying to repair their radio wave generator.

"Poor blighters!" Caroline had said. "I'm sure they're just following orders. I hope they have their solar flare shielding in place."

The other captain, a certain Andrew Straker, had recommended that Wallace hold off on his actions until they signaled that they were able to continue. Judging from the timestamp, the message had arrived just as Wallace was picking up his axe.

The pity of it was, if he had only received the message earlier, Nesbitt and his men might still be alive. She wrestled with the thought. It had been his choice to kill them; he could not excuse himself with an accident of timing. Gemma still found it difficult to excuse herself for Mr. Chapman's death, self-defence notwithstanding, now that she knew who he was.

Wallace had told the truth. There were no messages after that one, and no way to determine where the other ship was now without contacting them directly. Christophe had taken the reprieve in stride. Having shared more than one round of lager with Straker at the Badger and Tentacle in the past, he'd said, he was not eager to meet him again without the beneficial company of a nearby keg.

Christophe's next orders were rather creative, even by Brightman's standards. He had asked Gemma to encode a message to Straker from Wallace saying that he had, indeed, delayed his action and asking that they reply as soon as they were able. He then asked Humboldt -- whom he had transferred to the Wireless section for the time being -- to devise a method to track their position using their wireless signal in case they ever answered.

In the meantime, Humboldt had surmised, they could at least guess the other ship's position using the difference between the send and receive timestamps of the messages, if they bothered to reply. Humboldt was happy to have a question to keep him busy whilst he recovered from his own injuries. Boredom terrified the man.

A rattling of her wardrobe caught her attention. Caroline jumped at the sudden noise.

"Oh, it's just Maggie," Gemma said as the door opened and revealed a waving tentacle. "So that's how you've been getting into my room all this time! Why aren't you using the hallway now?"

"Everyone may know about me, Gemma," came Maggie's mental reply, "but not everyone is quite as accustomed to my cheerful face as you are. I would prefer to ease them into it."

She rolled her bulk out of the cabinet and onto the floor.

"Oh, hallo, Maggie," Caroline said.

"Caroline," Maggie replied with a strong blink of her eyes, her version of a nod. "How goes the decoding, ladies?"

Gemma wondered what voice Caroline heard in her head when Maggie spoke. Was it Jennie's voice she heard, as Gemma did? Or was it a completely different voice? Caroline pushed back her chair and stood for a good stretch and yawn.

"I'm punching the cards to get the book itself into the A.E.," she said as she pointed to the text on the desk. "Then I'll write some code that'll take the message from their cards and just print out the plaintext for us. Having to include the metadata, the page numbers and such, is a bit of a bother. It's going to take a while to get it all in, but I'm hoping that once it is done, it'll be faster than decoding them by hand."

"A book cipher? Oh, I love those! Which book?"

Maggie picked up the volume with a delicate flourish and held it up to one eye. She curled the end of one limb beneath it and flipped through the pages at an astonishing rate with yet another. She chuckled as she went.

"How charming!" she said. "What a darling little spy story."

"You can read that fast?"

"Of course."

Gemma tapped her chin, pondering possibilities. "Maggie, do you remember everything you read?"

"You mean, do I store it in my redundant memory?"

"Yes. Could you, say, remember what is on a given page, given line, given position?"

"If I read it with that kind of recall in mind, yes. I don't record everything automatically. It has to be deliberate."

"I wonder if you might do another favour for me. Would you read it again, store it that way, then read this message?" She held up a still-encoded message. "Decode it?"

Maggie flipped back to the front of the book and read it again. She then plucked the paper from Gemma's hand with a free limb and held it up to her other eye.

"Oh, Wallace has been a busy fellow," she observed as the blue orb tracked back and forth across the page. "And a bit naughty, I must say."

"Can you write it down for us?" asked Gemma.

"Or just type it up on the reader here?" asked Caroline.

"Certainly."

"Lovely!" Caroline exclaimed. "That'll save me a lot of drudgery. You're even better than an engine, Maggie!"

That comment, like a dart, shot into Gemma's mind and lodged in her grey matter as soon as the Boolean uttered it. It echoed some other thoughts that Gemma had had over time. The ideas tumbled over and over in her head... engines and code, code and engines...

"Speaking of code," Maggie said, "I have something else for you. The answer to your question."

"Question?" asked Caroline. "What question?"

Gemma held her breath. Her torso screamed at her, but she held it anyway. She did not know what answer to hope for.

"Yes. She is."

Gemma blew out the held gasp of air. Tears spilled down her face, both in relief at finally knowing and in dread at having to share the news.

"I... I don't get it," Caroline said. "What's wrong, Gemma? What question?"

Gemma patted an empty spot on the bed. "Come, sit here. I have some news for you. About Jennie."

"Jennie?"

"Shouldn't we tell Elias first?" asked Maggie.

"No, no, I want to know now. Oh, don't tease me!"

"I will go to him, then, and tell him now," replied Maggie. She placed the books and papers back on the desk and opened the cabinet door once more. "I will return later to finish our work. This will be easier if it comes from me. In person. And if he's already lying down."

In the orrery, the planets were silent, frozen in place since Rathbone's attack. There had been no time since then for repairs. Nigel stood at the rail in his dungarees and stared at the miniature *Fury* stalled in mid-air. The actual ship had never stopped moving, but its tiny twin was immobile. Instead of a kinetic sculpture, the orrery was now a tableau, stuck for a moment in time, like a painting, frozen in a splash of emerald, azure, and shades of crimson.

Nigel cradled a gigantic wrench against him. He looked weary, like a farmer surveying ice-squashed fields that had been in full bloom the day before. He would not look at Gemma. Maggie, sensitive to his feelings, was absent, leaving the task of revelation to others. Gemma had thought it would be happy news for the Boolean, that his child had a grandfather, one with as generous a heart as Dr. Pugh's.

"No," Nigel said. "No, that can't be. My Jennie was an Orphan. Like me. She told me her parents were dead. She knew for certain. Are you saying my wife lied to me?"

"That was no lie," Gemma said. "She told you what she thought was true."

Nigel snapped his head around to her and snarled, "And what would you know about it? You know far too much about her -- you've done too much for her. It can't just be for my sake. It's as if you knew her. Knew a side of her that I didn't."

Pugh squeezed her shoulder to hold her back, but the truth wailed for release. Even if it made him feel worse, Nigel needed to know. He needed to know what sort of monster stalked his child. Even the captain, had he been present, could not order her silence now. Secrecy would only fester inside of her until it was set free.

"I did know her," she replied.

She could hear Pugh sobbing softly behind her. He had known for many years what had happened to his child, but that did not soften the blow of hearing it again. Nigel's knuckles went white as she told him. The story wound out of her like a ball of Frau Knopf's yarn being sucked through Maggie's lightning-fast needles. Tears slid out from underneath the wire rims of his spectacles as the words spilled across the floor in a flood.

Brightman. Computers. Stealth. Codes. Secrets. Theft.

Death.

Nigel covered his ears and howled. "I don't want to hear any more! It's too fantastic! Too horrid! Not my sweet Jennie!"

"I knew her as Philippa."

"And you, Pugh," he sobbed, "what did you call her? What was her name?" His question echoed around the cold walls of the slumbering orrery. "What was her name?"

"Cora," he said, his voice that still, soft breeze after a storm. "My little Cora."

"Cora," Nigel repeated. "How did she die? I mean, *really* die? Did you know that was going to happen? Why didn't you tell me earlier? Perhaps we could have--"

"I didn't know anything until it was too late," Gemma sighed, her own vision slightly blurred. "I did not make the connection until--"

"Until you saw my pocket watch," he said, recollection dawning on his pain-twisted face. "It was like you had seen a ghost."

"I had, Nigel. I had seen a ghost. Brightman had told me, told all of us, that she was dead. My only friend in the world was gone. Oh, Nigel! I am sorry she is gone. I am sorry for the life we were forced to lead. But I am glad, so glad, to know that she had some portion of happiness with you."

"Did she? Did she, really? Did she love me, or was I just another job?"

"I don't know, Nigel. I honestly don't know. I don't know if Brightman sent her to you, or if she ran away and was tracked down later. I don't know how you met her. From time to time she had whispered to me that there was a better life out there." She choked for a moment and glanced at Dr. Pugh for a dose of strength. "I wasn't ready to believe that. I do believe that, now. And I want to believe that she loved you, that she was happy with you. Happy to become a mother, however briefly."

Pugh said, "I want to believe that, too. I've known you for some time, lad. I know you loved her well. I, too, am glad my Cora, Gemma's Philippa, and your Jennie, was with you, of all people."

"Was she truly with me? Can I even be sure that--"

Gemma stopped him. "I can never know anything for certain, but I would wager that she is your child. You have a father-in-law! A daughter! You have living family! That is more than most on this ship can boast!"

Pugh said, "There is a way to tell for certain, when we get home, if you have doubts. Maggie can--"

"Keep that beast away from me!" he bellowed. He flung the weighty wrench against the globe of Mars, and the fury of it dented a new crater in the crimson orb. "You cannot change what it is by giving it a name! Damn Mars! Damn the Martians! Damn the Invasion! And damn you!"

"Nigel--"

"Get out! Leave me be! Get out, get out, get out!"

* * *

As the days passed, they closed in on the Red Planet and picked up the pieces floating in the wake of Wallace's sabotage. Between Dr. Hansard's strict supervision and the maternal clucking of Frau Knopf, Gemma healed. Her bruises faded, and the complaining of her ribs softened to a whisper.

Dr. Pugh recovered as well. In their mutual convalescence, they took many walks in the Garden, which was undergoing a healing of its own after the power outage. Dr. Pugh told her tales of her famous father, and she told him about the life of his daughter. Arm in arm, they followed the paths that wound about the Gardens. They passed Herr Knopf as he fussed over his frostbitten cabbages and hovered hawk-like over Rathbone as the man set stone urns of petunias to rights. The former wireless officer -- and Brightman Boy -- had not a glance to spare her as she passed by.

She spent time with each member of the Cohort, at Pugh's urging, to learn about each one's research.

"It's all rather dry, Miss," the linguist said as he showed her the fruits of his labour. "Very technical, very efficient. The lack of metaphors makes the translation easier to understand, though."

"Had they no poetry with them? No novels?" Gemma asked. "We brought so much literature with us."

"Not a syllable, I'm afraid," he replied. "Not even the Martian version of a dirty limerick. They are brilliant engineers, but I am afraid their conversation at tea would be rather dreary."

Later she perched upon her lab stool and pored over the journals. She wished to solve Pugh's mystery of the *Nautilus* dates, but she also wanted to search for other clues about Aronnax himself. The last time she had been in this spot, she had not had a scrap of a hint about her parents' identities. Now, she read the words written by her father, one who had never known of her, either. What would they have made of each other if they had ever met, she wondered.

She brushed the dog-eared record of his famous journey under the seas with her fingertips. She allowed herself a light chuckle when she recalled that this man's daughter was on an even more perilous journey through a completely different kind of sea, with a man who was at once the son of his host and of his protégé.

Perhaps she should start a journal of her own, documenting this journey from a woman's point of view, like Nellie Bly...

"Good to see you smiling again."

She lifted her eyes to see Christophe lurking on the other side of the lab bench with a curious grin on his face and a book tucked under one arm.

He placed the book on the lab bench and pushed it towards her. The cloth on the cover was so faded that its original colour was difficult to determine. The frayed corners had seen better days. The gilt letters on the cover had been brushed by fingers one too many times, and she could barely make out the title: *Captain Stormfield's Visit to Mars and Other Tales*. She beamed when she saw the author's name.

"More Twain?" she asked. "I've never seen this one before."

"Yes! He wrote it after meeting Maggie."

"He met Maggie?"

"One of the few outside the labs to do so. It was a limited run, though. The TIA found it a bit too comical and bought up most of the copies. I thought you could use something relaxing to read. Journals can be rather heavy at times, especially that one. I have several books, but I thought that *Physical Geography of the Sea and Its Meteorology* might have limited application on Mars." He lowered his voice, and hope shone in his eyes. "And I thought we should have something to discuss if by some chance we have another... midnight salon."

He was there again, the laughing boy that she had found in the gazebo. This man had been her mission, but she had only discovered that fact when she had broken free of it. Oh! If she were still under Brightman's sway, how easy it would be to obey right now. That mélange of command and mischief playing around the edges of his mouth...

She focused on the book, unable to answer him. She opened the cover. Her fingers drifted across the flyleaf, which was wrinkled and freckled with age.

"It's inscribed to you," she said, "by the author himself!"

"Heh, yes, it is. He and Tesla were great pals back in the day. He spent a lot of time in the labs, when I was a lad."

"You must have been very young at the time."

"I was. But I have an excellent memory, if nothing else. Couldn't have made it through my academy exams, otherwise."

She regarded him with narrowed eyes, watching the playfulness nearly pouring out of his ears.

"Why am I not surprised?" she purred.

They both burst into a laughing fit, ignoring the curious stares of the other scientists in the room. She felt a flicker of an undefined warmth kindling somewhere near her toes that was working its way up into her belly.

She clamped down on the feeling, hard. It was too close. It was too close to what Brightman had wanted of her. She would not give Brightman that. She would not destroy that earnest face. He had once thought she was a lady, but that disguise was only a candy-coating over bitter bones. Even with all he knew about her now, he still pursued her, perhaps even more than when he thought her to be an innocent. But without Brightman's control, she was drained of everything she had ever known, even of the cynicism that Brightman had poured into her Girls with every glance, every word, every cup of tea. Gemma had become a hollow vessel, waiting to be filled with she knew not what.

She turned some of the pages and examined the illustrations. There was much affection surrounding this volume. He was lending her a treasure, a slice of his heart. She continued to examine the book, mostly to avoid his gaze, and discovered a CDV wedged between two pages. She turned it over to see the image of an elderly professor, with spectacles perched on his nose between twinkling eyes. Otherwise, he had the same unsmiling face that everyone had in portraits from that time.

She read the caption aloud: "Professor Aronnax."

"Yes," he said. "I thought you might like a picture of him. I had to trade three different Nelsons and a Sophie for it. Our new first mate drives a hard bargain."

She studied it more closely, looking for traces of herself in his face. The spectacles made it hard to tell, but they did have the same slight upturn in the corner of their eyes.

"Thank you," she said.

This was a gift, even greater than that of the loan of the book. This was one treasure she could not refuse. She closed the book and pushed it back towards him, but he simply pulled out his pocket watch and muttered something about being late to a meeting with Hui.

"Silly mission," he said as he walked away, "always getting in the way. I will see you at tea, my lady."

CHRISTOPHE

Now that they had settled back into a routine -- drilling their orbital insertion and targeting procedures -- Christophe resumed his midnight readings in the gazebo. He hoped, night after night, to see Gemma emerge out of the darkness and sit beside him. He missed the Gemma that had laughed with him in the still of the night a lifetime ago. But night after night, she did not appear. He lamented the fact to Maggie as they toured the orchard.

"It is good to walk in the light," Maggie said. "Ship's day is so lovely."

They passed beneath apple trees that had managed to avoid freezing during the power outage. Maggie tottered along beside him, using some of her tentacles as legs, with the tips of her tendrils curled into long feet. When they were alone, she would drape a free limb about his shoulders; but if others were about, she merely strolled beside him and allowed him the dignity of his command.

Christophe replied to her in the privacy of his mind, giving any of the crew wandering about the impression that they were strolling arm-in-tentacle in silence.

"We seem to have come to some sort of détente, after all that has happened," he said.

"That is good. I know you are fond of her."

"Certainly! Ever since I met her. There is something new around every corner with her. She is like no one else I have ever known. You've talked to her. Has she said anything--"

"She is still healing," Maggie replied. The sound of her voice in his head was gentle but firm.

"She seemed much better at tea today," he said. "Dr. Hansard said--"

"Christophe," Maggie said, "those are not the wounds I mean."

"What do you mean, then?"

"I sometimes see past a person's words. Not everyone's, of course. Wallace has found a way to shut me out, and Rathbone is a complete mess. But with some people, I see memories and feelings. I value privacy, and I will not violate hers. I will say only this: she suffers. Deeply. Far more deeply than even she knows. She was never loved, save by one, and that one is long gone from her."

Maggie paused for a moment to pick up a wayward basket of petunias. She repacked the soil around the flowers and hung the basket on its hook on the ironwork pole beside the path. She rubbed her limbs together to dislodge the soil. She retrieved a lost blossom and held it in one tentacle as she started walking again.

She continued, "We all take some comfort in knowing the story of our lives. Even if the story is horrible, at least we have a sense of continuity. But she has had her story ripped away. Her life was a lie. How would you feel if someone told you that you were not my little bud?"

"I could not even imagine it!" His face contorted in imagined pain. "How disconcerting!"

Mr. Owen, enjoying some rare off-duty time, appeared on the path ahead of them as he walked in their direction. He froze for a moment, eyes wide and jaw so slack it nearly brushed the ground below him. Finally, he managed a watery salute, dove down another path, and disappeared into the cherry grove.

Maggie merely shrugged as they watched the branches rattle in the man's wake. "Nor I," she said. "Imagine how she feels, discovering the opposite. That someone who claimed she was an orphan was really her mother. Someone that should have loved her as I love you, as Elias loves you, used her in horrid and unnatural ways. She never knew a mother's love, and very little of any other kind of love, except for a single friend that is now lost to her."

"A friend who was my sister."

"The same. That one was as dear to her as any sister or brother."

"Like Miguel was to me."

"Yes. Dear, dear Miguel." She fell silent for a moment, and her tentacles went limp with sorrow. She twitched and resumed her walk. "She has lost what made her feel important. What gave her life meaning -- her teacher, her mission here--"

"Her mission," he said, his voice distant. "In all the kerfuffle, I had forgotten all about it."

"I will leave it up to her to tell you what it really was. Suffice it to say, she will not carry it out. All that is over. Everything she knew and valued until she set foot on the ship no longer matters to her. And now, she must rebuild herself from the ground up."

"I could help her with that."

"Perhaps, but not yet in the way you wish. She needs care and support as she does so, but for the most part this is something she has to do herself. Far too many others have done the defining for her. It will take time." She squeezed his hand with the tip of her limb. "You ask her to make a leap, when she cannot yet see the other side of the chasm. Let her build a bridge there. Let her learn the language before you ask her to speak it. Remember what the priest said about love? She now sees glimmers of what he meant, but just glimmers. Be her friend, as you are now, until she is able to understand more."

He licked the corner of his lips, as if to wipe away the frown that threatened to pull them down. "And if she is never ready?"

"Then she is never ready. Look elsewhere for what you seek. It may be that she is like me and has no need to mate. Or will always associate such things with a life she no longer wants. It was a kind of slavery, my bud. She had to play many roles. But never herself. Warm embraces were thresholds to secrets. Kisses, merely keys. Romance was just a tool, a means to someone else's ends. She needs time, and space, to reframe her thinking, and see love for what it truly is, in all its forms. If you care for her -- not just want her -- you will give her that space."

"I've never had to do that before." He shook his head. "I'm supposed to be the hero here! At least according to all of those wretched CDVs. I'm supposed to *do* something."

"You can do something," said Maggie. "You can be her friend."

"I'm not sure I know how to be just friends with a woman."

"Then you need to learn that language as well."

Not long afterward, just days shy of their destination, Christophe spent the evening with *The Prince and the Pauper*. Prince Edward was just inviting the uncannily similar-looking Tom into the palace when a small figure emerged out of the darkness and climbed the gazebo stairs. She held a familiar book in her hands.

Christophe sat up straighter on the bench to make room for her. She sat down next to him, not quite close enough for their knees to touch. She held the book out to him.

"Finished already?" he asked in as casual a voice as he could muster as he took it from her, careful not to brush her hands with his fingers.

"Yes," she replied. "Quite the thrilling tale. Thank you."

He waited a moment for further commentary, but none came. He shifted in his seat, unsure of what to say next. He prayed that she could not smell his breath. He had given up the Men-T-Fresh Tonic of late, and he found that he was more comfortable without the slightly burning sensation of it in his mouth. Besides, if a man were not courting a girl, what use would it be? He shifted in his seat again when he realized she was still staring at him.

"You didn't come here just to return a book," he said.

"No," she replied softly.

He stacked both books on his other side and asked, "What can I do for you, Gemma? Do you require yet another infusion of Twain? There is plenty more."

She laughed, and he could feel the frost between them melt a little.

"I admit, the distraction was welcome," she replied. "Between everything that has happened and my work for Dr. Pugh, I've needed... needed something."

"And what does old Elias have you working on these days? More Code of Life?"

"That and another project. Sort of a pet topic of his. I've encountered something rather odd in my reading. I had hoped it was just an error, but--"

"Oh, now, let me guess. The Nemo paradox? That old chestnut? How did it go, again?" He hunched over, elbow on knee, chin on fist, in a parody of Rodin's famous statue. "On the one hand, old Aronnax, your father, writes in a journal that he met Captain Nobody -- one of *my* fathers, as rumour has it -- back in 1867. They parted ways in 1868 when the *Nautilus* went down in a maelstrom off the coast of Norway. Am I right so far?" He switched elbows and knees to his other side. "On the other hand, we have Cyrus Smith, the engineer who claims to have landed on Lincoln Island in 1865 after escaping from the Confederates in a balloon in the middle of a hurricane. And it's a mysterious place, this Lincoln Island, as it is home to the now-retired Captain Nobody. He is their enigmatic benefactor for four years, until they meet him in 1869, just before he shuffles off this mortal coil, along with the *Nautilus*. Do I have it right?"

"Yes! Have you read both journals?"

He chuckled. "More often than I've read Twain. Like you, I've wanted to know more about my other progenitor. Quite a mystery, isn't it, that he had a seven-month adventure with Aronnax whilst he was nursemaiding Smith?"

She shot him a sly smile and continued for him. "And that Smith claims to have read Aronnax's account before it even happened? I'm inclined to chalk it all up to errors in translation at this point, unless someone actually traveled in time like that fellow." She wiped a joyous tear from the corner of her eye as she pointed at the book she had returned. "But that's not the biggest mystery of all. I don't think Pugh is interested in dates."

"Oh, really?" he asked with an arched eyebrow. "What, pray tell, do you think the good professor really wants to know?"

She narrowed her eyes at him, and he could feel her gaze examining his face -- not an altogether unpleasant experience. Hope rose in his chest.

"Aronnax seemed to have no inkling of Nemo's origins. However, Smith says that Nemo revealed that his real name was Dakkar, a Prince of India." She pointed at him. "You, my good Captain, are quite the handsome fellow, but you look nothing like a Prince of India."

He nodded. "I have thought that, too. But Maggie states that she made no mistake, that she used his Code--"

"That is where things get dicey," she replied. "This whole paradox revolves around assumptions, evidence, and assumptions about evidence. I believe Maggie when she says she used the Code she was given. But how can we be sure it was his? Perhaps she was given someone else's by mistake? Nemo supposedly died -- twice -- decades ago! With no body to be found. No Code to compare against. Just some hair sample out of nowhere." She wrinkled her nose in thought. "By the way, no one has stated how that sample was acquired. Did someone from either encounter nip a lock of hair from him?"

"I believe Smith did, just before they scuttled the *Nautilus*. At least, that's what I am told."

"That particular tidbit wasn't in the journal. And how did we -- meaning Pugh and Maggie -- get hold of that sample from Smith?"

"I don't know. A family secret, perhaps."

"Perhaps," she replied with a smile. "Or perhaps they are not entirely sure themselves. It could be Smith himself! Very well, then, at this point we will merely have to think of your 'other' father as Mr. Mystery. Perhaps we will have a better shot at determining his identity that way."

"Then, perhaps," he said quietly, "you can figure out what went wrong with me."

"Wrong?" She leaned back as she pronounced the word, as if she had tasted something foul. "Wrong? I would not say that. I would not say that at all." She crossed her arms and harrumphed, then spoke again. "Don't worry for a moment about what Code you may or may not have. It's your actions that count. That is why this is just a pet project, I'm sure. Besides, Pugh and Maggie are your family. You led us through the power outage safely. You're about to get us to Mars! You are the first spacefaring captain in history! You did that with your head, your heart, and your backbone, not your Code."

Chastised, he grinned at her sheepishly. "Well, I didn't do it alone."

"No one does." She cleared her throat and studied her hands. "At least, no one should."

"May I remind you, you're not alone, either? Maggie has pretty well adopted you for her own, and I think Yeoman McLure would punch anyone in the face who said you were any less than family. Elias adores you, and you have given him some peace where his missing daughter is concerned." It was his turn to look away. "And my sister. The one I never knew I had." He looked back at her. "You never really were alone, as long as you had her friendship. She was to you what Miguel was to me."

They finally looked up at each other again, and he felt a tug inside of him at the pained expression on her face.

"I'm glad she had you," he continued, "just as I am glad that she had Mr. Davies. I wish I had known her. I would have liked to have had a sister." With a shyness he had not felt in many years, he took one of Gemma's hands in his own larger one and held it lightly. "Would you tell me about her? Tell me about my sister?"

They talked until the darkness in the Gardens faded into the ship's artificial dawn. When they heard Herr Knopf muttering his way through the cabbage patch, they winked at each other like conspirators and slipped onto their separate paths to the day that awaited them.

GEMMA

"I just don't think I was meant for this, that's all," Gemma said as the crochet hook glared at her in the flickering firelight.

She tossed it onto the low table in the middle of their circle. She tugged at her brown lab jacket, feeling grateful that her ribs had healed enough to wear her own clothing again. The pirate blouse -- freshly laundered by Frau Knopf -- had long since found its way into the depths of Old Dependable.

Gemma glanced across the table at Maggie, the seventh member of the circle seated at last, who was working her way through a massive pile of wool. With one pair of tentacles, she stitched the last few rows of the scarf that Gemma had seen back in the nest, its calligraphic "M" fluttering as she moved. Yet another pair of limbs had started a completely separate piece in the same colour, with the roots of a "G" scrolling out of her needles. Every so often, yet another tentacle would slip in a third needle to twist the yarn and form the letters.

"Space is cold," was the only explanation Maggie would give for it as she worked and swayed to the velvet sound pouring out of the gramophone. In Wallace's absence, the unlabeled albums had slipped out of their hiding place and onto the shelves, resting in the light. They had enjoyed more than one airing during tea time.

"Nothing against Vivaldi," Frau Knopf had said as she had lowered the needle onto the record just after Gemma had arrived, "but a little bit goes a long way. But the blues? The blues sings about life, what goes wrong, what we do to each other. You cannot fix what you do not know is broken, *Ja*? I think any *Volk* that can sing the blues about itself, that *Volk* is going to be all right, in the end. This music will be out in the open back home, and soon. You'll see."

Caroline chirped at Maggie. "So you were the ghost, all along!" The Boolean sat next to Knopf, who was winding a skein of yarn about the young lady's outstretched hands. "You were the one always skittering about."

"I'm afraid so."

Gemma was pleased that Caroline had taken to Maggie's means of communication so quickly. All those scientific romances the girl was fond of reading must have prepared her for it.

The Boolean frowned. "What shall I report back to the Psychical Society, then? I surely can't tell them about Maggie. Do I tell them there weren't any ghosts, after all? Or that it was bugs from the Garden creeping about in the air ducts?"

Frau Knopf stopped winding for a moment and fingered the cameo at her throat. Her gaze was focused somewhere in the distance. "There are always ghosts, Fraulein. Even on Mars."

"That would really be something to report! Ghosts on Mars. But whose ghosts, I wonder?"

"You could have your own lecture tour with that," Gemma replied. "Like Nellie Bly after her trip round the world."

Caroline gasped with excitement. "And you could do it with me! Wouldn't it be grand?"

"Oh, it would," said Maggie. "'To Mars and Back'. But from a woman's point of view!"

"*Ja*," said Frau Knopf. "*Ja*, we can't rely on the men to say anything important."

Gemma rubbed her chin. It would certainly get Brightman's attention, which might or might not be deliciously wicked. A lecture by Gemma Aronnax, doubly so.

Gemma said, "Perhaps we should start with a journal. Let's be proper scientists about this."

"And proper journalists!" Caroline replied.

The pipephone speaker crackled to life, and a tinny version of Christophe's voice emerged.

"Attention all hands. We have a visual on Mars. We should enter orbit within forty-eight hours."

Maggie reached for Gemma's hand with one snaky limb and held it tightly.

"Planet, ho!" she sang.

CHRISTOPHE

The last of the debris had been cleared, and the floor of Gun Control shone as brightly as it had the day they had launched. Only a few stubborn patches of char remained here and there, and they would soon be gone. The controls of Hui's new weapon occupied the space that once housed the now-ravaged heat ray.

Christophe rested his palm against the new steel panel on the wall and tried to sense what lay underneath; he tried to detect where the ship had absorbed Cervantes into its very bones. Miguel had seeped into the ship that he had cared for and shepherded since before her maiden voyage. It had been as dear to him as the *Kiwi Clipper* was to Christophe. He understood that now. The *Thunder Child's Fury* no longer felt like a stranger.

"All is quiet here," he whispered. "We have heard neither hails nor calls from the Red Planet." Christophe stroked the wall with the tips of his long fingers. "You've done well, old sport. You've gotten us this far. Just hold us together a little while longer. Just a little while. We'll do what we need to do, and then we'll go home."

He leaned his forehead against the steel's welcoming but unyielding coolness. With closed eyes, he listened to the hum of the Oberths and let the sound wash over him like the tide flowing its way towards shore. Until Maggie came to fetch him, Christophe strained his ears to hear an answer in the *Fury*'s enduring song.

293

GEMMA

"It certainly looks peaceful," remarked Bidarhalli.

"Where are they?" asked Hui.

Along with the rest of the Cohort, Gemma gazed down at their destination from the orrery observation window. After forty long days and forty even longer nights, the *Thunder Child's Fury* had reached her goal at last, on the second day of October. With all that had happened on the way, they had almost forgotten where they were going. But now it was here, in front of them and undeniable. The ship had sidled up to the planet like a child ready to nurse from its many-times-greater mother.

The rest of the crew were at battle stations. The tension was so thick that Frau Knopf could have sliced it, toasted it, and served it for tea. Captain Moreau had drilled them over and over again in preparation for any number of conceivable scenarios. They had prepared, in fact, for anything but this.

They had prepared for anything and everything except for... *nothing*.

From the soft semi-darkness of the orrery, the Cohort watched the polar caps glisten as the ship slipped by through the quiet sky in a near-polar orbit. Craters and canyons pocked the face of the planet, and vast dry plains of soil and rock stretched out beneath them like an Arean Danae. As they passed over the North Pole and sailed towards the South Pole over the Martian equator, they saw no oceans. There were no rivers, no Martian version of the Nile. Lowell's famous canals were nowhere to be seen, and the red circles on the conference room maps were reduced to so much wasted ink. Taking photograph after photograph with Alfieri's telescope, for once pointed down at the ground instead of at the sky, they had found neither roads nor cities. Nothing moved. There was more life in the *Fury*'s Garden than on the Red Planet entire.

Nothing.

As they orbited the planet, they chased day into night, looking for any lights that might pierce the darkness. They crossed into day again, still alone, and saw fresh landscape that had rotated into the sunlight. Dust storms larger than Great Britain scoured the surface. A deep scar cut across Mars' face, a deep wound that, if it had been any deeper, would have cleaved that world in two. Even practical Gemma felt that some great hand had reached out from the stars and clawed the very heart out of the rusted rock.

There was no sense of menace. There were no angry nests of Invaders threatening to break loose upon them. There was simply a scarred pearl hanging in the heart of the night. The only people that Gemma could see were the reflections of her fellows in the observation window, peering round each other like a clutch of nervous hens straining to see a fox in the bushes.

But the hens saw no foxes. There was nothing but dust and rust.

"So beautiful!" Gemma said.

Once the shock of not being attacked had worn off, she had opened a blank journal and started scribbling about in it. She was lost in a fever of sketching each view of the planet as they plowed across the Martian sky.

"I agree," said Shaw as he mopped the sweat from his forehead with his kerchief. "Unfortunately, we are not here for the Cook's Tour. Where could they be? Maggie, have you any theories?"

"No," Maggie mumbled into their heads. She chewed on the end of a trembling tentacle with the side of her beak. "I haven't the foggiest."

The pipephone on the wall squawked, and Gemma picked up the handset. "Llewellyn."

Dr. Pugh's voice crackled over the line. "Seeing anything from down there yet, lass?"

"All's quiet here, Dr. Pugh."

"How's Maggie?"

Gemma cast a sidelong glance at her new friend. "All right, aside from a touch of the jitters. How is everyone on the bridge?"

"Feeling like Maggie. We haven't seen a thing, either. Any thoughts from our resident geologist?" There was no mistaking the teasing edge in his voice.

"Pffft," she sputtered back. "Perhaps underground? The surface seems rather bleak. I don't even see ruins of where things *used* to be."

"I agree with you. But what about launch facilities for the cylinders? Or factories to produce the Black Smoke? Where do they cultivate the Red Weed? Where did they manufacture the weapons they used against us? Could all that be underground?"

"What about that great scar of a canyon? Could they have facilities built into its walls?"

"It's a possibility." The rest of what he said was muffled, as if he were addressing someone on the bridge. "The captain has requested that you and Maggie join us in his ready room."

"But--"

"I have a feeling that Mars will still be down there when we're finished."

She replaced the handset. Maggie must have overheard the conversation, for she stood up on two of her tentacles and waited. Gemma managed one last glimpse at the waiting planet below them. She could almost hear the stars whispering to her again, now that they were here.

"It's just begging to be explored, isn't it?" Gemma asked.

"It's certainly begging for something," Maggie replied.

Christophe and Dr. Pugh joined Gemma and Maggie in the ready room, where they clustered around one end of the table.

"Did they leave?" Pugh mused aloud. "Did they know we were coming? Could our one ship have frightened them away?"

"I highly doubt that," said Christophe. "I do remember that not too long after the Invasion, we saw some of them head towards Venus. Is it possible that they all left?"

"Oh, heavens, I'm not ready to turn around and hoof it all the way to Venus," Pugh moaned. "I'm out of steam as it is."

Gemma said, "Even if they did journey to Venus, wouldn't some infrastructure be left behind? We're not seeing any ruins or remains. It's like they were never here."

"Frankly," Maggie chimed in, "I am relieved."

Gemma asked, "What if we did meet some other Martians like you, Maggie? Ones that would talk to you?"

"Oh, my!" she exclaimed, one tentacle waggling nervously in the air. "I don't know what I would say. What would we have to talk about?"

Pugh pushed away from the table and rested his long legs on a neighboring chair. Folding his arms across his middle, he rolled his neck back onto the top of the chair and studied the ceiling. He chuckled, almost giddy in his relief. "You could always teach them how to knit."

Maggie's laugh felt pleasant in Gemma's brain. "I do not think we brought that much yarn."

"Knitting," Gemma mused. Her eyes widened as realizations dovetailed into place. She stood with the force of her next word. "Knitting!"

"What are you going on about?" asked Pugh as he rolled a weary face towards her.

"The Invaders. They don't knit."

"I certainly wouldn't expect them to."

"I think the Martians are remarkable for what they didn't bring,"

Gemma said with a shiver. "The cylinders in which they traveled were unadorned. In all the information we've managed to uncover in their memory Code, we haven't found one ounce of culture. No art, no music." She picked up a CDV that someone had left on the table. Christophe's face beamed at them in sepia tones as she waved it about. "No cards to trade. No tales of great Martian heroes to inspire them as they went forth. They didn't bring anything to read or do as we did. No recreational materials at all! Certainly no Cultural Officers. They didn't need them. They don't get bored." She slapped the CDV down upon the table. "In our heady rush to tear apart their technology, we overlooked the most powerful bit of all: the Martians themselves. They are not aliens."

When the others merely stared at her in a confused, blank silence, she continued. "At least not in the way we think of them. Caroline stated it best: they are like analytical engines. I'd wager my entire CDV collection that that's exactly what they are."

"You mean, *living* analytical engines?" asked Christophe.

"Yes! A sort of manufactured intelligence."

"That would imply that someone did the manufacturing," said Pugh.

"Yes," Gemma replied. "Someone else. Perhaps somewhere else. Someone else sent the Invaders to us."

"They simply used Mars as a base camp? A staging area? What evidence do you have?" Christophe asked. "That is quite an extraordinary extrapolation."

Gemma narrowed her eyes as she reviewed the flurry of ideas in her head. "Remember the plans that they found that were the basis for the *Fury*? The plans for the gravity plates?" She pointed to Maggie. "Maggie's body follows their typical design, even if she acts more like us. She was a ballet dancer when the gravity was off. As if null gravity *is* her natural environment. Why would they need gravity plates? Why have those complicated ship designs at all when a simple cylinder meets their needs? Unless those plans were for someone else? Their masters, perhaps?"

Gemma paced the length of the room, and her thoughts churned as she marched. "Look, the planet below us is the only lead we have. We have to go down there and investigate it. We came all this way. We have lost so much just to get here." She paused and looked into Christophe's eyes, hoping he would see the reflections of Jennie and Cervantes in her own. "It is dangerous, yes! But so was building this ship in the first place. So was leaving our home world and flinging ourselves out among the stars. We have to eliminate the possibility that there is someone else behind the Invaders, at the very least. We must do something; we must make the rest of that danger worth it."

"What do you propose?"

"That we take the *Iron Wind* down to the surface. We do not have to land. Just get a closer look. She can fly in an atmosphere, yes?"

"Of course," Christophe said. "But where would we start? Mars may be smaller than Earth, but it's still a lot of country to explore."

Gemma rifled through her notebook and stopped on a page of sketches. She plunked the book down and pointed to her drawing of the nearly planet-wide rift.

"I suggest we start here. Shoot the rift and search for any signs of life in the walls, past or present. It would be an excellent place in which to shelter from those dust storms we saw earlier."

"That is still a rather large territory," said Pugh. "It's thousands of kilometres long. It would be like flying the North American continent from end to end."

Gemma peered more closely at her sketch. She stabbed at the wider portion in the centre with her finger. "Look at these side-chasms here. Some of them are far narrower than the main canyon. Quite a cozy place in which to conceal a base."

"You have an interesting notion of 'cozy'," Christophe replied. "But why not check out the poles first? That's where the water is concentrated, even if it is all ice."

"Too cold," Maggie said with a shiver. "And I do not require much water, apart from what I get when I feed. I suppose the same would hold for them."

"But they would need more than just drinking water, surely," said Pugh. "Industry needs water, coolant!"

"I'm not sure we can assume their needs are like ours, but they could have underground sources as well," Gemma said. "However, I suggest that the ship monitor the poles for any activity whilst we poke around in the canyon. Have Alfieri put that telescope of his to work."

"And if they attack us while we're on the surface? The *Iron Wind* is unarmed. It's not a combat vessel. The *Fury* won't be of much aid. If we crash, it is over. We will have no means of rescue."

"That is a risk," said Gemma. "We would not have much hope to fight back, even if we were armed, as most likely we would be outnumbered. We would need only a small crew for the craft, so we can minimize the risk. But honestly, I believe that if they were going to attack, they would have already. We've been orbiting in plain sight for hours and hours. And before you say that it's too dangerous for me, just remember that of all the members of your crew, I am the only one to have lived in harm's way my entire life. At least now that danger will be for something meaningful!"

Christophe regarded her for a moment as he wrestled internally with the idea. "It will take a few days to fly it from end to end. Are you ready for close quarters with me for that long?"

"Close quarters with you?" Gemma asked, firing a stern look back at him.

"I will chaperone, if you like," said Maggie, "though I'm not keen on going down there."

He met her stare with a determined smile. "I'm piloting the *Iron Wind*. I didn't come all this way for nothing."

Gemma could not help but recall the last time she had been on this deck. She hoped for a less painful experience this time. Her ribs ached a little as she scanned the crew that had gathered to see them off. That took her mind back even further. When she had left Earth, there had been no one to say farewell to, except perhaps the technician that had belted her into the launch pod. This time, she had had a steady stream of well-wishers, from Caroline to the Knopfs to Hui. How different! The thought made her ribs ache even more, but for a different reason.

She plucked at the seam of her trousers. Unused to such clothing, nonetheless she had yielded to Caroline's insistence that they would be more flexible and useful than her skirts. Christophe himself had appeared in a flight suit that she had never seen before, one that was slim-fitting but allowed much freedom of movement. Despite its practical cut, he still managed to look rather dapper -- which given Caroline's silent reaction to it, was having its intended effect upon the female of the species. Gemma allowed herself a moment to watch him move in it, and then she snorted as she recalled their near-miss in the orrery. She told herself that it had just been the longing for warmth after a funeral, and that was all.

She fingered the edge of her notebook -- a fresh one with plenty of room for new sketches -- and watched Maggie converse with Dr. Hansard as they moved towards the vessel's hatch. She could not see the good doctor's face, and she could not hear Maggie's responses in her head. Gemma smiled, though, as Humboldt appeared in their path, took one of Maggie's tentacles in his hand, bowed over it, and kissed it lightly.

"Oh my!"

Gemma heard the bubbling response this time. Maggie shivered and jiggled her knitting bag, which was clutched tightly in another limb. Whether it was with delight or disgust, Gemma could not tell.

She felt a warmth next to her, and she turned to the source of it. Christophe beamed down at her with his most disarming grin as he set the bulky ditty bag in his right hand on the floor.

"Looking forward to stretching my legs, so to speak," he said. "I haven't piloted the *Iron Wind* since our trip to the moon." He leaned down and whispered, "I am glad that you and Maggie will be with me."

Gemma inclined her head towards him. "As am I."

Mr. Pritchard approached them next and saluted Christophe. Gemma could see a slight tremor in the man's hand as he lowered it.

"All set, Mr. Pritchard?" Christophe asked. "Or should I say, *Acting Captain* Pritchard?"

"All set, sir," he replied. "And I hope I'll be just first mate again soon. Be careful down there, sir. And take care of my two friends here." He nodded his head in Gemma's direction. "I do wish Mr. Cervantes could have been here."

Gemma watched as Christophe gazed up into the steel rafters of the cargo bay. He said, "Oh, he is here, Captain. He is." Shaking off the dreaminess of his voice, he clasped Pritchard's hand and shook it. "I'll fly better knowing the *Fury* is in your capable hands, Ron. We will be back before you know it. Let me know the moment you hear from Admiral Thorvaldson, should he respond."

As they continued to converse, Gemma felt a hand on her shoulder. Pugh loomed over her with a wan smile on his face.

"Come back safely, child. And watch out for my son, would you?" He winked at her. "There is more than one reason why he is the *Fury*'s captain instead of her pilot."

When the hatch sealed behind her, Gemma had a quick flash of memory back to the last time she had entered a small craft with this man. It seemed more than forty days ago. She smiled at Maggie, who was attempting to secure herself behind the pilot's seat. Yes, far more than forty days ago.

"It's fine if you are a little nervous, Miss Llewellyn. I certainly am," Christophe said through a shaky smile. "I haven't done *this* before."

The ride down was a haze of bumps and jolts that Gemma would rather forget. The ride up from Earth in the small capsule had been heaven compared to this, and now she was thankful that her first ride had been sans viewports. She clutched a small paper sack in her hand and prayed she would not revisit the heavy breakfast that Frau Knopf had forced upon her.

The features of the Red Planet grew as they neared the surface. The Rift started as a sketch on a crimson map, then it was a dry riverbed, and then it yawned like a hungry beast below them. Light and time, past and present, were merging at last, as Alfieri had promised; Gemma was about to discover what happened when they collided.

As they descended, Christophe angled their course so that they would enter the gigantic corridor near its centre and then turn north into the niche. She sketched and wrote as quickly as she could in her notebook. She used the CDV of Aronnax that Christophe had given her as a bookmark as she worked.

The lack of blue in the sky and the lack of green on the ground shocked her. Even the sun shone differently here, as if she were viewing the world through smoked glasses. Everything was dimmer; even the shadows were thin and weak. Dry mountains thrust up above them as they dropped lower and lower. The peaks faded into the distance in a haze of dust.

"So, Maggie, what do you reckon?" Christophe asked. "Does it look like home to you?"

A few of her tentacles twitched before she answered. "The sooner I get back to New Zealand, the better."

They passed over gullies that had not seen water in ages. There was not a blade of grass to be seen, nor any sign of the Red Weed that the Martians had spread upon the Earth, nor the treasure that the crew had dreamt of hauling home. Caroline had been correct; the entire landscape was one large patch of rust.

Rocky waves rolled beneath their path, like an ocean frozen in time. Some of the crests reached far into the sky, but they were still lower than the impossibly high cliff walls. As they plunged down into the canyon, they found the ground even farther below them than they had anticipated.

"The canyon walls are kilometres high," Christophe observed. "I do not believe we'll be able to scan an entire section of wall in a single pass."

"Let us start close to the ground, then," Gemma said. "We can pass back through if we don't find anything down low."

Hours later, Gemma unbuckled her harness and stood up. She stretched and yawned. Her neck was stiff, and her eyes ached. The wonder of a new world had rubbed off, and a routine boredom had replaced its lustre. Rocks and soil, soil and rocks. Rocks shaped by no other hand than wind itself, wind and time. Perhaps water had carved away at them, ages ago, but of a sentient design or plan, there was no sign at all.

She rubbed her weary eyes. Squeezing past Maggie's bulk, she took a few short steps to the back of the cabin to work the kinks out of her tense muscles.

"What sort of a name is Moreau, anyway?" she asked, just to have something to say.

"Pardon?" Christophe blinked at the sudden question.

"Just curious. I get that Pugh couldn't really give you his name without risk of exposing project Orion. But why choose Moreau?"

Christophe emitted an amused grunt. "I had always hoped that I was named after the artist, Gustave Moreau. Turns out it was a bit of a sick scientific joke by the other scientists on the project. Some wild tale going round about a mad vivisectionist named Moreau that attempted to turn animals into people. As the story goes, it didn't turn out well for anybody."

"I read the journal articles on his experiments long after they started calling Christophe that," Maggie growled. "The man was depraved. I was most displeased. But by then it was too late."

"Jennie told me such a story, once," Gemma replied, "but his name had escaped me, until now."

"I assure you, we're no relation!"

"I'd stick with the painter story, for my own sanity. Though I suppose it's no worse than my own mother not giving me her name. I am not sure where she got 'Llewellyn', anyway."

"I suppose 'Aronnax' would have been too obvious."

The awkward silence that followed was relieved by the wireless clamouring for their attention.

"Still nothing," Christophe said into the handheld microphone. "However, we have a long way to go."

"Take a rest when you need to," came Pugh's crackling voice. "Show Llewellyn how to fly that bucket so you two can trade off and catch a few winks."

Gemma took to the controls as easily as Maggie had to null gravity. Learning was a welcome relief to her brain after the unending tedium of the canyon landscape. She cast a glance out of the viewport every few minutes to check for any signs of habitation. She did not know what to hope for. At least Nothing was peaceful, if a bit boring.

When he was satisfied that she would not crash them into the canyon walls, Christophe leaned back in his chair and dozed. They had not taken his lanky form into account when they had designed the cramped bunks just aft of the tiny bridge. His heavy breathing -- just short of a snore -- accompanied the clicking of Maggie's ever-present needles. She worked row after row as Gemma piloted the craft and scanned the passing cliff wall. Gemma found the signs of life welcome in a ghost town that had neither ghosts nor town, and Maggie's knitting was less worrisome than her tendency to nibble on the edge of her tentacles in her more anxious moments.

Sleeping whilst a woman was at the tiller? Gemma was certain Christophe had never done that before, either. She blinked into the stillness, which was broken only by his breathing and the rumbling of the small craft's engines. She spotted something odd in the distance, something that did not belong in the empty countryside.

"Maggie, do you see what I see? I am not asleep, am I?"

The clicking stopped. Maggie scooted forward to the space between and just behind the seats.

"I see it, too," she said. "That does not look natural."

Rooted in the north rim was the end of an arch. About a mile to the south it turned towards the ground and pushed into the crimson floor of the canyon. From a distance, it had blended into the background, but as they pulled ever closer to it, it looked less natural and more artificial. Gemma had to bite back the phrase "man-made".

Maggie tapped Christophe's shoulder. He started awake, and only his harness kept him from jumping up. He shook off the sleep quickly, as any seasoned sea captain would.

"Martians?" he asked.

"Not quite. That thing." Gemma pointed ahead. "What do you make of it?"

They were much closer now. Dust and corrosion had robbed it of its gleam, but it was definitely made of metal and not rock.

"Christophe, will you take the controls? I'd like to focus on the structure."

With a nod, he kept them on course with the arch dead ahead. Gemma tensed with anticipation as it loomed higher and higher above them.

"Shall I pass through it, o geologist?" he asked with a wink.

Gemma chewed her lip. This wasn't quite the same as deliberately mucking up a calculation or sabotaging an experiment by swapping distilled water with acid. This was an entirely different world. Caution -- despite her earlier speech on the ship -- was called for.

"Can we turn? Parallel it on this side and get a closer look at the top of the arch?"

"I get a nasty feeling just looking at it," Maggie broke in. "The thought of flying through that opening? Ugh." With a shudder, she dug into her knitting bag and retrieved a second set of needles.

"Very well," Christophe said.

He eased the nose of the craft up and angled them towards the top of the structure. He banked gently at its anchor point to the wall and ran parallel with it. Neither door nor hatch presented itself.

"What an odd structure!" Christophe said. "Even Martians need maintenance hatches, surely."

They reached the outer edge. He executed a slow turn to wrap them around to the far side.

"Perhaps it is not a building?" asked Gemma. "Perhaps it is a device or a machine?"

"Possibly. At any rate, it's the only sign of habitation that we've found. There are no signs of windows set into the rock adjoining it. If it were a machine, wouldn't there be, say, a control area close by? Even if they don't need tea breaks, they do need somewhere to do their work."

Gemma squinted as she studied the structure from this side. "Nothing here, either. Perhaps we should examine it underneath the main arm?"

"That would be an odd place for a hatch."

"Not if they can climb like me," said Maggie. "Or if they could fly up to it and dock there."

Christophe scratched at the scruffy spots on his chin. "Let us report in, then give it a shot."

Gemma continued to squint out the viewport at their jagged course as she listened to the grumpily affectionate banter between the captain and the man she now knew as his father. But now it was a comfort instead of an annoyance.

"Be careful, lad."

"Will do. We are heading in now. Everyone buckled in?"

The radio crackled for a moment, and then Christophe said, "Elias, it looks as if--"

ELIAS

The transmission dissolved into a sudden silence. Dr. Pugh strained his ears, fiddled with the knobs, and bulged his tired eyes as he fought to hear another syllable.

"Christophe?" he shouted into the microphone. "Christophe! What happened?"

Gasps erupted behind him. Pritchard's hand shook his shoulder with an unexpected gentleness.

"Dr. Pugh," he said in a hoarse whisper, "look up."

The scientist turned to look at the viewport, where a bright light, centred on the North rim of the canyon, flared out at him, bright as the sun.

"No, no!" he screamed as the light began to fade, as if it were dragging his family away with it.

His knees buckled beneath him. If the new captain's strong arms had not caught him, he would have collapsed onto the deck. Pritchard eased him into a chair before taking up the microphone. He called for the captain, again and again, until the *Fury* crossed the terminator into the dark night of Mars.

Silence.

The bridge crew held a collective breath and gazed down into the blackness.

Dr. Pugh moaned, and his gnarled hands cradled his ancient face. "Oh, Christophe! Maggie! Gemma! My son! Oh, no, my son!"

CHRISTOPHE

"Elias, it looks as if--"

Christophe dropped the handset as the thin Martian air in front of them shimmered. A curtain of light unfurled from the top arm of the structure, but they were so close that he could not turn in time to avoid it. He started to bank, but instead he collided with the brilliant net at an awkward angle. The light flared, bright as the sun, penetrating the small craft with all its strength. The pain of it forced him to call out. He could hear Maggie shrieking and even stoic Gemma crying out his name next to him. The light burnt its way past his eyelids.

He was blind. They were flying blind. They were still in the air, but for how long?

GEMMA

Tentacles that Gemma could not see supported her shoulders and legs as her harness fell away from her.

"I have you, love," came Maggie's voice.

Gemma blinked, awake at last, and tried to clear her vision of the lingering outlines of light -- outlines of images that could not truly exist. Her eyes still burned from the light, so she had not been unconscious for long.

"Be still," Maggie continued. "You just had the wind knocked out of you, is all."

Gemma could hear Christophe's muffled voice in the background.

"Yes," Maggie responded to him, "she is uninjured. She is awake, but groggy."

The images on her singed retina lingered. A rainbow of phantoms crawled over the cabin in front of her, but even they were starting to fade. Maggie cradled her like an infant above the floor.

"I believe I can stand now, Maggie," Gemma said with a shaky voice.

"Careful," Maggie warned as she lowered her to the deck. "We are not level. Christophe and I are fine, though. I believe the *Iron Wind* was our only true casualty." She retrieved one set of knitting needles from behind a broken control panel and worked them for a moment before realizing that they were empty. The yarn had slipped off them and rolled out of sight. She gnawed on the tip of one of them as she said, "Christophe is aft, checking on our supplies."

Gemma balanced as she stood on her own. There was enough of a tilt that she had to pay attention to her stance, but that was all. She turned to the viewport and saw only the wall of rock that had ended their journey so suddenly.

Gemma rubbed her collarbone, which she knew bore marks from the force of the harness keeping her from flying out of her seat.

"What *is* working?" she asked. "Can we still contact the *Fury*? Perhaps we can think of something. If we still have the extra supplies that Wallace--"

"Mark down the radio as the second casualty," Christophe said as he made his way down into the main cabin. He fidgeted with a large-barreled pistol in his hands. "Even the redundant unit is shot." He looked down at her with world-weary eyes. "I am happy to see you are uninjured. I wish I could say the same for our long-term prospects. Even if we could signal the ship, there is no way they could fetch us from the surface."

"Maggie," Gemma asked, "can you contact Pugh?"

"I have been trying, but I can get no answer. Same with Elsa and Caroline. It is as if they aren't there. I have never done it from this far away before, though, so I am not sure what that means."

"Keep trying," Gemma said. "If you can contact them, perhaps the *Fury* can convince the *Orestes* to get here and use their dropship."

Christophe flashed her a weary smile, and for a moment, he was the lad in the Gardens again. "You never give up, do you?"

"It's not over 'til it's over, Captain." She nodded at the pistol, visions of Cervantes joining the fading lights dancing on her retina. "I don't think it's yet time for *that*."

He gazed down at the weapon. "Oh! Flare gun. I thought I might use one of the pressure suits and have a run out. We need to see if we can at least let the ship know we're alive. It's not very powerful, and they may not see it, but so far it is all we have. Not exactly a lot of wood about for a large bonfire or any of the usual Robinson Crusoe solutions."

"We should wait for nightfall," Gemma said, trying to still the shakiness in her voice. "And for when they pass over us, to give us the best chance... perhaps we'll see their running lights overhead."

He set the flare gun aside and peered at his watch. "I'm not sure if we will see them, but we can look. I believe it will be sunset before too long, and they should be passing over this area not long after that." He took her hand and then took one of Maggie's tentacles. "I'm sorry, ladies. I should not have led us down here without a backup plan."

"It was my idea."

"And it was my call. I'm the captain." He slumped. "Was the captain. Pritchard is in charge now, and his duty is to do what's best for the *Fury*."

Gemma swallowed the sudden panic that threatened to shake her to pieces. Terror would serve no purpose now. Brightman had ground that into her over a lifetime.

One bright thought outshone the dread that hung over her like a thundercloud: she was as far away from Brightman as she could possibly get. At least she did not have to deal with that particular horror. Gemma would rather face an entire horde of Martian machines than take on one more mission for that monster.

The thought buoyed her. There were still Girls under the woman's control. Gemma had to get back. She would not die in a boat, like the Lady of Shalott. She would live, and she would break Brightman's curse. She had to free them, the way she had been freed, free them to see a larger world. Free them to seek their own destinies rather than continually nick secrets in the service of another. Free to seek the stars themselves, if they so desired.

"Let us suit up, then," Gemma said. "I will go with you. As ship's geologist, I have a duty to collect some samples. Surely we have time for that, Captain."

He gave her hand a squeeze and then led them all aft to the small airlock. He opened a storage locker that contained two heavy suits. Gemma's eyes widened as she examined each piece, from the massive gloves to the copper clad helmets to the strange backpacks that were to supply them with air in the thin Martian atmosphere. They were far more complex than the ones they had worn on Launch Day.

"They are based on designs we found on the *Nautilus*," Christophe said. "Slightly upgraded, of course. The original ones were for underwater use, for great external pressures. We have the opposite problem here. But we should be able to make short jaunts out of the ship before--"

Maggie waved his words away with one tentacle as she helped Gemma shoulder her way into the smallest of the suits.

"There isn't one for me, of course," Maggie interrupted. She pointed at her own bulk. "I don't believe I will need one. I believe whoever designed this body in the first place did so with multiple environments in mind."

"I agree," Gemma said. "Still, you do have some active Human Code in there. Your eyes, for example, are not like theirs. Not sure how they'll respond to the lower pressure."

"Yes," Christophe said as he holstered the flare gun into the suit's belt. He picked up the helmet and aimed it for his head. "Let us check things out first, and we will see if it is safe for you, mum."

He retrieved a brass-encased block of instruments from the closet. A barometer and a thermometer gleamed alongside several other sensors on its front panel. "Are you going to be all right alone?"

"Of course. I am never truly alone. And, as Emily Dickinson would say, 'I dwell in Possibility.'"

Maggie helped him settle the helmet into place and activated the magnetic locks that would hold it on through the wildest of dust storms. She did the same for Gemma.

"Be careful, you two. I love you both."

Clutching a storage bag as a makeshift sample collector, Gemma followed Christophe into the small airlock and readied herself for more of the rumpled and jagged landscape. He reached for the control panel to open the door and paused. He turned as much as the small chamber would allow the bulky suit to move. All she could see were his eyes, where a boyish mixture of pride and curiosity danced. He touched her hand, though she could not feel it through the glove.

"You are the first Terran scientist to set foot on Mars, Gemma. Even if no one but us will ever know, you are the first. We made it. Even if we never leave here, we made it."

She touched his hand back and gave him a warm smile. "And you are the first sailor, Christophe. Let us see what we can see, my friend."

As the door hissed open, Gemma looked down at the ground, concentrating on it so she would not fall. Even minor injuries could be deadly now. Still focused on the ground as she hopped down from the boulder beneath the craft, she saw what must have been the sole patch of green on Mars.

Christophe reached the ground ahead of her. He gasped with the effort of moving in the weighted boots, meant to keep them from bouncing so much in the lighter gravity of the Red Planet. She settled beside him and finally looked up. She gasped too, but it had nothing to do with her exertion.

The Red Planet was no longer Red.

Gemma gazed up into the first blue sky that she had seen in forty days, a sky so blue that she could have dived into it for a luxurious swim. Spires of glass and metal pierced that never-ending blue in the distance, and the world about them shimmered with living light.

This world was not empty, after all...

The adventures of the crew of the *Thunder Child's Fury* continue in Book 2: *The Mysterious Planet of Captain Moreau*, to be released in 2016.

ACKNOWLEDGEMENTS

Writing feels like a very lonely enterprise at times, but no book is written in a vacuum. There are always people along the way to give you a helping hand and a lot of hope. I had so many people assisting me and encouraging me in my years-long journey that a full list would be a mile long at this point. A big hearty thank-you to everyone and especially...

My dear husband, T. D. Raufson, for making this dream possible and for managing the process with me.

My parents, Gary & Beverly Smith - thank you for always encouraging creativity in your children. You have always cheered us on and never, ever called any of us crazy for the artistic endeavors we took on. Thank you for encouraging us to read whatever we could get our hands on, whether it was the Bible or Jane Austen or Alan Dean Foster or our favorite comic books. You helped prepare me for this journey from very early on.

My patient beta readers: David Thurmond, Eve Taggart, Jeff Smith, Jason Smith, and fellow indie author K.S. Daniels. You are all awesome! I loved working with each of you on this!

The Bromfield family (Chris, Lisa, Courtney, & Chris Jr.) and David & Robin Lawyer, for all their love and encouragement.

Author Elise Stokes, for checking up on my progress from time to time. You really helped when I was stuck in the doldrums!

Margie Cox (the idea for this book was hatched at your annual party) for all your encouragement and writing advice, Grace Moss, Jessica Moss, JaBarr Lasley-King, Jessica Smith, John Lemay, Paul Charles, Frank Hui, and all my friends in the Superhero Costuming Forum. Your creative energies are matchless!

Dr. Allen Hansard, for the use of his name.

Sandy Talbott

Keith Cleveland, for the Teddy Roosevelt speech poster. It helped me through some tough spots!

My former co-workers (and still friends) who encouraged me to follow the dream.

Debbie at The Cover Collection, for all her hard work on my beautiful covers and for all the encouragement over the last year.

Author A. C. Crispin - I took your writing class at DragonCon years ago, and it meant a lot to me. Thank you for all the beautiful stories you told over the years.

Thanks to Franklin Chang-Diaz for inventing the VASIMR technology, which served as the basis for the Oberth Engine design.

Thanks to Keith Lofstrom for his research on the potential for Launch Loop systems.

I am grateful for the many men and women who spent their lives, and in some cases gave their lives, to get the human race into space. I am especially thankful for Sally Ride, Ph.D., the first American woman in space.

Many thanks to Jules Verne and H. G. Wells, for writing the works that inspired this novel and have inspired generations of readers and artists.

And to you, dear reader, for giving my little story a chance.

ABOUT THE AUTHOR

K.T. Hunter is a lifelong fan of science fiction, from Verne to Wells to Scalzi. She received her B.S. in Computer Science from UT Chattanooga in 1993. She released her first novel, *20 Million Leagues Over the Sea*, in June 2015. She lives in Tennessee with her husband, author T. D. Raufson, and their cats.